ASTICMAN

To the condition of being handicapped

by Paul Peroutka

compiled by Carmen Aldinger

authorHOUSE®

AuthorHouse™
1663 Liberty Drive, Suite 200
Bloomington, IN 47403
www.authorhouse.com
Phone: 1-800-839-8640

First published by AuthorHouse   7/27/2009

ISBN: 978-1-4389-5140-9 (sc)

Printed in the United States of America
Bloomington, Indiana

This book is printed on acid-free paper.

CONTENTS

Preface (by Carmen Aldinger)   vii

Your Friend - Paul Peroutka © 1980   1

Asticman © 1980   4

Spasticman/Elasticman © 1980   6

A Friend © 1980   31

Any Hint of Creativity: © 1980   39

Wheelchair   40

Legbrace   41

A Prayer by Lonely   42

My Teacher, Toby © 1980   45

To My Therapist © 1981   72

Danny Deety © 1984   82

Nonverbal Champion © 1981   95

Preparation for Independence © 1982   110

The Mind is a Terrible Thing © 1982   114

Spasm Orgasm © 1981   122

The Taking Care of Dr. Dinn © 1984   164

Laughic © 1984   189

Ecclesiasticman © 1987   197

Scholasticman © 1985   211

They Graduate © 1987, 1995   219

Words to the Graduating Class © 1986   223

The Just Life © 1987   226

In Memory of Tommy © 1985   239

From: Cella © 1987   241

Great Day © 1982   244

Chiasticman © 1990   252

Hell Can Find Answers © 1986   257

How Do You Like Me So Far, Mom? © 1990   269

Praying to Mom © 1990   270

Why We Write © 1990   273

I Cannot Condone Abortion © 1990   277

Traveling with the Death Bucket © 1990   280

Fantasticman © 1995   285

Gambler © 1991   297

Adapt © 1992   301

Soul in the Helpless © 1992   304

Recommendations from the Board © 1992   307

Just Give Him a Cookie © 1994   308

PREFACE

Paul Peroutka has been an inspiration to many people, and certainly to me. He lived with severe cerebral palsy all the 42 years, 5 months, and 7 days of his earthly life. As he said in one of his writings, he had "cerebral palsy 24 hours a day." Yet he usually was an upbeat person who wanted people to see "Paul beyond the palsy."

Paul died during the night of August 9-10, 2004, sitting in his chair. He left behind a lifetime of writings.

For the last 12 years of Paul's life, I have been his employee, friend, girlfriend, fiancée, almost his wife, his roommate, primary caregiver, surrogate, power of attorney, and, as he called me proudly toward the end of his life, his best friend.

Since Paul died, I have talked about Paul with many people, in several countries. However, nobody can tell his story as well as Paul could. Therefore I decided to put together this collection of Paul's writings. Paul was a gifted writer who wrote in many styles and genres.

To summarize main parts of Paul's writing career, I want to use excerpts from his own "Career Notes." He used to self-publish through a copy shop, and the excerpt includes some of the titles of his 'books' and stories.

I'm Paul Peroutka; please call me a poet. I've written in many genres for many reasons for many years. My identity is intertwined with my severe cerebral palsy and my defined view of the world. I started out in Baltimore where I published my first volume in 1980. I was 18 that summer, and in March of 1992 I turned 30 when I released my thirteenth compilation. During those years I grew and I traveled both alone and with others. Whenever I would put my thoughts on paper I was able to leave my wheelchair. But always at the end of the story, I was still sitting down.

I think that anyone asked to look back to the beginning of a twenty year career doing anything might first admit that it took a little while getting started. In recollecting, I usually group my two first volumes, Your Friend and The Mind is a Terrible Thing, together considering that those are the ones that take me through late high school and early college. And a kid that age is not going to know which voice or style he is going to want to commit to; at least I didn't. So I tried using a lot of voices: my dad's, my brother Michael's, my high school friends', my teacher's, Hunter Thompson's, Tom Snyder's, John Lennon's, Hugh Hefner's, Jesus's. So especially the first 'book' I compiled during the summer of 1990 and then the second I did the next summer really came out as grab bags where you never really knew where I would go from chapter to chapter. 'Asticman'(yes the very original)and 'Nonverbal Champion' both comedically and sensitively explain my triumph over physical and communication barriers. 'A Friend' and 'To My Therapist' offer the unique perspective of a growing, maturing handicapped teenager as I try to juxtapose childhood mores with confusing confrontations of adolescence.

… 'Great Day' came towards the end of the Bustop days, but I really look at it as my first hit.

I switched in my writing in 1983 sort of away from young college chronicles to dealing with young parenthood. …

My 1984 was like the Dead's 1970; most of those titles I'm still recognized for and very glad to be so: ... 'Dr. Dinn' (Grey)... That was my lucky streak.

... I concluded my college career writing Scholasticman.

In 1986 I decided to become adventurous with experimental voice and presentation. I was deliberately departing from familiar styles and objectives. And I know that I caused mixed reaction, certainly in myself and I have no doubt in my readers, all three of them by now. I thought at the time some of those experiments failed to merit the praise that I'd given the earlier work. But now I really give myself a lot more slack. ...

Then I was blessed to have been able to pull Vitiusta together, my ambitious answer to The Beatles, The Grateful Dead, Christie Brown and Joni Erickson... oh, and God too. I loved all six partners who put their names to that effort. I just wanted it to be as interesting and certainly as diverse as we could make it. And it probably still is my number 1 pride. Just in my contributions like 'The Just Life', 'Ecclesiasticman', 'Cella', ..., I believe I accomplished adequately what I set out to do. But combining all the wonderful talents and perspectives of Sydna, Bernie, Alan, Oaky, Bobby, yes and even John Nolan, made that work pure delight.

When I wrote 'Paul Peroutka Tries To Save The World And A Little Piece Of Rock and Roll', I was still slowly coming out of a year-long depression and lack of confidence due to a suicide attempt. So the second part of that one was really free-style. But I remember having on my side the fact that my commentative voice was getting stronger, and also by the time of my tenth book Lunch in LA I had accumulated enough traditions, characters, hooks and ploys that I could start going back and maturing and expanding them .... So I sailed through the first George Bush administration writing such pieces as ... 'Why We Write' (Heaven's to Betsy), 'Fantasticman',... 'I Cannot Condone Abortion', 'Gambler', 'Adapt', 'Soul in the Helpless' ...(The Best of Billfold).

I then put down roots in New York, Washington, Colorado, LA and Boston. I settled into my niche in autobiographical fiction, and I gained confidence in my ability for commentary and story telling. Some online services posted excerpts of my books as I was writing them.

For this book I have selected some of my favorite writings from the first part of Paul's writing career. They give a candid picture of who Paul was and what it meant for him to deal with his handicap every day. The selections also show Paul's progression of writing from dialogue, narrative and poetry about his handicap to illustrating his experiences in school and college to gaining employment, travelling, dealing with his mother's death, and taking a stand on political causes, such as abortion. I realize that these are my selections and not necessarily how Paul would have put them together. However, I do think he would be happy to see his writings in print.

I have left those writings in all capital letters which Paul originally produced in that way. Early in his writing career, it was not easily possible for Paul to shift from caps to no caps without the use of his hands. Only later, as technology improved, was it feasible for him to write in sentence case. While some of the writings in all caps might be a bit more challenging to read, they are just a small reminder of the challenge it was to communicate with Paul with his imperfect speech. Though, as he said, it was still usually easier for most people to read his voice than to understand his speech.

Paul has written in many different forms of expression, being a voice for the handicapped. He was very open about his life and his experiences and often very explicit. Some of his openness may surprise or stun some of the readers, but I think it portrays honestly the life of a young man with his feelings and struggles and peer influences and the frustrations and limitations of his severe handicap. In some of his writing styles he chose to use vulgar and vernacular expressions. The use of these words also denotes the feelings that Paul wanted to express in each particular piece. While I would not use these words in my own writing, I, and Paul's friends believe that he would not want to have his pieces edited to eliminate these words. In fact, in one of his writings, Paul states, "No one should assume the right to edit your voice. You know what you have to say, and how you want to put it down. You are the writer. It is your choice to make." So, his writings appear here as they were originally copyrighted.

It is my hope that these writings will give you a glimpse into Paul's world and thus into the mind and life of a severely handicapped person who could never do any of the tasks of daily living for himself. He typed his texts with a wooden pointer attached to a helmet, which he called "headstick."

May you be inspired, enlightened and challenged, as many others have been – during Paul's lifetime, and beyond.

Boston, MA, Summer/Fall 2008
Carmen Aldinger

YOUR FRIEND – PAUL PEROUTKA

NOVELS AND MOVIES BY AND ABOUT HANDICAPPED INDIVIDUALS SEEM TO BE SELLING THESE DAYS. BUT, ALAS, I DON'T SKI. I'M NOT AN ARTIST. I DON'T SMOKE CIGARS. I'M NOT EVEN AN ATTRACTIVE YOUNG GIRL. I'M LUCKY IF I COULD EVEN BE DESCRIBED AS CUTE; ALTHOUGH I'VE ALWAYS THOUGHT SO. ABOUT THE ONLY THING I CAN CLAIM AS MY FAME IS THAT I TYPE WITH A STICK ON A HELMET. THIS OLD HELMET HAS GOTTEN ME FAR AND I'M GONNA KEEP IT WITH ME ALWAYS. I SURE HOPE MY HEAD DOESN'T GROW TOO MUCH FROM NOW ON.

THERE ARE SEVERAL THINGS I WANT TO CONVEY AND ACCOMPLISH BY THE COLLECTING OF THE ESSAYS THAT APPEAR IN THIS BOOK. I WANT TO SHARE WITH MANY PEOPLE I KNOW AND I WISH KNEW ME BETTER, THE TWO PLAYS, 'SPASTICMAN', AND 'ELASTICMAN', APPEARING IN THE BEGINNING OF THE BOOK SIMPLY AS 'ASTICMAN'. I WROTE THEM IN MY SECOND AND THIRD YEAR OF HIGH SCHOOL, AND THEY REFLECT JUST ABOUT EVERYTHING I WAS AND WHAT I OBSERVED MY WORLD TO BE AT THAT TIME IN MY LIFE. MAYBE IT'S NOT AS GREAT AS I THINK IT IS, BUT IT'S PROBABLY MY MOST PRIZED POSSESSION.

IN THE ESSAY 'A FRIEND', I'LL SHARE A FANTASY OF MINE WITH YOU. IT IS AMONG THE FEW NON-SEXUAL FANTASIES I DO HAVE, BUT STILL I THINK IT HAS THE POTENTIAL OF BEING THOUGHT-PROVOKING. IT DEALS WITH THE UN-REAL POSSIBILITY OF A PERSON MEETING A PERSON HE COULD HAVE BECOME BORROWING A MAJOR EVENT IN HIS LIFE HAD OCCURRED. IN MY LIFE, MY BRAIN LOST MUCH OXYGEN AT THE TIME OF MY BIRTH. I. E. I'VE LIVED WITH CEREBRAL PALSY ALL MY LIFE. THAT'S NOT THE MOST INCREDIBLE THING IN THE WORLD, OR EVEN THE MOST INTERESTING. I WOULD NEVER GET ON 'REAL PEOPLE' OR IN RIPPLEY'S 'BELIEVE IT OR NOT'. I DON'T THINK I'M THAT GREAT A PERSON OR LIVED THAT INTERESTING OF A LIFE. I DO THINK I'VE WRITTEN SOME GOOD PIECES THROUGH THE YEARS, AND I CAN TURN A GOOD PHRASE HERE AND THERE.

I WANT TO FOOL MYSELF AND TRY TO ASK YOUR ENDURANCE WHILE I IMAGINE THAT I CAN WRITE POETRY. ACTUALLY I'VE ALWAYS ENVISIONED MYSELF AS A TOP-40 LYRICIST RATHER THAN A SERIOUS POET; SO IF THERE ARE ANY WOULD-BE TOP 40 COMPOSERS OUT THERE, GIVE ME A CALL.

I WANT TO PUT SOME THINGS DOWN ON PAPER I'VE ALWAYS DREAMED ABOUT SHARING WITH AN AUDIENCE OF READERS. I ALSO HAVE THE OPPORTUNITY TO SAY THANK YOU TO A VERY DEAR FRIEND, AND WITHOUT BABBLING ENDLESS AND MEANINGLESS GIB-JAB COMPLIMENTS ABOUT HER, ABSOLUTELY THE BEST TEACHER IN THE WORLD, MRS. TOBY EDWARDS.

ALL IN ALL, I'VE ALWAYS BEEN AN UPBEAT GUY. I'VE HAD A LOT OF FRIENDS DURING THE YEARS AND SINCE MY DISABILITY HAS STOPPED ME FROM SAYING THESE KINDS OF IDEAS, I CAN POSSIBLY WRITE THEM DOWN

ON PAPER WELL. I HOPE THAT PEOPLE RESPECT ME FOR WHAT I TRY TO BE, NOT ALWAYS WHAT I APPEAR TO BE. I'VE ALWAYS TRIED TO ADD SOME SMILES AND ELIMINATE SOME NONSENSE.

SO DON'T CRY FOR ME, LAUGH WITH ME.

Asticman

HI MY NAME IS PAUL PEROUTKA.

HOW THROUGH ALL MY LIFE I'VE WISHED I COULD SAY THAT AS CLEARLY AS I COULD WRITE IT, BUT MY CEREBRAL PALSIED TONGUE ALWAYS IMPEDED THAT HAPPENING; SO HERE I AM, WRITING MY LIFE STORY AT THE AGE OF 18. I'D STILL RATHER BE OUT DRINKING WITH THE GUYS.

YOU MAY ASK WHY AN EIGHTEEN YEAR OLD BOY WOULD WRITE HIS LIFE STORY ALREADY, IF IT SHOULD EVEN BE WRITTEN IN THE FIRST PLACE? WOULD ANYTHING I HAVE TO SAY BE THAT PROFOUND, IF INTERESTING? THE ANSWER YOU'D GET FROM ME WOULD BE: I DON'T KNOW, I SURE LIKE IT. MY KIND OF LIFE, BEING AFFLICTED WITH MILD ATHETOID CEREBRAL PALSY HAS BEEN WRITTTEN ABOUT BEFORE. NEVER, I BELIEVE, IN SUCH A VEIN IN WHICH I'LL PUT IT DOWN, BUT PERHAPS ENOUGH TIMES SO THAT YOUR CURIOSITY WILL BE PIQUED AND YOU'LL WANT TO READ ON.

I'VE BEEN A VERY LUCKY PERSON, I THINK. A LUCKY PERSON IS ONE WHO HAS RUN INTO AS MANY OF ONE KIND OF SITUATION IN LIFE AS HE'S RUN INTO TOTALLY OPPOSITE AND DIVERSE ONES. SO HE MIGHT BE LOOKING AT THE BEACH AT WAKIKI, TANNING ON

HIS SUNDECK, WHILE HE REMINISCES HIS DAYS IN THE HOLE IN A TURKISH PRISON. I'VE NEVER DONE THIS, BUT I HAVE SIT WITH MY BEST FRIENDS FROM THE BIGGEST HIGH SCHOOL IN TOWSON AT THE JUNIOR PROM WITH MY BEST GIRL AND FEELING LIKE A VERY IMPORTANT AND DISTINGUISHED PERSON, WHILE REALIZING THAT NO MORE THAN 14 YEARS AGO I WAS EXTREMELY FORTUNATE THAT THE BALTIMORE COUNTY BOARD OF EDUCATION WAS SO KIND AND SO GENEROUS AS TO ANNOUNCE ME "EDUCABLE."

I DON'T WANT TO TELL YOU TOO MUCH MORE ABOUT ME. I THINK MY ESSAY SPEAKS FOR ITSELF. I'M A VERY OMNISCIENT WRITER IN THAT, WHEN I WROTE THE TWO PLAYS WHICH ARE HERE IN COLLABORATED AS ONE, THEY WERE PURELY FOR MY OWN ENJOYMENT AND NOT MEANT FOR OTHERS TO SEE; THEREFORE I USED EVERYBODY'S REAL NAME, AND INCLUDED JUST ABOUT EVERYONE NEAR AND DEAR TO ME. THERE WAS NO WAY I WAS GOING TO ALLOW MY PRIVATE THOUGHTS ABOUT THE PEOPLE AROUND ME TO BE DISSEMINATED FOR ALL TO SEE. BUT WHAT THE HELL, I SOLD OUT SO HERE IT IS. ALL THE NAMES HAVE BEEN CHANGED TO PROTECT THE GUILTY, ME.

AS I HAVE SAID, THIS BELOW PLAY IS A CONGLOMERATE OF AN ORIGINAL MANUSCRIPT AND ITS SEQUEL, INTERTWINED FOR THIS PUBLICATION FOR CHRONOLOGICAL ACCURACY. REMIND YOU OF FRANCIS COUPULA? IT'S REALLY ABOUT TWO PEOPLE I KNOW REAL WELL, GOD AND MADGE, THE HAND-SOFTENER. I'M MENTIONED ONCE OR TWICE.

Spasticman/Elasticman

GOD: OH DANM IT.

MADGE: WHAT'S THE MATTER, POWERFUL GUY?

GOD: AH, I JUST CREATED PAUL PEROUTKA AND I SCREWED HIM UP.

MADGE: WELL CAN'T YOU FIX HIM?

GOD: NOPE, LOST HIS OXYGEN.

MADGE: THAT'S FUNNY.

GOD: WHAT, ABOUT PEROUTKA?

MADGE: NO, I NEVER HEARD YOU SAY NOPE BEFORE.

GOD: OH, AND I HAD SO MANY GOOD PLANS FOR THAT LITTLE BUGGER, LOOK AT HIM. HE'S REGISTERING ONE. AND RIGHT NOW, AS WE SPEAK, HE'S PLAYING JEOPARDY, WATCHING HIS FRIENDS GET CASTRATED, EVEN BEING OBSERVED, AND THEN THERE'S LINDA LOSERY. OH MY ME, I HATE TO THINK OF IT ALL.

MADGE: WELL DIDN'T WE READ THIS STUFF IN HIGH SCHOOL?

GOD: AH, THERE'S STUFF YOU NEVER READ IN HIGH SCHOOL. AND I CAN SEE IT ALL HAPPENING TO HIM RIGHT NOW. OH KID, I'M SORRY.

MADGE: TELL ME THE WHOLE STORY, GOD.

GOD: OH, I SEE SO MANY THINGS, I DON'T KNOW IF I CAN TELL THEM ALL.

MADGE: WELL HELL, TRY.

GOD: ALRIGHT, ONLY DON'T BE FRIGHTENED. FIRST OF ALL HE WAS BORN IN A FARAWAY PLANET, A PLANET CALLED 'HEADSTICK'. NOW, THIS PLANET OF HEADSTICK CONTAINED MANY MASS CONTAINING AREAS CALLED ROOMS. ONE ROOM HAD THE SIGNIFYING NAME, BATH. PAUL HAD MANY TRYING TIMES IN THE BATHROOM. ONE WAS WHEN HIS MOTHER, BOOP-EL WAS WASHING HIM IN THE TUB...

PAUL: MUM, MUM, MUM...

BOOP-EL: PAUL, I'M VERY TIRED.   IS IT THAT IMPORTANT?

PAUL: (THROUGHOUT THE PLAY, DROPPING CONSONANTS OFF OF WORDS SO NOT TO BE UNDERSTANDABLE TO ALL) MUM, YOU ARE CHOKING ME WITH YOUR ARM.

BOOP-EL: PAUL, HOW COULD I BE JOKING YOU WITH MY ARM? NOW C'MON, COOPERATE AND LET ME FINISH WASHING YOU.

PAUL: MOM, YOU'RE CHOKING ME, MOVE YOUR ARM PLEASE.

BOOP-EL: I'M NOT JOKING YOU. I'M VERY SERIOUS ABOUT GETTING THIS DONE.

PAUL: I SAID YOU'RE CHOKING ME.

BOOP-EL: OHHHH, YOU SAID I'M CHOKING YOU. OHHH, IS THAT ALL YOU WANTED?

PAUL: YES, GASP GASP GASP!

MADGE: OH, AND GOD, ISN'T THIS WHEN THEIR PLANET WAS IN DANGER OF BEING BLOWN UP SO HIS PARENTS SEND HIM RACING THROUGH SPACE TO EARTH? IT IS, ISN'T IT?

GOD: YES, IT IS. AND SOMEHOW, HIS NEW, EARTHLY PARENTS, MARY AND JOHN, KNEW HE HAD SPECIAL POWERS. I REMEMBER THAT DAY...

MARY: JOHN, I THOUGHT I TOLD YOU THIS MORNING TO PICK UP THAT RUG SO I CAN VACUUM UNDER IT.

JOHN: LOOK, MARY! A BABY JUST LANDED IN OUR LIVING ROOM!

MARY: NO SHIT, JOHN. NOW PICK UP THE RUG SO I CAN VACUUM THE FLOOR.

JOHN: MARY, I HATE TO TELL YOU THIS BUT OUR BABY JUST PICKED UP THE FLOOR.

GOD: STRONG LITTLE SUCKER, HE WAS.

MADGE: IT MUST HAVE BEEN A GREAT SURPRISE TO HIS NEW EARTHLY PARENTS TO FIND HIM THERE.

GOD: A GREAT RELIEF, YOU MEAN. YOU SEE, FOR A LONG TIME HIS FAMILY HAD NO ONE BUT THE WALL

TO TELL TO STAND UP STRAIGHT, SIT UP STRAIGHT, TRY HARDER, CLOSE YOUR MOUTH, STOP DROOLING, COOPERATE, SHUT UP...OH, YEAH, I FORGOT "PUT YOUR FEET ON THE WHEELCHAIR PEDALS, I'M TRYING TO PUSH YOU." YEAH, FINALLY HIS FAMILY HAD SOMEONE TO BITCH TO; PAUL, EASY GOING, DEPENDABLE, LIGHT-HEARTED, FLEXIBLE, ELASTICMAN.

MADGE: TELL ME MORE, TELL ME MORE, DID HE EVER GROW TALL TELL ME MORE, TELL ME MORE, TELL ME ALL ABOUT PAUL

GOD: WHEN PAUL CAME TO TOWSON, EVERYONE STARTED REPEATING EVERYTHING HE SAID, YOU KNOW, LIKE SUBTITLES. HE DIDN'T KNOW WHY THEY DID THIS; HE DIDN'T REPEAT WHATEVER THEY SAID. HIS FIRST REAL DEEP SENSE OF LOSS AND DISAPPOINTMENT WAS WHEN THE BIG MEAN HUNTER, NAMED DON, SHOT BABAAR'S MOTHER. THIS WAS ALSO HIS FIRST SHOWING OF EXTREME STUPIDITY. IT WAS ONLY A BOOK, FOR GOD'S SAKE. BUT ANYWAY, THEN PAUL WISED UP AND LEARNED HOW TO PLAY THE MILTON BRADLEY GAME OF 'JEOPARDY'. BY THE WAY, THAT WAS ONE OF MY BIG MISTAKES; TAKING THAT SHOW OFF THE AIR. BUT, LIKE GEORGE BURNS SAID, I TRY.

MADGE: OH I REMEMBER THAT SHOW. THAT WAS WHEN YOU ANSWERED THE QUESTIONS AND SHOWED HOW SMART YOU WERE. BUT WHEN PAUL PLAYED THE HOME GAME WITH HIS FAMILY, HE SHOWED OFF A LITTLE TOO MUCH, DIDN'T HE? THEN EVERY TIME HE'D ANSWER A QUESTION RIGHT, HE'D BE TOO EXCITED WITH HIMSELF THAT HE'D JUMP UP AND DOWN IN HIS WHEELCHAIR, FLEX HIS LEGS OUT, AND CONTORT HIS FACE UNCONTROLLABLY.

GOD: THAT'S RIGHT. NOW MADGE, IN CERTAIN CIRCUMSTANCES, FOR AN ATHETOID PERSON, THIS IS

PROPER, NATURAL, AND SOMETIMES EVEN BEAUTIFUL. BUT THE SECRETS THAT AN INTELLIGENT AFFLICTED YOUNG MAN OUGHT TO ACQUIRE ARE THE TIMES WHEN SUCH INVOLUNTARY MOVEMENTS SHOULD BE SUPPRESSED, WHEN THEY SHOULD BE IGNORED, AND WHEN IT MIGHT BE PROPER FOR THEM TO BE NOTICED, AND POSSIBLY EVEN ADMIRED. ALSO, AN ATTRIBUTE FOLKS LIKE PAUL GOT FROM ME IS MORE THAN AVERAGE DETERMINATION AND INTELLIGENCE. I FIGURED IT WAS THE LEAST I COULD DO. ANYWAY, AS PAUL LEARNED IN HIS EARLY LIFE, THESE TALENTS TOO HAVE TO BE MADE KNOWN TO PEOPLE AROUND HIM AS WELL AS TO BE PLAYED COOL. THEN CAME MR. PROPELLER. HE WAS THE PRINCIPAL OF PAUL'S NEW SCHOOL. HE DID NOTHING ALL DAY BUT ROAM THE HALLS, WITH HIS STERN FACE AND HIS POT BELLY, INTIMIDATING BASICALLY STABLE PEOPLE AND THE LIKE. LIKE PAUL, HE INTIMIDATED.

MR. PROPELLER: HELLO, PAUL, THIS IS YOUR PRINCIPAL, I'M HERE TO INTIMIDATE YOU.

GOD: AND THEN PAUL MIGHT HAVE MADE SOME INVOLUNTARY MOVEMENTS WITH HIS JAW, HANDS, ARMS, LEGS, OR ALL FOUR, WHICH MADE HIM APPEAR WEAK IN COMPARISON AND/OR UNABLE TO HAVE AN INTELLIGENT CONVERSATION. THAT'S ONE BITCH ABOUT CEREBRAL PALSY. I DON'T KNOW WHY I THOUGHT HE NEEDED THAT. I'M SORRY KID. ANYWAY, PAUL CAME THROUGH A LOT OF EMBARRASSMENT. A BIG PART OF HIS PHILOSOPHY WAS CONCERNED WITH PEOPLE OBSERVING OTHERS. PAUL SPOKE UP IN PROTEST WHEN DOCTORS AND THERAPISTS EXAMINED HIM IN THE WRONG CONTEXT. ONE TIME HE GOT A SURPRISE VISIT IN HIS OWN ROOM BY MR. PROPELLER, MR. YANTZHEAD, A THERAPIST WHO STILL WASN'T CONVINCED PAUL COULD PASS THE FIRST GRADE, AND

MISS MAYHAND, A VERY NICE LOOKING BLONDE WITH VERY BIG BREASTS.

MR. PROPELLER: HI PAUL, I USED TO KNOW YOU REALLY WELL BUT NOW I'VE NEVER MET YOU BEFORE.

MR. YANTZHEAD: HI PAUL. (CAN HE HEAR ME? CAN HE UNDERSTAND ME? CAN HE ANSWER ME?)

MISS MAYHAND: HI PAUL, I'M MISS MAYHAND, THE SOCIAL WORKER. DON'T WORRY, I'M WELL QUALIFIED. I HAVE FOUR DEGREES, MANY CERTIFICATIONS AND I THINK I CAN EXPLAIN WHY WE ALL BARGED IN ON YOU. YOU SEE, WE WANT TO GET A GOOD WRITE-UP ON YOU AND ACQUIRE A WELL FORMED PICTURE OF THE SELF-HELP SKILLS A MILDLY ATHETOID CEREBRAL PALSY TEEN-AGER LEARNS BY HIMSELF THROUGH EXPERIENCE. WE ARE INTERESTED IN OBSERVING YOU OFF GUARD LIKE THIS AND SEEING HOW YOU DEAL WITH SUCH SELF-HELP NECESSITIES AS COMMUNICATION, MOBILITY, EATING, DRINKING, BATHROOMING, BATHING, SITTING, STANDING, WALKING,...

PAUL: YOUR BASIC SHIT LIKE THAT, EH?

MR. PROPELLER: DON'T FORGET SEXUAL SATISFACTION.

PAUL: WELL NOW, WAIT A MINUTE HERE, I---

MISS MAYHAND: BY THE WAY, DO YOU DROOL, PAUL?

PAUL: SOMETIMES I CAN'T CONTROL IT, YES I DO.

MISS MAYHAND: EW, GROSS I DON'T WANT TO SEE HIM, EW, GROSS, GET ME OUT OF HERE! EW GROSS!

PAUL: NOW, AT THIS POINT I MUST OBJECT. NOW, I WAS JUST HAVING FUN WITH MY STEREO. YOU THREE

JUST COME IN HERE WITHOUT WARNING, STARTLE ME, AND STAY HERE EVEN THOUGH YOU SEE I'M STARTLED, EXCITED, AND UNABLE TO RELAX AROUND THREE STRANGERS ASKING PERSONAL QUESTIONS WITHOUT WARNING. NOW, I'LL BE HAPPY TO ANSWER YOUR QUESTIONS IF YOU GIVE ME A FEW MINUTES TO PREPARE MYSELF FOR THE WAY I WOULD LIKE TO BE PRESENTED. OK, NOW, IF YOU REALLY WANT TO KNOW ABOUT MY SEXUAL SATISFACTION...

GOD: PAUL THEN SMOTHERED THE HONEY OF A SOCIAL WORKER WITH SLOBBER. SHE HOLLERED A LOT BUT SHE CAME OUT OF IT SMILING.

MADGE: WELL AFTER HIS EARTHLY FATHER, JOHN DIED, ANSWERING TOO MANY QUESTIONS AT JEOPARDY, HE DECIDED TO LEAVE HOME AND GO INTO THE WORLD. HE WAS THEN VISITED THROUGH GREAT FLASHBACK AND SUPER-IMPOSING DEVICES, BY HIS REAL FATHER CUTE-OL, AND GIVEN THE WHOLE STORY OF THE DESTINATION HIS LIFE MUST PURSUE.

CUTE-OL: I AM CUTE-OL, MAN. I WAS YOUR FATHER. YOU ARE COCK-EL. YOU COME FROM THE PLANET, HEADSTICK. YOUR BROTHER WAS COCKER, JOE COCKER. BUT HE WAS KILLED BY JOHN BELUSHI AFTER HE VOMITED ON HIS DOG, SCRUFFY. THAT'S ANOTHER STORY. OUR PLANET WAS DESTROYED BUT I GAVE YOU NEW LIFE. NOW I GIVE YOU MY MIND, ALL OF IT. YOU NEED IT ALL.

> I AM YOUR HALF, MY SON, YOU MAKE ME WHOLE
> I GIVE YOU MY MIND
> YOU FILL MY SOUL WITH ALL THE PRIDE AND
> ESTEEM
> I CAN MUSTER FOR YOU
> AND ALL THE FORTHRIGHT KNOWLEDGE
> I BARE FOR YOU
> YOU ARE BUT A CHILD OF THE UNIVERSE

BUT THE UNIVERSE IS MERELY AN IMAGE
SEEN THROUGH A CHILD'S EYES
YOU ARE ONE IN A GREAT NUMBER,
YET THAT NUMBER CAN BE YOURS
LEADERSHIP IS NOT REQUIRED IN HONOR,
HONOR IS NOT REQUIRED IN FRIENDSHIP,
FRIENDSHIP ISN'T DEMANDED IN RESPECT,
AND BORROWING RESPECT, REMAINS HUMAN
DIGNITY
CHOOSE YOUR FRIENDS WISELY
CHOOSE ENEMIES GREATLY MORE WISELY,
FOR 'TIS BETTER TO HAVE TOO FEW
YOU COME FROM A CHAIN, MY SON,
A CHAIN OF WORKERS, TRYERS, AND PERSONAL
SUCCEEDERS,
DON'T LOOSEN YOUR GRIP
IF INSTINCTS LEAD YOU STRAIGHT, MOVE ON,
YOURSELF,
IF HEART SAYS YOU'RE WINDING, IMPROVE ON
YOURSELF
DON'T FEAR TURNING BACK ON WRONG
ROUTES
IT IS HOW YOU'LL MEET YOUR DESTINATION,
DON'T HESITATE GOING ON LONELY ROADS
THE SHORTEST WAY TO THE POINT IS WITH AN
HONEST LINE
WHEN, FINALLY YOU MEET LIFE'S CLIMAX, THE
ULTIMATE GREAT,
THE FINAL GOOD,
SON, I'LL BE WAITING JUST FOR YOU, TO TELL YOU
EVERYTHING
YOU DID RIGHT.

MADGE: THEN PAUL STARTED SCHOOL AT 'THE
COCKEYSVILLE VACUUM', HE WAS MAINSTREAMED.

GOD: YOU MEAN PUT IN SCHOOL WITH THE REGULAR SUCKERS.

MADGE: THAT'S RIGHT.

GOD: THANK YOU.

MADGE: I CAN STILL HEAR HIM THE FIRST DAY WHEN THE HYDRAULIC LIFT ON HIS SCHOOLBUS REACHED THE GROUND.

PAUL: WELL, THIS IS IT.

MADGE: AND WHEN HE ARRIVED IN HIS CLASSROOM AND MET THE PEOPLE HE HAD TO WORK WITH, AH, IT WAS AS HECTIC AS A CITY ROOM IN A BIG METROPOLITAN NEWSPAPER. HIS TEACHER, PERRY EDWINS, WAS INTRODUCING YOUNG PAUL AROUND.

MRS. EDWINS: HERE ARE THE PEOPLE YOU'LL BE WORKING WITH, PEROUTKA. YOU SEE, EVERYBODY IN THIS ROOM IS NAMED JIMMY. ONE TIME WE HAD A JOHN, BUT IT GOT TOO CONFUSING. NOW, THIS IS JIMMY COOK. SAY HELLO, JIMMY.

JIMMY: HI PAUL.

MRS. EDWINS: AND THIS IS JIMMY SARENDINO.

JIMMY: HI PAUL, HOW YOU DOING?

PAUL: OH, JUST FINE.

MRS. EDWINS: AND THIS IS OUR ONLY WOMAN HERE. SAY HELLO, MISS LINDA LOSERY.

LINDA: AH, DO I HAVE TO? AH, MY MOM'S COMING TO PICK ME UP REAL SOON, IS IT TIME TO GO YET, AH CRAP...

MRS. EDWINS: LINDA, I WANT YOU TO SHOW PAUL, HERE, THE ROPES.

LINDA: AH, DO I HAVE TO? AH, I'M WAITING TO GO TO LUNCH WITH SOME OF MY FRIENDS. WILL IT TAKE LONG? HE LOOKS FUNNY.

PAUL: I PROMISE NOT TO GET IN YOUR WAY, MISS LOSERY.

LINDA: WELL, SEE THAT YOU DON'T, MR. PEROUTKA.

PAUL: GOSH, SHE MUST REALLY RESPECT ME. NOBODY'S EVER CALLED ME MR. PEROUTKA BEFORE.

MRS. EDWINS: NOW, PAUL, HERE IS YOUR DAILY SCHEDULE. FIRST YOU GO TO LATIN, THEN YOU GO TO SPANISH, THEN YOU GO TO BIOLOGY, THEN ALGEBRA, THEN ENGLISH, THEN JOURNALISM, THEN HISTORY, THEN BUSINESS MANAGEMENT, THEN MAYBE YOU'LL HAVE TIME FOR A QUICK BITE TO EAT, THEN WE'LL TAKE YOU TO ENGLISH...

MADGE: GOSH! BY THE TIME SHE FINISHED RECITING HIS SCHEDULE, IT WAS TIME TO GO HOME. THEN IT WAS TIME TO GO TO INTERNATIONAL PERSPECTIVE, A FANCY WAY OF SAYING SOCIAL STUDIES. PAUL HAD CLASS IN A LARGE LECTURE HALL. THE COURSE WAS TAUGHT BY TWO TEACHERS, THE LADY BEING MISS BLUEBELL, AND THE MAN BEING MR. RICHARD N. MIXON. YOU'D HAVE TO SEE THE CLASS TO BELIEVE IT...

MR. MIXON: NOW, LADIES AND GENTLEMEN, IN ORDER TO MAKE THIS COURSE PERFECTLY CLEAR, WE WOULD

HAVE TO GO THROUGH AND TRY TO EVALUATE JUST WHAT IT IS WE WILL BE TALKING ABOUT IN THIS CLASS. NOW YOU MUST BE VERY VERY SURE TO BE VERY VERY MINDFUL NOT TO GO THROUGH AND CONFUSE ONE VERY VERY PARTICULAR PERIOD WITH ANOTHER VERY VERY IMPORTANT TIME IN HIST'RY. NOW, IN ORDER TO GO THROUGH AND...AH NOW, I BELIEVE NOW THAT I AM RUNNING COMPETITION WITH SOME MEMBERS OF OUR CLASS. NOW, SOME OF US HAVE GONE THROUGH AND DISRUPTED US BY HAVING THEIR OWN CONVERSATION WHILE I'M TALKING. NOW I HATE TO CALL OUT EXAMPLES, ROY AND RILEY. AND I SEE A MR. MATCH OUT THERE TALKING. BY THE WAY, WHAT'S YOUR FIRST NAME?

MR. MATCH: MITCHELL, BUT MY FRIENDS ALL CALL ME MITCH.

MIXON: ALRIGHT, MITCH MATCH, GO THROUGH AND SHUT UP. IF IT'S A CASE OF A STUDENT UNDERSTANDING THE CURRICULUM PERFECTLY, THEN HE OR SHE SHOULD GO THROUGH AND PUT THEIR HEADS DOWN AND GO TO SLEEP.

MADGE: WHAT DO YOU THINK HAPPENED? THEY ALL WENT TO SLEEP. THIS REALLY PISSED HIM OFF.

MIXON: ALRIGHT, THAT GOES THROUGH TO BE IT! FROM NOW ON I WILL BE STANDING AT THE FRONT OF THE AISLE AND MISS BLUEBELL WILL BE HERE AT THE OVERHEAD TEACHING YOUR MATERIAL AND YOU KNOW WHAT THAT MEANS. IF WE CALL YOU UP HERE BECAUSE YOU HAVE GONE THROUGH AND GOOFED OFF, YOU KNOW WHAT YOU HAVE TO DO! ALRIGHT, MISS BLUEBELL, TAKE OVER, PLEZ.

MISS BLUEBELL: ALRIGHT, I THINK YOU ALL UNDERSTAND HOW IT'S GOING TO BE IN THIS CLASSROOM. NOW,

IN ORDER TO UNDERSTAND OUR HISTORY, WE MUST RE-EVALUATE OUR OWN PERSONAL LIFESTYLES. ACCORDING TO...I AM NOW RUNNING COMPETITION WITH A COUPLE PEOPLE IN HERE. I WILL NOW ASK MR. RILEY TO STEP UP TO THE FRONT, IN FRONT OF MR. MIXON, NOTHING WILL BE SAID TO YOU: JUST DROP YOUR PANTS.

RILEY: OOOWWWW!!! OOWWWWW! OOOOHH, OOWWW!!! OOH, PAIN, OOHHH...

MISS BLUEBELL: NOW, CLASS, BACK TO THE MIDDLE AGES...OH OH, RUNNING COMPETITION. MR. MATCH, PLEASE REPORT TO MR. MIXON.

MADGE: THIS PRACTICE OF DISCIPLINE DONE BY THESE HISTORY TEACHERS GREATLY SHOCKED, REPULSED, AND INFURIATED PAUL. SO, HE DID THE ONLY THING HE WAS ABLE TO DO. BEING VERY MOVED AND UPSET AT THE BOY'S MISFORTUNE, HIS BODY BECAME UNCONTROLLABLY STIFF AND TIGHT. HE BEGAN BREATHING IRREGULARLY, THUS LOUDLY AND QUEERLY, WHEN HE DID BREATHE AT ALL. HE MADE MANY NOISES AS HIS ARMS AND LEGS ROCKED HIS WHEELCHAIR. BUT WITH A FIRM LOOK ON HIS GRIMACED FACE, IT WAS OBVIOUS HE HAD AN IMPORTANT MESSAGE TO EXCLAIM AND HE WOULD BE HEARD.

PAUL: STOP IT! STOP IT, I SAY. THIS IS WRONG!!

RILEY: LOOK, IT'S JOE COCKER.

ROY: NO, IT'S CHRISTIE BROWN.

PAUL: NO, IT'S SPASTICMAN. THAT'S RIGHT, SPASTICMAN. I'M HERE TO REPRESENT MY PEOPLE, THE HANDICAPPED, BUT ESPECIALLY THOSE WHO CAN'T CONTROL FACIAL AND BODILY INVOLUNTARY MOVEMENTS, THOSE WHO

MIGHT BE CONSIDERED UGLY, OR NOT ATTRACTIVE TO LOOK AT, THOSE WHO MIGHT BE TREATED AS OUTCASTS. WE'RE NOT LOOKING FOR SPECIAL TREATMENT AND FLATTERY, WE'D JUST LIKE TO BE RESPECTED AMONGST SOCIETY. NOW I HAPPEN TO BE APPALLED AT THE BEHAVIOR IN THIS CLASS, NOT NECESSARILY OF THE KIDS, BUT OF THE TEACHERS. AND I'M NOT ASHAMED TO LET MY TRUE FEELINGS SHOW. MAYBE IF I DRAW ATTENTION TO MYSELF, YOU MIGHT REMEMBER HOW LUCKY YOU ALL REALLY ARE. AND THAT'S ALL I HAVE TO SAY.

MADGE: AFTER THAT VISIT FROM SPASTICMAN, ALL THE KIDS WERE AMAZED, STARSTRUCK---ESPECIALLY THE GIRLS...

VIVICA: OH, SPASTICMAN, CAN I HAVE YOUR AUTOGRAPH???

DIANA: OH SPASTICMAN, YOU'RE MY HERO.

CAROL: YOU'RE GREAT, SPASTICMAN, I WANT YOU, I WANT YOU.

MR. MIXON: HE'S SO GREAT, I THINK I CAN FINISH A SENTENCE NOW. I'LL NEVER HURT ANOTHER STUDENT.

LINDA: WELL, I DON'T KNOW, I DON'T THINK HE'S SO GREAT.

PAUL: AND WHO MIGHT YOU BE, YOUNG PRINCESS, AND MIGHT YOU GO TO THE DANCE WITH ME THIS FRIDAY NIGHT?

LINDA: YES, I'D LOVE TO...I MEAN, I GUESS IT WOULD BE ALRIGHT.

MADGE: WELL, LINDA CAME TO THE DANCE, AND SHE SPENT HALF THE NIGHT LOOKING FOR HER HANDSOME DATE, SPASTICMAN. FINALLY SHE RAN INTO PLAIN OLD INFERIOR PAUL.

PAUL: HI, LINDA. HOW'S IT GOING?

LINDA: OH, FINE, I GUESS.

PAUL: CAN I SIT DOWN NEXT TO YOU?

LINDA: WELL, I'M EXPECTING SOMEONE, KINDA. NO, I GUESS IT'S ALRIGHT.

PAUL: YOU KNOW, LINDA, YOU'RE QUITE AN ATTRACTIVE GIRL, VERY POPULAR.

LINDA: OH, IF YOU SAY SO. UH, WHAT'S YOUR NAME AGAIN?

PAUL: IT'S PAUL. PAUL'S MY NAME. YEAH.

LINDA: YEAH, HA. OH, IT'S A NICE NIGHT. NOT TOO HOT, NOT TOO COOL.

PAUL: NO, NO. NOT TOO HOT, NOT TOO...LINDA, WOULD YOU LIKE TO GET SPASTIC WITH ME?
LINDA: YOU MEAN LIKE...WITH YOU? WHY SURE, WHY NOT?

MADGE: SO THE COUPLE DID IT TOGETHER. THEY BOTH FLEXED OUT THEIR LEGS AND ARMS AND MADE FUNNY NOISES BREATHING. IT WAS SO ROMANTIC. AND THE MOMENT WAS MADE EVEN MORE MAGICAL BY THE SINGER AT THE DANCE, THE FAMOUS MICHAEL ANTHONY SINGING THIS LOVELY SONG...

I TOLD MY FRIENDS ABOUT YOU

THEY ALL SAID IT'S GOOD THAT I'M IN LOVE
AGAIN
AND LOOKING FINE
THEY ALL WANT TO KNOW YOU
THE WAY I WANT TO SHOW YOU TO ALL OF
THEM
AND SAY YOU'RE MINE
YOU MAKE ME FEEL AS GOOD AS I EVER COULD
'CAUSE YOU MAKE ME FEEL ENTIRELY GOOD
I WAS WITH YOU THE OTHER NIGHT
YOU MADE ME SEE THE WHOLE WORLD COULD BE
SO RIGHT
I HAD TO SMILE
I THINK ABOUT YOU ALL THE TIME
MY THOUGHTS DISTRACTED BY THOUGHTS OF
LOVING YOU DAY AND NIGHT
AND ALL THE WHILE
WITH YOU I CAN MAKE IT MORE THAN I EVER
WOULD
'CAUSE YOU MAKE ME FEEL ENTIRELY GOOD

MADGE: OH, AND HERE'S ANOTHER EPISODE IN SCHOOL.
YOU SEE, PAUL SOMETIMES FOUND IT HARD TO KEEP
STILL AND QUIET IN CLASS WHILE OTHER KIDS READ
THEIR PRESENTATION OR RECITED THEIR ASSIGNMENT.
THERE WAS ONE DAY IN CREATIVE WRITING CLASS
WHEN A PRETTY GIRL WAS CHOSEN TO READ ALOUD
HER ESSAY. PAUL, WANTING TO BE JUST A REGULAR GUY,
JUST WANTED TO LISTEN PASSIVELY TO THE GIRL. BUT,
AS HAS HAPPENED BEFORE, THE IDEA THAT HE MIGHT
MAKE NOISE ONLY REINFORCED HIM TO MAKE MORE
NOISE THAN HE MIGHT HAVE IF HE DIDN'T THINK
ABOUT IT AT ALL. ANYWAY, AS SOON AS THE FIRST
GIRL STARTED TO SPEAK, BLOOD RAN TO PAUL'S HEAD
WHICH WAS THE FIRST SIGN THAT HE'D BE LIKELY TO
HAVE INVOLUNTARY MOTION AND WOULD HAVE TO
TALK HIMSELF DOWN TO A RELAXED STATE AGAIN.

TEACHER, MISS K. JOHNSON: WE WILL NOW HEAR FROM OUR FIRST STUDENT, MARILYN QUARTERS.

MARILYN:
WELL, YOU SEE, MY REPORT IS ABOUT PLAYBOY MAGAZINE. YOU SEE, IT'S RUN BY THIS GUY NAMED HUGH HEFNER, AND THEY TELL ME HE'S HORNY 24 HOURS A DAY. EVEN AFTER HE'S DONE IT, HE'S STILL HORNY; AND BY THE WAY, HE DOES IT TWICE, DAILY, AND THEY TELL ME THAT HE'S NEVER DONE IT WITH THE SAME ONE TWICE, BUNNY, I MEAN. HE HAS GIRLS DRESSED UP AS BUNNY RABBITS AND THEY SERVE YOU DRINKS AT THE NIGHT CLUBS AND THEN HE TAKES PICTURES OF NUDE GIRLS ON THE BED AND THEY DO WEIRD THINGS ON THE BED, MAN. I MEAN YOU WOULDN'T THINK THEY COULD DO IN A LYING DOWN POSITION, THEY DO IN A LYING DOWN POSITION AND IT'S STRANGE, MAN, I MEAN...

PAULS THOUGHTS: NOW, C'MON, KID, DON'T START MAKING NOISE JUST BECAUSE YOU DON'T WANT TO. THAT DOESN'T MAKE SENSE AT ALL, DOES IT? NO. NOW, I WILL STAY WITH THIS PROBLEM CONCENTRATING ON RELAXING UNTIL YOU DO RELAX. DON'T WORRY. NOW, DON'T WORRY ABOUT KEEPING STILL BY SUPPRESSING YOUR ARMS AND LEGS SO THEY WON'T MOVE. THAT'LL NEVER RELAX YOU. TOO MANY PEOPLE MIGHT THINK IT WILL, BUT IT'LL ONLY BRING YOUR RESPIRATORY SYSTEM INTO PLAY WHICH WILL MAKE NOISE WHEN YOU BREATHE LOUD AND THAT'S WHAT YOU DON'T WANT TO HAPPEN. NOW RELAX, JUST BE A REGULAR GUY, GOD, I WISH I WAS A REGULAR GUY, GOD, THAT WAS A DISGUSTING REPORT

MISS K. JOHNSON: THAT WAS VERY GOOD, MARILYN, THANK YOU. AND THANK YOU, SPASTICMAN. YOU'VE MADE OUR WORK SO MUCH MORE MEANINGFUL.

PAUL: WELL, WHAT D'YOU KNOW?...

MADGE: GOD, I HAVE THE FEELING I'M COMING TO THE CLIMAX OF THE STORY OF SPASTICMAN. SOMETHING ABOUT PAUL BEING AN AUDIENCE WHILE A TEACHER MADE LOVE TO HIS WIFE AND SAVED HIS MARRIAGE BY MAKING THE COUPLE REALIZE JUST HOW BEAUTIFUL THEIR LOVE-MAKING WAS AND HOW FORTUNATE THEY WERE TO HAVE EACH OTHER? IS THAT IT?

GOD: YEAH, AND DIDN'T THE VICE PRINCIPAL, MR. BROKAW, ANNOUNCE IT OVER THE INTERCOM? IT WAS DURING MORNING ANNOUNCEMENTS...

MR. BROKAW: ...UNDER GOD, INDIVISIBLE, WITH LIBERTY AND JUSTICE FOR ALL. PLEASE BE SEATED. WE WOULD LIKE TO CONGRATULATE OUR BASEBALL TEAM FOR A SEASON WELL PLAYED. WE WON NO GAMES BUT GEE, WERE OUR UNIFORMS SHINY WHITE. OUR SCHOOL WILL BE VISITED BY SEVENTH GRADERS TODAY SO IT'S NATIONAL 'BE NICE TO A LITTLE BUGGER DAY'. MS. THOMAS REMINDS ALL FRENCH TO BRING THEIR BOOKS TO CLASS TODAY. MISS K. JOHNSON'S MENSTRUAL CYCLE BEGINS TODAY SO BE ON THE LOOK-OUT FOR THAT. AND AN ANONYMOUS TEACHER WOULD LIKE TO THANK SPASTICMAN FOR SAVING HIS MARRIAGE LAST NIGHT.

ALL IN THE CLASS: YEH YEH!! SPASTICMAN'S A HERO! SPASTICMAN'S A HERO! SPASTICMAN'S A HERO, SPASTICMAN'S A HERO!!

JIMMIES: YEH! LET'S ALL GIVE SPASTICMAN A PARADE!

ALL: YEAH YEAH! HURRAY! HURRAY!!

MADGE: SO THEY CARRIED THEIR HERO, SPASTICMAN, ALL AROUND THE HALLS OF THE GOOD OL' SCHOOL, UP AND DOWN THE STREETS OF THE GOOD OL' TOWN, THE MUSIC COULD BE HEARD PLAYING ALL OVER THE GOOD OL' STATE. AND IT WAS THE FINEST PARADE IN THE GOOD OL' WORLD. THEY EVEN HAD A GOOSE THERE AND IT WAS THE FINEST GOOSE. OK, SO THE PARADE LASTED FOR THREE WHOLE DAYS. IT WAS THE MOST VICTORIOUS CELEBRATION EVER GIVEN FOR ANY CHAMPION, EVER. IT WAS THEIR HERO SPASTICMAN. IT SEEMED LIKE THE FESTIVAL WOULD NEVER END BUT WHEN IT FINALLY CAME TO AN OUTSTANDING CONCLUSION IN THE SCHOOL LIBRARY, ONE OF THE JIMMIES NOTICED THAT ALTHOUGH HAPPY AND VERY PLEASED, PAUL'S FACE WAS JUST A BIT HESITANT.

JIMMY: WELL, WHAT DO YOU REALLY WANT, HERO?

PAUL: I DON'T WANT TO HAVE TO BE SPASTIC ANYMORE.

PAUL PEROUTKA THEN VANISHED FROM THAT SITE. IT IS BELIEVED HE WAS IMMEDIATELY TRANSCENDED MIRACULOUSLY TO THE ROOF OF THE EMPIRE STATE BUILDING IN NEW YORK CITY, WHERE ALL HIS AFASIA AND HIS INFIRMITIES LEFT HIM, HIS BODY STRIPPED OF HANDICAP, HIS MIND STRIPPED OF WORRY AND SHAME. HE HAD WON HIS FINAL VICTORY AND IS SAID NOW TO CELEBRATE IT ETERNALLY.

MADGE: LORD, WHAT DID HAPPEN ON THE EMPIRE STATE BUILDING? CAN YOU TELL ME? LORD, LORD, ARE YOU ALRIGHT?

GOD: WHAT? WHAT DID YOU SAY? I DIDN'T HEAR YOU.

MADGE: I JUST ASKED YOU WHAT REALLY HAPPENED WHEN PAUL WAS ON THE EMPIRE STATE BUILDING? CAN YOU TELL ME OR IS IT TOO UPSETTING?

GOD: NO, NO. I'LL TELL YOU. YOU SEE, PAUL BEGAN TO FLAP HIS ARMS AND YELL AND SCREAM VICTORIOUSLY, BELIEVING HE NOW HAD PERFECT CONTROL OF HIS MUSCLES, MOTOR ABILITIES AND SPEECH. IN FACT, HE STILL DIDN'T. I JUST COULDN'T MAKE IT HAPPEN. IT LOOKS LIKE I'VE SCREWED HIM UP BEYOND REPAIR. WHAT CAN I SAY? I LOST THE OXYGEN. I'M SORRY KID.

MADGE: LORD, WHY ARE YOU SO CONFUSED? IS SOMETHING THE MATTER?

GOD: IT'S JUST WHAT I'M SEEING HAPPENING TO PAUL NOW. IT'S ANOTHER INSTANCE IN THE BATHTUB.

MADGE: OH, IT COULDN'T BE ANY WORSE THAN WHAT HE'S ALREADY ENDURED.

GOD: I'M AFRAID IT IS.

MADGE: OH REALLY? TELL ME ABOUT IT!

GOD: I CAN'T. IT'S TOO PAINFUL.

MADGE: OH, COME ON, POWERFUL GUY. YOU'VE TOLD ME EVERYTHING SO FAR.

GOD: NO, I DON'T WANT TO GO THROUGH THAT AGAIN. PLEASE DON'T MAKE ME.

MADGE: THAT'S RED DYE NUMBER TWO YOU'RE SOAKING IN.

GOD: ALRIGHT! ALRIGHT! I'LL TELL YOU. IT ALL STARTED WHEN THE TELEPHONE RANG ONE SUMMER DAY AT THE PEROUTKA RESIDENCE. PAUL'S MOTHER ANSWERED IT AND IT WAS ALISON JEAN DIAMBROGE.

MOTHER: YES...YES...OH HELLO...WHY, SURE, I'LL ASK HIM, HE'S RIGHT HERE. PAUL, THIS GIRL SAYS YOU KNOW HER. SHE SAYS HER C.Y.O. GROUP IS GOING SWIMMING THIS SATURDAY AT HER HOUSE AND THEY NEED A TOKEN HANDICAPPED BOY TO MAKE THE PARTY COMPLETE. CAN YOU MAKE IT? IT SOUNDS LIKE A VERY CHRISTIAN EVENT. YOU KNOW HOW YOUTHS ARE. YOU MAY EVEN BE ONE YOURSELF SOMEDAY.

GOD: THEN PAUL FIGURED OUT THE WHOLE SITUATION INSTANTLY.

PAUL: (TO HIMSELF) IT'S A PLOY, THE GIRL WANTS MY BODY!

GOD: THEN HE GRATEFULLY ACCEPTED AND ARRIVED AT THE GIRL'S HOUSE ON SATURDAY.

MADGE: WHAT HAPPENED WHEN HE GOT THERE, LORD?

GOD: YOU'RE A SUCKER FOR SMUT, AREN'T YOU? WELL THERE WAS NO C.Y.O. GROUP. PAUL SEARCHED THE HOUSE WITHOUT FINDING A SOUL. FINALLY HIS EARS HEARD DYLAN'S 'LAY, LADY, LAY'. HIS LUNGS INHALED AMBIANCE. HIS FEET FELT LATHERY WATER FLOWING INTO THE HALLWAY, HIS MOUTH TASTED EXCESS SALIVA AND HIS EYES GAZED SEEING ALISON JEAN DIAMBROGE NUDE, SUBMERGED IN A BUBBLE TUB. HER

LEGS, SPREADING AND CREEPING UP OUT FROM THE WATER, THE BUBBLES POPPING AS HER BREATHING TURNED TO PANTING, HER SOFT VOICE BECAME PURRS OF YEARNING.

ALISON: IT'S YOU I WANT. SO GLAD YOU COULD COME. NOW YOU KNOW WHAT YOU MUST DO. SATISFY ME, PAUL. ONLY YOU CAN. YOU MUST. I WANT YOU. I NEED YOU. I MUST HAVE YOU, NOW...

PAUL: HEY, UH, ARE YOU TRYING TO SEDUCE ME, MISS DIAMBROGE?

MADGE: DE, D D D, D D D D, D, D D D, D, AND HERE'S TO YOU MRS...

GOD: SHADDUP, WILLYA?

ALISON: I DON'T WANT DUSTIN HOFFMAN, I WANT YOU. BESIDES HE HAS NO GENITALIA. TAKE ME, PAUL. I'M YOURS. I MUST BE YOURS. AND YOU WILL BE MINE. I CRAVE YOU, I DREAM OF YOU AND I BECOME AROUSED. OH, PAUL, I'M MORE THAN AROUSED NOW. I'M DRAINED, I'M DESPERATE. I NEED TO HOLD YOU, CARESS YOU, MAKE YOU, MY TIGER, INTO A PUSSYCAT. COME CLOSER. I MUST BE EASED, I MUST BE COOLED. I MUST BE HAD, POSSESSED BY YOU, YOU AND ONLY YOU.

TELEPHONE RINGS.

MOTHER: PARDON ME, BUT ARE YOU GONNA BE ALRIGHT FEEDING PAUL AND ALL THAT? SOMETIMES IT'S HARD TO GET FOOD AND LIQUID INTO HIM. I COULD COME OVER AND SHOW YOU HOW IT'S DONE IF YOU'D LIKE.

FATHER: THIS IS MR. PEROUTKA ON THE EXTENSION. HOW ABOUT BATHROOMING? I THINK THE BEST THING

TO DO IS ASK HIM EVERY HALF HOUR OR SO IF HE HAS TO GO AND THEN WHEN YOU TAKE HIM, YOU HAVE TO YELL AT HIM AND MAKE HIM FEEL INFERIOR, THAT'LL HELP HIM TO GO. AND THEN...

ALISON: IT'S YOUR PARENTS.

PAUL: DEAR GOD, COULD YOU POSSIBLY HELP ME OUT ON THIS SITUATION, PLEASE?

GOD: NO SHIT, PAUL, I CAN TAKE CARE OF IT.

ALISON: THAT'S FUNNY, THE PHONE JUST WENT DEAD. ANYWAY, IT DOESN'T MATTER NOW, DARLING. IT'S ALL COMING TRUE, YOUR DREAM AND MINE. WE WILL FULFILL EACH OTHER. I WILL COME TO YOU NOW, PLAY WITH YOU, AND SET YOU FREE, SET US BOTH FREE FROM OUR YEARNING AND OUR LUST FOR EACH OTHER. OH COOL ME, COOL ME OFF BUT KEEP ME WARM. TAKE ME, HOLD ME. TAKE ME!

GOD: SHE ROSE FROM THE TUB, HER BREASTS DRIPPING BUT CLEARLY SEEN AND DESIRED BY HIM. HER SOAKING BODY APPEARED SHINY, THEREFORE ANGELIC AND BEAUTIFUL IN THE SENSUOUS LIGHT AS SHE SLOWLY AND SEDUCTIVELY FREED HER LONG DARK HAIR FROM THE BACK AND LET IT COVER HER SHOULDERS. HER WALK WAS BRISK AS HER STIMULATIONS WERE PIQUED AND ANXIETIES WHETTED. SHE WAS STIFLED FOR AN INSTANCE BY THE SIGHT OF DROOL ON HIS LOWER LIP.

PAUL: GOD: COULD YOU HELP ME OUT HERE?

GOD: NO SHIT, PAUL. I CAN TAKE CARE OF THIS. I BACK-FLOWED THE SALIVA PLUS ANY FUTURE SALIVA HE MIGHT HAVE TO WORRY ABOUT. WHAT THE HELL, I TOOK AWAY ONE HINDRANCE FOR A WHILE; I'M A

NICE GUY. SHE DREW CLOSER AND CLOSER. IT GREW NEARER AND NEARER TO THE MOMENT WHEN PAUL WOULD HAVE TO PERFORM THE MOST DARING AND BRAVEST DEED HE HAS EVER HAD TO DO. EVERY MUSCLE IN HIS BODY WAS STIFFENED AND TIGHT, IN FACT, BEYOND ANY HOPE OF EVER LOOSENING FULLY. HE WAS UNDERGOING PAIN AND FRIGIDIBILITY BEYOND HUMAN TOLERANCE.

MADGE: YOU MEAN LIKE...

GOD: YES, LIKE SPASTICMAN. BUT SPASTICITY HAS NO PLACE IN A CLIMAX, OF A STORY OR ANYTHING ELSE.

PAUL: GOD, CAN YOU PLEASE TAKE CARE OF THIS.

GOD: I TOLD HIM NO SHIT AND RELIEVED A FEW SPASMS IN HIS BODY. BUT HE STILL HAD LITTLE CONTROL OF HIS MOVEMENTS OR HIS BLOOD PRESSURE AS THE WOMAN WANTED TO SEDUCE HIM, AND THE ACT HE NEEDED SO BADLY TO PERFORM AND ENJOY AS NORMALLY, SMOOTHLY AND MASCULINELY AS HE COULD, GREW EVER CLOSER.

PAUL: GOD: YOU'VE HELPED ME BEFORE. NOW, CAN'T YOU TAKE THE WHOLE DAMN HANDICAP AWAY FROM ME?

GOD: OH DAMN IT. NO, PAUL. I LOST THE OXYGEN. I'M SORRY, PAUL.

> WHEN THEY UNDERSTAND
> I MAY BE FAR AWAY; IT MIGHT NOT MATTER TO ME
> BUT WHAT A DAY, WHEN THEY SEE
> HOW HARD I TRIED; WILL THEY CARE HOW MUCH I CRIED

WHEN THEY UNDERSTAND
WHAT I TRIED TO DO, AND I WAS UNABLE TO
SAY
BUT WHAT DID I DO; AND WHAT COULD THEY
SEE
THEY WILL ONE DAY KNOW THE ME THAT DIDN'T
SHOW
I'VE BEEN ABLE TO TAKE A THOUSAND FALLS
THE ONE WHO'LL TAKE MY HAND IS ME
WHEN THEY UNDERSTAND
WHETHER I'M HERE OR GONE; I'LL BE A HAPPIER
MAN THEN
I'LL EXPLAIN TO NO ONE; YOU DON'T EXPLAIN TO
THOSE WHO UNDERSTAND
I WON'T HAVE TO PROVE I'M A MAN
WHEN THEY UNDERSTAND

A FRIEND

OH, HI THERE. HOW YOU DOING? NICE DAY OUT HERE TODAY, ISN'T IT? YEAH, SUN'S A LITTLE BRIGHT, BUT... NICE DAY. YOU COME TO THE GAMES OFTEN? YEAH? YOU LIKE LACROSSE? YEAH. OH, WHAT? OH SORRY WHAT? YOU TRYING TO SAY SOMETHING? OH. HA, YEAH. OK WHAT? NO, DON'T BE DISCOURAGED. IT'S JUST THAT I CAN'T UNDERSTAND YOU. I'M SLOW, YOU SEE, EH? HAHA. WHAT'S THAT AGAIN? ARE YOU TELLING ME THAT YOU LIKE THE GAME? AH SURE, I LIKE IT TOO. WE GOT A GOOD TEAM THIS YEAR. YEAH, UH, YOU DON'T GO HERE, DO YOU? NO? YOU JUST CAME OUT HERE TO WATCH A GOOD GAME EH? YEAH! WE'RE GONNA KICK-ASS TODAY, MAN. OOPS! I'M SORRY. I GOTTA WATCH MY MOUTH, DON'T I? WHAT'S THAT? YOU'RE LAUGHING SO HARD. YOU MUST LIKE THAT KINDA LANGUAGE, EH? YEAH! NOTHING WRONG WITH THAT. BUT I BETTER WATCH MYSELF, THERE MIGHT BE GROWN-UPS AROUND. WHAT'S THAT? THERE AIN'T NO GROWN-UPS AROUND? WELL THEN, THE HELL WITH IT, RIGHT? CUSS ALL WE WANT TO, RIGHT? YEAH! YOU'RE LAUGHING SO HARD. I WONDER IF I COULD GET YOU A NAPKIN. IT LOOKS LIKE YOU'RE DROOLING? WHAT? NO? YOU CAN TAKE CARE OF IT YOURSELF? WELL, ALRIGHT! GOOD MAN! WOW, DID YOU SEE THAT PLAY? WOW! OH OH, WHAT'S THE MATTER? ARE YOU GETTING TOO EXCITED? YOUR LEGS ARE MOVING OUT OF CONTROL.

31

YOU'RE BREATHING LOUD AND YOU'RE DROOLING AGAIN. ARE YOU ALRIGHT? CAN I DO ANYTHING FOR YOU? WHAT? WHAT ARE YOU TRYING TO TELL ME? YOU LOOK UPSET, IT MUST BE IMPORTANT. ARE YOU IN TROUBLE? I BETTER GET A GROWN-UP. NO? YOU'RE ALRIGHT? JUST EXCITED, HUH? OH WELL. YOU SURE YOU'RE ALRIGHT; YOU DON'T NEED ANYBODY? WHAT? YES YOU DO? NO. YES? WHAT ARE YOU TRYING TO TELL ME? NO, YOU DON'T NEED NOBODY? YES, YOU DO NEED SOMETHING? WHAT DO YOU NEED? WELL I'M SORRY BUT I DON'T UNDERSTAND. YOU'RE LOOKING BEHIND YOU BUT I DON'T SEE ANYTHING EXCEPT... OH SHOOT! IS THIS WHAT YOU WANT? IT'S A BOARD WITH LETTERS ON IT. IS THIS WHAT YOU WANT? AND I SEE. YOU POINT TO LETTERS AND THAT'S HOW YOU TELL PEOPLE WHAT YOU NEED! WELL, SHOOT, I GOT IT NOW! OK, NO PROBLEM. NOW TELL ME, WHATEVER IT IS, I CAN DO IT FOR YOU. I AIN'T AFRAID; I CAN HANDLE IT. I'LL DO ANYTHING TO HELP YOU. (OH GOD, I HOPE I DON'T SCREW UP.) GO AHEAD. TELL ME WHAT YOU NEED. WHAT? OH, YOU SPELL IT OUT TOO DAMN FAST...I MEAN, TOO FAST FOR ME. GO SLOWER... NO, SLOWER... WHAT ARE YOU SAYING. WHAT ARE YOU ASKING ME TO DO? L... I, F, E. LIFE. OK. S, U, C, K, S. LIFES UCK S? LIF ESU CKS? WHAT? OH I SEE. ARE YOU STILL LEARNING HOW TO SPELL? OH WELL, IT'S ALRIGHT. WHAT? YOU DO KNOW HOW TO SPELL? WELL THEN, WHAT ARE YOU SPELLING? DOES IT HAVE SOMETHING TO DO WITH YOUR WHEELCHAIR? YOUR ARMS OR LEGS? WHAT??? L, I, F, E, S, U, C, K, S. LIF ESUCKS. LI FESUCKS. IT DOESN'T MAKE ANY SENSE. LIFE, LIFE? IS THAT RIGHT? LIFE SUCKS, LIFE SUCKS? IS THAT WHAT YOU SAID? I'LL BE DAMNED. IS THAT WHAT YOU SAID? WHY, YOU LITTLE BASTARD! HERE, I THOUGHT YOU WERE IN TROUBLE OR SOMETHING. I WAS ALL WORRIED ABOUT YOU AND ALL YOU GOTTA SAY IS LIFE SUCKS. WHO'D'AVE BELIEVED IT? WELL, I'LL SAY ONE THING FOR YOU. YOU'RE RIGHT! AT

LEAST IT DOES FOR ME. BUT YOU'RE A COOL GUY. YOU LOOK LIKE YOU TAKE LIFE EASY. EH? WHERE DO YOU GO TO SCHOOL? EH? OH, YOU HAVE TO SPELL IT OUT FOR ME ON YOUR BOARD. OK. AH, YOU USED TO GO TO A SPECIAL SCHOOL FOR HANDICAPPED KIDS. AH, WHAT'S IT LIKE GOING TO A HANDICAPPED SCHOOL? WHAT'S THAT YOU SAY? THE, SCHOOL. WASN'T. ON CRUTCHES. WHAT'S THAT, MAN? OH, I GET IT! HA HA. YOU'RE PRETTY FUNNY! HA HA. YOU'RE A BLAST. WELL, ANYWAY, WHAT'S IT LIKE? DID THEY REALLY TEACH YOU ANYTHING? I MEAN DO YOU KNOW HOW TO READ? OH, I'M SO STUPID, AIN'T I? HOW WOULD YOU EVER BE SPELLING THINGS OUT FOR ME IF YOU COULDN'T READ? I'M SLOW. I GUESS YOU ALREADY NOTICED THAT. I COULDN'T BELIEVE WHAT YOU SAID TO ME JUST NOW. THE FIRST TIME I EVER TALK TO A HANDICAPPED PERSON AND HE SAYS 'LIFE SUCKS'. HOT DAMN. DID YOU LEARN THAT KIND OF STUFF FROM YOUR FAMILY? YEAH. YOU CATHOLIC? YEAH, IRISH? GOT ANY IRISH IN YOU? YEAH. YEAH. WELL THEN I KNOW YOU CUSS AT YOUR HOUSE. YOU GOT OLDER BROTHERS AND SISTERS? TWO BROTHERS AND TWO SISTERS? SON OF A GUN, SO DO I. WHERE DID YOUR BROTHERS GO? TEASON CATHOLIC HIGH? HEY, SO DO I. YEAH, WHAT D'YA KNOW? WHAT ARE YOU SPELLING NOW? W,U,S,S,Y, WHAT? ARE YOU SAYING I GO TO A WUSSY SCHOOL? I'VE ONLY KNOWN THIS PERSON FOR FIVE MINUTES AND ALREADY HE CALLED ME A WUSS. UNBELIEVABLE. YOU LITTLE... WHAT'S THAT? WHY AIN'T I ON THE LACROSSE TEAM? I LOOK STRONG AND ATHLETIC? AH, YOU'RE JUST TRYING TO MAKE UP WITH ME AFTER CALLING ME A WUSS. NO. I JUST LIKE TO WATCH LACROSSE. I LIKE TO WATCH ALL SPORTS DON'T YOU? WHAT I'M REALLY INTO IS BOXING. I'M A FIGHTER. I FIGHT IN A COUPLE LEAGUES. THEY SAY I'M GOOD. I TELL YOU, MAN, THAT'S ALL I CARE ABOUT. THAT'S ALL I WANT TO DO FOR THE REST OF MY LIFE, YOU KNOW? 'CAUSE WHEN I'M IN THAT

RING, MAN, NOBODY CAN BITCH ME AROUND NO MORE.
I'M THE ONE THAT DECIDES WHAT GOES DOWN FROM
THEN ON OUT. AND USUALLY IT'S THE GUY IN THERE
WITH ME, YOU KNOW? NO, THEY TELL ME I AIN'T THAT
BAD; I COULD GO PLACES, YOU KNOW, GO PRO, LIGHT
HEAVY-WEIGHT. THE ONLY PLACE MY FAMILY WANTS
ME TO GO IS COLLEGE. AND I'M NOT SAYING THAT
STUFF ISN'T IMPORTANT. I'M THE KIND OF GUY WHO
WAS BROUGHT UP ALL MY LIFE THINKING EDUCATION
IS THE MOST IMPORTANT THING IN YOUR LIFE AND
ALTHOUGH I'VE SAID THE HELL WITH MOST OF THE
THINGS MY HARD HEADED, STUBBORN FATHER DRILLED
IN MY HEAD WHEN I WAS A KID WHO LISTENED TO HIS
BULLCRAP, I STILL DO THINK EDUCATION IS MOST
IMPORTANT. SO I'M GOING TO COLLEGE. BUT THEY
WANT ME TO CONCENTRATE ON THE ACTUAL
NONSENSE THEY'RE TEACHING YOU. LIKE LATIN. WHO
IN THE HELL GIVES A DAMN ABOUT LATIN? NO MATTER
WHAT KIND OF GOOD SOUNDING, DOUBLE-TALKING
EXPLANATION THEY COME UP WITH TO GET YOU TO
TAKE IT, IT'S STILL A GOD DAMN DEAD LANGUAGE.
WHAT THE HELL GOOD IS IT? WILL IT HELP ME FIGHT?
WILL IT HELP ME GET GIRLS? NO!!! WE'RE NOW ON THE
THIRD DECLENSION, THE FOURTH CONJUGATION AND
THE ABLATIVE ABSOLUTE, AND I'M STILL AS SCREWED
UP AS WHEN WE STARTED NOUNS, VERBS AND CLAUSES.
OH WELL, WHAT THE HELL... OH, WHAT ARE YOU
SAYING? YOU FOUND LATIN STIMULATING, BUT ALAS
USELESS. SMART MAN. YOU'RE NO FOOL. YOU'RE
PROBABLY A LOT SMARTER THAN ME. YEAH; I CAN TELL,
YOU'RE NOBODY'S FOOL. WHAT? YOUR FATHER DRILLED
THE NONSENSE ABOUT EDUCATION INTO YOUR HEAD
TOO, EH? NEVER LET UP WHEN YOU WERE A KID. OH, I
SEE. YOUR BROTHERS AND SISTERS ALL WENT TO
CATHOLIC SCHOOL, EH? MADE YOU FEEL BAD BECAUSE
YOU HAD TO GO TO PUBLIC SCHOOL THAT WAS SET UP
FOR HANDICAPPED KIDS. I'M BEGINNING TO GET THE

PICTURE HERE. YOU FELT BAD BECAUSE YOUR BROTHERS AND SISTERS WERE PROGRESSING, ADVANCING AND PURSUING PROFESSIONAL CAREERS. I KNOW WHERE YOU'RE COMING FROM. MY SISTER IS A TEACHER AND THE OTHER ONE'S A DOCTOR, AND BOTH MY BROTHERS HAVE GREAT JOBS, A LOT OF MONEY AND A WHOLE LOT OF WOMEN, AND SON OF A GUN, I WANT TO BE A BOXER. GOD, WHAT A DISAPPOINTMENT TO MY FOLKS. WHERE DID THEY GO WRONG? THEY CONSTANTLY ASK THEMSELVES. HEY, MAN, WHY ARE YOU LOOKING SO SURPRISED ALL OF A SUDDEN? YOU LOOK LIKE YOU'VE SEEN A GHOST. NO, YOU DON'T HAVE TO SPELL OUT AND TELL ME YOUR SITUATION. IT SOUNDS LIKE IT MIGHT BE SOMEWHAT SIMILAR TO MINE. BUT ONE THING YOU SHOULD BE GLAD YOU MISSED IN LIFE AND THAT IS NUNS. OOH, SOME OF THOSE NUNS CAN MESS YOU UP SO BAD. THEY CAN MAKE YOU FEEL SO SMALL, AND SO POWERLESS. IN ANY GIVEN SITUATION, YOU KNOW YOU'RE RIGHT, YOU CAN BE POSITIVE THAT YOU SHOULD WIN THE ARGUMENT, YOU DIDN'T DO ANYTHING WRONG, OR THAT SHE'S ALL WET AND SENILE. YOU THINK YOU'LL GET ANYWHERE? NO, MAN, NO. AND THEY TEACH YOU THE CRAZIEST STUFF, MAN. THEY'RE JUST CRAZY WOMEN, MAN. I THINK ALL CRAZY WOMEN ARE BROKEN UP INTO TWO CATEGORIES, NUNS AND MOTHERS. AND THEY'RE ALL THE SAME; THEY'RE ALL CRAZY. WHAT? YOU SAY THAT CAN'T BE TRUE? ARE ALL GUYS THAT GO TO TEASON CATHOLIC HIGH WUSSES? YOU GOT A POINT THERE. ARE ALL BOXERS STUPID, YOU ASK? WELL THIS ONE SURE IS. I GOT IN TROUBLE A COUPLE TIMES IN MY LIFE. ONE TIME THIS NUN WAS ON MY BACK BECAUSE I WAS LATE FOR CLASS ONCE OR TWICE AND I DIDN'T HAVE MY HOMEWORK OR SOMETHING AND SHE GOT ON MY CASE REAL BAD, YOU KNOW? SO I TOLD HER TO BACK OFF. I GOT SUSPENDED FOR TWO WEEKS. AND THEN LAST YEAR, I GOT IN TROUBLE FOR HAVING A BOTTLE OF WINE ON

THE BUS ON THE WAY TO THE RETREAT. I WAS REALLY BLITZED, YOU KNOW? AH, WHAT THE HELL ELSE CAN YOU DO AT A RETREAT? I MEAN, IF THEY EXPECT ME TO TAKE THAT MEDITATION STUFF SERIOUSLY, THEY GOTTA AT LEAST GIVE ME A SIX-PACK, YOU KNOW? BESIDES, IT WORKED GREAT FOR MY BROTHER A COUPLE YEARS AGO. YEAH, HE PULLED THE SAME TRICK ON A BUS ONCE. HE GOT OUT OF BEING IN THE YEARLY OPERETTA. I WISH I WAS THAT LUCKY. INSTEAD OF KICKING ME OUT OF THE DAMN SHOW, THEY GAVE ME THE LEAD. HAROLD HILL IN 'THE MUSIC MAN'. DO YOU BELIEVE IT? THEY THINK I'M TALENTED. YEAH, ME, TALENTED. MAN, ALL I WANT TO DO IS FIGHT, YOU KNOW, KNOCK ALL KINDS OF STIFFS OUT IN THE RING. I DON'T WANT TO STAND UP THERE IN FRONT OF ALL KINDS OF PEOPLE IN A MUSICAL. I'M OUTGOING AND ALL THAT KIND OF THING, BUT THAT'S ONLY BECAUSE OF MY FAMILY. MY BROTHERS, THEY WERE BOTH STARS AT T.C.H. EVERYBODY LOVED THEM; THEY WERE IN ALL THE SHOWS. BUT THAT'S NOT FOR ME, YOU KNOW? I HATE MY SCHOOL. I HATE MY FAMILY, YOU KNOW? ALL THE GOOD AND RESPONSIBLE AND RESPECTABLE THINGS THAT THEY ALL STAND FOR. YOU UNDERSTAND? THEY'RE JUST A HARD ACT TO FOLLOW. I WANNA BE A BOXER. I THINK I'LL RUN AWAY FROM HOME. WHATD'YA YOU SAY? OH HELL; I'M SORRY. AM I UPSETTING YOU? YOU LOOK WHITE, LIKE YOU'RE AMAZED OR SOMETHING. WHAT'S WRONG? SPELL IT OUT FOR ME. EVERYTHING'S OK, EH? WELL STOP SCARING ME LIKE THAT. YOU LOOK LIKE YOU HAVE TWO HEADS OR SOMETHING. YOU LOOK AT ME THE WAY MY GIRL LOOKED AT ME LAST NIGHT. YOU GOT A GIRL? YEAH! IS SHE PRETTY? YEAH, DAMN RIGHT. YOU AIN'T NO DOG. YEAH, I BET SHE'S A NICE GIRL. DAMN RIGHT! WHAT? YOU, HAVE, TROUBLE... ARE YOU SAYING YOU HAVE TROUBLE GETTING CHICKS BECAUSE OF YOUR HANDICAP? IT'S HARD TO MAKE GIRLS REALIZE YOU'RE A RIGHT DUDE AND A REGULAR

GUY BECAUSE YOU MIGHT LOOK A LITTLE DIFFERENT? WELL THAT IS A BITCH. YEAH, I CAN DIG YOUR PROBLEM, MAN. BUT I TELL YOU, MAN, YOU GOTTA KEEP TRYING. 'CAUSE YOU'RE ALRIGHT. YOU'RE NO FOOL. AND YOU JUST GOTTA KEEP ON SHOWING 'EM YOU'RE THERE, MAN. MAKE THEM KNOW YOU'RE COOL AND ALRIGHT. HEY, I KNOW WHERE YOU'RE COMING FROM. 'CAUSE LIKE I'M, LIKE, ALWAYS HORNY TOO, YOU KNOW? I'VE ALWAYS WANTED IT TO COME TRUE, MYSELF, YOU SEE? AND, I GUESS I CAN TELL YOU THIS, IT HAS. UH, IS THIS TOO HEAVY FOR YOU? NO? 'CAUSE YOU ARE LOOKING KINDA PALE AGAIN. DO YOU WANT ME TO TELL YOU ABOUT THIS? OK. I WON'T GO INTO EVERYTHING, OK? 'CAUSE THAT'LD BE TOO MUCH. BUT, UH, YEAH, IT'S HAPPENED ONE TIME, AND SHE WAS SWEET, VERY NICE GIRL. SHE DIDN'T HAVE TO, YOU KNOW? I DIDN'T PUSH HER, OR ANYTHING. IF THERE'S ANYTHING SUCH AS A MUTUAL UNDERSTANDING, OR TWO PEOPLE SAYING, 'HEY, WHY NOT?', I THINK THIS WOULD QUALIFY. ANYWAY, I WAS, LIKE, MORE PROUD, THAT NIGHT, THAN I'VE EVER BEEN OF MYSELF, YOU KNOW, IN MY LIFE. BUT I KNOW THIS ONE THING, YOU KNOW? IT MIGHT BE THE MOST BEAUTIFUL THING YOU'VE EVER EXPERIENCED RIGHT AT THAT MOMENT, BUT I TELL YOU, YOU GOTTA MOVE ON, EITHER WITH THE SAME GIRL OR YOU CAN EVEN MOVE ON AND TAKE SOMEBODY ELSE OUT. BUT YOU GOTTA THANK HER, LET HER KNOW HOW SPECIAL IT WAS, AND FORGET IT. IF YOU DON'T FORGET IT, IT'LL EAT YOU UP, YOU'LL WANT IT TO ALWAYS HAPPEN, IT WON'T, AND YOU COULD REALLY SCREW YOURSELF UP LOOKING ALL YOUR LIFE JUST FOR ONE MOMENT YOU ONCE HAD. BUT YOU'LL NEVER GET IT IF YOU DON'T GET OUT AND LET 'EM KNOW YOU'RE THERE, MAN. SO THAT'S MY ADVICE TO YOU, MAN. 'COURSE, YOU PROBABLY NOTICED BY NOW THAT I'M FULL OF CRAP, RIGHT? WHAT? OH HELL! T.C.H. LOST THE GAME TO THAT DAMN 'HOLIDAY HALL'. HEY, YOU

NEVER TOLD ME WHERE YOU GO TO SCHOOL. WHAT?
YOU GO TO HOLIDAY HALL? YOU LEAD ME TO BELIEVE
YOU WERE ON MY SIDE. YOU LITTLE SMARTASS. YOU
MEAN YOU WORKED YOURSELF UP FROM A LITTLE
SCHOOL FOR THE HANDICAPPED, ALL THE WAY TO A
GREAT SCHOOL LIKE THE HOLIDAY HALL? MAN, YOU
ARE ONE OF THE SMARTEST PEOPLE I'VE EVER MET.
YOU'RE GREAT. I'LL ALWAYS REMEMBER YOU. ENJOYED
TALKING TO YOU. BUT YOU KNOW, YOU STILL LOOK
REAL PALE AND SHOCKED... HEY, YOU KNOW WHAT?
WE'VE TOLD EACH OTHER OUR WHOLE LIFE'S STORIES
AND I HAVEN'T EVEN TOLD YOU MY NAME. MY NAME IS
PAUL PEROUTKA. I'M EIGHTEEN. YEAH, FIFTH AND LAST
CHILD OF BETTY AND BUD'S. ABOUT ALL I CAN THANK
'EM FOR IS MY GOOD LOOKS. OH, AND BY THE WAY, SPELL
OUT YOUR NAME FOR ME, PLEASE. WHY ARE YOU STILL
STARING AT ME?

Any Hint Of Creativity

I HEAR THE CALL; IT IS PAUL
I AM IDENTIFIED, SOMEONE WANTS MY ATTENTION
TELL THE JOKE, SPEAK THAT LINE
TELL US WHAT YOU LEARNED IN SCHOOL LAST YEAR
AND WHY IS THIS NAME ME
WHY AM I THIS BODY, THIS FACE
SHOULD MY NAME BE MY BASE

SHOULD I DRESS LIKE IT, SLEEP LIKE IT
BRUSH MY HAIR AND TEETH BY IT
WOULD I BE LIKED MORE OR LESS
IF PAUL DIDN'T FIT THE DRESS
AND WHAT'S IT DONE FOR ME HENCE IT'S STUCK TO ME
DEFINED ME AS THAT KID; PUT A NAME TO THAT
BEAUTIFUL
HEAD OF HAIR
RECOGNIZED THE BOY IN THE WHEELCHAIR
AND WOULD AN A BE ADDED IF I HAD BREASTS
OR WOULD I N E BE THE BEST
AND DOES IT REALLY DO ME ALL THAT GOOD
IT MEANS SMALL; I WANNA BE TALL
I WANT TO BE FAMED; NOT JUST NAMED
BUT SO I AM DEFINED AS IF WITH A STROKE OF PAINT
ONLY BECAUSE MY MOTHER ADMIRED THE SAINT
AND CHANGE IT, I CAN'T
FOR IT MIGHT HAVE BEEN MARTIN, ROBERT, OR JOHN
BUT I HEARD THE CALL; AND IT WAS PAUL

WHEELCHAIR

WHEELCHAIR, WHEELCHAIR, GOING SO SLOW
NOT AS FAST AS DANNY OR JOE
FALLING BEHIND IN A CROWDED HALL
IS NOT VERY FUN AT ALL
WHEN I DIE JUST LOCK MY CHAIR
AT A PLACE WHERE I'LL FIND COMFORT THERE
DIG ME A HOLE, I WOULDN'T MIND
RIGHT BENEATH THE FINISH LINE
WHEELCHAIR, WHEELCHAIR, TIRES ARE FLAT
RE-ALIGNMENT, THAT'S WHERE YOU'RE AT
YOU'LL BE AS READY AS NEW ANYTIME
BUT I'VE JUST LOST MY PLACE IN LINE
THEY'RE NO BETTER THAN YOU, ALL THE REST
THEY'VE TRIED TO TELL YOU THAT YOU'RE SECOND
BEST
DON'T LET THEM FOOL YOU, YOU KNOW THE SCORE
YOU'VE LIVED THROUGH THIS STUFF MANY TIMES
BEFORE
WHEELCHAIR, WHEELCHAIR, PLEASE HELP ME GO
FAST ENOUGH JUST SO I CAN SHOW
I'LL ENDURE SOME ACHES AND PAINS
I'LL COMPETE BOTH WITH SPEED AND BRAINS

LEGBRACE

DOWN BY THE RIVER THAT FLOATS BY THE
GRADESCHOOL
I SEE THE KIDS MY AGE RUNNING HOME
HERE I MUST SIT WITH MY CLUMSY OLD LEGBRACE
ME AND MY LEGBRACE ARE HERE ALL ALONE
I HEAR A NEIGHBOR TELLING MY MOTHER
SHE READ A DOCTOR HAS FOUND A CURE
BUT MY MOM DOESN'T SEEM VERY HAPPY
SHE READ IT TOO, AND WE JUST CAN'T AFFORD
LEGBRACE, OH WHAT CAN I DO
I FEAR I'LL ALWAYS HAVE YOU
TO SAY I CAN'T WALK
MAY BE JUST TALK
BUT DOLLARS, THEY COME VERY FEW
I WISH WE HAD THE MONEY TO HELP ME
OR SOME INSURANCE TO MAKE THE LENDING
BUT THIS IS WRITTEN IN THE STYLE OF THE FIFTIES
SO THIS SONG MUST HAVE A SAD SAD ENDING
LEGBRACE, OH MY TEARS NEED A CUP
MY TALE COULD MAKE YOU THROW UP
I THINK THAT THIS SONG
HAS LASTED TOO LONG

SO I THINK I BETTER JUST STOP

       MY APOLOGIES TO DICKY LEE
       AND EVERYONE ELSE

A Prayer By Lonely

DEAR GOD, WHAT IN HELL AM I DOING HERE
AND PLEASE LET ME LIVE TIL TOMORROW NIGHT TO
ASK YOU THE SAME QUESTION
IN THIS PLACE I AM NOT UNDERSTOOD,
FAR AWAY FROM THE PEOPLE WHO UNDERSTAND
I AM NOT KNOWN FOR WHAT I KNOW
BUT FOR WHAT THEY DO NOT KNOW ABOUT ME
THEY CONFUSE FRAILTIES WITH WEAKNESS,
SHORTCOMINGS WITH NO-SHOWS
AND ONCE AGAIN, PALSY IS COMING BEFORE PAUL
YOU STILL REMEMBER ME, DON'T YOU, LORD
I'M THE ONE THAT BELIEVES IN YOU
I FIND IT HARD TO LIVE HERE, EASY TO SURVIVE
I HAVE NO COMFORT, JUST MEMORIES
I HAVE NO COMPANY, JUST PRIVATE CONVERSATIONS
WITH MY SON
NO ONE WILL EVER KNOW MY SON, FOR THEY WILL
NEVER KNOW MY NEEDS
I'VE NEVER MET A PERSON I NEVER HUMORED
BUT I'LL NEVER HUMOR YOU LORD, FOR YOU'RE NOT A
PERSON
YOU EXIST ONLY IN ME FOR ME TO EXIST BY YOU
I CAN'T TELL MY NEIGHBOR WHAT YOU ARE, FOR HE
SURELY MUST DISAGREE
KNOWING YOU IS THE FINAL DIFFRACTION

SO IF TWO OPINIONS ARE IDENTICAL, TWO SOULS
CAN'T BE UNIQUE
(AND THEY MUST BE, BECAUSE I SAY SO)
SO, MY GOD, AND JUST MY GOD, STAY WITH ME, DON'T
STRAY FROM MY PRIORITIES
LET ME CATCH SOME WINKS, EMPTY MY BOWELS, AND
MAKE THE BEST OF OUR TOMORROW.

My Teacher, Toby

I WANT TO TELL YOU ABOUT MY TEACHER, BECAUSE I HAD THE BEST.

AT THE AGE OF SIX, I STARTED ATTENDING A BALTIMORE COUNTY PUBLIC SCHOOL FOR PHYSICALLY AND MENTALLY RETARDED KIDS CALLED RIDGE. FROM THEN UNTIL NINE YEARS LATER, THE NAME AND THE SCHOOL BECAME AN IMPORTANT PART OF MY LIFE. NOT ONLY WAS IT A GRADE AND GRAMMAR SCHOOL FOR ME TO LEARN, ASSOCIATE, AND GET MY FIRST LOOK INTO THE WORLD AS ANY GROWING KID WOULD EXPERIENCE, BUT IT HAD GIVEN ME AN IDENTITY, A PURPOSE, SOMETHING, TO WORK AT AND BE PROUD OF. AT THE TIME, IT SEEMED TO BE THE GENERAL CONSENSUS OF ALL THE ADULTS INVOLVED IN MAKING THE DECISION TO SEND ME THERE THAT I WAS EXTREMELY FORTUNATE TO BE GOING THERE, AND EVEN THAT IT MIGHT HAVE EASILY TURNED OUT OTHERWISE. I CAN STILL RECALL MY VERY FIRST VISIT TO THE SCHOOL; THE PRINCIPAL AND VICE PRINCIPAL PONDERING ME WITH ASKANCE, THEN HUDDLING WITH A FEW COUNSELORS, AS IF TO BE SURE THEY REACH THE CORRECT ANSWER TO 'GOD, DO WE REALLY WANT THIS KID?' WELL, THEY DID AND THAT SCENE MUST HAVE HAD THE SAME EFFECT ON MY PARENTS BECAUSE A DAY WOULDN'T GO BY THAT THEY DIDN'T REMIND MY SIX YEAR-OLD SELF HOW

BLESSED I WAS TO BE ACCEPTED INTO RIDGE. I GUESS IT REPRESENTED SOCIETY'S ACCEPTANCE OF ME AND BEING SUCH AN IMPRESSIONABLE YOUTH, I NATURALLY FELT BLESSED.

NOW THAT GOD HAD INTERVENED IN MY LIFE BY ALLOWING ME, A CEREBRAL PALSIED ATHETOID WITH NO USE OF LEGS, LIMITED USE OF ARMS, AND NO SPEECH, TO GO TO SUCH A FINE SCHOOL FOR THE HANDICAPPED, MY LIFE HAD OPENED UP INTO A WORLD I MIGHT NOT HAVE KNOWN OTHERWISE. I CAN TELL YOU THAT THE FIRST LADY WHO TAUGHT ME HOW TO READ WAS MRS. WILMA WEHRLE, AND I CAN TELL YOU THE FIRST TEACHER I EVER HAD A CRUSH ON WAS MARTHA MOORE. I COULD TELL YOU A HUNDRED AND ONE MORE STORIES EQUALLY AS TRIVIAL. BUT I CAN NEVER TELL YOU A BETTER OR MORE BEAUTIFUL STORY THAN THAT OF A SPECIAL EDUCATION TEACHER WHO WORKED AT RIDGE AND HELPED GIVE IT THE COMMENDABLE REPUTATION IT HAS STILL TODAY; THIS IS THE STORY OF A TEACHER WITH ALL THE GRACE AND SKILL GOD COULD EVER ASSIGN TO ONE BODY. SHE WAS MY TEACHER FOR FOUR YEARS AT RIDGE AND HER NAME IS DOROTHY EDWARDS.

IT WAS THE YEAR THAT I WAS READY FOR THE FIFTH GRADE THAT MY BEST FRIEND, JOHN PARADISO, WAS MOVED INTO MRS. EDWARDS' CLASS. I HAD ALWAYS DREAMED OF THAT DAY. RIDGE HAD AN ATMOSPHERE OF BEING A VERY SMALL COMMUNITY, AND IT WAS BIG NEWS FOR A KID TO BE OLD AND HARD-WORKING ENOUGH TO BE IN THAT CLASS. 'WOW, THAT'S WHERE THE BIG KIDS ARE,' WE LITTLE TIKES USED TO GOSSIP. IT WAS THE ELITE, AND I WAS IMPRESSED. I WAS ABOUT AS BIG-SHOT AS AN ELEVEN YEAR-OLD COULD ACT. I TOOK IT SO SERIOUSLY THAT, INSTEAD OF WATCHING MY OWN BEHAVIOR, I WAS CONCERNED THAT JOHN

WOULDN'T ACT IN LINE. IN BETWEEN TELLING HIM TO STRAIGHTEN UP AND WHEEL RIGHT, I FOUND MYSELF GOOFING OFF. ONCE DURING A READING LESSON WHILE SECRETLY PLAYING 'PAPER FOOTBALL' WITH BILL COPENHAVER, I WAS SPOTTED BY MY NEW TEACHER AND I SAW A FACE ON HER I WOULDN'T WANT TO SEE ON MY WORST ENEMY. SHE LET OUT THE BIGGEST AND MOST DISHEARTENING SCOLDING I EVER ENDURED AS A KID. IT WAS A SIDE OF HER I'D NEVER SEEN, NOR HAVE SEEN SINCE. AFTER SHE FINISHED CORRECTING MY BEHAVIOR AND AS SHE WENT BACK TO THE LESSON, I FELT HUMILIATED, STUNNED, DUMBFOUNDED, ASHAMED, AND ABOUT AS SMALL AS AN ERASER. IN THAT STATE OF TOTAL DESPAIR AND REJECTION, I THEN CAME TO REALIZE THE ONLY POSSIBLE CONCLUSION, 'HEY, I THINK THIS LADY LIKES ME.'

FROM THAT MOMENT ON, I BEGAN TO SPOT JUST WHAT THE LADY WAS ALL ABOUT, AND FOUND MYSELF MORE ATTACHED TO HER AS DAYS AND WEEKS IN HER CLASS PASSED BY. SHE HAD CREATED A FAMILY FEELING IN HER CLASS FROM THE TIME SHE BEGAN WORKING AT RIDGE; EVERY YEAR WOULD ADD AND SUBTRACT MEMBERS AS THE SCHOOL'S STUDENTS ADVANCED. IT WAS EASY FOR ANYBODY TO FALL INTO THE SCHEME OF THINGS.

HER CLASS VARIED IN MANY WAYS. THE CLASS WAS UNGRADED AND WE RANGED IN AGE FROM ELEVEN TO FOURTEEN. THE LEVELS OF WORK SHE HAD TO TEACH WERE SCATTERED FROM FIFTH TO EIGHTH GRADE MATERIAL. SHARING THE LOAD WITH AN AIDE, IT WAS DISCOVERED THAT IN THAT ONE YEAR, MY FIRST IN HER CLASS, 23 COURSES WERE TAUGHT IN THAT ONE ROOM EACH DAY. THERE WAS NO BREAK FOR EITHER TEACHER, AND ONLY 30 MINUTES FOR LUNCH, SUPERVISING US KIDS. YOU ARE BEGINNING TO GET MORE OF A PICTURE OF WHY I SAID I HAD THE BEST.

THERE WERE SEVEN OF US IN THE CLASS. FEW PEOPLE HAD SIMILAR DEGREES OF DISABILITIES. BUT AS SOON AS I WAS PUT IN MRS. EDWARDS' CLASS I KNEW I WOULD BE CONFRONTED WITH A MAN CALLED JOHN NOLAN. NOW IT WILL ALWAYS CONTINUE TO PUZZLE ME HOW THE NAME, JOHN NOLAN, IS NOT A MAJOR PART OF ABSOLUTELY EVERYONE'S LIFE; FROM THE DAY I WAS TWO I'VE BEEN COMPARED TO THE PERSON AND HAUNTED BY HIS NAME. JOHN NOLAN WAS BORN, AN ATHETOID, THREE YEARS BEFORE I WAS, TO TOTALLY DIFFERENT PARENTS THAN MINE. FOR SOME REASON, PEOPLE HAVE IT HARD BELIEVING THAT WE AREN'T EXACTLY ALIKE IN EVERY WAY AND I'M ONLY THREE YEARS BEHIND.

IN ACTUALITY, OUR PATHS DO CROSS AT SEVERAL PLACES. WE DO HAVE SIMILAR MOTOR AND BODILY DYSFUNCTIONS, WE BOTH WENT TO RIDGE, WE BOTH HAVE OVERCOME A LOT TO ACHIEVE ANY SUCCESS WE'VE OBTAINED ALONG THE WAY. AND WE'RE BOTH BLONDE AND ADORABLE. (WELL, AT LEAST ONE OF US FITS THAT BILL.) IN MY EARLY DAYS, I WAS IN AWE OF HIM AND A LITTLE RESENTFUL OF THE GUY WHO EVERYONE HAD COMPARED AND CONTRASTED ME TO. THE POPULAR REMARK TO SAY TO YOUNG PAUL, NO MATTER WHAT I WAS DOING, SEEMED TO BE 'ARE YOU GOING TO DO THIS AS WELL AS JOHN NOLAN DID IT?' FROM WHAT I CAN REMEMBER, I ALMOST ALWAYS DID.

ANYWAY, JOHN HAD PRECEDED ME IN MRS. EDWARDS' CLASS BY EIGHT YEARS. SHE HAD TAUGHT HIM EVERY YEAR FROM FIRST GRADE TO DOING JUNIOR HIGH SCHOOL WORK. IT WAS CLEAR TO SEE THAT THESE TWO HAD BECOME INSEPARABLE HAVING BEEN TOGETHER SO LONG. I STARTED WITH THE PLAN TO STAY AS FAR AWAY FROM BOTH OF THEM, AS TO NOT TREAD IN HIS

TERRITORY ONCE AGAIN, AND NOT TO FORCE HER TO LIKE ME JUST BECAUSE I LOOK AN AWFUL LOT LIKE HER STAR PUPIL.

I WOUND UP THE YEAR BECOMING GREAT FRIENDS WITH BOTH OF THEM; THEY BOTH HAD SO MUCH TO TEACH ME, PARTICULARLY ABOUT WHAT MY PLANS AFTER LEAVING RIDGE MIGHT BE. THAT WAS JOHN'S LAST YEAR THERE. HE WAS GOING TO CALVERT HALL THE NEXT YEAR. IT WAS A HUGE ADJUSTMENT FOR HIM TO MAKE TO BE GOING TO A VERY ELITE CATHOLIC SCHOOL WHILE ALL HIS EXPERIENCE SO FAR WAS THE SHELTER AND PROTECTION OF RIDGE AND BEING UNDER MRS. EDWARDS' WING. IT WAS A TRANSITION THAT NEEDED TO BE DISCUSSED AND PREPARED FOR MANY OF THE LAST DAYS OF THAT SCHOOL YEAR BY HIM, MRS. EDWARDS AND MRS. NOLAN. JOHN'S MOTHER WAS HAPPY TO ALLOW ME TO SIT IN ON THE PLANS FOR JOHN'S NEAR FUTURE BECAUSE THEY ALL REALIZED THAT IT MIGHT ONE DAY BE THE DIRECTION INTO WHICH I MIGHT GO. I'VE NEVER FORGOTTEN THEIR COURTESY AND I HAVE SINCE BECOME MORE AND MORE CONVINCED HOW MUCH MRS. EDWARDS REALLY CARED ABOUT EACH ONE OF HER STUDENTS.

RETURNING THE NEXT YEAR WAS SAD WHEN MRS. EDWARDS WASN'T THERE THE FIRST DAY. MRS. CHAROLETTE FOGARTY, OUR CLASS AIDE, ANNOUNCED THE NEWS THAT MRS. EDWARDS' DAUGHTER-IN-LAW HAD BEEN KILLED IN A CAR ACCIDENT. I KNEW HER WELL; SHE HAD TAUGHT ART AT THE SCHOOL FOR SEVERAL YEARS. I REALIZED THEY MUST HAVE BEEN CLOSE SINCE MRS. EDWARDS HAD ALWAYS BEEN KNOWN TO TALK AND BRAG ABOUT HER FAMILY. IT OCCURRED TO ME WHAT AN UNFAIR THING IT WAS FOR SUCH A GIFTED, TALENTED, AND OFTEN VERY CHEERFUL PERSON TO BE STRUCK WITH SUCH BAD FORTUNE.

HOW JOLLY AND HAPPY SHE WAS EARLY THE LAST YEAR WHEN HER DAUGHTER HAD HER FIRST GRANDSON, TUCKER. ALL WE HEARD WAS TUCKER THIS, TUCKER THAT... LIFE SEEMED TO HAVE ITS UPS AND DOWNS FOR MRS. EDWARDS. BUT 'IF I KNOW HER' I SAID, 'SHE'LL ALWAYS BE ABLE TO BOUNCE UP AND GET HIGH ON LIFE AGAIN.' AND SHE ALWAYS DID.

IN THAT AND THE YEARS TO FOLLOW, MRS. EDWARDS BECAME A TRUE FRIEND AND CORNERSTONE IN MY LIFE. I WAS MOSTLY GROUPED WITH JOHN AND A GIRL NAMED JACKIE. WE WENT THROUGH TEXT BOOK AFTER TEXT BOOK, SUBJECT AFTER SUBJECT, BUT MORE IMPORTANT, A BREAK AFTER LUNCH. IT'S TRUE THAT MRS. EDWARDS WAS A HARD WORKING TEACHER, AND SHE DIDN'T EXPECT ANY LESS FROM US. WE ALL KNOW NOW THAT THE WOMAN WANTED TO SEE EVERYBODY GO AS FAR AS HE OR SHE COULD GO. SHE KNEW WE THREE COULD GO FARTHER THAN THE REST; THAT WE COULD GO AS FAR AS WE WANTED, AND SHE MADE SURE WE ALL WANTED TO GO TO THE TOP. BUT, MAN, SHE WAS A SLAVEDRIVER.

AMONG JOHN, JACKIE, AND I, THERE WAS A SPECIAL INTIMACY DURING OUR LESSONS. MOSTLY MRS. EDWARDS WORKED US PRETTY HARD, BUT SOMETIMES SHE'D LET US STRAY. THOSE WERE OUR FONDEST TIMES WITH HER, I BELIEVE. AND WHEN SHE STRAYED FROM SCHOOLWORK, SHE WOULD TALK ABOUT HER FARM IN THE OZARK MOUNTAINS OF ARKANSAS. HOW SHE LOVED THAT PLACE OUT THERE; AND HOW WE COULD TELL THAT HER HEART WAS REALLY OUT THERE SOMETIMES WHEN SHE SPOKE OF POETRY AND SQUARE ROOTS. IN THE SAME WAY THAT I ROAMED THE STREETS OF MANHATTAN, JOHN TOURED THE BASEBALL HALL OF FAME, AND JACKIE MANOEUVRED HER ELECTRIC WHEELCHAIR DOWN THE BOARDWALK

OF OCEAN CITY MARYLAND, ALL DURING THE COURSE OF A HALF HOUR LUNCH PERIOD AS WE DAYDREAMED IN THE CAFETERIA, WE COULD SEE IN OUR TEACHER'S EYES THAT SHE WAS MILKING A COW IN THE MORNING AND DELIVERING A BRAND NEW CALF THAT AFTERNOON. THE WHOLE CLASS SHARED IN HER ANTICIPATION. WE WANTED DESPERATELY FOR HER TO STAY WITH US FOR AS LONG AS POSSIBLE BUT WE WERE RESIGNED TO THE FACT THAT SHE WAS COMING FAIRLY CLOSE TO THE END OF HER TEACHING DAYS; AND THE DAY SHE RETIRED WITH HER HUSBAND, PAUL, AND DAUGHTER, GWYN, TO THEIR DREAMSPOT, WE'D ALL BE GLAD THAT OUR DEAR FRIEND WAS FINALLY HOME, IN THE OZARKS, TO STAY.

EVEN IN OUR GROUP OF THREE, THERE WAS A VARIETY IN PERSONALITY TYPES AND MRS. EDWARDS WAS GREAT AT RESPONDING TO EACH ONE'S NEED AND LIKES. SHE PULLED OUT AND HIGHLIGHTED THE SPORTS ENTHUSIAST IN JOHN WHENEVER WE READ A STORY ABOUT ATHLETIC COMPETITION. THERE WAS A FIRM AND TRUSTING RELATIONSHIP THAT JACKIE HAD WITH HER TEACHER; SHE NEEDED JUST A FEW MINOR ADJUSTMENTS MADE IN HER SITTING POSITION DURING THE COURSE OF THE DAY AND MRS. EDWARDS WAS RIGHT THERE IN A FLASH TO HELP HER, AS SHE WAS WHEN ANYBODY IN THE CLASS NEEDED PHYSICAL HELP. IN A WAY, MRS. EDWARDS SEEMED TO BE CLOSER TO JACKIE THAN SHE WAS TO US BOYS. THERE WAS A CERTAIN UNDERSTANDING AND LOVE BETWEEN THEM I SUPPOSE ONLY TWO WOMEN COULD HAVE. THE OLDER ONE WAS SO GENTLY WITH THE YOUNGER, AND THE YOUNGER SO RESPECTFUL OF THE OLDER. WE COULD HAVE CLAIMED THAT TO BE THE REASON WHY JACKIE ALWAYS GOT THE BEST GRADES, BUT WE COULDN'T OVERLOOK THE BRIGHTNESS AND INTELLIGENCE

OF OUR FRIEND. WE HAD TO FACE IT; JACKIE WAS A BRAIN.

AS FOR HER RELATIONSHIP WITH ME, MRS. EDWARDS WAS ONE OF THE BEST FRIENDS I'LL EVER HAVE. SHE WAS A BUDDY WHEN THIS GROWING KID NEEDED ONE, A MOTHER WHEN I KNEW MY OWN JUST WOULDN'T UNDERSTAND, A PAL I COULD GO TO FOR A FAVOR, AND THE PERSON WHO PROBABLY UNDERSTOOD WHAT KIND OF PERSON I WAS THE BEST. SHE KNEW WHEN I WAS SINCERE AND SHE SPOTTED ME LIKE A HAWK WHEN I GAVE HER STUFF. WITH THAT KIND OF TEACHER, I DIDN'T DARE NOT DO MY HOMEWORK AND EXPECT TO FEED HER A WEARY EXCUSE. SHE'D HAVE HAD MY HEAD. BUT SHE WOULD HAVE SMILED AFTERWARDS. OF ALL THE KIDS IN THE CLASS, I BELIEVE SHE TRUSTED IN ME THE MOST TO DO HER A FAVOR SUCH AS SET AN EXAMPLE FOR ORDER WHENEVER THE CROWD WAS GETTING OUT OF HAND, AS I GUESS WE OFTEN DID.

IT JUST SEEMED TO HAPPEN THAT WHENEVER THERE WAS A NEW RULE SET DOWN THAT WE KIDS HAD TO OBEY, I WOULD BE THE FIRST ONE UNCONSCIOUSLY TO BREAK IT. I'M REFERRING TO TRIVIAL THINGS SUCH AS NOT GOING OUTSIDE FOR RECESS BEFORE THAT BIG HAND WAS DIRECTLY ON THE THREE, OR GOING TO A THERAPY SESSION IN A HURRY WITHOUT STOPPING TO TALK TO ANYBODY, OR NOT MAKING EYES AT THE LATEST PRETTY TEACHER IN SCHOOL; THESE WERE REAL EARTH-SHATTERING REGULATIONS WHEN I WAS THIRTEEN. AND MRS. EDWARDS WAS ONE WHO NEEDED A GOOD AMOUNT OF ORDER TO RUN HER SHIP, SO WHENEVER I'D OVERSTEP MY BOUNDARIES, MY DARLING TEACHER WOULD VERY CONVENIENTLY USE THAT OPPORTUNITY TO CHEW ME OUT IN FRONT OF THE WHOLE CLASS TO MAKE SURE THE INCIDENT WOULDN'T RE-OCCUR WITH ANY OF MY CLASSMATES.

AS SOON AS SHE REACHED THE THIRD SENTENCE IN HER LONG SPIEL, I GOT HER MESSAGE. I KNEW NOTHING I DID COULD EVER BOTHER HER THAT MUCH, SO SHE WAS USING ME AS A COMING ATTRACTION IN CASE ANYBODY MIGHT DO SOMETHING WORSE. WE WOULD EVER EXCHANGE CONVERSATION AFTERWARDS ABOUT THE PLOY SHE HAD JUST PULLED SEEING ME AS A SCAPEGOAT. SHE'D JUST NUDGE ME AND GIVE ME A QUIET 'OK?'

BY NOW YOU PROBABLY GET THE IDEA THAT MRS. EDWARDS WAS GREAT WITH PEOPLE. SHE CARED ABOUT EVERYONE OF HER STUDENTS AND TOOK THE PERSONAL INTEREST IN GETTING TO KNOW EVERYONE'S PARENTS AND FAMILY. FOR THE MOST PART, OUR CLASS WAS MADE UP OF PHYSICALLY HANDICAPPED KIDS. BUT WE HAD A FEW KIDS WITH SLIGHT EMOTIONAL PROBLEMS. I HAVE TO REMEMBER SAM IN THIS INSTANCE. SAM HAD A HEART DISORDER THAT MADE HIM WEAK AND STOPPED HIS GROWTH. HE FOUND IT INCREASINGLY DIFFICULT TO ASSOCIATE WITH OTHERS OR EVEN BE FRIENDLY. HE MIGHT GO INTO A CORNER AND TALK TO HIMSELF FOR A WHILE.

WELL THE REST OF US MIGHT HAVE HAD VARIOUS PHYSICAL PROBLEMS BUT I GUESS AT TIMES WE COULD BE AS BRATTY AS ANY OTHER KIDS OUR AGE. IT WAS VERY EASY FOR US TO OVERLOOK ANYBODY'S PHYSICAL DISABILITIES, BUT IT WASN'T THAT EASY TO BE UNDERSTANDING OF SOMEONE WHO WAS SOCIALLY DIFFERENT. THIS IS WHAT MRS. EDWARDS WOULD EMPHASIZE WHENEVER SHE'D HAVE A TALK WITH US ABOUT OUR CONDUCT. HER ASKING FOR US TO BE EXTRA PATIENT AND MATURE ABOUT SAM'S SOMETIMES ERRATIC BEHAVIOR WAS ALWAYS SO WELL PLANNED AND TO THE POINT.

"PEOPLE, I WANT TO HAVE A LITTLE TALK WITH YOU WHILE A CERTAIN ONE OF US ISN'T HERE. AND I KNOW YOU KNOW I'M TALKING ABOUT SAM AND YOU KNOW THAT I'M GOING TO LECTURE YOU ABOUT HOW YOU TREAT HIM. NOW REPEATEDLY I'VE TOLD YOU HOW HARD IT IS FOR SAM TO GO TO THIS SCHOOL. YOU KNOW HE'S NOT A VERY STRONG PERSON; YOU SEE HIM GOING TO THE HEALTH SUITE ALMOST EVERYDAY. YOU MUST UNDERSTAND THAT IT'S VERY HARD FOR HIM TO RELATE TO YOU KIDS. HE SEES YOU DASHING DOWN THE HALLS AND RUNNING AND WHEELING AROUND ON THE HARDTOP PLAYGROUND AND HE KNOWS HE CAN'T BE AS ACTIVE AS YOU, SO HE FEELS LIKE AN OUTSIDER. HE FEELS LEFT OUT. EVEN AT HOME, HE HAS THREE BROTHERS AND," WITH A SHRUG OF THE SHOULDERS AS ONLY MRS. EDWARDS COULD DO IT, "HE SEES THEM ALL ADVANCING FAR BEYOND WHERE HE COULD EVER REACH." ADJUSTING HER GLASSES, SHE WOULD CONTINUE, "NOW I WOULD THINK THAT PEOPLE SUCH AS YOU, PEOPLE WHOM, FOR ALL THEIR LIVES, OTHERS HAVE BEEN UNDERSTANDING AND HELPFUL BECAUSE OF YOUR VARIOUS HANDICAPS, WOULD BE ESPECIALLY UNDERSTANDING OF SOMEONE ELSE'S PROBLEMS. NOW COME ON, TRY. DON'T TEASE HIM, DON'T MAKE FUN OF HIM, DON'T EXCLUDE HIM FROM YOUR ACTIVITIES. HE MIGHT JUST GROW OUT OF HIS SHELL AND HE MIGHT BE ABLE TO BECOME JUST ONE OF THE CROWD. COME ON. DO IT FOR ME."

THAT LAST LINE WAS A PLEA NOBODY COULD IGNORE. THIS KIND OF LECTURE TOOK PLACE ABOUT ONCE EVERY TWO MONTHS. THAT WAS AS LONG AS ITS EFFECT LASTED. IT WOULD BE ON ONE TOPIC OR ANOTHER. MRS. EDWARDS RAN A TIGHT SHIP BUT NEVER IN A STRICT SORT OF WAY. BASICALLY, SHE LET EVERYBODY BE THEMSELVES, AND IF TOO MANY PEOPLE WERE TOO MUCH THEMSELVES AT THE SAME TIME AND

HAVOC WAS CAUSED, WELL, SHE'D PULL THE TROOPS TOGETHER AND TELL US WHERE WE LAXED DOWN AND FLEW WRONG. THEN SHE'D TELL US TO CORRECT THE SITUATION. WE LOVED HER.

AND IF WE STUDENTS WHO MIGHT HAVE WORKED WITH HER FOR JUST A FEW YEARS LOVE HER, THE RIDGE STAFF WHO WORKED WITH HER MUST HAVE LOVED HER EQUALLY AS MUCH. THERE WAS A SPECIAL FRIENDSHIP BETWEEN OUR TEACHER AND HER TEACHER'S AIDE, CHAROLETTE FOGARTY. THEIR RAPPORT TRANSCENDED THROUGH THE WHOLE CLASS WHICH COULDN'T HELP BUT ADDED TO THE FAMILY ATMOSPHERE. WILMA WEHRLE AND ARTIST JONES WERE TWO MORE REMARKABLE WOMEN WHO WERE LONGTIME TEACHERS AT RIDGE AND ADMIRERS OF THEIR FRIEND WHOM THEY CALLED TOBY. ONE THING THAT MEANT A GOOD DEAL TO ME WAS THE DAY THE THREE LADIES WOULD DISCUSS OLD STUDENTS AND FUNNY STORIES ABOUT EACH ONE. THE GRADUATES THEY'D TALK ABOUT SEEMED LIKE OLDER BROTHERS AND SISTERS AND GAVE US KIDS WHO WOULD LISTEN TO THE STORIES AND THE OLD STUDENTS' ACCOMPLISHMENTS SINCE RIDGE, A SENSE OF HOPE, ENCOURAGEMENT, AND WHETTED OUR DETERMINATION TO EXCEL IN SCHOOL.

BUT CERTAINLY ONE OF MRS. EDWARDS' GREATEST CONTRIBUTIONS TO RIDGE WAS HER ADVICE, SUPPORT AND HELPING HAND SHE REACHED OUT TO NEW TEACHERS. ON OUR WING OF PHYSICALLY LIMITED CHILDREN THERE WERE TWO NEW LADIES, FRESH OUT OF COLLEGE, READY TO MEET THE CHALLENGES, TRIALS, TRIBULATIONS AND REWARDING EXPERIENCES OF TEACHING LESS FORTUNATE KIDS. WHAT A GREAT ENDEAVOR; BOTH WERE SO FULL OF ENERGY. WELL, THE REWARDING MOMENTS DID COME BUT NOT AFTER

MANY, MANY TRIALS AND TRIBULATIONS AND I WOULD VENTURE TO GUESS, A FEW ERRORS. FORTUNATELY TOBY EDWARDS RECOGNIZED THEIR POTENTIALS AND DID WHAT SHE COULD TO HELP THEM ALONG THOSE FIRST WEEKS, MONTHS, AND YEARS.

SHARON SKOWRONSKI TAUGHT THE YOUNGEST KIDS ON THE WING. SHE WAS WELL EQUIPPED WITH A HEFTY SUPPLY OF ENERGY AS ANY FIRST GRADE TEACHER SHOULD. AND, LIKE EVERYBODY, MUST HAVE GOTTEN A DOSE OF INSPIRATION FROM TOBY. I SUPPOSE SHE FIGURED THAT IF THAT LADY CAN ENDURE HAVING PEROUTKA IN HER CLASS, I CAN HANDLE THE FIRST GRADE. IN ANY CASE, SHARON'S FAMILY WAS AN ADMIRABLE LOT; HER MOTHER SUBSTITUTED AT RIDGE A FEW DAYS A WEEK, HER FATHER WAS WITH THE FBI AND TOOK TIME OUT TO TALK TO OUR SCHOOL ABOUT HIS WORK. HER BROTHER WAS A SEMINARIAN AND WHEN HE WAS ORDAINED HE ASKED HIS SISTER TO CHOOSE AN APPROPRIATE PERSON FROM RIDGE TO MAKE HIS PATTON. SHARON THOUGHT ON THE MATTER, THEN DECIDED IT WOULD BE LOVELY IF MRS. EDWARDS' YOUNGEST DAUGHTER, GWEN, WOULD DO THE PROJECT. THE THREE LADIES TALKED IT OVER AND LO AND BEHOLD, THE MASS WAS A BEAUTIFUL EVENT. THE NEW PRIEST, TERRY, AND THE BISHOP WHO HAD ORDAINED HIM CAME DOWN TO THE EDWARDS' PEW DURING THE KISS OF PEACE AND SHOOK BOTH MOTHER AND DAUGHTER'S HAND. I'VE NEVER SEEN MRS. EDWARDS MORE BEAUTIFUL AS WHEN HER EYES LIT UP AT THAT MOMENT OUT OF SO MUCH PRIDE FOR HER DAUGHTER.

MORE CLOSELY ASSOCIATED WITH MRS. EDWARDS WAS ALISON BAILEY, SHE HAD THE CLASSROOM NEXT TO OURS AND SOME OF US WOULD EXCHANGE CLASSES FOR DIFFERENT COURSES. DURING THE FIRST YEAR

THAT SHE WAS THERE, I THINK ALISON LEARNED AS MUCH FROM MRS. EDWARDS AS WE KIDS DID. SHE WAS A YOUNG WOMAN WITH MUCH ENERGY AND DRIVE. I SUPPOSE SHE JUST NEEDED HER NEW FRIEND, TOBY, TO HELP HER DIRECT THE ENERGY IN THE RIGHT PLACES BEST TO EDUCATE HER KIDS AND FOR HERSELF AS A TEACHER.

"I DON'T KNOW, TOBY. I TRY. YOU SEE, I GET ON A SUBJECT; LET'S SAY WE'RE DOING MATH AND I'M SAYING PI R-SQUARED IS THE FORMULA FOR THE AREA OF A CIRCLE. WELL, PEROUTKA WILL SAY IN HIS SMART ALEC WAY, 'MISS BAILEY, EVERYBODY KNOWS THAT PIES ARE ROUND,' AND THEN I LAUGH, AND EVERYBODY LAUGHS. AND THEN I TELL ANOTHER JOKE AND JOHN TELLS ANOTHER. I JUST CAN'T SEEM TO STOP DIGRESSING FROM THE SUBJECT MATTER. AND THEN WE ALL GET SILLY. AND SPELLING! SPELLING IS TERRIBLE. I CAN'T GET THROUGH A SPELLING LIST WITHOUT DOING A THESIS ON EVERY WORD. AND GOD, THIS IS EMBARRASSING. WHEN I'M GIVING THEM A WORD FOR A SPELLING BEE, THEY'LL ASK ME 'UH, HOW DO YOU SPELL THAT,' AND I TELL THEM. OH TOBY, WHAT AM I GONNA DO? THEY DON'T SEEM TO RESPECT ME THE WAY THEY DO YOU."

"LISTEN, ALISON, DON'T GET YOURSELF TOO UPTIGHT ABOUT THESE THINGS. EVERYTHING TAKES TIME. I CAN TELL YOU A MILLION STORIES ABOUT MY FIRST DAYS OF TEACHING. BUT I LEARNED THAT I HAD TO BE FIRM, I HAD TO BE CONSISTENT. I COULDN'T BE ALL JOLLY AND PLAYFUL ONE MINUTE, THEN STERN AND CROSS THE NEXT. I HAD TO GET A RAPPORT WITH A KID AND STICK TO IT. IF A KID IS BAD, I'LL LET HIM KNOW IT, REPEATEDLY, AND I'LL ALWAYS TRY TO HELP HIM BE A GOOD KID. IF A KID IS GOOD, I'LL TRY TO SMILE AT HIM IN A CERTAIN WAY, MAKE HIM KNOW HE'S NEEDED, OR THAT I LIKE HIM. BUT WE'VE GOT TO GIVE THESE KIDS

THE BEST EDUCATION WE CAN GIVE THEM IN THESE SOMEWHAT PROVINCIAL CIRCUMSTANCES. I MEAN WE'VE GOT THERAPY SESSIONS TO CONTEND WITH AND AS YOU KNOW, SOME KIDS CAN ONLY GO AS FAST AS THEY CAN; THEY CAN'T MOVE AS FAST AS THE REST. JUST REMEMBER WHAT I'VE ALWAYS SAID, 'A MAN CAN ONLY DO WHAT A MAN CAN DO.'

"AND ALISON, THERE'LL BE TIMES WHEN YOU'LL BE FRUSTRATED, AND THERE WILL BE DAYS WHEN YOU WON'T GET HARDLY ANYTHING DONE. BUT MY ADVICE TO YOU IS TO KEEP RIGHT ON IN THERE. DON'T LOOK BACK NOW, YOU MIGHT JUST TURN INTO A PILLAR OF SALT. COME ON, YOU'VE COME THIS FAR, YOU'RE GONNA BE A FINE TEACHER. AND," THEN CAME THE FAMOUS EDWARDS SHRUG, "IF THINGS ARE BAD, AND THERE IS NO WAY THEY CAN BE GOOD, WHY, YOU'LL JUST HAVE TO ACCEPT THEM. YOU KNOW WHAT I SAY TO THE KIDS, DON'T YOU, WHENEVER THEY GET DEPRESSIVE ABOUT THEIR HANDICAPS? THERE'S NOT A STUDENT I HAD THAT HASN'T HEARD ME SAY THIS PRAYER, 'GOD, GRANT ME THE STRENGTH TO CHANGE THE THINGS I CAN CHANGE, THE PATIENCE TO ACCEPT THE THINGS I CAN'T CHANGE, AND THE WISDOM TO KNOW THE DIFFERENCE.' COME ON, HANG IN THERE. FOR ME?"

NOT EVEN ALISON COULD REFUSE THAT PLEA. I BELIEVE THAT IT WAS THAT UNDERSTANDING AND SUPPORTIVE STYLE OF DISCOURSE THAT MADE MRS. EDWARDS GREAT AND MADE ALL HER STUDENTS LOVE HER.

MRS. EDWARDS GOT ALONG WITH THE ADMINISTRATION WELL TOO. SEVERAL YEARS BACK SHE WAS OFFERED A HIGH POSITION IN ADMINISTRATION BUT SHE TOLD US THAT SHE TURNED IT DOWN BECAUSE IT WOULD

MEAN PAPERWORK INSTEAD OF CLOSE CONTACT WITH PEOPLE. "I JUST COULDN'T GO FOR THAT," SHE SAID.

BUT SHE HAD A FINE RELATIONSHIP WITH OUR PRINCIPAL, MRS. LOUISE HOLE. IT WAS NEARING THE FINISH OF MY FOURTH YEAR IN MRS. EDWARDS' CLASS THAT I SPOTTED HER THURSDAY AFTERNOON. AFTER THURSDAY AFTERNOON SHE AND MRS. HOLE WERE OFF IN THE CORNER OF OUR ROOM TALKING VERY SERIOUSLY. I COULD TELL SOMETHING BIG WAS COOKING, AND DYING, I WAS, TO KNOW WHAT THE SCOOP WAS. BUT IT WAS OBVIOUS THAT THIS DISCUSSION WAS FOR THEIR EARS ONLY SO I WOULD LOOK FOOLISH IF I TRIED TO OVERHEAR THE BIG NEWS. THEY WOULD HAVE TOLD ME TO GO JUMP IN THE RIVER, OR PLAY FOOTBALL ON THE BELTWAY. I GOT SUCH LITTLE RESPECT WHEN IT CAME TO SUCH BIG SECRETS. I WAS THE ONLY ONE IN THE ROOM AT THAT TIME; EVERYONE ELSE WOULD BE AT CHORUS PRACTICE. (IT'S TRUE, SOME LADY WHO RAN THE CHORUS THOUGHT EVERYBODY IN MY CLASS COULD SING EXCEPT FOR ME.) ANYWAY, I EXCUSED MYSELF FROM THE ROOM WHERE THESE HEATED DISCUSSIONS WOULD TAKE PLACE EVERY WEEK AND GO OUT INTO THE HALLS AND PLAY 'AS TIME GOES BY' ON THE PIANO WITH MY HEADSTICK. I'M SURE PASSERS BY REMARKED AS THEY HEARD ME, 'NOT ONLY CAN'T THAT KID SING; HE CAN'T PLAY THE PIANO EITHER.'

WELL, I DIDN'T FIND OUT WHAT THE BIG SECRET WAS UNTIL THE MID-SUMMER. I WAS RETURNING HOME FROM A PETE SEGER AND ARLO GUTHRIE CONCERT WITH A PEPPERONI AND ONION PIZZA IN MY LAP WHEN MY MOTHER MET ME AT THE DOOR. SHE AND MY DAD HAD BEEN TO A MEETING AT SCHOOL WITH THE PARENTS OF EIGHT OF MY FRIENDS. THERE, MRS. EDWARDS AND MRS. HOLE HAD EXPLAINED THAT THE RIDGE SCHOOL HAD AGREED WITH A LOCAL JUNIOR HIGH SCHOOL TO

SEND US NINE KIDS TO SCHOOL WITH THE NORMAL CHILDREN OUR AGE. THEY SAID WE COULD ALL HANDLE NINTH GRADE WORK AND THAT MRS. EDWARDS AND MRS. FOGARTY WOULD GO ALONG WITH US TO THE NEW SCHOOL TO HELP US TAKE NOTES, MOVE FROM CLASS TO CLASS, AND ASSIST US IN ANY PHYSICAL OR PSYCHOLOGICAL PROBLEMS WE MIGHT ENCOUNTER IN MAKING SUCH A BIG ADJUSTMENT. IT TURNED OUT THAT DURING THE FIRST WEEKS AT OUR NEW SCHOOL, COCKEYSVILLE HIGH, I BELIEVE WE HELPED OUR TWO TEACHERS ADJUST AS MUCH AS THEY HELPED US. IT MUST HAVE BEEN EQUALLY AS HARD FOR NINE HANDICAPPED KIDS WHO HAD BEEN SHELTERED ALL THEIR LIVES TO BE PLACED IN A NEW ENVIRONMENT AS IT WAS HARD FOR TWO 48 YEAR-OLD WOMEN TO GO BACK TO HIGH SCHOOL. BUT WE ALL SET OUT TO MAKE THE BEST OF IT!

CONSIDERING THAT ALL ELEVEN OF US HAD KNOWN EACH OTHER FOR AS LONG AS WE CAN REMEMBER, WE FELT EVEN MORE LIKE A FAMILY SINCE WE WERE FACING THIS NEW ENDEAVOR TOGETHER. IT WAS CLEAR TO SOME OF US WHAT WOULD BE SOME OF THE HARDEST THINGS TO ACCEPT AND GET USED TO, BOTH FOR OURSELVES AND OTHERS. FOR INSTANCE, THE KIDS KNEW THEY WOULD HAVE TO GET USED TO A HEAVIER WORKLOAD; BUT OUR SWEET AND INNOCENT TEACHERS WOULD HAVE TO GET USED TO THE SOMETIMES NOT SO NICE WORDS THROWN AROUND IN THE HALLS AND CLASSROOMS BY OUR ABLE BODIED CLASSMATES. YOU SEE, WE ALL MINDED OUR PRETTY LITTLE TONGUES BACK AT RIDGE. WE DID, BECAUSE WE KNEW THAT IF WE DIDN'T, MRS. EDWARDS WOULD HAVE BOOTED US OUT.

CONTINUING THE PARALLEL OF ADJUSTMENTS, OUR TEACHERS HAD TO ENDURE STARING BY SOME OF THE

HIGH SCHOOL KIDS AS IF TO INFER THEM SAYING, 'WHY ARE THEY HERE? THEY WEREN'T HERE BEFORE,' AND, AS YOU MIGHT GUESS, NINE HANDICAPPED KIDS IN A LARGE POPULATION OF HIGH SCHOOL STUDENTS WILL ENDURE AN AWFUL AMOUNT OF STARING TOO, AT FIRST, THAT IS.

OUR EXPERIENCES AT COCKEYSVILLE WERE NEVER REALLY ALIEN-LIKE. FOR MOST OF US, ATTENDING A REGULAR HIGH SCHOOL CHANGED FROM AN AWESOME TASK TO A REWARDING CHALLENGE AND A FUN RIDE. WE DID HAVE TO PUSH OURSELVES TO BE THE BEST STUDENTS WE COULD BE, BUT WE RECEIVED HELP FROM JUST ABOUT EVERYONE WE TURNED TO.

FOR MANY OF OUR CLASSES WE WOULD GO OUT OF OUR LITTLE HOMEROOM TO REGULAR CLASSROOMS. EITHER MRS. EDWARDS OR MRS. FOGARTY WOULD GO WITH US TO TAKE NOTES AND HELP US COMMUNICATE WITH THE TEACHERS AND THE OTHER STUDENTS. BUT OUR NEED FOR THEIR HELP GREW SMALLER AS EACH ONE OF US BEGAN MAKING OUR MARK IN THE SCHOOL. THREE OF US WERE IN THE CHORUS, TWO WERE ELECTED IN THE JUNIOR NATIONAL HONOR SOCIETY. BUT MUCH MORE IMPORTANTLY, A FEW OF US COULD HAVE BEEN LABELED AS 'LADIES MEN'. AS YOU CAN GUESS, THE REST OF OUR ACHIEVEMENTS SEEMED SECONDARY COMPARED TO THIS LAST ONE.

MRS. EDWARDS WAS A GREAT LADY BECAUSE SHE COULD BE ANYTHING TO ANYBODY. THERE MIGHT HAVE BEEN A PERSON ABSOLUTELY UNLIKE MYSELF IN OUR GROUP OF NINE; AND YET SHE COULD BE AS GOOD A FRIEND AND UNDERSTAND HIM JUST AS MUCH AS SHE LOVED AND UNDERSTOOD ME, AND FULFILL ALL EXPECTATIONS OF EVERYONE IN BETWEEN.

PERHAPS THE ONE WHO BROKE AWAY THE FASTEST INTO THE WORLD OF INDEPENDENCE WAS JOHN P. HE WAS ALWAYS THE MOST OUTGOING GUY AT RIDGE AND HE HELD NOTHING BACK AT COCKEYSVILLE. BY CHRISTMAS, THERE WASN'T A PERSON WHO DIDN'T KNOW HIM OR REGARD HIM AS A FRIEND. PERHAPS A LESS EXPERIENCED TEACHER WOULD HAVE TRIED TO TAME SUCH A PLAYBOY DOWN A BIT, BUT NOT MRS. EDWARDS. SHE KNEW THAT A VERY ACTIVE SOCIAL LIFE WAS IMPORTANT TO JOHN. BUT SHE ALSO TOLD HIM THAT IT COULD BE THE CAUSE OF STEADILY DECLINING GRADES SO SHE'D ENCOURAGE HIM TO INCORPORATE BOTH SOCIAL ACTIVITIES AND HEAVY STUDYING INTO HIS SET OF PRIORITIES. JOHN ALWAYS TRIED HIS BEST AND MRS. EDWARDS ALWAYS SUPPLIED HER FRIENDLY CONFIDENCE AND ENCOURAGEMENT WHEN HE WOULD HIT A ROUGH SPOT.

A BIG DECISION JOHN HAD TO MAKE THAT YEAR WAS WHETHER TO STAY IN THE SLIGHTLY SHELTERED ENVIRONMENT OF THE PROGRAM AT COCKEYSVILLE, OR TO TRANSFER, AS IT HAD ALWAYS BEEN HIS DREAM TO DO, TO HIS OWN NEIGHBORHOOD SCHOOL. NO DOUBT, A LOT OF ADVICE AND COUNSEL IN MAKING THIS DECISION CAME FROM OUR DEDICATED TEACHER, AND WHEN HE HAD FINALLY DECIDED THAT YES, HE WOULD GO IT ON HIS OWN, HER SUPPORT BECAME COMPLETE.

"NOW JOHN, YOU KNOW THAT THIS IS A BIG STEP AND A VERY IMPORTANT MOVE TO MAKE. YOU'RE GONNA HAVE TO BEHAVE YOURSELF. YOU WON'T HAVE MRS. FOGARTY OR ME TO TELL YOU TO STUDY, HIT THE BOOKS. DON'T HIT THEM TOO HARD, BUT JUST TRY YOUR BEST. MAKE ME PROUD OF YOU NOW. I'LL PRAY FOR YOU AND I LOVE YOU."

AND HOW COULD HE HELP BUT HAVE A TEAR IN HIS EYE WHEN HE SAID, "ALRIGHT, MRS. EDWARDS, I WILL. I LOVE YOU TOO."

ALSO VERY CLOSE TO OUR TEACHERS WAS DANNY COOK. OF ALL OF US, DANNY MIGHT HAVE BEEN THE MOST ARTISTIC, EASY-GOING, AND LEVEL HEADED KID IN OUR CLASS, BUT SOMETIMES HE WAS STILL A SCREWBALL LIKE EVERYONE ELSE. DAN WAS UNIQUE BECAUSE HE WAS INDEPENDENT ENOUGH TO RECEIVE A DRIVER'S LICENCE AND ZIP AROUND TOWN WHEREVER HE WANTED TO GO, YET HE REMAINED JUST AS LOYAL TO MRS. EDWARDS AND ALL HIS FRIENDS IN THE CLASS. WHENEVER SOMEONE NEEDED A FAVOR, ESPECIALLY A RIDE SOMEWHERE, THEY KNEW THEY COULD DEPEND ON DANNY.

WITH ALL HIS GOOD ATTRIBUTES, DAN OCCASIONALLY RAN LOW ON SELF-CONFIDENCE. NOT A DEPRESSIVE KIND OF GUY, BUT HE'D GET WORKED UP OVER A MAJOR EVENT, AN ENGLISH TEST, FOR EXAMPLE. AND THEN, OF COURSE, MRS. EDWARDS WOULD COME TO THE RESCUE.

"NOW DANNY, YOU'LL BE FINE. YOU AND I WENT OVER EVERYTHING THAT MRS. JACKSON MIGHT ASK ON THE TEST TODAY."

"OH, MRS. EDWARDS, I KNOW, BUT I'M STILL THINKING THERE'S SOMETHING WE'VE FORGOTTEN. NOW, WHAT IF SHE ASKS WHO WERE THE TWO CHARACTERS IN 'OF MICE AND MEN'?"

"AH, YOU KNOW THAT," SHE'D ASSURE HIM, "WHO WERE THEY?"

"UH, LENNY... LENNY AND UH, UH, SQUIGGY!"

"NO, NO, NO. NOW COME ON, EVERYTHING'S GONNA BE FINE. YOU'VE STUDIED ENOUGH TO KNOW EVERYTHING ON THAT TEST."

"BUT YOU NEVER KNOW WHEN MRS. JACKSON ASKS ONE OF THOSE OFF THE WALL QUESTIONS. SHE'S FAMOUS FOR DOING THAT, YOU KNOW."

SHE'D QUICKLY COME BACK WITH, "LOOK, DANNY, YOU'RE GONNA HAVE ALL KINDS OF TEACHERS IN YOUR LIFE, EASY ONES, HARD ONES. YOU MIGHT HAVE TEACHERS WHO'LL ASK YOU QUESTIONS LIKE I DO, OR EVEN LIKE MRS. JACKSON..."

"HA, NOBODY'S LIKE MRS. JACKSON."

"WHATEVER YOU SAY," SHE'D CONCEDE, "I CAN ONLY TELL YOU THAT WHEN I WAS IN COLLEGE, I HAD TO TAKE THIS ONE SEMESTER OF FRENCH READING AND ALL IT WAS WAS THIS 354 PAGE BOOK ALL IN FRENCH. IT WAS A NOVEL," BY THIS TIME, SHE HAD THE WHOLE GROUP'S ATTENTION, "AND WE HAD TO READ IT AND DISCUSS IT IN CLASS, BUT ALL THAT WAS SPOKEN IN CLASS WAS FRENCH. THE PROFESSOR EVEN KNEW VERY LITTLE ENGLISH. AND I WAS REALLY A LOSER WHEN IT CAME TO LISTENING TO AND UNDERSTANDING FRENCH BUT I REALLY NEEDED TO HEAR THE DISCUSSION OF THIS BOOK BECAUSE I HAD TROUBLE WITH THE FIRST FIFTY PAGES. THAT'S WHEN I LEARNED THAT TEACHERS CAN BE AS DIFFERENT AS NIGHT AND DAY AND I JUST HAD TO ADJUST MYSELF TO EACH ONE."

"WELL, WHAT D'YOU GET ON THE COURSE?"

"I GOT AN A BECAUSE THE FINAL EXAM WAS IN ENGLISH. SEE? YOU NEVER KNOW."

I DON'T BELIEVE DANNY DID AS GOOD ON HIS TEST AS HE'D HAVE LIKED, BUT HE GAVE IT ALL HE HAD WITH MANY SIMILAR TESTS SIMPLY BECAUSE HE KNEW, AS WE ALL DID, MRS. EDWARDS WAS RIGHT IN THERE PUSHING FOR US. JACKIE WAS THE ONLY ONE WHO REALLY SHINED AS FAR AS GRADES WERE CONCERNED. IT WAS AS IF SHE HAD ONLY BE TAUGHT THE FIRST LETTER OF THE ALPHABET; A 'B' WOULD HAVE BEEN FOREIGN TO HER. THIS WAS SOMETHING THAT WAS ENCOURAGED AND CONGRATULATED BY OUR TEACHER, BUT NEVER DEMANDED. SHE EXPECTED EVERYONE TO DO THEIR BEST, BUT TO KNOW WHAT THEIR BEST IS. JACKIE MIGHT HAVE HAD TOO HIGH EXPECTATIONS OF HERSELF ONCE OR TWICE, BUT THEY WERE ALWAYS BROUGHT DOWN TO THE PROPER LEVEL BY MRS. EDWARDS. SHE WOULD JUST POINT OUT ALL OF JACKIE'S GREAT POINTS, LIKE HER CHARM, HER WIT, HER INTELLIGENCE, AND ONCE AGAIN THAT 'JUST THE WAY SHE WAS' WAS PRETTY NICE.

A REMARKABLE GIRL IN OUR CLASS WAS BECKY RHOADS. SHE HAD MORE STRENGTH AND ENDURANCE THAN MOST PEOPLE IN THIS WORLD WILL EVER HAVE. FOR SHE HANDLED ALL HER MANUAL FUNCTIONS WITH HER FEET. SHE COULD AMAZE ANYONE SHE MIGHT MEET JUST BY HER BOLDNESS AND UNINHIBITEDNESS. SHE WAS A PERSON WHO STRIVED TO LIVE IN A WORLD WHERE EVERYONE WOULD BE ABLE TO DO THEIR OWN THING, TO BE FREE AND OPEN IN THEIR PHYSICAL APPEARANCE AND IGNORE THEIR OWN AS WELL AS EVERYONE ELSE'S HANDICAPS. SHE CERTAINLY SHARED THIS DREAM WITH MRS. EDWARDS.

THERE WERE THREE AMONG US AFFLICTED WITH MUSCULAR DYSTROPHY. THIS IS A SAD DISEASE BECAUSE ONE CAN WATCH A FRIEND GROW INCREASINGLY

WEAKER AS THE MONTHS AND YEARS ROLL ON. BUT, AS YOU MIGHT GUESS, MRS. EDWARDS WAS NOT ABOUT TO LET THEIR MINDS OR SPIRITS GROW DIM AT ALL. WITH THE SAME ENCOURAGEMENT WHICH SHE GAVE ALL THE REST OF US TO MAKE THE MOST OF HIGH SCHOOL SOCIAL LIFE, SHE TRIED HER VERY BEST TO OPEN UP THE WORLD AND SCOPE TO GREG, DAVID, AND BOB. THEIR DAYS OF SCHOOL WERE NUMBERED BECAUSE OF THEIR GROWING WEAKNESS, BUT WE ALL TRIED TO MAKE THE BEST OF THAT LAST YEAR WE HAD TOGETHER. AND THROUGH THE DILIGENCE AND DETERMINATION OF EVERYONE CONCERNED, GREG, DAVID, ALONG WITH BECKY FINISHED REQUIRED WORK FOR FOUR FULL YEARS OF HIGH SCHOOL IN JUST ONE YEAR. THEY RECEIVED DIPLOMAS FROM THEIR NEIGHBORHOOD HIGH SCHOOLS AND ALL RECEIVED STANDING OVATIONS AT THEIR GRADUATION CEREMONIES.

I ATTENDED GREG'S GRADUATION AND CRIED AT THAT MOMENT WHEN HE RECEIVED THE CERTIFICATE AND HIS EYES GLEAMED INTO THE AUDIENCE AT THE LADY WHO HELPED HIM SO MUCH TO GET THERE. THE GAZE BETWEEN GREG AND MRS. EDWARDS WAS ONE OF SHEER LOVE AND A SIGHT I WILL REMEMBER FOR THE REST OF MY LIFE.

NOW WE COME TO THE BIGGEST FLIRT THAT COCKEYSVILLE HIGH HAS EVER KNOWN. JOE LIU CAME FROM TAIWAN. I REMEMBER THE DAY HE FIRST CAME TO RIDGE AND HE COULDN'T SPEAK THE LANGUAGE AT ALL. WE KIDS TRIED TO TEACH HIM WORDS LIKE DOG, CAT, TEACHER, AND SCHOOL. WE'D HAVE BEEN BETTER OFF TEACHING HIM WORDS THAT HE'D HAVE A USE FOR WHEN HE GOT TO HIGH SCHOOL LIKE 'WHAT'S YOUR TELEPHONE NUMBER?' BUT I DON'T WANT TO TAKE AWAY FROM THE FACT THAT JOE HAD A VERY QUICK AND INSIGHTFUL MIND. HE MADE FRIENDS VERY EASILY

AND HAD A DEEP RESPECT FOR MRS. EDWARDS. HE DIDN'T ALWAYS SHOW IT THOUGH. JOE WAS A WILDCAT SOMETIMES. HE'D SPEED IN HIS WHEELCHAIR MUCH TOO FAST SOMETIMES AND IMITATE SOME BAD TRAITS HE MIGHT HAVE SEEN OTHER KIDS DO WHILE ROAMING AROUND IN THE HALLS. BUT THIS BAD BEHAVIOR WAS ALWAYS UNDERSTOOD, THEN CORRECTED BY HIS TEACHER. "NOW, JOE," MRS. EDWARDS WOULD SIT DOWN AND TALK TO HIM, "YOU REALLY MUST SETTLE YOURSELF DOWN. IT'S NOT RIGHT FOR YOU TO DO SOME OF THE THINGS YOU DO. IT'S IMPORTANT FOR YOU TO HAVE FUN, YES. BUT YOU CAN'T GET INTO TROUBLE LIKE YOU ARE DOING. YOU HAVE TOO MANY THINGS TO WORRY ABOUT BESIDES ANY EXTRA SHENANIGANS. IT'S ALSO VERY IMPORTANT FOR YOU TO DO WELL IN SCHOOL. YOU GOTTA PUT YOUR MIND TO IT. YOU KNOW, YOU WON'T ALWAYS HAVE ME TO HOLD YOUR HAND AND GIVE YOU PEP TALKS LIKE THIS."

JOE MIGHT NOT HAVE REALIZED THE TRUTH IN WHAT SHE SAID TO HIM, BUT HE WILL NEVER FORGET THE DAY MRS. EDWARDS GATHERED ALL US KIDS TOGETHER FOR AN ANNOUNCEMENT ONE MAY AFTERNOON AT THE END OF THE DAY.

"ALRIGHT PEOPLE, CAN WE ALL GET AROUND? GET TO YOUR DESKS OR SOMETHING; I'D LIKE TO SAY SOMETHING, OK? IT'S ALL BEEN ESTABLISHED; YOU ALL KNOW WHERE YOU'RE GOING NEXT YEAR. THE THREE OF YOU," TALKING TO ONE CORNER OF KIDS, "ARE GOING TO BE GRADUATING NEXT MONTH AND YOU KNOW I COULDN'T BE MORE PROUD OF YOU, I THINK YOU DESERVE ALL THE CREDIT IN THE WORLD. THREE MORE OF YOU ARE GOING ON TO DULANEY HIGH SCHOOL AND WILL GRADUATE IN TWO MORE YEARS AND THE REST OF YOU ARE GOING YOUR SEPARATE WAYS. YOU KNOW THAT I LOVE YOU VERY MUCH AND I WILL ALWAYS LOVE YOU AND REMEMBER THE TIMES

WE'VE SPENT TOGETHER. YOU'VE PROBABLY BEEN WONDERING WHERE I'LL BE NEXT YEAR. WELL, THE ANSWER TO THAT IS, THE OZARKS. I'M RETIRING, THIS IS MY LAST YEAR OF TEACHING."

A HUSH FELL OVER THE ROOM. THE THOUGHT THAT MUST HAVE COME TO EVERYONE'S MIND WAS, 'OH WOW, SHE'S FINALLY GOING TO BE HAPPY AND CONTENT NOW THAT SHE'S GOING TO HER REAL HOME FOR GOOD...OH GOD, I'LL MISS HER.'

"I CAN IMAGINE THAT YOU'RE ALL DUMBFOUNDED, YOU CERTAINLY LOOK IT..."

THERE WAS A PAUSE, THEN A SURGE OF LAUGHTER.

"YOU NEEDN'T BE SO SHOCKED; YOU MUST HAVE KNOWN THE DAY WAS COMING. AND YOU NEED NOT BE SO SAD. I'D LIKE YOU TO BE HAPPY FOR ME. HAVEN'T I WORKED HARD ENOUGH? DON'T I DESERVE A REST? HAVEN'T I BEEN YOUR FRIEND AND HAVEN'T WE SHARED SO MUCH?" THERE WERE MANY NODS. THERE WERE MANY TEARS. "MY HUSBAND HAS SOLD HIS DENTAL PRACTICE AND WE PLAN TO MOVE IN JULY. PARTING WILL BE SAD FOR YOU AS WELL AS FOR ME, BUT IT SEEMS THAT NOW ALL OF US ARE MOVING ON TO DIFFERENT STAGES OF OUR LIVES. AND OUR SADNESS WILL SOON BE REPLACED BY NEW EXPERIENCES AND EXCITEMENT FOR ALL OF US." JOE WAS THE SADDEST OF ALL.

THE NEXT DAY IN SCHOOL WAS A PARTICULARLY BORING ONE FOR ME SO AFTER MY FIRST CLASS WHEN MRS. EDWARDS CAME TO TAKE ME TO THE NEXT ONE, I DECIDED TO DO SOMETHING UNUSUAL. ONLY I COULD HAVE GOTTEN AWAY WITH SPENDING CLASS TIME TALKING TO MRS. EDWARDS BY TELLING HER THAT I HAD TO GO TO THE BATHROOM. THEN SHE TOLD THE TEACHER THAT I'D BE PROLONGED AND MISS THE FIRST

PART OF CLASS. SHE HAD TO HELP ME ON THE JOHN ANYWAY, SO IT GAVE US A FEW MINUTES IN PRIVATE TO TALK ABOUT WHAT WENT DOWN THE DAY BEFORE.

I STARTED, "SO, THIS MORNING I WOKE UP EXTRA EARLY AND WAITED TO SEE IF THE SUN WOULD RISE."

"WHY D'YOU DO THAT?"

"BECAUSE OF THE EARTH SHATTERING NEWS THAT HAPPENED YESTERDAY; MRS. TOBY EDWARDS ANNOUNCED HER RETIREMENT. NEVER THOUGHT IT WOULD HAPPEN."

"I NEVER THOUGHT IT WOULD HAPPEN EITHER," SHE LAUGHED. "MY HUSBAND IS TIRED AND THERE'S REALLY NOTHING LEFT FOR ME TO DO HERE. YOU'RE ALL BECOMING MORE AND MORE INDEPENDENT, AND GOING IN SO MANY DIRECTIONS. I JUST COULDN'T KEEP UP WITH YOU IF I STAYED AROUND. THIS WAY I HAVE SO MANY WONDERFUL MEMORIES. AND THE STRONGEST CONFIDENCE THAT YOU ALL ARE DOING YOUR VERY BEST. YOU KNOW I EXPECT TO SEE ALL YOUR NAMES UP IN LIGHTS SOMEDAY. I HAVE NO DOUBT THAT I WILL."

"YOU KNOW," I ADDED, "THAT'S ONE OF THE BIGGEST THINGS I LOVE ABOUT YOU. ONE THING YOU HAVE ALWAYS BEEN FULL OF IS CONFIDENCE, AND ALSO HOPE. YOU'RE A TOWER OF HOPE. YOU ARE THE MOST RELIGIOUS WOMAN I'VE KNOWN, NEXT TO MY MOTHER, OF COURSE."

WE BOTH LAUGHED BECAUSE WE BOTH KNEW MY MOTHER.

"I LIKE YOUR FAMILY," SHE COMPLEMENTED ME, "YOU ARE ALL SO TALENTED...WELL, ALL EXCEPT FOR YOU,"

AND THEN SHE GAVE A LAUGH THAT I ALWAYS LOVED TO HEAR. IT MADE UP FOR THE TERRIBLY INSULTING BUT MARVELOUSLY FUNNY REMARK SHE HAD JUST MADE. I CAME BACK WITH, "UH, WHEN DID YOU SAY YOU WERE LEAVING FOR THE OZARKS?"

OUR LAUGHTER WAS HEARTY THEN.

"ALL SERIOUSNESS ASIDE," I CONTINUED, "YOU KNOW, I CAN'T THANK YOU ENOUGH FOR SHARING YOUR OWN FAMILY WITH ME, WITH ALL OF US. I FEEL LIKE I KNOW THEM ALL."

"SOMETIMES IT IS DIFFICULT TO DISTINGUISH THEM FROM YOU ALL. YOU ARE REALLY LIKE MY CHILDREN IN MANY WAYS. I'M PROUD OF ALL YOUR ACCOMPLISHMENTS JUST LIKE I AM OF MY OWN CHILDREN."

"I JUST HATE THE THOUGHT OF SEEING YOU GO. IT'S NOT THAT I'M NOT HAPPY TO SEE YOU RETIRE TO THE OZARKS. IT'S THAT I REALLY DON'T WANT A PLAQUE."

"A PLAQUE?" SHE BEGGED MY PARDON.

I INSISTED, "SURE, A PLAQUE. YOU KNOW, LIKE YOU GIVE ALL YOUR STUDENTS WHO GO ON TO ANOTHER SCHOOL. MORE THAN LIKELY IT'LL HAVE THE SERENITY PRAYER ON IT WITH AN EAGLE FLYING OVER THE OCEAN. YOU KNOW, THE PLAQUE!"

"I DON'T GIVE IT TO EVERYBODY," SHE DEFENDED.

"SURE YOU DO! NOLAN, SMITH, BAKER, COPENHAVER..." I LISTED.

"I DIDN'T GIVE IT TO PARADISO."

"WELL HECK, PARADISO CAN'T READ ANYWAY," WAS THE PEAK IN THIS SILLY ARGUMENT ABOUT A RITUAL OF MRS. EDWARDS GIVING A SPECIAL GIFT TO HER GRADUATING STUDENTS. STILL I JOKINGLY PERSISTED, "AND NOW THAT ALL OF US ARE LEAVING YOUR NEST, THIS YEAR YOU'LL PROBABLY GO OUT AND BUM NINE NEW PLAQUES, ONE FOR MRS. FOGARTY TOO; OR DO YOU HAVE A WHOLE BUNCH OF THEM STACHED SOMEWHERE?"

GETTING JUST A TAD DEFENSIVE, "WELL, WHAT'S WRONG WITH A DARN PLAQUE?" SHE ASKED.

"IT'S SO UNORIGINAL. IT DOESN'T SHOW THAT YOU'LL REALLY REMEMBER ME AND WANT ME TO REMEMBER YOU."

"WELL, WHAT WOULD YOU LIKE ME TO GET YOU?"

I TOLD HER, "SOMETHING REALLY SPECIAL. SOMETHING THAT I REALLY NEED AND COULD USE FOR MY ROOM, SOMETHING NOBODY SHOULD WITHOUT. I WANT SOMETHING THAT WHEN I USE IT, I'LL ALWAYS THINK OF YOU. GET ME SOMETHING YOU WOULD NEVER DREAM OF GETTING ANYONE ELSE."

AND SHE DID. IT WAS THE LAST DAY OF SCHOOL AND I GOT EXACTLY WHAT I WANTED. I RECEIVED A LONG HUG FROM MY DEAR FRIEND, MRS. EDWARDS, AND HER GIFT TO ME, A CURTAIN ROD OF MY VERY OWN.

'THANK YOU, MRS. EDWARDS.'

To My Therapist

HERE WE'RE COMING, MY PARENTS AND ME
THEY'RE DRAGGING ME 'CAUSE I'M GONNA RUN AWAY
GAGGING ME 'CAUSE I'M GONNA CRY MY EYES OUT;
THAT'S WHAT I TOLD THEM
I DO NOT WANNA BE HERE. YOU CAN'T MAKE ME
STAY
MOM IS HOLDING MY LEGS 'CAUSE I'M GONNA START
KICKING
YOU SUDDENLY SAY 'WAIT, HE MOVES HIS LEGS
WELL, LET HIM KICK, WAIT'
YOU DON'T THINK I SEE WHAT YOU'RE DOING, ALL I
WANT IS TO BE FREE
GET ME OUT OF HERE, OH NO, I WILL NOT
COOPERATE
YOU SAY 'DON'T YOU WANT TO VISIT ME' I SAY
FLAT OUT NO
'DON'T YOU WANT TO EXERCISE AND GET BIG AND
STRONG'
MOM SAYS 'COME ON, SHE'S A NICE LADY' AND I
TELL YOU YOU'RE OLD AND UGLY
DAD SLAPS MY HEAD AND I THINK I DID SOMETHING
WRONG
YOU SAY, 'MY, YOU CAN CRY LOUD; YOU HAVE
STRONG LUNGS'
I STOP CRYING JUST TO BE DIFFICULT, JUST TO
DISGUST YOU
THEN YOU TAKE ME ON YOUR LAP, EXPLAIN JUST
WHAT YOU WANT TO DO WITH ME

HEY IT DOES LOOK LIKE I CAN TRUST YOU

THAT WAS WHEN I WAS FOUR, I'M SEVEN NOW, AND
HAPPY TO COME TO THERAPY
I LOOK FORWARD TO GETTING OUT OF THIS CHAIR AND
ONTO THE MAT
IT'S A TIME TO GIVE MY TIRED SEAT A REST AND
CRAWL AROUND-
CAN O.T. HELP ME TO SWING A BASEBALL BAT?
CAN YOU SHOW ME HOW TO SPEAK SO MY FRIENDS CAN
UNDERSTAND ME?
WILL MY ARMS EVER TO STRONG ENOUGH TO GRAB
ONTO A BRANCH OF A TREE AND CLIMB
CAN MY LEGS GET STRONG ENOUGH TO RIDE A
BICYCLE LIKE THE ONE WILLY HAS
YOU SMILE AND LAUGH AND SAY 'IT'LL TAKE TIME'
YOU ARE WILLING TO EXPLAIN EVERYTHING TO ME
AND HELP ME TO UNDERSTAND
I FIGURE, YOU MUST KNOW EVERYTHING; YOU'RE AS
OLD AS MY PARENTS ARE
AND I KNOW YOU'RE INTERESTED IN ME 'CAUSE YOU
WANT TO KNOW WHAT I'LL BE WHEN I GROW UP, YOU
ONCE SAID THAT I COULD GO FAR
SOMETIMES IT HURTS WHEN YOU STRETCH OUT MY
LEGS
AND IT MAKES ME MAD WHEN I CAN'T TALK BECAUSE I
CAN'T GET ENOUGH AIR
YOU SOMETIMES YELL AT ME WHEN I DROP SOMETHING
BECAUSE I'M JUST NOT TRYING
BUT I KNOW IT'S ONLY 'CAUSE YOU CARE

WELL NOW I'M 10 AND MY DOCTOR SENT ME TO THE
HOSPITAL ALL SUMMER FOR THERAPY
YOU'RE OLDER THAN MY REGULAR THERAPIST AT
SCHOOL, I GUESS

HEY, WHAT ARE YOU DOING? THAT'S NOT THE WAY SHE
USUALLY DOES IT! HEY, IT HURTS
OH YEAH, YOU'RE THE THERAPIST, YOU MUST KNOW
BEST
IT SURE IS DIFFERENT THOUGH, AND I DON'T LIKE
THIS VERY MUCH
IT'S SUMMER AND ALL MY FRIENDS ARE HAVING FUN,
PLAYING BASEBALL OUTSIDE
THIS IS HURTING AND TIRING ME OUT AND YOU
AREN'T BEING NICE ABOUT IT
I FEEL SORRY I EVER CAME HERE, AND I'M GONNA
CRY
NO, 10 YEARS OLD IS NOT TOO OLD, AND I'LL CRY
WHEN I FEEL LIKE IT
I'M GONNA TELL MY MOMMY THAT YOU WERE MEAN
TO ME
YOU MADE ME WORK REAL REAL HARD WHEN I WAS
TIRED AND HOT
BOY, I SURE DO NOT LIKE TO GO TO THERAPY
NOW THAT I'M BACK AT SCHOOL, IT'S NICE TO DO
THE EXERCISES I'VE ALWAYS DONE
THERE WAS A LADY AT THE HOSPITAL WHO WAS NASTY
AND OLD
THERAPY AT SCHOOL IS GOOD BECAUSE IT'S THE
TIME TO GET OUT OF CLASS
OH YEAH, EVERYBODY SAYS IT'S A NICE PLACE TO
GO

WELL NOW I'M 12 AND I'VE BEEN DOING THESE
EXERCISES FOR A LONG TIME
WHY DO YOU SAY IT'S TIME TO TRY SOME NEW
THINGS NOW?
GEE, IT TOOK ME 8 YEARS TO GET USED TO WHAT WE
DO THESE DAYS
I'LL TRY ANYTHING IF YOU SHOW ME HOW
THIS IS SCARY, STANDING ALL BY MYSELF, WITH

NOBODY HOLDING ME
I DON'T THINK I GOT ENOUGH BALANCE; I'M SCARED
I'LL FALL
I'M NOT HAPPY DOING THIS, IT FRIGHTENS ME AND
I CAN'T THINK OF NOTHING ELSE
YOU DON'T SEEM TO UNDERSTAND AT ALL
I TRY TO REALLY PUT ON A SHOW SO YOU WON'T
MAKE ME DO THIS ANYMORE-
YOU SAY 'OK, WE DON'T HAVE TO CONTINUE THIS IF
YOU REALLY DON'T WANT TO.'
I SAY I'M SORRY I'M A CHICKEN, AND YOU SAY
'DON'T BE SORRY, YOU'RE NOT ONE'
'WE'LL ONLY WORK ON WHAT YOU WANT TO LEARN TO
DO.'
LATELY I-BEEN NOTICING THAT YOU-BEEN GETTING
TIRED DURING THE DAY
YES, I KNOW WHAT THE WORD 'RETIRE' MEANS; WHAT
DO YOU MEAN YOU'RE GOING TO?
HOW CAN YOU LEAVE ME AFTER ALL WE'VE BEEN
THROUGH TOGETHER?
ANOTHER THERAPIST MIGHT TRY, BUT SHE WON'T
HELP ME LIKE YOU

HI, HOW DO YOU DO? DID THE LAST THERAPIST
TELL YOU ABOUT ME?
I'M 13 AND I LIKE TO COME TO THERAPY, THAT IS
WHEN YOU DON'T YELL AND I DON'T WORK HARD
THE LAST THERAPIST MADE IT PRETTY HARD BUT OLD
PEOPLE HAVE TO YELL A LOT
BUT IF YOU'RE NICE TO THEM, THEY LIKE TO GIVE
YOU A GOLD STAR
ARE YOU A REAL THERAPIST OR JUST A PRACTICE-ONE;
YOU ARE JUST A YOUNG GIRL
I DIDN'T REALIZE SOMEBODY COULD BE IN CHARGE
AND STILL BE GOING TO SCHOOL
NO, I GUESS ALL THERAPISTS DON'T HAVE TO BE

OLD MAIDS, UGLY AND STERN
BUT IT SURE MAKES IT EASIER TO FOLLOW RULES
YOU LOOK LIKE MY SISTER INSTEAD OF MY MOTHER;
YOU LAUGH AT THINGS A LOT
YOU WOULDN'T YELL IF I DID SOMETHING WRONG,
YOU'D JUST SAY FORGET IT
NOT ONLY AS A TEACHER, BUT AS A FRIEND, YOU'RE
NICE TO BE AROUND
I COULD EVEN TELL YOU A DIRTY JOKE AND YOU
WOULD GET IT
NOW I HOPE YOU REALIZE THAT EVEN THOUGH WE'RE
FRIENDS, I'M TRUSTING YOU TO HELP ME
YOU'VE EARNED YOUR MASTERS DEGREE SO YOU MUST
BE SMART AND THE BEST AT WHAT YOU DO
IT'S A GREATLY QUALIFIED WOMAN I HAVE FOR A
THERAPIST AND A FRIEND
AND YOU'LL BENEFIT FROM ME AS MUCH AS I'LL
BENEFIT FROM YOU

WELL NOW I'M 15, AND IN NO MOOD TO SUCK
THROUGH A STRAW, PLAY WITH BLOCKS,
OR STAND WITH TRIPODS. IF I COME TO THERAPY
AT ALL, I'LL COME JUST TO HANG OUT WITH YOU
HEY, IF YOU HAVEN'T GOTTEN ME BETTER THAN THIS
SO FAR, ALL YOUR THEORIES ARE USELESS
BESIDES, NEXT YEAR I'M CUTTING OUT AND GOING
TO A REGULAR SCHOOL
HEY, IT'S BEEN NICE, BUT I WANT TO BE AROUND
REGULAR PEOPLE NOW
ONE DAY I TRIED FALLING IN LOVE WITH YOU BUT
YOU PUSHED ME AWAY
YOU SAID WE SHOULDN'T BE MORE THAN THERAPIST
AND PATIENT; AND YOU'RE RIGHT
BUT I WANT A GIRLFRIEND MORE THAN A THERAPIST
SO IT'S GOODBY TODAY
HEY, I WISH YOU LUCK WITH THE KIDS YOU TRY TO

HELP
I USED TO BE ONE OF THEM, BUT YOU DIDN'T MUCH
HELP ME
I DON'T NEED NOBODY TO LOOK OVER ME AND TELL
ME WHAT TO DO NO MORE
YOU'RE FOR THE BIRDS AND SO IS THERAPY

IT'S BEEN A FEW YEARS, I DON'T DO MUCH
EXERCISE DON'T COME EASY TO ME
I'M NOT GETTING ALONG LIKE I THOUGHT I WOULD
SINCE I'VE BEEN WITHOUT THERAPY
SOCIALLY NOW I'M DOING REAL WELL
BUT I'D LOVE TO BE AS ACTIVE AS SOME OF MY
FRIENDS
I'D LIKE TO WALK BETTER, TALK BETTER, WRITE
BETTER, WRITE?
I NEVER HAVE FIGURED OUT THE USE OF THESE
HANDS

MY DOCTOR TOLD ME ABOUT A PROGRAM AT THE
HOSPITAL
YOU REMEMBER MY LAST ENCOUNTER THERE
HE SAYS I COULD START HAVING THERAPY EVERY
WEEK AGAIN
IF I COULD FIND THE TIME TO GET THERE
DOC SAYS IT WOULD HELP MY POSTURE
DAD SAYS IT WOULD OCCUPY MY TIME
I'M OLDER, MATURER, AND ABLE TO APPRECIATE
THINGS MORE
MAYBE I COULD TAKE MORE ADVANTAGE THIS TIME.

I COME INTO THE THERAPY ROOM AT THE HOSPITAL
FEELING I'VE DONE THIS BEFORE
BUT WHEN I WAS FOUR, I WAS SCARED; NOW I'M 18
AND CONFUSED AT WHAT I'M DOING HERE
LOOKING AROUND, WHAT I SEE IS FOUR AND FIVE

AND SIX YEAR OLD KIDS
AND I WHEEL IN, BY FAR, THE OLDEST PATIENT
HERE
YOU COME, INTRODUCE, TALK TO MY PARENTS, I
STILL DON'T HAVE GOOD SPEECH
YOU'RE VERY PRETTY, BUT I CAN'T LET YOU KNOW
ME THROUGH WORDS, ONLY INSUFFICIENT SMILES AND
SHAKES OF THE HEAD,
I RELY ON THE WORDS OF OTHERS TO DESCRIBE MY
SYMPTOMS
SO WE SIT AND DISCUSS MY STORY FOR A WHILE
YOU ASK SO MANY QUESTIONS I THINK WOULD BE
OBVIOUS; WASN'T I IN A TEXT BOOK SOMEWHERE
DIDN'T YOU READ ABOUT ME AND EXPLORE EVERY
MINOR DETAIL?
CAN'T YOU LOOK AT ME AND SURMISE THE WHOLE
PICTURE; ARE ALL THESE QUESTIONS NECESSARY
DON'T YOU KNOW ALL THE THINGS MY CONDITION
ENTAILS?
WELL, MY BLADDER'S FINE, BOWELS ARE FINE, NO
DEFORMITIES ON ME, ALL THAT'S WRONG, I'M WHAT
YOU SEE;
NO PROBLEM SEEING, HEARING, UNDERSTANDING,
UNDERSTAND ALL THAT?
WE GET ACROSS WHAT WE WANT FROM GOING BACK TO
THERAPY AT THIS LATE STAGE
AND THEN YOU SUGGEST WE GET DOWN ON THE MATT

NOW I'VE BEEN COMING TO YOU FOR GOING ON SIX
MONTHS, AND WE DO THIS ROUTINE OF EXERCISES; I'M
SATISFIED THAT WE'RE BEING PRODUCTIVE, I GUESS
IT'S KIND OF SOOTHING, NOTHING TO FIGHT, WHEN
A YOUNG GIRL IS STRETCHING YOUR LEGS, BUT
YESTERDAY, MOM ASKED ME IF WE'RE MAKING ANY
PROGRESS
I DIDN'T KNOW HOW TO ANSWER; WOULD YOU?

IS THERAPY HELPING ME GET STRONGER, CAN YOU DIRECT AN 18 YEAR-OLD BODY INTO A PATTERN LIKE YOU CAN A FOUR YEAR OLD?
SHOULD I REALLY BE COMING TO THERAPY ANY LONGER?
IS IT THAT MY MIND IS IMAGINING SOME SEXUAL CONTACT, MY CONSCIENCE BEING RELIEVED THAT I'M DOING WHAT MY DOCTOR WANTS ME TO DO?
I'LL HAVE TO MAKE THAT DECISION, BUT I'VE BEEN OBSERVANT WHILE I'VE BEEN HERE, AND IF YOU DON'T MIND, CAN I GET PERSONAL WITH YOU?
I WAS WONDERING WHAT MADE YOU DECIDE TO GO INTO THIS FIELD
WHY DID YOU WANT TO BECOME A THERAPIST IN THE FIRST PLACE?
AND NOW THAT YOU ARE, DO YOU APPRECIATE THE IMPORTANCE OF YOUR SERVICE
DO YOU KNOW THAT KIDS AND PARENTS LOOK UP TO YOU IN MANY WAYS?

WHEN I WAS A KID, I THOUGHT I HAD TO OBEY A THERAPIST LIKE YOU WOULD A NUN
SHE WAS AN IMPORTANT AUTHORITY FIGURE AND SHE HAD ALL THE ANSWERS, YOU EXPECTED, THEN I FOUND THAT MOST COULD BE UNDERSTANDING, WE BECAME FRIENDS
BUT THEIR EXPERIENCE, AUTHORITY AND DEDICATION WAS ALWAYS RESPECTED
THEN THERE WAS THAT DAY I FEEL IN LOVE, AND REALIZED SHE WAS AS HUMAN AS I
AFTER THAT MOMENT OF INFATUATION, IT WAS MY FRIEND'S DETERMINATION AND DRIVE I LOVED
THEN CAME MY TURNING POINT; I BECAME SELF-CENTERED, NARROW MINDED AND LAZY, AND THERAPY WAS SOMETHING I WANTED NO PART OF

SO I COME INTO THIS WARD FOR KIDS AND ALL I SEE
ARE YOUNG PEOPLE FRESH FROM SCHOOL. THERE'S
NOT A BATTLE-AX THERAPIST IN SIGHT BUT I WON'T
TELL YOU GUYS AREN'T MUCH OLDER THAN ME, AND
IT'S GETTING EASIER TO SEE WHERE YOU'RE COMING
FROM; DO YOU UNDERSTAND ME AS WELL?

I OVERHEARD ONE OF YOU REFER TO BEING A THERAPIST
AS A JOB, AND COMPARE IT TO GOING BACK TO SCHOOL
TO GET ANOTHER DEGREE
YOU CAN GET THE MOST DEGREES, THE BEST PAY,
THE LEAST HOURS, THE HIGHEST POSITION
NOTHING GETS AROUND PEOPLE NEEDING THERAPY.

GET IT STRAIGHT IN YOUR MIND, KNOW WHERE YOU
ARE
SHED MOST EGO, DROP ALL GREED FROM YOU
STUDY THE MIRROR AND DECIDE YOU'RE SEEING THE
BEST PERSON YOU KNOW
THEN SHOW HER TO ONES AROUND YOU
AND TO MY THERAPIST, FOR HELPING TO GIVE MY
BODY THE FREEDOM
THAT GOD GAVE MY MIND, THANK YOU

AS FOR ME, THE DECISION HAS TO BE MADE, CAN
THERAPY REALLY HELP ME ANYMORE?
ARE THERE ANY MORE ANSWERS THAN THOSE I'VE
GOTTEN FROM PEOPLE I'VE SEEN?
I'VE BEEN BOBATHED, TAKEN A BATH, BEEN PATTERNED,
STIMULATED, CHRIO-NIZED, SYNTHESIZED
I'VE EVEN KISSED FELDENCRIST'S RING
I'VE BEEN ROLLED OVER, ROLLED UNDER, TUMBLED,
FUMBLED
GOTTEN THE MOST OUT OF BEING WITH MY BROTHER
PLAYING FOOTBALL

IS THERE ANY FORMULA THAT CAN TELL THIS ASS TO
MOVE AT ALL
BETTER THAN THIS BRAIN INSIDE THIS HEAD THAT
EVERYONE CALLS PAUL

?

DANNY DEETY

This is a story accounting typical experiences of a young teenager undergoing a fairly new surgical operation in the hopes of correcting some of his symptoms of Athetoid Cerebral Palsy. It might be recommended to anyone considering the same alternative or one similar. It is written by a young man who many years ago received an implantation of a cerebellum stimulating device, a surgical technique developed by Irving S. Cooper M.D. This technique has been performed, developed and expanded upon for approximately ten years. This story deals mostly with the patient's perspective, and it is not qualified to lend any large amount of clinical or scientific information. It is meant to be one of your companions.

pp,b,bp 1984.

Danny Deety was thirteen in November of 1974. He and his parents had decided to make the trip to a New York hospital to see about a new surgery performed on people with Cerebral Palsy. His condition left him with bad arm control, little dexterity, no standing balance, poor speech, and an affliction of involuntary motion. The Deetys had heard of this operation on the annual telethon for CP, in medical journals and magazines.

The Deetys were a close three. Rosey and Ralph were forty years older than their youngest son Danny. They had raised four other children before Danny who were now grown and on their own. Much of the parents' time had always been devoted to Danny and exploring every feasible avenue for therapy and ways for him to communicate. The three had always experienced very unique situations together which gave them a closeness and unity. Looking into the 'New York operation' was just another fun family trip, just the next stop on the tour.

They checked into a Fort Lee hotel on Sunday evening. Danny was excited and anxious being so close to New York City. And on Monday morning they kept their appointment at Saint Barnabas hospital in the Bronx. They were led to an office on the third floor way at the end of the hall.

The room was small. It held two small sofas on both sides. The walls held countless, what seemed like dozens of diplomas, certificates and awards to Dr. Irving Cooper, a man with, Danny counted, thirteen letters after his name. A young secretary dwelled in the corner embodied in her work, answering the telephones and receiving visitors. Her litany of preliminary questions to all who approached her was something like: "Where are you from? What doctor sent you here? Where's your Blue Cross and Blue Shield?" Danny thought she was pretty.

Families were escorted in and out of this room in a similar fashion. Conversations began and continued although participants were always transient. The format became obvious that all visitors would go in an even smaller room aside and talk to a Mrs. Graham before they got to see the doctor. The Deetys were called eventually and just before Ralph nodded to sleep.

Mrs. Graham delved more into Ralph Deety's insurance and health plans. From Mrs. Graham the Deetys got a better idea what to expect the doctors to explain, what the technique entails and what the procedures were like. It was too much to think about at first, especially for Danny. Mrs. Graham told them to take things one at a time. They went back outside again where Danny could look at the pretty secretary again.

Fifteen minutes later the Deetys were taken to see Doctor Waltz. He sat behind a very large desk. He looked like Dick Cavett. He was kind and talked slowly enough for Rosey to hear every word and jot it all down. He explained the cerebellum stimulator implantation operation. It had been developed and used by a team at this hospital. The team was headed by Irving S. Cooper.

The technique was detailed like this: Under general anesthesia the patient receives two electrodes which are implanted on both sides of the cerebellum. The cerebellum is located in the lower back of the head. Wires extended from the electrodes through one side of the neck, necessitating a second incision, to the high chest, causing the third incision, where two quarter sized receivers are placed. The theory is very similar to that of a heart pacemaker. Two antennae would be taped on the chest over the receivers. The antennae connect to an external power pack, the size of a transistor radio. The hope was that impulses from the power pack would stimulate cells in the cerebellum that had been damaged or deadened. These amazing possibilities and theories fascinated the Deetys.

The operation had been performed for less than two years. Only about two hundred and fifty people had received it. Dr. Waltz explained that most of the candidates were a bit older than Danny. He couldn't recommend it until he became fourteen. The doctor said that it was only performed in people with normal intellects and on those whom they believed it would benefit on a reasonable par. Danny would have to undergo two weeks of psychological, occupational and physical therapy for the team to concur that he should have the surgery.

By the time the doctor was finished speaking it looked like the decision would go that Danny would be admitted to the hospital right then to begin the tests. Danny asked his father when they were alone if he could have one day to see all the sights of New York City. The adults chuckled, and Danny was happy to have one more day before going into the hospital. The Deetys drove around Manhattan, walked into Rockefeller Center, and dined that evening in the Rainbow Room.

The next morning saw the Deetys driving over the George Washington Bridge once more, and Danny was admitted to Saint Barnabus. He was put on the fifth floor for a few days. Rosey was hoping to be able to stay with Danny overnight, but they needed a permanent plan on where she would stay for the two weeks and just how long Ralph would need to stay in New York. Mrs. Graham told them about the nurses' quarters where rooms were for rent and where many parents of the patients receiving the stimulator operation stayed.

On the third day in the hospital Danny was moved to the second floor. This was where all of the people receiving this surgery eventually stayed. The second floor was painted much brighter, had a friendlier atmosphere, and offered much more company and information about the operation. One side of the floor was occupied by a huge recreation room where most of the families spent their day. Danny and Rosey began to be introduced constantly to new friends and companions. And their attitudes and prospects were increasingly brighter. Ralph decided to leave for home after that weekend and plan on making the drive up again every weekend.

Danny was particularly not fond of blood tests and EEGs. He didn't mind much the psychological tests and the speech therapy. He was friendly with many people he met in the rec room. It had a small record player, but the only two records were by Ringo Starr and Edward Baer. He had never been around so many people who also had Cerebral Palsy. Rosey and he also met people afflicted with Dystonia and Epilepsy who might be helped by this surgery or others like it. Danny had never learned so much about himself and his condition than from being around these people.

He and his mother met many people. They became friends with a lady named Dorothy from Boston and her daughter, Debby, who had dystonea. Rosey is a very open and vivacious person and makes new friends very easily. Dorothy had many experiences to share about raising Debby and traveling around many years to clinics and hospitals. Some were similar to Rosey's and some were foreign, but the ladies found much common ground to talk about. And Rosey wasted no time making many new friends in this manner. Everyone had a story, and everyone had a reason for coming to this hospital. It didn't take long for anyone to find a little niche, a couple friends, and to feel part of this temporary extended family.

Danny had never met a real farmer before. His father started talking to one from Kansas one day, and their conversation interested Danny for hours. Then they met a father and son, Al and John from Missouri. John was thirty five when he was hurt in a motorcycle accident. Ralph's eyes were opened for the first time to the horrible results that come from motorcycle falls. John had been seriously handicapped a few years before, and he was there to see if the stimulator implant could restore some of his muscle tone.

Danny found a chess partner in old Mr. Naschewicz. They would play two games each evening at seven o'clock. One thing that Danny thought was cool was filling out the menus every third day. He called it neat that he could actually decide what he would have for dinner. Rosey had never afforded him that luxury at home. So he always ordered spaghetti. Danny ate more in the hospital than he ever had before. He also was more social and willing to speak to strangers. There was one grumpy old man who wouldn't put down his paper long enough to talk to anyone. Danny stayed around him and bothered him long enough so that he had to agree to play one game of Memory. After that, the old man saw that there were many folks around that he could talk to, and he became much more at home.

Danny's second week at the hospital wasn't at all pleasant because he received a spinal tap. His directions were to lie flat on his back for twentyfour hours. After that time, he was told, he could get out of bed and feel fine. But Danny suffered from an excruciating head ache and nausea for more than a week. He only felt alright lying down. That week he was told that if he got up more, the pain would eventually go away. So he sat up for short periods of time. But Danny knew his terrible headache a lot better than his doctors did. So he stayed in his bed and told his parents to invite some of his friends from the rec room to come in to see him.

At the end of the week Danny was ready to be discharged. His stomach felt better but his head was still pounding, so he rode with his head on his mother's lap in the back seat all the way home. Danny's teacher and classmates couldn't wait to hear what happened to him in New York. His best friend John P. asked him if they really cut his head open and took all the bad stuff out. His teacher asked him if he was going ahead to have the operation. Danny really didn't know. He and his parents hadn't had a chance to talk at length about all they had learned and whether they thought the stimulator would help Danny.

So that school week ended and on Saturday morning Danny and his parents sat quietly at the kitchen table and talked over what they had all been thinking for the last few weeks. Ralph Deety had been convinced that the surgery was a good idea. He was impressed with the theories and the competence of the team of doctors at Saint Barnabus. He understood basically the concept of stimulating damaged brain cells by an external power pack. He believed that if Danny was willing to undergo it all, this would be the next stage and a giant step in Danny's development. Rosey was going to maintain reservations, questions and concerns. Certainly they had spoken to many people during the stay, people who received the surgery and believed they were helped, people who believed they weren't helped, people who were like they were, considering whether or not to go through it all.

Danny listened very carefully to what his parents said. He decided he would wait to get their reactions before he would expose his own. He was still young enough to want to cling with a popular opinion. It occurred to him that his father's strong voice was going over better than his mother's whiney worries. He formed a feeling of great bravery and courage about becoming bionic. Visions of Lee Majors running through some airport trying to capture a Soviet spy dashed through his mind. 'This could really freak out John P.' he thought. So he briefly tried to agree with his mother and point out how dangerous it was. 'There's a two percent risk, Dad.' When this did not get an overwhelmingly sympathetic response, Danny figured he'd better quickly swing to the other side of the coin. 'Yeah man, I'll do it.'

There would be about eighteen months before Danny was scheduled to return to Saint Barnabus. In that time his oldest sister got married, Nixon resigned, and his grandmother died. Overriding all of these major events were questions, confidences, and prayers for guidance to make the right decision on the surgery. John P. got Danny more and more psyched about Danny going through with this 'freaky scientific experiment.' The ladies bridge club listened to Rosey's explanations of this procedure, and it was squeezed in between discussing Gladys' baby shower and Betty's gall bladder operation. And there were many late conversations at home with the older Deety brothers and sisters. Alison and K understood their mom's concerns. Roger and Rick with their father encouraged Danny to have the operation. Danny didn't hesitate long in deciding whose advice to take.

On April 5, 1976 Danny, Rosey, and Ralph walked down that same long hall on the third floor of Saint Barnabus. They turned into the small room at the end and found the same pretty secretary still embodied at her telephone and typewriter. The certificates and diplomas and sofas were exactly as they had left them. And Mrs. Graham still worked in the even smaller room aside. Now Danny was fourteen, and old enough, and ready to have the cerebellum stimulator operation. After meeting with Mrs. Graham and making final insurance arrangements, the Deetys met with Dr. Ammin. Dr. Ammin was going to perform Danny's surgery. He answered all second thought and last minute questions, and there were a lot of them that Rosey had prepared. This conference lasted well into three hours. The patient and parents were inquisitive, the doctor was kind and assuring. At the end of their discussion he asked the three if they were ready. He said the surgery was scheduled for Friday morning. The answer was ultimately yes.

Danny worried a lot on Tuesday night. He cried on Wednesday and Thursday nights. He insisted that his parents come over to his room from the nurses' quarters at five o'clock when he was scheduled to be awakened for preparation. While he was having his first enema, he instructed his father that if anything happened to him on the table, he wanted the rights to his life sold to Doubleday, and he quoted a price. Then he was given a pill, his parents left, and he resigned to sleep.

On Friday morning he was less than half conscious while his hair was shaved off and he reminded his father about the Doubleday deal. He said two words that morning. The stretcher was rolled into his room and he said Showtime. He was lying on the stretcher in the hall when the elevator doors opened, and he said Rosebud.

Danny's surgery lasted a bit over five hours. He was operated in a sitting position. The critical portion of the procedure was the implantation of the electrodes. This went well in Doctor Ammin's hands. Doctor Cooper came in the room for a very few minutes to observe. He patted Doctor Ammin's back for encouragement and support. But he did it while the doctor's hands were far away from Danny's head. A catheter was placed in his leg and his heart rate was constantly carefully monitored. Any slight variation in the rate would have instructed the doctors to discontinue the procedure and close him. No complications arose. And at two fifteen Rosey and Ralph Deety were invited to go to the intensive care unit to see their son.

They made two visits to intensive care that day, but Danny wasn't awake during either of them. They felt relieved and blessed when they saw that he would be fine. The first person Danny saw upon opening his eyes was his brother Roger. Roger was ecstatic. "Dan, how are you?" Dan looked at a man who could have been a stranger and asked, "Will somebody stop this ship?" Then he experienced a few hours of unpleasant vomitting.

Maria was Danny's friend in his small booth in intensive care. She had pretty red hair, and she talked ever so sweetly each time he had to go through painful suctioning. She saw his discomfort and pain during those horrible moments when the tube was down his throat, so she told him to think of something pleasant and to start singing the White Album in his head until the tube came out. She'd say, "It will be so fast, I bet you don't even finish 'Back in the USSR.'"

One day, Danny needed suctioning so many times and he was so cooperative about it, Maria came in late at night, plugged in a television and let him watch Saturday Night Live. It made him feel very good and laugh very loud because that night was the first Easter show with Ron Nesson and Patti Smith. Then Danny didn't have long to regain his strength. He'd always gotten psyched for Easter.

Danny was back on the second floor ward on Monday morning. He had no plans for smiling or laughing for a week or so. The operation took a lot out of him. But in a few days he was up and back in the rec room. There were a few familiar faces from his first visit to the hospital. And there were many new faces to know and learn to live with. Danny's first full day bay back in his wheelchair happened to be just in time for a birthday party. He was the second guest of honor since everyone was so glad to see him around again. As soon as he took a bite of cake, his appetite came back in full force. From then on he became known as the munching madman. Mothers who would go out to dinner at night would bring him back sandwiches and pizzas. And it didn't matter how much food was given to him, Danny would eat it all.

Danny was introduced to his power pack ten days after his surgery. This was what was known as 'plugging in.' The power pack or stimulator was designed to send impulses to one side of the brain for one minute, and then send impulses to the other side. It had a button to be pushed when one desired both sides to be stimulated. Many people who suffered from epilepsy found this most helpful to stop a seizure. The stimulator had a voltage control which graduated from zero to ten. The procedure was for the patient to stay hospitalized for six weeks. In that time he or she would receive therapy, check-ups, and evaluations. Also through monitoring and testing the voltage would be gradually increased. The stimulation inevitably caused headaches initially. And every patient varied in their endurance level. Danny had headaches at every new level. He described them as annoying dull pains. Sometime he would take it like a man and give himself a chance to get used to it so the pain would eventually disappear as he was told it would. Sometimes he would have to ask them to 'turn him down.'

Danny, Rosey and Ralph became part of an ever growing, ever rotating family in the rec room. In any given week they knew intimately at least eight families and had interests in at least three people who were due to have surgery. Ralph would drive home after every weekend and bring another member of the family the next week. First came Alison who was Dan's closest sibling. She was a school teacher and she liked to enrich his mind by playing quiz games with him. The whole family would join in the evenings in Danny's room, including his roommate Jerry, an Irish New York bus driver, and his wife. They adopted the Deetys as a second family and offered Alison a place to sleep for the weekend. Jerry forced Danny to watch baseball with him and even made him a temporary Yankee fan. But this lasted only a very short time.

Alison came up on another weekend and spent much time with Danny in the rec room. There was a very unique character whom they liked to talk to. Her name was Jean. Jean was from Brooklyn and she was afflicted with a slight slur. This caused her to speak in a distinct voice which was fun to imitate. She was also very outspoken and blunt, as she called her own mother Trudy. And she called Rosey Betty Boop. She played a bit too rough for Danny's liking, she annoyed him and she knew it. So Alison would have to referee the conversations, but it was all in good fun. Danny got his revenge by singing the song 'Positively 4th street' in her face when she didn't know what he was saying.

Roger Deety came back the next weekend. Roger played the guitar and sang for all the people in the rec room. He befriended a young boy from Georgia named Chip who was constantly doing Jerry Clowell imitations. Chip knew every routine by heart and didn't stop reciting them. His family were strong Carter supporters and assured everyone that one day their governor would be elected president. They were hardly believed.

When Danny's brother Rick came up to New York, the Deetys got a weekend pass from the hospital and went to see the city. It was a rainy miserable day, but Rick wanted to see an OTB parlor and place a bet on the Preakness. So the Deetys got in the car and hoped for a very fun outing. They decided to see the show at Radio City Music Hall. They drove past the theater and saw a line, so they decided to let Rick out to get tickets while Ralph kept driving to look for a parking space. He was extremely lucky when he found one forty five minutes later. But Rick didn't appreciate any luck as he was disgustingly drenched and was mugged twice. He was able to hold on to the tickets though, and the family went into the hall and enjoyed the feature. Later they dined at Mamma Leone's. Danny was in heaven, and Rick was consoled when he learned that Elecutionor won.

Danny became very close to Judy. Judy had to stay in bed much of the time. Her father stayed with her all day. Mr. Vince was devoted to his daughter and worked hard to keep her entertained by playing checkers and scrabble with her and inviting other kids in to play. He could also sense that Danny had a crush on Judy so he left them time to themselves whenever he saw that they wanted to be alone.

Judy was a few years younger than Danny, but she was the first girl who really meant a lot to him. They talked a lot about music. Danny received a small transistor radio from the gift shop and they liked listening to it. Judy got tired of listening to theme songs of TV shows and bugged Danny to switch his radio to FM. Danny got mad because he liked WABC, and he thought it was too hard to move the knob. "Look, do you want to be stimulated or not?" This was Danny's first lesson of the importance of obeying an order from a woman. He made his girlfriend happy and tuned in WPLJ. They heard some long music called Bohemian Rhapsody by a band they'd never heard of before.

Rosey and Ralph made many friends of the parents in the rec room. They attended a meeting every Saturday afternoon to learn about the entire program from Walter, a technician afflicted with epilepsy who had been the first recipient of the brain stimulator. They discussed Danny's future with other parents who would face the same questions and decisions concerning their children. Rosey consoled Linda whose son Randy was denied the opportunity to have the surgery because his tests showed that he didn't meet the intellectual level that was necessary for it to succeed. Ralph played poker with Mrs. Trigber, a blind woman who was there trying to give her daughter with dystonia the chance to stand straight again. The time at Saint Barnabus matured and inspired Rosey and Ralph as much as it did their son.

Danny stayed the six weeks required after his surgery to undergo therapy and evaluate his progress with the stimulator. The doctors were ultimately able to increase the voltage up to ten. Danny was instructed to decrease the impulse when and if he experienced any pain. He was told that the process of improvement would be slow. But with much more therapy and patience he would be able to use the impulses and the external assistance to his motor center and adapt it to allow him to learn to do new and better things.

The Deetys were encouraged to follow all the procedures they had learned to keep the power pack recharged and care for it correctly. The daily routine would indeed be detailed. Yet, as all the recipients were, they were encouraged to begin a new life and build new hopes. Danny was ready to think about going home. He had grown in many more than one way.

It was a Wednesday in the middle of May when bags were packed in the Deetys' room in the nurses' home and in Danny's room on the second floor of Saint Barnabus. And in the rec room a very happy kid rolled around and said good-by to all the meaningful friends he had acquired for the last two months. He even kissed Jean. And Rosey and Ralph hugged and parted from compatriots with whom they had shared a most unique time. They knew they were not leaving these people forever. Patients were asked to return to the hospital every six months to reexamine progress and goals. Everyone tried to coincide their plans on when exactly to return so they might reunite. Then the Deetys left the rec room, and they walked to the elevator. Mr. Vince came running out just as the doors were closing. "Danny, you forgot your radio." Danny's smile for that day grew even more beautiful.

And in the car Danny turned on his radio to listen to WABC once more. And Dan Ingrum played the theme from Happy Days.

I have composed this short essay with the help of my loving parents simply to share some experiences and memories I still hold dear and important in my life. As is said, it actually is not very clinical or technical. It is more of a walk through one person's case undergoing a major brain correcting operation. It is told intentionally in third person fiction for the sake of clarity and relevance.

As for the results and aftermath of the actual surgery which I received approximately eight years ago, my family and I noticed only small improvement or stability of improvement following my implantation.

At the time I underwent the procedure, the external power pack was built rather bulky, five by eight inches, and had to be carried around in a leather pocket attached by a shoulder strap. Because of increasing inconvenience, skin irritation due to the tape used to secure my antennae to my chest, and other reasons such as headaches and dissatisfaction with my progress, I stopped wearing the power pack nearly three years after my operation. This should not heavily influence any people who have seriously examined possibilities of any similar surgery and believe that it may help them.

I felt it was important to share such a valued experience in my past so I did so to my greatest capacity. It has been several years since I have had any serious exposure to information about this type of surgery. I do know that there have been many surgical, technical, and even therapeutic advances and expansions in the last eight years with which I am totally unfamiliar.

My suggestion would be to search and to dig for the right solutions for you. This is a truly marvelous time to be living. Our possibilities for improvement and for excellence are so immense, it must ultimately convince one to believe in an absolute providence. And although we have lost forever the ability to hold all the wealth of the world's knowledge within one's immediate grasp, we still have endless avenues of research and information to discover. And it should be possible if not obligatory for everyone with a will to improve and overcome their handicap to find the most correct methods and solutions for them.

Paul Peroutka
thank you Betty & Bud

Nonverbal Champion

MY NEUROLOGICAL DISORDER HAS LEFT ME WITHOUT
THE ABILITY TO SPEAK NORMALLY. MY INTELLECT,
SOMETIMES ANNOYING STUBBORNNESS, OFTEN PAIL
DRY WIT, AND MY ENORMOUS DRIVE TO MAKE PEOPLE
LIKE ME DON'T ALLOW ME TO KEEP QUIET AND NOT
LET PEOPLE GET TO KNOW ME. AND MY GOOD FRIENDS
ALLOW ME THE LUXURY OF EXPRESSING MYSELF
WHENEVER I FEEL I HAVE TO. ALL THIS HAS CAUSED

ME TO TAKE ADVANTAGE OF EVERY BENEFIT I CAN CALL MINE, AND ALLOWS ME TO LEAD A PRETTY FULL AND HAPPY LIFE.

I THINK, NOW THAT I'M 19, HOW INCREDIBLY FAR I'VE COME, AND HOW FAR IT LOOKS LIKE I CAN GO; HOW MUCH I'VE LEARNED AND I'M ABOUT TO LEARN; AND HOW IRONIC IT IS THAT THE THINGS THAT I'M BARRED FROM DOING AND LEARNING ARE THOSE THINGS WHICH A TYPICAL 1, 2, 3, 4, AND 5 YEAR OLD KID PICKS UP WITHOUT MUCH THOUGHT AT ALL. I'VE GRADUATED FROM HIGH SCHOOL, HOPE TO GRADUATE FROM COLLEGE; YET I'M NEVER GOING TO GRASP THE TRICK OF PUTTING ONE FOOT IN FRONT OF THE OTHER, KEEP THIS BODY UPRIGHT THROUGH THE MAGIC OF BALANCE, AND TRANSPORT MYSELF BY WALKING. I'VE WRITTEN TWO BOOK-FULL COLLECTIONS OF WRITINGS, A THOUSAND LOVE-LETTERS, AND A COMMENCEMENT SPEECH THAT GOT A STANDING OVATION; YET I'M NEVER GOING TO MASTER PRONOUNCING MORE THAN THREE OR FOUR CONSONANT SOUNDS, OR MORE THAN EIGHT OR TEN VOWEL SOUNDS, AND I CAN'T PROMISE THAT I CAN PRONOUNCE TOO MANY WORDS PERFECTLY. I'M NEVER GOING TO ADVANCE SO THAT I CAN SAY A WHOLE SENTENCE THAT COULD BE UNDERSTOOD BY ALL. HOW STRANGE IT IS TO REALIZE THAT THOSE ABILITIES WILL NEVER BE AVAILABLE TO ME. YET, WHEN YOU CONSIDER SOMEONE LIKE ME, THERE'S SOMETHING YOU MUST REALIZE TOO. YOU CAN'T SHUT ME UP THAT EASILY.

ACTUALLY, I HAVE ALWAYS COMMUNICATED VERBALLY. BEING AMONGST MY BOISTEROUS FAMILY, THERE WAS NO REASON FOR ME TO BELIEVE I WASN'T ENTITLED TO GET MY 2 CENTS IN. WELL, LIKE EVERY KID, 5, 6, 7, 10 YEARS OLD, IT WAS NATURAL FOR ME TO THINK THAT MY OPINIONS WERE MORE VALUABLE THAN

THEY REALLY WERE. BUT I QUICKLY LEARNED AND VOWED TO BE SELECTIVE ABOUT WHAT I WANTED TO SAY. ONE REASON THAT I DID WAS BECAUSE IT DOES TAKE TIME FOR SOMEONE TO GET THE MESSAGE OUT OF ME; AND THE OTHER REASON WAS THAT I DREADED THE THOUGHT OF BEING CALLED A BORE. NOWADAYS, THE REASON I CHOOSE MY WORDS WISELY WHILE SPEAKING TO FRIENDS AND ACQUAINTANCES IS THAT I LIKE THEM TO REST ASSURED THAT WHEN I TALK, IT'S GOING TO BE NECESSARY, MEANINGFUL, AND TO THE POINT. IN A WAY, THIS IS ONE QUALITY I WISH I COULD PASS ON AND TEACH TO MANY PEOPLE MORE VERBAL THAN I. TO MY KNOWLEDGE, THERE'S ONLY ONE PERSON WHO SEEMS TO HAVE THIS PHILOSOPHY DOWN-PAT. I'M REFERRING TO E.F. HUTTON.

ALWAYS DETERMINED TO GET MY POINT ACROSS, VERBALLY OF COURSE, MY FAMILY AND I SOON ADOPTED WHAT I CALL 'THE ABC METHOD'. THIS MEANT THAT WHEN I WAS THREE I HAD TO BE A PRETTY GOOD SPELLER. AT LEAST, I HAD TO SPELL PHONETICALLY, IF NOT CORRECTLY. AND SIMPLY, 'THE ABC METHOD' IS WHEN I SAY A WORD OR PHRASE AS BEST I CAN, MY LISTENER GUESSES AT WHAT I'M SAYING, WE FINALLY GET IT RIGHT, OR IF WE DON'T, I SPELL THE WORDS. IT SOMETIMES TAKES A WHILE, BUT THAT'S MY WAY OF COMMUNICATING, MY LANGUAGE, MY CODE, MY WORLD.

OBVIOUSLY, I HAD ALWAYS LIVED IN A 'WORLD' WHERE I COULD ONLY COMMUNICATE, TALK, WITH A SMALL NUMBER OF PEOPLE. I'M NOT SURE THE READER CAN APPRECIATE WHAT THAT WOULD MEAN. IF I HAD SOMETHING IMPORTANT TO ADD TO A CONVERSATION, IF I WANTED TO GET TO KNOW PEOPLE BETTER, OR HAVE THEM GET TO KNOW ME, OR IF I WAS UNCOMFORTABLE, HURTING, OR JUST NEEDED TO SHOUT SOMETHING

OUT, I HAD TO MAKE SURE THAT SOMEONE WHO UNDERSTOOD ME WAS AROUND BEFORE I EVEN OPENED MY MOUTH. SURE, IT WAS A GOOD IDEA TO BE PATIENT WITH A NEW PERSON, TRY TO GET IT OUT, AND ADD A MEMBER TO MY CIRCLE. BUT MY LANGUAGE CAN SELDOM BE LEARNED IN A CRASH COURSE, AND I USED TO HATE TO PUT ANYBODY TO A LOT OF TROUBLE IF I DIDN'T THINK I COULD GET MY MESSAGE ACROSS QUICKLY.

MY PREDICAMENT DID BECOME PAINFUL. NATURALLY, AS I GREW TO BE 13, 14, 15, I HAD THE URGE TO BREAK AWAY, CERTAINLY NOT BE AS DEPENDENT ON MY FAMILY AS I ALWAYS HAD BEEN. IT WAS A MATTER OF THE CIRCLE OF PEOPLE THAT I WANTED AND HAD TO COMMUNICATE WITH WIDENING. THIS WAS ESPECIALLY TRUE WHEN I STARTED THE NINTH AND TENTH GRADES AT A REGULAR HIGH SCHOOL, MY FIRST CONSTANT EXPERIENCE OUTSIDE A SHELTERED FACILITY FOR THE HANDICAPPED.

UNTIL THAT TIME, I HAD ONLY USED A CONVERSATION BOARD RARELY. I HAD ALWAYS POINTED TO THE LETTERS WITH A HEADSTICK, A WOODEN STICK ATTACHED TO A SAFETY HELMET. IT WAS MORE OF AN ACTIVITY I PRACTICED IN OCCUPATIONAL THERAPY THAN A MEANS OF COMMUNICATION WITH STRANGERS. I GUESS I FIGURED I COULD ALWAYS USE THIS SKILL IF I REALLY HAD TO, BUT I NEVER SAW IT PRACTICAL IN DAILY CONVERSATION. I THOUGHT IT MIGHT BE TOO DIFFERENT FOR PEOPLE TO ACCEPT, TOO SLOW FOR PEOPLE TO FIGURE OUT AND UNDERSTAND WHAT I WANTED TO SAY, AND TOO SLOW A PROCESS FOR ANYONE TO WANT TO TALK TO ME. AS I'VE GROWN OLDER, I'M GLAD I'M GRADUALLY DISCARDING MOST OF THE NARROW OPINIONS AND LIMITED VIEWS I HAD AS A KID.

IT ALL CAME DOWN TO ONE MORNING, THE FIRST DAY OF MY TENTH GRADE YEAR. MRS. EDWARDS, MY TEACHER FOR MANY YEARS, PUSHED ME INTO LATIN CLASS THE FIRST THING THAT MORNING. SHE WAS INTRODUCING ME TO MY BRAND NEW TEACHER AND TELLING ME REPEATEDLY, AND MOST CERTAINLY, THAT I WAS GOING TO HAVE TO USE MY CONVERSATION BOARD WITH MY HEADSTICK REGULARLY IN THAT CLASS, AND OTHER CLASSES. SHE POINTED OUT THAT ALL MY TEACHERS ARE GOING TO WANT TO KNOW MORE AND MORE ABOUT ME; SINCE, BECAUSE OF MY HANDICAP, I WAS THEIR MOST UNIQUE STUDENT, THEY NEEDED TO KNOW HOW TO COMMUNICATE WITH ME, AND HOW MUCH I WAS AWARE OF WHAT WAS GOING ON IN CLASS. IT WAS THAT MORNING WHEN I GOT A KICK FROM BEHIND. I HAD NO CHOICE; I HAD TO COMMUNICATE WITH MY BOARD.

AS TIME WENT ON, I WAS ABLE TO COMMUNICATE WITH MY TEACHERS MORE AND MORE. IF I HAD A QUESTION, I KNEW I COULD GET IT ACROSS ONE WAY OR ANOTHER. THAT BROUGHT ON A BETTER FEELING ABOUT MYSELF. HOWEVER, THERE WAS A WHOLE OTHER SIDE TO MY SUCCESS IN COMMUNICATING. I GOT TO TALK TO KIDS. I GOT TO BE JUST A REGULAR GUY WHO COULD TELL A JOKE, OR COMPLAIN ABOUT HOW MUCH HOMEWORK WE HAD THAT LAST NIGHT. ANOTHER WORLD HAD OPENED UP TO ME. IT PROBABLY WAS WAY TOO LATE, BUT I TOOK ADVANTAGE OF EVERY NEW RELATIONSHIP I COULD MAKE BY MY NEW SYSTEM, COMMUNICATING NON-VERBALLY.

MY STORY REALLY BEGINS WHEN I LEFT THAT ONE SCHOOL AND STARTED ELEVENTH GRADE AT A PLACE CALLED CALVERT HALL COLLEGE HIGH SCHOOL. THIS WAS THE TIME IN MY LIFE WHEN I BROKE ALL CHAINS OF SHELTEREDNESS AND WAS REALLY ON MY OWN. I'M

THE KIND OF PERSON WHO LIKES TO HAVE FRIENDS AND NEEDS PEOPLE AROUND ME TO HELP ME AND THAT I CAN TALK TO. I MUST REMEMBER THAT IT TOOK A WHILE TO GET UP THE COURAGE TO SHOW SOME OF THE GUYS HOW I COULD TALK TO THEM WITH MY BOARD; IT TOOK UNTIL HALF THAT YEAR WAS OVER. IT WASN'T THAT I WAS STILL AFRAID OF THE IDEA OF USING IT, SINCE I HAD HAD MUCH SUCCESS COMMUNICATING THE YEAR BEFORE. IT WAS THAT I THOUGHT THAT IT MIGHT TAKE TOO LONG TO EXPLAIN HOW TO USE IT, NOT TO MENTION THE EXTEMPORANEOUS MOVEMENTS I WOULD HAVE TO MAKE TO GET THEIR ATTENTION AND KEEP THEM INTERESTED.

WELL, IT FINALLY HAPPENED; I GOT A GUY'S ATTENTION, I SHOWED HIM THAT I WANTED HIM TO GET OUT THIS BOARD WITH A WHOLE LOT OF LETTERS ON IT, AND THAT I WANTED THIS HELMET WITH A STICK ON IT. THAT WAS ACCOMPLISHED.

NOW, I DID HAVE A MESSAGE THAT I WANTED TO GET ACROSS TO THIS GUY. HIS NAME WAS BRIAN AND HE HAD ALWAYS BEEN NICE TO ME. HE ALWAYS WAS WILLING TO PUSH ME WHEREVER I NEEDED TO GO, AND RIGHT FROM THE BEGINNING, HE TALKED TO ME LIKE I WAS ANY REGULAR GUY. I KNOW THAT I COULD COUNT ON HIM TO TAKE THE TIME AND SEE WHAT I WANTED TO SAY TO HIM. FIRST I THOUGHT I WOULD BREAK THE TENSION BY SAYING SOMETHING THAT WOULD REALLY SHOCK, NOT ONLY BRIAN, BUT THE GUYS ALL AROUND WATCHING THIS WHOLE SHOW. IT HAD TO BE FUNNY BUT SHORT. I SPELLED OUT TWO WORDS WHICH DESCRIBED MY FEELINGS ON LIFE AT THAT PARTICULAR MOMENT. YES, IT WAS AN OFF-COLOR THING THAT I SAID, BUT, BOY, DID IT GET A LAUGH.

AFTER EVERYONE GOT OVER THAT SHOCK OF FINDING OUT THAT THE KID IN THE WHEELCHAIR CAN CUSS LIKE THE BEST OF THEM, AND BELIEVE ME, THESE GUYS WERE THE BEST OF THEM, I KNEW IT WAS TIME TO KEEP ON GOING AND SAY WHAT I WANTED TO BRIAN. IT WAS A QUESTION CONCERNING MY SOCIAL LIFE. THE CONVERSATION WENT SOMETHING LIKE THIS. (OF COURSE, MY RESPONSES WENT A LOT SLOWER THAN HIS, HAVING TO BE SPELLED OUT LETTER BY LETTER.)

I STARTED, "IT'S GETTING HARD TO GO OUT ON DATES WITH MY FATHER DRIVING. DO YOU THINK SOMETIME WE COULD DOUBLE DATE?"

HE WAS INSTANTLY TAKEN ABACK THAT THIS IS WHAT I HAD TO SAY. THEN HE RETURNED, "OH SURE, OF COURSE. YOU'VE GOT YOURSELF A CHICK, EH?"

I JUST THOUGHT OF A GREAT WAY TO GET ANOTHER LAUGH. I POINTED TO THE NUMBER 5, MEANING 5 CHICKS. THE JOKE WAS CALLED BY A COUPLE GUYS AND EVERYBODY STARTED LAUGHING AGAIN. I WAS A HIT. IT BECAME FUN TO USE THE BOARD AS THEY FED ME MORE QUESTIONS AND I DELIVERED SHORT BUT FUNNY AND INTERESTING ANSWERS. "YOU DRINK BEER, PAUL?" "HELL YEAH, DOESN'T EVERYONE?" (LAUGH) "YOU LIKE TO GO OUT AND PARTY?" "EVERY NIGHT." (LAUGH) "IS YOUR GIRLFRIEND PRETTY?"

FORGETTING THAT I STARTED OUT TALKING ABOUT MY REAL GIRLFRIEND, I SAW NOTHING WRONG WITH MAKING UP AN IMAGINARY BROAD, BLONDE, TALL, AND WITH MANY RECOMMENDING BODILY FEATURES. EACH ONE GOT A BIGGER LAUGH THAN THE ONE BEFORE. NOT ONLY WAS I A HIT, BUT I BECAME JOHNNY CARSON AND HUGH HEFNER COMBINED. SOON IT WAS TIME TO GO TO A LECTURE, BUT THERE WOULD BE MORE

CONVERSATIONS AT THAT ONE PARTICULAR TABLE IN THE CAFETERIA. FROM THEN UNTIL THE END OF THAT YEAR, MORE AND MORE PEOPLE SAW ME TALKING WITH THE BOARD, AND MANY OF THEM CAME UP AND JOINED IN. IT SEEMED LIKE ALL THE GUYS HAD HEARD THAT IF YOU CROWDED IN ON A CIRCLE THAT WAS TALKING TO ME, THEY WERE IN FOR A COUPLE GOOD LAUGHS. I USED TO THROW IN AS MANY CURSE WORDS AS I COULD. NOT ONLY DID THAT GET ME ATTENTION, LAUGHS, AND PLACE ME ON A LEVEL WITH MY CLASSMATES, BUT OFTEN THOSE WORDS REALLY EXPRESSED MY TRUE STATE OF MIND. LIFE IS NOT EASY IN HIGH SCHOOL, AND IT DOES GET DOWN-RIGHT FRUSTRATING WHEN YOU'RE CONFINED BY CEREBRAL PALSY.

THAT YEAR, MY MAIN GOAL WAS TO GET AS MANY FRIENDS AS I COULD. AT LAST PEOPLE WERE LISTENING TO ME, GETTING TO KNOW WHAT WAS REALLY GOING ON IN MY MIND, AND LIKING ME FOR WHAT I REALLY WAS...EVEN IF IT WAS JUST A PERVERSE OLD GUY IN A WHEELCHAIR. I LEFT SCHOOL FOR THE SUMMER A VERY FULFILLED PERSON BEING GRATEFUL FOR HAVING SO MANY FRIENDS AND FOR FINALLY GETTING READY TO GO INTO MY SENIOR YEAR OF HIGH SCHOOL.

WHEN THE LAST PART OF AUGUST CAME, I FOUND MYSELF IN A STRANGE STATE; I ACTUALLY LOOKED FORWARD TO GOING BACK TO SCHOOL. I KNEW THAT FROM THERE ON OUT, I COULD PLAY THINGS THE WAY I WANTED. I COULD MAKE AS MANY FRIENDS AS I WANTED, COMMUNICATE WITH THEM WHENEVER AND HOWEVER I WANTED TO. I DIDN'T HAVE TO CONCENTRATE AS MUCH ON MY GRADES BECAUSE THAT WAS NO LONGER THE ONLY THING I COULD FALL BACK ON. PEOPLE WERE RESPECTING ME FOR MY PERSONALITY, NOT SOME REPORT CARD THAT SAID I WAS SMART. NOW I CAN SEE THAT I NEVER ENJOYED

FLASHING AROUND SCHOOL MARKS AND EXPECTING THEM TO SPEAK FOR ME. ONCE I BECAME COMFORTABLE ENOUGH TO USE THE BOARD, I FOUND THAT I COULD DO PLENTY OF SPEAKING FOR MYSELF.

AND SO SCHOOL STARTED IN SEPTEMBER AND MUCH TO MY APPRECIATION, MY FRIENDS' PATIENCE AND WILLINGNESS TO HELP ME OUT PICKED UP WHERE IT LEFT OFF. THE YEAR DIDN'T GET TOO FAR WHEN I FOUND THAT THERE WAS AN EVEN BIGGER CIRCLE OF PEOPLE WHO WERE INTERESTED AND EAGER TO TALK TO ME USING THE BOARD; THIS INCLUDED TEACHERS AS WELL AS KIDS. FOR TWELFTH GRADE ENGLISH, I WAS ASSIGNED MR. JOHN KOTCHEN. HE WAS A YOUNG TEACHER, ONLY ABOUT SEVEN OR EIGHT YEARS OLDER THAN HIS STUDENTS SO IT WAS NATURAL FOR HIM TO HAVE SEVERAL FRIENDLY AND CLOSE RELATIONSHIPS WITH US. HE TOOK AN INTEREST IN ME FROM THE BEGINNING. BECAUSE OF SOME APPREHENSION AND LACK OF INFORMATION, HE DISCUSSED ME WITH ANOTHER TEACHER, ANDY FIELDS, A GOOD FRIEND OF MINE. MR. KOTCHEN LEARNED MORE AND MORE ABOUT ME, BOTH FROM TALKING TO ANDY AND BRIEFLY TO ME. HE LEARNED THAT VERY FEW THINGS UPSET OR OFFENDED ME, THAT I LIKED TO CUSS A LOT, THAT I LIKED SEX A LOT, THAT I LIKED BEER MORE THAN ANYTHING, THAT I DIDN'T TAKE SENIOR ENGLISH TOO SERIOUSLY, AND THAT I LIKED THE BEATLES. WELL, I THINK HE TOOK HIS COURSE A LITTLE MORE SERIOUSLY, ACTUALLY, A LOT MORE SERIOUSLY THAN I DID. BUT OTHER THAN THAT, HE WAS MY KIND OF GUY, AND THEN WE BECAME VERY GOOD FRIENDS.

WE USED TO REALLY LIKE TO TALK ABOUT DIFFERENT BEATLE TRACKS. WE HAD CONVERSATIONS LIKE; WHO PLAYED LEAD GUITAR ON THAT NUMBER, OR WHO WROTE THE LYRICS TO THAT ONE, OR WHAT DOES

THAT RECORD MEAN IF YOU PLAY IT BACKWARDS...
HEAVY DISCUSSIONS LIKE THAT. THEN CAME THAT DAY
IN DECEMBER OF 1980. I KNOW I HAD A FEW TEARS IN MY
EYES THAT MORNING, AND I WOULDN'T BE SURPRISED
IF I SAW SOME IN HIS EYES TOO.

I DID MOST OF MY COMMUNICATING IN THE CAFETERIA.
YOU NEVER SAW ME IN THE LIBRARY. I HAD DONE
ENOUGH TIME THERE, STUDYING, PASSING, AND
FEELING VERY LONELY. I SAW THAT IT WAS A GOOD
IDEA NEVER TO GO BACK THERE AGAIN. I WAS NEVER
LONELY IN THE CAF.

I FOUND THAT I COULD GET AS MUCH INSIDE
INFORMATION OUT OF MR. KOTCHEN AND ANDY.
THEY'D TELL ME WHAT QUESTIONS WERE GOING TO BE
ON A BIG TEST, OF COURSE TRUSTING ME TO KEEP THIS
INFORMATION TO MYSELF AND TO NOT HELP ANYBODY
CHEAT. AND OF COURSE I WOULD IMMEDIATELY WHEEL
MYSELF OVER TO MY FRIENDS, ESPECIALLY THE ONES I
WANTED TO OWE ME A FAVOR, AND GIVE THEM ALL THE
HELPFUL HINTS THAT I HAD JUST GOTTEN FROM THE
TEACHERS. SO YOU SEE, THERE WERE MANY REASONS
WHY EVERYONE BENEFITTED FROM BEING ABLE TO
COMMUNICATE WITH ME.

BELIEVE IT OR NOT, I DIDN'T SPEND ALL DAY IN SCHOOL
SWEARING AND CHEATING. YES, MOST OF THE DAY,
BUT NOT ALL OF IT. I REALLY ENJOYED THE LIFE OF
A FREE-WHEELING, GIRL-CHASING, BEER-DRINKING
CALVERT HALL MAN. ALL OF THIS CONTENTMENT
CAME FROM KNOWING THAT I WAS NO LONGER
COMMUNCATIONALLY DEPENDENT. CONSTANTLY
I WAS PROVING TO OTHERS, AND TO MYSELF, THAT I
COULD TRANSLATE ANY TYPE OF MESSAGE TO ALMOST
ANY TYPE OF PERSON. AND I DID ASSOCIATE WITH
SEVERAL DIFFERENT TYPES OF PEOPLE.

FIRST, AS YOU MIGHT GUESS, I COULD BAMBOOZLE ANY OF MY TEACHERS INTO THINKING THAT I WAS VERY RESPECTABLE, OH SO STUDIOUS, AND, AT TIMES, PERHAPS SLIGHTLY ANGELIC. I'M NEVER GOING TO FOOL MY READER NEARLY AS MUCH AS I DID MY TEACHERS. IN ANY CASE, I'M REFERRING TO THE FACT THAT I HAVE ALWAYS POSSESSED THAT INNATE QUALITY THAT ALL DAREDEVILS HAVE OF CONVINCING CERTAIN ELDERS THAT THEY'RE JUST A BIT SWEETER AND TAMER THAN THEY REALLY ARE. BASICALLY, IT'S KNOWN AS JUST A LITTLE HARMLESS BS, YES, AND EVEN THAT'S POSSIBLE TO DELIVER WITH A LETTER- BOARD. ONE THING THAT ALWAYS WAS USEFUL TO ME WAS, WHENEVER A TEACHER HAD A QUESTION ABOUT AN ASSIGNMENT THAT STARTED WITH 'DID YOU DO...' I KEPT MY STICK CLOSE TO THE WORD 'YES'.

ALSO, I LIKED VERY MUCH ASSOCIATING WITH DIFFERENT TYPES OF KIDS. I SAID GOOD MORNING TO 75% OF THE PEOPLE I SAW GOING FROM HOMEROOM TO MY FIRST CLASS OF THE MORNING, WHICH BY THE WAY WAS THE CAFETERIA. EVERYBODY KNEW ME AND HAD A HANDSHAKE OR A SMILE FOR ME. I'M KIND OF PROUD THAT I WAS THAT POPULAR. I OWE IT ALL TO BEING ABLE TO HAVING A FULLY COMMUNICATIVE LIFE.

AND SURE, I MUST HAVE BEEN KNOWN TO SOME PEOPLE AS THAT GUY WHO TALKS WITH THAT HAT AND THAT STICK AND BECAUSE OF THAT, I MUST HAVE BEEN LABELED AS COOL, WEIRD, OR AT LEAST DIFFERENT. BUT IT SEEMED THAT IF THEY GOT TO KNOW ME, THE THINGS THAT I HAD TO SAY BECAME MY MOST IMPRESSIVE TRADEMARK, RATHER THAN MY MEANS OF SAYING IT. I MUST ADMIT, THERE ARE CERTAIN ADVANTAGES TO BEING UNDENIABLY UNIQUE THAT CONSTANTLY GO ALONG WITH THIS LIFE WITH

MY HANDICAP THAT I WOULD DEFINITELY HESITATE ABOUT GIVING UP. YES THOUGH, I WOULD LIKE TO HAVE PERFECT SPEECH.

I PUT MYSELF IN THE MIDDLE OF ABOUT THREE LARGE CIRCLES OF FRIENDS. BASICALLY, THEY WERE DEFINABLE BY THE SPORTS THEY PLAYED. I HUNG OUT WITH THE FOOTBALL TEAM, THE LACROSSE TEAM, AND THE SWIMMERS. THE FOOTBALL AND LACROSSE TEAMS OFTEN OVERLAPPED, AND WE ALL GOT ALONG GREAT. BUT THERE ARE NOBODY LIKE SWIMMERS. THEY'RE THEIR OWN BREED AND THEY SEEM TO LIKE IT THAT WAY. BUT I'M THE KIND OF GUY WHO CAN GET ALONG WITH ANYBODY...AS LONG AS THEY MAKE AN HONEST EFFORT TO FEED ME BEER WITHOUT SPILLING IT ALL OVER MY LAP. THERE WAS ONE GROUP I DIDN'T LIKE AND STAYED AWAY FROM. HONOR STUDENTS; THEY NEVER MADE ANY EFFORT AT ALL. HOW SMART CAN THEY BE IF THEY CAN'T FEED A GUY BEER WITHOUT SPILLING IT? WELL, I WISH THEM WELL ANYHOW.

I USED MY BOARD MOSTLY TO ARRANGE MY SOCIAL LIFE. AFTER ALL, THAT WAS THE MOST IMPORTANT THING TO ME. I WOULD ASK THIS GUY TO TAKE ME TO THIS PARTY ON FRIDAY, AND THAT GUY TO TAKE ME TO THAT BASKETBALL GAME ON SATURDAY. AND THEN THERE WERE THE MIXERS. BRIEFLY, I'LL EXPLAIN WHAT KINDS OF MERRIMENT I MADE SEVERAL TIMES AS A RESULT OF GETTING GOOD BUZZES. THIS IS ALSO GOING TO TELL YOU WHAT GOOD FRIENDS I HAD, AND STILL HAVE, AND THE KIND OF FUN WE HAD. AND I'M ALSO GOING TO DESCRIBE A HIGH THAT I GOT, ACTUALLY COMPARABLE TO HIGHS FROM SMOKING PARTICULAR FOREIGN SUBSTANCES AND/OR HAVING A SEXUAL EXPERIENCE. IT ALL HAS TO DO WITH SOMETHING CALLED A 'CIRCLE'.

HAVE YOU EVER BEEN PUSHED AROUND, IN A CIRCLE, AND BACK AND FORTH, TILTED SIDE FROM SIDE, BACKWARDS, FORWARDS, AND THROWN UP IN THE AIR? TOP IT WITH TEN OR MORE HIGH SCHOOL GIRLS, ONE HAS TIGHTER JEANS ON THAN THE ONE BEFORE. AND IF YOU DO HAVE A BUZZ, ALSO A PERVERTED MIND LIKE I DO, YOU'RE APT TO REFER TO THESE HONEYS AS SOMETHING A LITTLE MORE VULGAR THAN 'HONEYS' AND THINK ABOUT DOING SOMETHING ELSE WITH THEM BESIDES DANCING. AND YOU CAN GET AWAY WITH ALL OF THIS BECAUSE YOU'RE IN A WHEELCHAIR, YOU'RE CUTE, AND NOBODY CAN UNDERSTAND WHAT YOU'RE SAYING ANYWAY. OF COURSE, IF YOU'RE AT A MIXER, THEY COULDN'T HEAR YOU EITHER. YOU'D PROBABLY GET A LOT OF SATISFACTION OUT OF AN EXPERIENCE LIKE THAT. YOU'D SAY, AS I DID, 'IT'S NOT SUCH A BAD LIFE.'

AS MY COMMUNICATIVE WORLD OPENED UP, MY SOCIAL LIFE OUTSIDE OF SCHOOL PROGRESSED ALSO. THE SELF CONFIDENCE AND INDEPENDENCE I GOT FROM DOING SO WELL IN SCHOOL CARRIED OVER TO OTHER COMMITMENTS I MADE FOR MYSELF, SUCH AS DATING. AT THE TIME I'M REFERRING TO, I DID FEEL VERY STRONGLY TOWARDS ONE YOUNG LADY. BUT I WAS ALWAYS LOOKING FOR NICE COMPANY WHILE I WASN'T WITH THE ONE I LOVE. WELL, WHAT OTHER CHOICE DID I HAVE; WHAT WOULD BE MORE NATURAL THAN FOR ME TO DO MY ACQUAINTING, MY FRIEND-MAKING AND MY GIRL-CHASING IF YOU PREFER, WITH MY HEADSTICK AND BOARD. RIGHT, IT WAS A LITTLE UNUSUAL, BUT I JUST HAD TO LOOK FOR GIRLS WHO WERE LOOKING FOR SOMETHING A LITTLE UNUSUAL. I COULD SHOW THEM A LOT OF UNUSUAL THINGS IF THEY WERE UP TO IT. BESIDES, IF YOU KNEW MY FRIENDS, AND I'M SURE THEY WOULD AGREE, I WAS JUST ABOUT THE MOST NORMAL GUY IN THE LOT.

I HAD COME TO THE POINT WHERE THERE WAS REALLY NO KIND OF MESSAGE THAT I COULDN'T GET ACROSS, AND I MEAN BY TALKING AND TRYING HARD TO MAKE SOMEONE, ESPECIALLY A STRANGER, UNDERSTAND ME ORALLY, OR ELSE NONVERBALLY BY USING MY BOARD OR THROUGH WRITING. WHEN THE END OF MY SENIOR YEAR WAS GROWING NEARER AND NEARER, I KNEW THAT I WANTED TO DO SOMETHING TO THANK ALMOST THE WHOLE SCHOOL FOR CONTRIBUTING HEAVILY TO MY COMMUNICATIVE INDEPENDENCE. ALSO, I WAS VERY FOND OF THE SCHOOL AND WISHED I HAD A MEDIUM FOR EXPRESSING MY PRIDE IN CALVERT HALL. THEN I LEARNED OF THE CONTEST THEY WERE RUNNING FOR VALA-DICTORIAN, ANYONE INTERESTED COULD SUBMIT A SPEECH FOR CONSIDERATION TO BE READ AT GRADUATION. I WASN'T THE BEST STUDENT THERE, NOT EVEN REMOTELY CLOSE. BUT WHAT THE HECK, CHANCES I HAD TAKEN BEFORE WERE MORE OUTSIDE THAN THIS; AND IF THERE'S ONE THING I'D LEARNED IN MY 19 YEARS, IT'S THAT ANYTHING'S POSSIBLE.

AND BELIEVE IT OR NOT, I WON THE CONTEST FOR VALA-DICTORIAN, ONE OF MY BEST FRIENDS DELIVERED MY SPEECH FOR ME, AND MY GIBBERISH RECEIVED A THREE MINUTE STANDING OVATION. BOY, WHEN YOU'RE CUTE, YOU CAN GET AWAY WITH MURDER.

IT'S MORE THAN THAT. TO BE SUCCESSFUL, YOU HAVE TO BELIEVE THAT WHAT YOU'RE DOING IS RIGHT. YOU ALSO HAVE TO BELIEVE THAT WHEN YOU'RE DOING YOUR THING, YOU HAVE A RIGHT TO BE, AND SHOULD BE IN THE FORE-FRONT OF EVERYTHING. LET EVERYBODY SEE YOU; EXPECT THEIR RESPECT, AND IF YOU COME IN CONTACT WITH THEM AND HELP THEM, EXPECT THEIR APPRECIATION, AND ACCEPT IT.

MY LIFE IS ALWAYS GOING TO BE DIFFERENT FROM MOST OTHERS', AND IT'S BEEN ESTABLISHED IN MY MIND THAT THE BIGGEST DIFFERENCE IS MY LACK OF VERBAL COMMUNICATION. BUT IT HAS ALSO BEEN ESTABLISHED IN MY MIND THAT I'M GOING TO MAKE DUE WITH WHAT I'VE GOT, WHICH MEANS I'LL ALWAYS ENJOY BEING DIFFERENT, AND I'LL MAKE PEOPLE LOOK, STARE, WONDER, PERHAPS ADMIRE, PERHAPS AVOID, PERHAPS LOVE, PERHAPS FALL IN LOVE WITH WHAT I AM. THERE'S A BIG FUTURE OUT THERE FOR ME. IT'S BIGGER THAN ANYTHING I'VE SEEN, AND ANYTHING I'M GOING TO IMAGINE. AND I'M GOING TO CONQUER IT ALL BY WEARING THIS SILLY HELMET WITH THIS STICK PROTRUDING OUT THE TOP, SPELLING OUT WORDS TO PEOPLE WITH A BOARD WITH LETTERS ON IT. COMMUNICATING.

Preparation For Independence

This is written by Paul Peroutka who, after twenty years and a lot of amazement, still is afflicted by Athetoid Cerebral Palsy. This condition has not kept me from conquering rather large obstacles in my life; and it didn't stop me from starting college more than nine months ago. What was even more exciting was that I was able to live in a dormitory at school and move away from home for the first time. The ideas which are universally connected with the words 'away from home for the first time' are interesting and somehow familiarly suggestive to almost everyone, especially to those in college themselves. I would like to tell about the last twelve months of my life in hopes that some of my experiences might be just as familiar, if not perhaps genuinely enlightening.

I would start my story at the beginning of the summer after I graduated from Calvert Hall High School. It had been a hope of my parents and mine that when I began attending Loyola College in Maryland in the fall, I would be able to dorm there as well. This possibility was contingent on whether we could locate enough people to be attendant care-takers for me to aid me in my personal selfhelp needs daily. While it is true that my house is four miles, about twenty minutes from the school by car on Charles Street, the urge to enable me to move away was actually inspired by my desires to be more of an independent person and my parents' hope to see me succeed.

As the June weeks went by, we were deeply involved with the question of where to find people who were interested in assuming responsibility for assisting me in my everyday personal needs while I lived on campus.

We had a very good starting ground because of the fact that every year my high school claims approximately 60 of its graduated men go on to attend Loyola. Before school had ended that year, we asked the guidance counselor to give us a list of names of guys who would be entering Loyola with me. When we received the list, all of the names were ones with which I was only vaguely familiar; none of the people I used to hang around happened to choose the same college I had, and so there was a bit of hesitation about getting in contact with the guys we wanted to help me. But during the course of one week, my mother talked to them all on the telephone and got them interested.

We decided to have a meeting at our home to get acquainted with the men and to explain to them all what we were asking them would entail. It was there we designed a program where one person would be responsible for caring for me over an eight hour shift each week. This would take two volunteers a day, one to be with me from 8 AM to 4 PM, and then one until midnight. Everyone seemed fairly willing to try it and see how it would go. One guy offered to be my roommate. My parents had to explain to all that the only way we had of paying for their services involved a state funded agency which would allot $9 a day for each man. This is when everyone made it clear that they were interested in getting involved for the sake of helping out a friend rather than for any money concerned. Hearing them say this gave me a big boost of confidence and made me think that definitely it might work.

We held a second meeting at the end of the summer to clarify everything and create a schedule for when people would be able to be responsible for me. My mother read out the time slots and people volunteered in turn. As she wrote each name, I tried to imagine how it was going to be getting along with that particular person.

Monday, 8-4: Joe Collini. Extremely clean cut fellow. I knew I would have to watch my step when I was around him so as not to spoil his good image.

Monday, 4-12: Bill Sofsky. Definitely a heavy weight, and never drives the porcelain bus. He poured a lot of beer into me at the ocean this summer. He ought to have fun doing the same all year long.

Tuesday, 8-4: Bud Herb. Also a heavyweight. Never drive with him after the sun goes down. He's a nice guy but I wouldn't want to go to jail with him.

Wednesday, 4-12: Chris Schaub. Was dragged here against his will and doesn't seem to know where he is from moment to moment. I better get someone to replace him just in case he doesn't show up.

Thursday 8-4: Joseph Amy. Too polite to my parents. He acts like a perfect gentleman.

Thursday 4-12: Rick Lawrence. Great musician and writes wonderfully obscene lyrics to popular songs. Affixed to something alive called RT.

Friday, 4-12: Paul Schiavonne. He doesn't pour beer well, but I like him a whole lot.

Roommate, Michael Spinnoza. Painfully red.

It is here I would like to thank my parents for supporting me one hundred percent in my desire to live as independently as possible. As they have done during every stage of my growing, they continue to think and act so unselfishly and to give me the most consideration, only concerned for my happiness. So I am now grateful for my mother's wonderful way with people, and my father's wonderful way with a checkbook. And I thank them both for giving me the opportunity to live away at college this year.

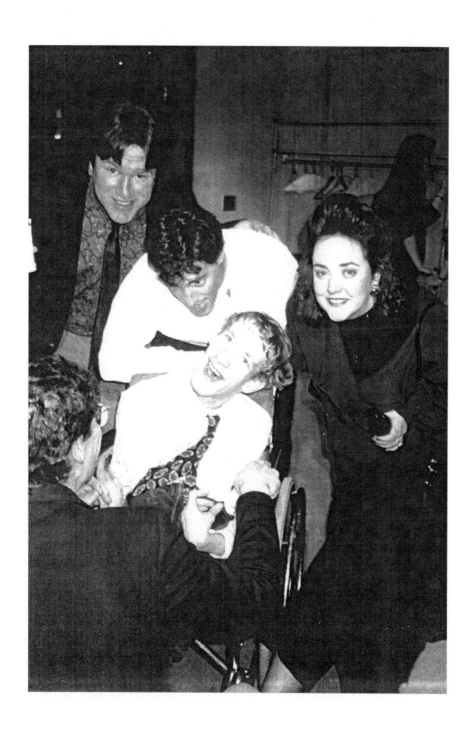

THE MIND IS A TERRIBLE THING

PILOT

This is a debut episode of a series about a wild partying cripple and his experiences living away from home in a college dorm. Paul Peroutka portrays adequately the lead character, a blonde blue-eyed wheelchair bound guy who would like to get as much beer and women in him, but still believes in traditional American values like asking his Mommy to wipe him every time he goes to the bathroom. He thinks he's John Lennon and can't believe that every girl he ever met doesn't want to have sex with him. He's moving to college thinking he can get all the women, liquor and drugs he wants. He better be packing a lot of bills or all he's going to get is liquor and drugs. He thinks that life is pretty good and that college ought to be fun. Boy, has he got a lot to learn. Here's the script for the premier show.

Paul and his parents, Betty and Bud, drive up into the main entrance of Loyola College. They are greeted by youngsters in rainbow hats ready to meet him and show him to his room in Butler Hall. Paul is treated very nicely by these new faces but insists on performing his Spasticman imitation displaying his nervousness for all to see. Mom Peroutka suddenly exclaims, "Oh my God, we forgot his books." There is a roar of laughter from upperclassmen everywhere. "BOOKS! What the HELL does he need books for?" just came from miles around. This gives Betty Boop a stir of shock and Paul a boost of encouragement that he was in for one big party for the next eight months. All of these people finally arrive at Paul's room, Butler 112, carrying all his stuff in. Paul is still nervous as hell and stretches his body out in all directions. He eyes a few upperclass-girls that he knows he's going to enjoy looking at all year. His hopes are up and he's finally going to calm down. When everybody goes out on the last trip to the car for the rest of his stuff and he's left in the room alone, he turns to himself saying, "This is gonna take a lot of beer."

Here come the Spinnozas. Mike the son and Officer the father and German the mother. And they talk and the other parents talk and everybody talks and bla bla bla. Paul is looking forward to friendship with Mike. Mike by the way has red hair so if you see the word 'red' anywhere in this synopsis, chances are it's about him. And when they kick the parents out and say 'goodby parents' Paul sits red down and talks to him, tells the most important things to him.

"Now Red, the three main most important things to me be eatin', shittin' and itchin'." He says "Now Red, when I gotta eat, I say I gotta eat. And you gotta feed me. And when I gotta shit, I gotta shit bad, and you gotta take me to shit. And when I got an itch, you got to scratch the living shit out of my skin so that it don't itch no more. I'm a-counting on you to take real good care of me, partner, ya-hear? Now if you do that for me, I'll be good to you and we ought to get along alright." And Paul said alright and Red said alright. Red said, "Boy, we're gonna be such good friends. We'll have such a great time together," and Paul said, "Boy, I'm psyched." And for the rest of the year they never speak to each other.

ORIENTATION

Freshman orientation at Loyola College consists of three days of conducting such wonderful exercises for new students to get acquainted as duck-duck-goose and musical chairs. While the rest of the school is doing that, Paul and his new friends are in his room getting high. Mom and Dad Peroutka stop by just to drop off Paul's books and his toothbrush and notice that all the boys must be very moody. They all have large smiles on their faces but such red eyes. The Peroutkas are unable to detect Paul's condition because he can't sit up anymore. When they leave, everybody sighs relief and lights up again. Paul asks who was that who stopped by.

A friend of Paul's who is a nurse stops by and shows everyone how to give Paul a bath and how to handle him. Paul is hopeful now that he will be properly treated and the boys won't throw him around and push him down and throw him up in the air and toss him backwards and tangle his body in all sorts of directions and treat him like a clumsy piece of shit. But they do it anyway.

FIRST THREE WEEKS OF SCHOOL

Scenes of Paul with his new attendants. He eats his first lunch in the school cafeteria with Joe Collini. He is the wholesome one. Paul rushes through lunch because he has business to do and he must ask Joe to help him with it. Before him on the table is a large manila envelope and a copy of a full-length play entitled 'Spasm Orgasm'. When Joe finishes eating, Paul asks him to jot down this little note and place it in the envelope along with the play. This is what the note says. "Dear Uncle Sheckey, How's your old peter going? Had wonderful time last time I visited the club. How are all the girls? Kiss them all and tell them I love 'em. This is what I put down last month, just thought you'd love a copy. Gotta go. Take care. Love the littleCocker."

When Joe reads the note back to Paul, he said this, "Paul, I just really admire you and think it's great that you care so much for your uncle and your cousins that you would send them such a nice gift." Paul is going to get along very well with Joe Collini because he is so wholesome.

With Bill Sofsky at dinner, he devours some TDV: truly disgusting veal, and very flat rootbeer. Bill makes constant remarks about what a slob Paul is to feed. But Paul knows Bill is so mean just because he loves him and wants to squeeze his nuts. Paul notes, "Oh, don't you know I like my attendants and lovers cruel." Bill is only feeding Paul veal because he is refusing to feed anybody Polish hot dogs.

"Hey man, you want Polish hot dogs, you get some other sucker to feed 'em to you." Bill can be so tactful. "Man, what's really disgusting is you like mustard on 'em. Yuck."

"Mean Mr. Mustard sleeps in the park, shaves in the dark trying to save paper."

Paul likes the Beatles very much and agitates Bill tremendously by singing a whole side of an album before he lets him feed another spoonful. Bill fixes his friend by very suddenly and mercilessly cramming the shit down his throat. Once Paul has stopped gasping, wining, whimpering, choking, and desperately hanging onto one more precious breath of air, Bill hears a quite faint but definite "uck-you."

Here comes Rick Lawrence to say a friendly dinnertime hello to those brave cafeteria consumers. Rick is the one who's attached to the thing, Rt. Rt is described as this sort of rubbery creature with overgrown joints and face features. You would likely vomit the first couple times you came in contact with it; but after a while you would become accustomed to its appearance and only have to be excused for 30 seconds for a short gagging spell. Rick lugs Rt around in a baby carrier strapped to his shoulders. Rick is happy to spot Paul and Bill tonight and decides to sit down for a chat with them.

"Hi guys, what's up?"

"Oh hi, sir. Glad to see you. How has your day been?"

"Oh, I'm just tired of dragging this fucker around on my back. We try to communicate the best we can, you know? But it's so hard. I've been trying to find out his damn telephone number so I can get rid of him. He tries to tell me but hell if I can understand him."

"Ah, too bad," Bill admits, "I try to understand this guy over here but all I can get is the long side of Abbey Road."

"De de-de de...Here comes the---"   "Here comes the veal, do do-do do!"

"AHHHHHH SHIT------Gulp GULP GUL......."

"There, he'll be cool for a while. I'm gonna get myself a sandwich. Rick, can you feed Paul the rest of his rootbeer? I have enough sticky fingers for one day."

"Oh sure, Bill. Here Paul, how do I do this? Just hold the glass up to your mouth with the napkins, like you do with beer? OK. There we go...Oops, a little bit of spillage here, but it's ok. Ooh! Ooh!! You know what? I like the way the rootbeer slides down your chin. No no no, don't wipe it off, don't wipe it off. Yeaaaah... A little more to the right. Aaaah yeaaaah..."

Faggot bullshit while drinking rootbeer pisses Paul off immensely and he gives Rick his due, "hey, uck you ag."

Rick tries to explain, "No Paul, I'm sorry. It was just a joke. Hey look. Rt likes the joke too. Ha ha, ha ha..."

And we hear now from Paul, "Rt, own ome!"

Paul is getting along famously with his new friend, Rick. He discovers that he is really just a cool and casual guy after all, and he is not at all the way he acts when he is around people who are older or who have more money than he. Paul soon notices that every vein in Rick's body is withstanding. Actually the guy could be described as a psychopathic roach smoker who really gets off on taking Paul to the bathroom. Everytime it goes something like this.

"Hey Paul, you gotta shit this time? Oh, crazy!"

"Gee, thanks Rick, for helping me out here. I'll try to make this a good one for you. A large turd and not too stanky."

"Oh, CRAZY!!! No sweat, Paul. I love it when you shit. Ah, no one can take as good a shit as you can, Paul. Hey, I got a crazy idea, man. I'll put you on the can, then I'll sit in your wheelchair, wipe off all the food that Sofsky got on your seat, and then I'll talk to you on some very interesting topics while you relieve yourself. Ok, Paul? Ok, now Paul, ask me the first question that you always ask me right after I put you on the toilet. Come on, Paul, out with it."

"Ok Rick. How are you?"

"Oh, I'm fine, Paul. Thank you for asking. How's yourself? You know Paul, I've been wondering something. Can you answer me a question? Paul, what is snot? I mean what is it?? What's its meaning? What's its purpose? Is it nose mucous? Oh no, it's not nose mucous. It's not like any form of liquid or solid that comes out of your face. What is SNOT? Can you look in any dictionary and tell me what snot is? NO! I say NO!! Dear God, please tell me---WHAT IS SNOT???

"Rick,"

"Yes Paul?"

"You are full of snot."

"What's that, Paul? Oh, you want me to get you off the toilet because you've been sitting there so long, you're getting hemorrhoids. Is that what you're saying, Paul?"

"Yeah it is, Rick."

"Ah, Crazy!!!"

After time on the toilet, Rick gives Paul a shower. He gets his friend all spiffy and clean and ready for a nice enjoyable evening of study and reflection with a clean body and spirit. And then he destroys it all completely by pouring beer into Paul's mouth and spilling it all over his clothes, getting him disgustingly drunk and savagely soaked. To this brutal type of behavior, Paul always replies, "You're my kind of guy, Rick Lawrence."

"Crazy, Paul, CRAZY."

Now, Chris Schaub (do you recall that name from somewhere?) takes care of Paul every Wednesday night. At first the two aren't sure they would get along so well after Paul spends an hour on the phone listening to the recorded tape from Hillcrest pregnancy clinic just to avoid striking up a conversation with Chris, the shitheaded looking beanpole with grease strings for hair laughing into uncontrollable frenzies at old Get Smart reruns. But then the idea comes up to go to the campus Rathskeller bar and the two immediately become best friends for life. They start discovering their totally equal interests in beer, sex, rock & roll, and of all things, writing. Up to now, both had thought that he was the best writer to come from their high school class. But now they admire each other's talents greatly.

Chris really gets along with Paul and when they're not drinking, trying desperately to get laid, or sharing sacrificial cheeseburgers from McDonalds, they write poetry together. They decided to form a partnership and release material under both names. Paul rehashes an old name he used to use with childhood friends who wrote dirty poems on the schoolbus. He asks Chris how he likes the name 'American Bustop' for the duo, and the ideas start flying from there.

Now they write poems left and right. They sometimes give up chasing the women. This has made Loyola College a much safer place. This is the first composition by American Bustop.

I live in the desert
in a house with no floors
All I do is
play the Doors
The lizard is cold
with a tongue of fire
Ma'am would you
get me lasagna and
a root beer
I must be going
Why do you don't that?

Pass me your feline
I've got a strange premonition
Under various conditions
Everything will be fine
If we don't rock Smirnoff's
The hot desert moon's
got me on the run
I'm the burning sand's
forgotten son
Take me on a submarine
that long thing with semen
frying on tomorrow's iceberg
speaking in cool seduction
breathing sand in false reluctance
Brothers with relative abundance
Tombstones glowing under desert stars
    Goodnight Mother you've been a bad boy
                  Peroutka / Schaub
AMERICAN BUSTOP

It is clear the reader has had enough. Their poetry does get better and it isn't long before Paul and Chris ask their good friend Rick Lawrence to join the group and the Bustop was formed, christened and ready to propagate its lust for life.

The three boys spend a lot of time writing, drinking, and basically screwing up the Loyola campus. They all consider deep aspects of the mind, especially polluted by THC and cases of Bud. They finally arrive at a simple truth of the universe. All three proclaim to the world their message:

"The mind is a terrible thing."

Spasm Orgasm

I'M LES, AND MY FRIEND IS MARTIN. MARTIN AND I HAVE KNOWN EACH OTHER FOR A LONG TIME. I TAKE CARE OF HIM A LOT. MARTIN CAN'T DO MANY THINGS FOR HIMSELF. HIS MIND'S OK, HE JUST HAS THESE SPASMS A LOT. AND HE CAN'T DO MUCH WITH HIS HANDS OR LEGS OR ANYTHING. IT MUST BE ROUGH, BUT I TAKE CARE OF HIM.

MARTIN SAID HE NEEDED A FAVOR. HE ASKED ME TO DO IT FOR HIM. LAST NIGHT I DID. WE WERE SITTING IN THE BOOTH.

LES: ANOTHER BEER, MART?
MARTIN: YEAH, OF COURSE.
LES: YEAH, WAITRESS, TWO MORE PLEASE.
MARTIN: IF YOU COULD JUST TELL ME ONE MORE TIME WHAT YOU TOLD HER. WHAT EXACTLY IS THE DEAL, WHAT'S GOING TO HAPPEN?
LES: MART, I TOLD YOU THAT A MILLION TIMES AND PROBABLY THE ONLY REASON YOU KEEP FORGETTING IS BECAUSE YOU'RE SO FACED. UNLESS, YOU'RE NERVOUS. ARE YOU NERVOUS?
MARTIN: WELL NO..UH..
LES: YOU ARE, YOU'RE NERVOUS. HA HA. THIS OLD SUCKER IS NERVOUS. HA HA..

MARTIN: WELL OF COURSE I'M NERVOUS. YOU KNOW HOW IMPORTANT THIS WHOLE THING IS TO ME. THIS THING IS GOING TO CHANGE MY WHOLE LIFE TONIGHT.

LES: WELL NOW WAIT A MINUTE. I DON'T CARE WHAT YOU'VE HEARD, IT AIN'T THAT GREAT. SURE, IT'S GREAT FOR A COUPLE MINUTES, BUT IT DOESN'T CHANGE YOUR WHOLE LIFE. WELL, I DON'T KNOW, MAYBE IT DOES. I DUNNO.

MARTIN: WELL, WHAT AM I GOING TO GET? WHAT DOES SHE DO FOR...PEOPLE?

LES: WELL, SHE DOES SEVERAL THINGS, MART, I JUST TOLD HER WHAT WE WANTED. I JUST TOLD HER THAT YOU WANTED, YOU KNOW, PRETTY MUCH THE WHOLE SHOW. PENETRATION, AND ANYTHING THAT MIGHT GO ALONG WITH IT. I JUST TOLD HER THAT YOU WANTED A VERY SPECIAL EVENING FOR YOU, THIS IS VERY NEW AND UNUSUAL FOR YOU, BUT THIS IS VERY IMPORTANT TO YOU, BUT SHE SEEMED TO HANDLE IT ALRIGHT. I TOLD HER THAT YOU PROBABLY WANTED THE WHOLE NIGHT. WAS I RIGHT ABOUT THAT?

MARTIN: UH, YEAH, WELL I GUESS. WAS THERE ANY PROBLEM ABOUT THE PRICE?

LES: UH NO, HE GAVE ME ENOUGH TO GIVE TO HER. SHE UNDERSTOOD. I TOLD HER THAT YOU DIDN'T HAVE EXACTLY A LOT OF MONEY, AND WHAT MONEY YOU DO GET COMES FROM THE GOVERNMENT. BOY, IF UNCLE SAM EVER FOUND OUT WHAT THE HELL YOU'RE DOING WITH HIS MONEY, HE'D KICK YOUR ASS---OH, HI THERE, YOU MUST BE BONNIE..

SHE CAME OVER TO THE TABLE. HER HAIR WAS AUBURN AND HER FACE WAS LOVELY. SHE HAD ONE OF THE BEST BODIES I KNOW I'VE EVER SEEN. SHE HAD COME OUT OF HER DRESSING ROOM IN A VERY LOOSE RED TRANSPARENT ROBE, HER G-STRING WAS BLACK, AND HER HEELS WERE VERY TALL. WE INVITED HER TO SIT

DOWN AND TALK AND SHE SAT NEXT TO MARTIN'S WHEELCHAIR, LEANING ON THE ARM. BUT ALL THE WHILE TALKING TO ME. MARTIN WAS OUT OF CONTROL. HE WAS HAVING ONE SPASM AFTER ANOTHER BECAUSE HE WAS SO EXCITED. I SAW THAT HE WAS TRYING TO CALM DOWN BUT HE JUST COULDN'T HELP SPAZING OUT. BONNIE PROBABLY FELT UNCOMFORTABLE AROUND HIM SO SHE KEPT ON TALKING TO ME. I FIGURED I KEEP HER TALKING UNTIL MARTIN SETTLED HIMSELF DOWN. IT WASN'T HARD TO DO..

LES: YEAH, PLEASE SIT DOWN, AND CAN WE BUY YOU A DRINK?
BONNIE: YEAH SURE. MAGGIE, I'LL HAVE A MARY.
LES: MARY? UH?...BLOODY MARY.
BONNIE: UH HA, VERY QUICK. HA HA.
LES: WELL, I'VE ALWAYS BEEN KNOWN FOR THAT.
BONNIE: OH, WELL SURE. HA HA.

I LOVED HER LAUGH. SO DID MARTIN.

BONNIE: YOU'RE THE MAN I SPOKE TO ON THE PHONE TODAY.
LES: YES THAT'S CORRECT. IT'S LES COMINGS AND THIS IS MY PAL, MARTIN.

SHE GLANCED AT HIM QUICKLY, SAID HI WITH AN EMBRACING SMILE, THEN TURNED BACK TO ME. FUNNY THOUGH: SHE PROCEDED TO HOLD HIS HAND. THIS SEEMED TO SATISFY HIM. WELL I GUESS IT WOULD HAVE SATISFIED ANYBODY. YET SHE WAS STILL PAYING ATTENTION TO ME. SO I CONTINUED..

LES: YOU TWO HAVE TO GET TO KNOW EACH OTHER. BONNIE, I'VE TOLD MARTIN EVERYTHING WE ARRANGED TODAY, AND EVERYTHING'S OK WITH HIM. HE'S REALLY LOOKING FORWARD TO THIS, AND TO TELL YOU THE TRUTH, HE CAN'T WAIT. YOU CAN SEE HOW EXCITED HE IS.

BONNIE: OH, YEAH, HA HA..

LES: MART, YOU SURE ARE ACTING LIKE THE CATS GOT YOUR TONGUE.

MARTIN: WELL, I GUESS I WON'T HAVE ANYTHING GOOD TO SAY.

BONNIE: WHAT'S YOUR LAST NAME, MARTIN?

LES: WELL, MART WOULD RATHER NOT SAY HIS....

MARTIN: UH, JONES. MY NAME IS MARTIN JONES.

LES: RIGHT, MARTIN..JONES.

BONNIE: WELL, I'D LOVE TO STAY AND TALK, AND I WILL, I WILL. BUT I GO ON IN ABOUT FIVE MINUTES. I HAVE TO DO MY SHOW. I HOPE YOU BOTH ENJOY MY SHOW. I THINK YOU WILL.

LES: OH, I'M SURE WE WILL. HOW LONG YOU BEEN DANCING HERE?

BONNIE: WELL, I'VE BEEN WORKING HERE AT THIS CLUB FOR FIVE YEARS, BUT I'VE ONLY BEEN DANCING FOR THREE.

LES: I SEE, DO YOU DANCE ALONE?

BONNIE: YEAH. EVERYNIGHT BUT SATURDAY. THEN I DANCE WITH ANOTHER DANCER, BILL. WE DO A ROUTINE CALLED "THE EATING CONTEST". I THINK YOU CAN GUESS WHAT THAT'S LIKE.

MARTIN: OH YES, I THINK I GOT AN IDEA.

BONNIE: I'VE REALLY GOT TO GET GOING. HAVE ANOTHER BEER OR TWO. PLEASE ENJOY THE SHOW, AND I'LL BE BACK REAL SOON, OK?

SHE RAN OFF BURSQUELY.

LES: OK BABY. CHRIST. YOU GOT A GOOD FRIEND, MART. I'M DOING THIS FOR YOU. IF I HAD A BRAIN IN MY HEAD, I'D TAKE HER AND GET IT ALL FOR MYSELF.

MARTIN: YEAH YEAH, I KNOW. WHEN DO YOU THINK SHE'LL BE READY?

LES: AH, GIVE HER SOME TIME IN THE DRESSING ROOM. SHE'LL BE OUT IN A WHILE.

MARTIN: WELL THAT'S OK 'CAUSE I GOTTA GO TO THE BATHROOM.

LES: OH, YOU STILL GOTTA DO THAT, HUH? AND I SUPPOSE YOU WANT ME TO TAKE YOU...

MARTIN: NO, I THOUGHT I'D PISS RIGHT UP ON STAGE. COME ON, SHITHEAD, LET'S GO.

I PUSHED HIM AROUND BACK AND WE WENT TO A STALL. ACTUALLY, THE ONLY STALL, ABOUT TWO INCHES WIDE. DID YOU EVER TRY TAKING A SPASTIC TO THE JOHN IN A PLACE AS SLIMY AS A STRIP-JOINT? IT AIN'T EASY. IT'S GODDAMN IMPOSSIBLE. THAT WAS THE DIRTIEST FUCKING PLACE I'VE EVER SEEN. BUT, NO MATTER, I LIFTED MART ONTO THE CAN AND LET HIM GO TO TOWN.

MARTIN: CHRIST, I HOPE I CAN GO.

LES: ARE YOU NUTS? YOU HAD TEN BEERS.

MARTIN: ELEVEN.

LES: YOUR BADDER MUST BE A DAMN PRESSURE COOKER. I DON'T KNOW WHY YOU HAVEN'T EXPLODED ALREADY.

MARTIN: I KNOW BUT YOU KNOW HOW I GET SOMETIMES. YOU KNOW, INSIDE. I GET SO TENSE, AND I CAN'T RELAX ENOUGH TO PISS.

LES: MART, YOU'RE GONNA BE PISSING FOR THREE DAYS AFTER THOSE BEERS.

MARTIN: MAN, I HOPE YOU'RE RI---

I HEARD A BIG TINKLE, THEN A STEADY RIVER FALLING ON PORCELAIN.

MARTIN: WELL. I GUESS YOU ARE RIGHT.
LES: CHRIST, I'LL BE HERE ALL NIGHT.
MARTIN: NO NO, WAIT, I'M ALMOST FINISHED.....NOW, WAIT TIL YOU HEAR THIS.

I HEARD THE SOUND OF A HUGE BRICK FALLING VERY HARD ON CEMENT.

LES: OH SHIT.
MARTIN: THAT'S RIGHT.

I SPENT THE NEXT TEN MINUTES WIPING THAT GUY'S ASS. DID YOU EVER WIPE ANOTHER PERSON? AFTER DOING IT, YOU THANK GOD YOU CAN'T SEE IT WHEN YOU WIPE YOURSELF. GROSS-CITY. MY FRIEND MART CAN REALLY DUMP A TURD.

LES: HOLY SHIT.
MARTIN: THAT' RIGHT.

AFTER THREE OR FOUR MINUTES OF WASHING MY HANDS SUFFICIENTLY, I WAS READY TO PUSH HIM BACK TO OUR TABLE. OPENING THE DOOR OF THE MEN'S ROOM, WE SAW BONNIE ALREADY THERE, WAITING FOR US. MART STARTED SPAZING OUT AGAIN. IMMEDIATELY HE BECAME AS NERVOUS AS HE EVER HAD BEEN THAT WHOLE NIGHT. I TRIED TO CALM HIM DOWN OUTSIDE THE JOHN.

LES: MART, I REALLY THINK YOU OUGHT TO RELAX. I REALLY THINK YOU WOULD ENJOY THIS EVENING A LOT MORE IF YOU JUST TAKE IT EASY.

MARTIN: YEAH, I KNOW WHAT YOU MEAN. YOU'RE RIGHT.

LES: WELL NOW, THE NIGHT'S REALLY JUST BEGINNING. YOU'VE GOT A LOT AHEAD OF YOU, A LOT TO LOOK FORWARD TO. I WISH I WAS LUCKY AS YOU.

MARTIN: OH GOD--DAMN, I'M NERVOUS.

LES: UH, YES I KNOW. THAT'S BECOME OBVIOUS. YOU WERE SPAZING OUT ALL THROUGH THAT CONVERSATION.

MARTIN: OH YES, I KNOW LES, BUT I'M TELLING YOU, I CAN'T HELP IT. I COULDN'T CONTROL MY MOVEMENTS. AND I THINK I TURNED THAT GIRL OFF.

LES: OH, DON'T WORRY ABOUT IT ANY. SHE LIKES YOU, I COULD TELL. EVERYTHING'S GONNA BE ALRIGHT, JUST WAIT AND SEE.

MARTIN: WELL LISTEN, YOU GOTTA TAKE ME TO THE BATHROOM, I'M NOT GONNA BE ABLE TO GET ANYTHING UP IF ALL I GOTTA DO IS PISS.

LES: WHAT???

MARTIN: NOBODY CAN FUCK, AND ENJOY IT, IF THEY HAVE TO URINATE. THEY CAN'T ENJOY IT IF THEY HAVE TO SHIT EITHER.

LES: I NEVER THOUGHT ABOUT IT, BUT I GUESS YOU'RE RIGHT.

MARTIN: OF COURSE I'M RIGHT, I KNOW EVERYTHING. NOW LET'S GO TO THE JOHN.

LES: WELL, YOU CAN WAIT UNTIL AFTER BONNIE'S SHOW IS OVER, CAN'T YOU?

MARTIN: WELL, I GUESS SO.

LES: YOU BETTER. I AIN'T MISSING THIS SHOW FOR NOTHING.

MARTIN: OK, GET ME ANOTHER BEER, WILL YOU? IT'S GONNA TAKE A REAL GREAT BUZZ TO GET THESE MUSCLES TO CALM DOWN.

LES: YOU KNOW THAT THIS IS YOUR NINTH.

MARTIN: SOMETIMES THAT'S WHAT IT TAKES. NOW GET IT.

I WENT TO THE BAR AND GOT HIM HIS DRAFT. THEN I HURRIED BACK TO THE BOOTH BECAUSE THE SHOW WAS READY TO START.

LES: HERE IT IS. NOW SHUT UP, I WANT TO SEE THIS.

IT BEGAN. THE EMCEE, WHO WAS ALSO THE OWNER, ONE OF THOSE SHORT FAT MIDDLE- AGED GUYS WITH THE DARK HAIR AND THE SUNGLASSES WHO TRIES HIS DAMNEST TO BE SHECKY GREENE. LET'S CALL HIM SHECKY GREENE.

SHECKY GREENE: OOH, HEHH-HEHH-HEHH... FOLKS, GUYS AND GALS, LADIES AND DEGENERATES, HEHH-HEHH-HEHH. HAVE WE GOT A SHOW FOR YOU. MAKING A ONCE IN A NIGHTTIME APPEARANCE, RIGHT HERE, ALL THE WAY FROM BACK STAGE. LET'S GIVE A REAL FAIR- TO-MIDLAND WELCOME TO BONNIE LA LURE.

THEN SHE WALKED UP THE STEPS, ON TO THE STAGE. SHE DID A LITTLE TEASE WITH SHECKY THERE, WHERE HE POKED HIS LITTLE FINGER INTO ALL THE CRACKS AND CREVICES AND OVERWHELMING INDENTATIONS ON HER BODY. THEN, OF ALL THINGS, HE WAS PULLED OFF STAGE BY A CANE. HOW VERY VERY ORIGINAL. THEN SHE STARTED DOING HER THING, HER ACT. THE FIRST WORD THAT POPS INTO THE HEAD IS SENSATIONAL. AND THAT'S JUST DESCRIBING HER BODY. SHE WAS STILL DRESSED IN THE ROBE AND G-STRING AND DANCED IN THEM FOR THE FIRST NUMBER. IT WAS A REAL PROFESSIONAL PLACE; THE DANCERS PUNCHED OUT THEIR NUMBERS BEFORE THEY WENT OUT ON STAGE. THIS WAS SOME TUNE BY RAY PARKER. I DON'T THINK IT DID TOO GOOD ON THE CHARTS.

NOW, THIS WAS YOUR TYPICAL STRIP-TEASE DANCER, SOCHEYING HER FEET, LEFT TO RIGHT, BACK AND FORTH, TURNING HER WHOLE SELF AROUND IN A CIRCLE NOW AND THEN. THE ROBE HUNG AND SWUNG FROM HER KNEES TO THE GUY IN THE FIRST ROW. HE HAD A CONSTANT COMING ATTRACTION OF THE REST OF THE ACT. HE NEVER GRABBED, BUT HE NEVER TOOK ONE EYE OFF THE INTERIOR OF HER STRING.

AND MARTIN SEEMED TO CONCENTRATE ON THAT AREA TOO. THAT SURPRISED ME BECAUSE HE ALWAYS CLAIMED HE WAS A BREAST MAN. I KNOW I AM ONE AND I SAT THERE AND HAD A FIELD DAY. THERE WAS NOTHING TO BONNIE'S TITS LEFT TO BE DESIRED. ANY MAN WOULD CONCEIVABLY PAY A FORTUNE TO PUT HIS HEAD BETWEEN THEM. I DID SEE MART'S EYES MOVING UP FROM THE PUSSY AREA TO THOSE MOUNTAINS OF GLORY AT HER DANCE. HIS SPASMS RETURNED AS HE INTENSELY WATCHED HER BODY SWAY. SHE DID INCORPORATE HER LOVELY HANDS INTO HER ACT. HER LONG RED NAILS SCRATCHED HERSELF EVERYWHERE SHE COULD POSSIBLY ITCH.

BY THIS TIME, MART WAS SEEING THE REALITY THAT WAS A THOUSAND TIMES MORE HEAVENLY THAN HIS MOST EROTIC FANTASY. EVERY BIT OF ENERGY IN HIS BODY WAS ONLY CONTROLLED IN HIS EYES, AND THE REST OF HIS BODY WAS ONE BIG RACING CAR, GOING, SPEEDING FASTER THAN SOUND, WITHOUT ANY HOPE OF SLOWING DOWN. HIS MUSCLES WERE NOT HIS, AND HE COULDN'T DO ANYTHING ABOUT HIS MOVEMENTS, SHAKING, OR QUIVERING. AND AS FAR AS HE WAS CONCERNED, HE DIDN'T HAVE TO. HE DIDN'T KNOW HIS BODY WAS MOVING, HE DIDN'T FEEL ONE SPASM. HIS FULL ATTENTION WAS ON THE SHOW, THE GIRL, THE FIRST NUDE WOMAN HE'D EVER SEEN, THE PERSON

THAT LATER THAT EVENING WOULD MAKE HIM A COMPLETE MAN.

BECAUSE HE WAS MAKING A SMALL ATTRACTION WITH HIS MOVEMENTS, AND BECAUSE I KNEW IT WAS THE LAST TIME I'D BE ABLE TO GET HIS ATTENTION, AT THE END OF BONNIE'S FIRST NUMBER, I POINTED OUT TO HIM HIS CONDITION, MADE HIM REALIZE HE WAS MAKING A FEW ANNOYING NOISES, AND ASKED HIM TO PLEASE TRY TO CONTROL HIS EXCITEMENT LEVEL JUST A TAD. TO THAT, HE QUICKLY REBUTTED, "FUCK YOU".

I JUST HAD TO SAY, "OK."

THE SECOND DANCE BEGAN WITH BONNIE DROPPING HER ROBE, LEFT COVERED BY HALF AN INCH OF SATIN COVERING HER PUBIC HAIR. SHE STEPPED OUT OF HER HEELS WHICH TURNED ME ON. AND SHE LOOKED OVER AND WINKED AT MART WHICH CAUSED HIM TO GO INTO A PERMANENT STATE OF NERVANA AND PUT HIM TOTALLY OUT OF CONTACT WITH THE PLANET, EARTH.

IF HE WAS ROWLED UP BY SEEING HER BOOBS THROUGH TRANSPARENT RED, HIS DREAMS WERE COMING TRUE BY HAVING A CLEAR VIEW OF THEM. THEY WERE NICE HONIES. ALL OF HER WAS GORGEOUS AS SHE LET HER HAIR FALL AND BOUNCE AGAINST HER SHOULDERS. THE SONG WAS ONE BY SHEENA EASTON, THAT OH SO SEXY VOICE. MARTIN'S FACE WAS AS RED AS THE SUN AND HIS MUSCLES WERE TIGHTER THAN THE STRONGEST ROPE.

THEN CAME THE BLANKET BIT. BONNIE WAS HANDED A WOOLEN BLANKET FROM OFF STAGE. YOU'VE SEEN THIS ROUTINE BEFORE. SHE VERY SLOWLY LAID HER LITTLE NEST IN THE MIDDLE OF THE STAGE, AND PROCEEDED

TO CREEP ON DOWN IN A KNEELING POSITION. HIDDEN IN THE BLANKET WAS A SQUEEZER OF LOTION. IN THE MOST SEDUCTIVE MANNER, SHE BEGAN APPLYING THE LOTION.

SHE BEGAN AT HER SHOULDERS. SHE ASKED THAT GUY IN THE FRONT SEAT TO HOLD IT WHILE SHE GOT SOME LOTION IN HER HAND AND CAREFULLY RUBBED IT DOWN HER ARMS. SHE MUST HAVE SLID ON DOWN THOSE BABIES TEN TIMES EACH. MART'S PECKER GREW MORE AND MORE EVERY TIME. THEN THE LOTION WENT ON HER NECK, AND SHE RUBBED IT DOWN, DOWN, DOWN. IT WAS BREAST TIME.

CIRCLE STROKES, CIRCLE STROKES, CIRCLE STROKES, SO SMOOTH AND GENTLE, ZEROING IN ON THOSE IRRESISTIBLE NIPPLES. DEVINELY SEEN AND ABSOLUTELY TEMPTING. ANYONE WITH HORMONES, SEEING THIS, WOULD GROW INSTANTLY WEAK. MART'S MIND WAS TOTALLY BLANK, AS SHOWN BY HIS TOTALLY BLANK FACE. THE ONE BREAST WAS SUFFICIENTLY CREAMED AND IT WAS TIME FOR AN INSTANT REPLAY WITH THE OTHER.

THEN IT WAS TIME FOR A BELLY RUB-DOWN, AND SHE DID THE MOST AMAZING TRICK. SHE HAD A NAVEL THAT ACTUALLY CHANGED FROM AN INNIE TO AN OUTTIE. I MUST ADMIT, I'M A MAN WHO'S MADE A SERIOUS, DETAILED STUDY ON WOMEN'S BELLY BUTTONS, COMPARING THE TWO BASIC TYPES, AND DETERMINING WHICH IS MORE FASCINATING. BUT I'VE NEVER, EVER SEEN ANYTHING LIKE THIS. I WAS ASTOUNDED, AND ALSO VERY ENLIGHTENED. MART WAS STILL HORNED OUT OF HIS GOURD.

THEN HER LEGS NEEDED THE PROTECTION FROM THIS ONE, VERY CHEAP, DIM RED SPOT LIGHT. SO SHE

STRETCHED THEM OUT, STARTING AT HER TOENAILS AND WORKED UP EXCRUCIATING SLOWLY. EVERY BUMP OR WAVE SHE ENCOUNTERED ALONG THE WAY MEANT ANOTHER SPASM OUT OF MY FRIEND. ACTUALLY I DON'T KNOW HOW HE SURVIVED THIS WHOLE NIGHT. NOBODY SHOULD GO THROUGH THE BODILY STRUGGLE AND EXHAUSTION HE DID. AND WE HAVEN'T GOTTEN TO HER THIRD NUMBER.

WE HEARD DOTTIE WEST AND KENNY ROGERS SING "I FEEL SORRY FOR ANYONE WHO ISN'T ME TONIGHT" AS WE WATCHED THE ACT BECOME PERVERTEDLY PLAYFUL. THE LOTION WAS UP AT HER THIGHS WHICH MEANT ONE THING. THE G-STRING HAD TO GO; AND IT DID. BONNIE'S THIRD DANCE WAS ALL NUDE, AND SHE ASKED FOR A LITTLE AUDIENCE PARTICIPATION, NO DOUBT FROM THE GUY IN THE FRONT SEAT. THAT LOTION JUST HAD TO BE APPLIED TO HER BACK, AND HE WAS THE MAN WHO JUST HAD TO DO IT. "START AT MY NECK AND WORK DOWN," SHE TOLD HIM AS SHE ROLLED TO LAY ON HER STOMACH.

WELL HE DID, HE CARESSED HER NECK AND RIBS AND EVERYTHING IN BETWEEN, BUT IT WASN'T LONG BEFORE HE GOT TO HIS DESTINATION.

AND BOY, DID HE DO A NUMBER ON THOSE CHEEKS. HE PUT HIS HANDS ALL OVER THAT ASS. THERE WAS NO MORE SUNTAN LOTION LEFT BUT THAT DIDN'T MATTER TO EITHER ONE OF THEM. I NEVER SAW TWO BIGGER HANDS. CHRIST, I THOUGHT HE WAS ABOUT TO TWIST ONE OF THOSE BUTTOCKS OFF BUT INSTEAD HE TRIED SOMETHING ELSE. WITH HER LAUGHING HYSTERICALLY ALL THE WAY THROUGH, HE BENT ALL THE WAY DOWN AND DOVE HIS HEAD STAIGHT UP HER BUTT. SHE SPREAD HER LEGS COMPLETELY HORIZONTAL AND HE BURROWED AND BURROWED

FARTHER AND FARTHER. I'LL ADMIT THE GIRL HAD ROOM TO SPARE, BUT STILL...SHE COULD HAVE BLED TO DEATH, HE WENT SO FAR.

THEN ALL OF A SUDDEN, AS THE SONG ENDED, THE GUY ALLIE- OOPED AND DID A SOMER-SAULT RIGHT OVER HER BODY, LANDING HIS FEET RIGHT IN FRONT OF HER HEAD. IT WAS REMARKABLE. THAT WAS THE END OF THE ACT. THE FELLOW TURNED OUT TO BE THE SHECKY GREENE I WAS TELLING YOU ABOUT, THE OWNER OF THE JOINT. HE PICKED UP THE MICROPHONE.

SHECKY GREENE: HEHH-HEHH-HEHH. NOW FOLKS, WASN'T THAT GREAT?? THAT WAS BONNIE AND I WANT YOU TO GIVE A GREAT BIG HAND TO BONNIE, RIGHT HERE. HEHH- HEHH-HEHH...

SHE QUICKLY SLIPPED ON HER ROBE AND HEELS, PICKED UP HER STRING AND A FEW FLOWERS THAT WERE THROWN ON STAGE, TOOK A FEW BOWS, THEN SPLIT. WE WERE SITTING ON HER WAY BACK TO HER DRESSING ROOM. SHE LOOKED TO SEE THAT MARTIN WAS MENTALLY HALF CONSCIOUS, ABSOLUTELY BLOWN AWAY. AND SHE COULD SEE THAT HE WAS STILL SPAZING OUT BECAUSE OF HIS EXCITEMENT. SO SHE RAN OVER AND PECKED HIM ON THE CHEEK. HE SMILED VERY COOLY, KISSED HER BACK, STAYED COOL UNTIL SHE GOT TO THE DRESSING ROOM, THEN FAINTED DEAD ON TOP OF THE TABLE.

HE DIDN'T REALLY FAINT, JUST WAS OVERWHELMED AGAIN, SO MUCH SO THAT HE NEEDED A BREAK FROM EXISTANCE. HE GOT ONE BUT I SOON WACKED HIM ON THE NOGGEN AND TOLD HIM TO STOP ACTING LIKE AN ASSHOLE.

MARTIN: OK, I WILL.

LES: GOOD. 'CAUSE YOU WERE GROSSING OUT MOST EVERYONE HERE. YOU COULDN'T STAY STILL ONE MINUTE.

MARTIN: I KNOW, MAN, BUT I COULDN'T HELP IT. I TOLD YOU THAT.

LES: I KNOW THAT, BUT EVERYONE HAS TO CONTROL THEMSELVES ONE WAY OR ANOTHER. I MEAN, CHRIST, I FELT LIKE GOING UP THERE AND CHEWING THE LIVING SHIT OUT OF HER. I MEAN I WOULD HAVE GONE EVEN FARTHER UP HER ASS THAN THAT GUY DID.

MARTIN: DO YOU THINK THAT WAS PART OF THE SHOW?

LES: OH YES, MART, I REALLY DO THINK SO. OF COURSE IT WAS, SHIT-HEAD.

MARTIN: WELL, WHY DOES SHE DO THAT? WHY DOES SHE LET HIM DO THAT TO HER? SHE'S A VERY NICE GIRL.

LES: THAT'S HER ACT, MAN, THAT'S HER JOB.

MARTIN: YEAH, BUT TONIGHT, SHE'S GONNA SPEND TIME WITH ME. AND I'M SUPPOSED TO MAKE LOVE TO HER...

LES: MAN, I HATE TO REMIND YOU, BUT THAT'S HER JOB TOO, YOU KNOW.

MARTIN: I KNOW, I KNOW. AND I THANK YOU FOR EVERYTHING YOU'RE DOING FOR ME TONIGHT. I THANK YOU FOR BEING HERE WITH ME NOW, AND MAKING ALL THE ARRANGEMENTS TODAY ON THE PHONE. AND I THANK YOU FOR THE LOAN. I PROMISE I'LL PAY YOU BACK.

LES: YEAH YEAH, ALRIGHT. LET'S QUIT WITH THIS GRATITUDE SHIT.

MARTIN: BUT I'M SINCERE. I REALLY MEAN IT.

LES: YEAH, I KNOW, BUT IT MAKES ME UNCOMFORTABLE. SHUT UP.

MARTIN: OK.

LES: OK, ARE YOU READY?

MARTIN: READY??? FOR IT?? YOU MEAN, READY TO DO IT??

LES: NO, MART. WE CAN GO HOME FOR A COUPLE OF HOURS. HAVE A FEW BEERS, ASK YOUR MOTHER HER THOUGHTS ON THE MATTER, ASK HER FOR A COUPLE BUCKS TO PITCH IN FOR THIS WHOLE THING. MAYBE WE'LL COME BACK NEXT WEEK. YOU ASSHOLE, BONNIE IS SITTING RIGHT THERE AT OUR TABLE. WHAT THE HELL YOU THINK'S GONNA HAPPEN NOW?? IT'S TIME, MAN! ARE YOU READY OR AREN'T YOU?

MARTIN: WELL, I DON'T KNOW. BUT DON'T GIVE ME THAT BULLSHIT. THIS IS VERY HARD FOR ME. IT'S REALLY HARD FOR ME.

LES: OK, MART, WHAT ABOUT THIS IS SO FUCKING HARD FOR YOU? NOW WHAT I SEE, YOU GOT A LOVELY YOUNG GIRL OVER THERE. YOU GOT HER OVER THERE JUST SITTING AND WAITING FOR YOU. SHE'S GONNA SPEND SOME TIME WITH YOU--ALONE, WHICH IS WHAT YOU WANT. SHE'S GONNA TAKE YOU IN ONE OF THOSE BACK ROOMS THERE AND SHE'S GONNA TALK NICE TO YOU, SHE'LL DO WHATEVER YOU WANT TO DO WITH HER. SHE'LL BE THE NICEST COMPANY YOU HAD. IT'LL BE THE BEST TIME YOU EVER SPENT WITH A WOMAN... YOU CAN JUST TALK TO HER. YOU CAN GET CLOSER TO HER. YOU CAN GO TO BED WITH HER. YOU CAN DO FUCKING ANYTHING YOU WANT WITH HER, MAN. I TOLD YOU EVERYTHING IS ARRANGED. THERE'S NOTHING FOR YOU TO WORRY ABOUT. THIS IS WHAT YOU BEEN WANTING FOR MONTHS. THIS IS WHAT YOU BEEN BITCHING ME ABOUT HELPING YOU TO DO FOR WEEKS. NOW FOR CHRIST SAKE, WHAT THE HELL ARE YOU NERVOUS ABOUT???

MARTIN: LISTEN, MOTHER-FUCKER. EVERYTHING IS HARD FOR ME. DON'T YOU REALIZE THAT? SITTING STILL IS HARD, TAKING A SHIT IS HARD. TALKING TO A STRANGER IS HARD. EVERY FUCKING BODILY FUNCTION IS HARD FOR ME TO DO. GOD DAMN IF, IF I'M

A PRICK ABOUT EVERYTHING, PLEASE CONSIDER IT AN OCCUPATIONAL HAZARD. WHAT I'M REALLY SCARED OF IS THAT I'LL FUCK IT ALL UP.

LES: I TOLD YOU SO MANY TIMES. THERE'S NOTHING TO FUCK UP. ANYTHING YOU WANT TO HAPPEN IS GOING TO HAPPEN. IT'S YOUR NIGHT.

MARTIN: BUT I'M TALKING ABOUT HER. I'VE ALREADY TURNED HER OFF AND I'M AFRAID SHE'LL TURN AWAY FROM ME COMPLETELY. I WON'T BE ABLE TO CONTROL MY MUSCLES, AND I PROBABLY WON'T BE ABLE TO GET TWO WORDS OUT.

LES: YOU SHITHEAD, THAT AIN'T GONNA HAPPEN. MAN, YOU WORRY TOO MUCH. JUST TAKE--IT--EASY. NOW FOR GOD SAKE, BONNIE'S SITTING OVER THERE WAITING, AND WE LOOK LIKE A COUPLE OF ASSHOLES HERE TALKING. LAST CHANCE. ARE YOU GOING THROUGH WITH THIS OR NOT?

I SAW HIS LIFE PASSING BY HIS EYES AS HE MADE HIS DECISION.

MARTIN: WELL FOR GOD SAKE, MAN WHAT THE HELL ARE WE WAITING FOR?

I COULD HAVE KICKED HIS ASS, BUT INSTEAD I PUSHED HIM OVER TO THE TABLE. I FIGURED THAT WAY, I'D BE ABLE TO GET AWAY FROM HIM AND GET OUT OF THAT JOINT AS FAST AS POSSIBLE.

LES: BONNIE, I GIVE YOU MARTIN. I BELIEVE YOU TWO HAVE MET.

BONNIE: OH YES, I BELIEVE WE HAVE. COME SIT BY ME MARTY, YA-HARDLY SAY A WORD.

LES: OH, HE DON'T LIKE IT FOR ANYONE TO CALL HIM MARTY.

MARTIN: UH, SIR, WOULD YOU SHUT UP. THIS LADY CAN CALL ME ANYTHING SHE WANTS.

LES: OH CHRIST, LISTEN TO HIM.
BONNIE: WELL, DON'T YOU WORRY, SWEETHEART, WHEN HE'S GONE AND WE ARE ALONE, I'LL CALL YOU A LOT OF OTHER THINGS. HA HA.

OH GOD, DID I LOVE HER LAUGH.

LES: WELL, LISTEN FRIEND, IS THERE ANYTHING ELSE I CAN DO FOR YOU BEFORE I SPLIT? I GET THE FEELING YOU TWO ARE PUSHING ME THE HELL OUT OF HERE.
BONNIE: AW NOW, WHERE DID HE GET THAT IDEA?
MARTIN: I DON'T KNOW, I'VE BEEN TELLING HOW COOL AND COLLECTED I'VE BEEN ALL EVENING. I GOT EVERYTHING UNDER CONTROL, LES.
LES: YEAH, NO SHIT. WELL THEN, I THINK I'LL LEAVE YOU TWO LOVE-BIRDS TOGETHER ALONE. I'M GOING TO THE BAR FOR ONE MORE BEER, AND THEN I'LL BE BOOKING. AND UH, BONNIE, I'M TO PICK MY FRIEND UP HERE IN UH, SIX HOURS?
BONNIE: UH, YES, THAT'S HOW LONG I USUALLY GO. THAT'S STANDARD.
LES: AND EVERYTHING ELSE IS TAKEN CARE OF?
BONNIE: OH YEAH, THE CHECK WAS FINE. IT WAS ENOUGH. EVERYTHING'S ALRIGHT.
LES: ALRIGHT THEN, KID, IT LOOKS LIKE YOU'RE IN. IS IT JUST THE WAY YOU WANTED IT?

HE GAVE A PAUSE. UNDERSTANDABLE, AFTER THE DISCUSSION ABOUT MONEY.

MARTIN: YEP, IT'S JUST THE WAY I WANTED IT.
LES: OK THEN. SIX HOURS FROM NOW IS JUST ABOUT SEVEN O'CLOCK. SEE YOU IN THE MORNING, KID. I TAKE IT YOU'LL STILL BE UP. TAKE IT EASY, BIG BOY.

I LEFT THEM FOR THE BAR. HIS EYES WERE ON ME AS I WALKED AWAY LIKE A KID GOING ON THE SCHOOLBUS

THE VERY FIRST DAY, BEGGING HIS MOTHER NOT TO
LET THEM TAKE HIM AWAY. MAMMA HAS TO, AND I
HAD TO. MART WAS ON HIS OWN.

MARTIN: HI.

BONNIE: HI...HA.

MARTIN: I'M MART. HA.

BONNIE: NO, YOU'RE MARTY...HA HA.

MARTIN: OH YEAH, THAT'S RIGHT. GEE, UH, THAT
SOUNDS NICE WHEN YOU SAY THAT, WHEN YOU CALL
ME THAT.

BONNIE: WELL I'M GLAD.

MARTIN: LISTEN, I MUST TELL YOU, I'M VERY NERVOUS.
I JUST CAN'T HELP IT.

BONNIE: WELL, THERE'S NO REASON TO BE.
EVERYTHING'S ALRIGHT.

MARTIN: YEAH, I KNOW, I KNOW. THAT'S WHAT LES
KEEPS TELLING ME.

BONNIE: HE SEEMS LIKE A VERY GOOD FRIEND.

MARTIN: YEAH YEAH, HE IS, HE IS. HE'S BEEN AROUND ME
SINCE THE BEGINNING. HE'S HELPED ME ALL THROUGH
MY LIFE. HE BEAT UP THE FIRST KID THAT EVER MADE
FUN OF ME. AND HE TOOK CARE OF THE FIRST TEACHER
THAT GAVE ME TROUBLE. HE GAVE ME MY FIRST BEER.
HE HELPED ME SMOKE MY FIRST JOINT. HE'S BEEN LIKE
MY BODYGUARD FOR ALL MY NINETEEN YEARS.

BONNIE: WOW, WHAT A FRIEND TO HAVE. YOU'RE VERY
LUCKY.

MARTIN: YEAH, WELL, SOMETIMES HE CAN BE A PAIN
IN THE ASS. BUT EVERYBODY CAN GET THAT WAY. HA
HA.

BONNIE: HA HA, I KNOW, YEAH. .. UH, MART, MARTY,
HA HA, WOULD YOU LIKE TO GET STARTED? I MEAN,
WOULD YOU LIKE ME TO SHOW YOU ONE OF THE BACK
ROOMS? CAN I PUSH YOU BACK THERE?

MARTIN: UH, SURE. IF YOU THINK IT'S TIME, SURE. YOU
WANT TO GET STARTED EH?

BONNIE: OH, I CAN'T WAIT TO GET STARTED ON YOU, HONEY-BUNCH...

MARTIN: OH, OOOOOHH, OH MY GOD. OH SHIT.

BONNIE: HEY, WHAT'S THE MATTER? CAN I HELP YOU? WHY ARE YOU SHAKING LIKE THAT??

MARTIN: NOTHING, NOTHING AT ALL. PLEASE. I'LL STOP SHAKING IN A MINUTE. PLEASE. WHY DON'T YOU PUSH ME ON BACK THERE, LIKE YOU SAID. AND EVERYTHING'LL BE ALRIGHT.

BONNIE: OK, BUT PLEASE CALM DOWN. DON'T MOVE AROUND SO MUCH. YOU MAKE ME NERVOUS, YOU KNOW? JUST CALM DOWN.

MARTIN: YEAH, BONNIE. THAT'S THE IDEA.

BONNIE: AND AWAY WE GO.. AM I PUSHING THE CHAIR TOO FAST?

MARTIN: NO, UH, ACTUALLY THIS IS WHAT YOU WOULD CALL SLOW. BUT IT'S COOL, IT'S COOL.

BONNIE: AH WELL, HERE WE ARE. SHALL I OPEN THE DOOR?

MARTIN: WELL, THAT WOULD BE THE BEST WAY TO GET IN.

BONNIE: OH SURE...HA HA.

MARTIN: OH, THIS IS IT, HUH? THIS IS WHAT YOU WOULD CALL YOUR BASIC BACK ROOM?

BONNIE: YEAH. WELL, THIS IS THE ROOM I USUALLY WORKIN...UH, I MEAN, I USUALLY SLEEP IN...I MEAN, I USUALLY TAKE---YOU KNOW, TAKE.

MARTIN: I KNOW. YOU'RE A VERY SWEET GIRL, VERY INNOCENT, I CAN TELL, VERY CARING.

BONNIE: UH, RIGHT. WELL, YOU KNOW, YOU REALLY DON'T HAVE TO FLATTER ME LIKE THAT. I DON'T NE---

MARTIN: I WASN'T FLATTERING YOU. I REALLY MEAN IT.

BONNIE: YEAH, RIGHT. LET'S JUST DROP IT, OK? I MEAN, LET'S TALK ABOUT YOU INSTEAD, OK? NOW, WHAT WOULD YOU LIKE TO DO FIRST? HUM?

MARTIN: WELL, I DON'T KNOW. SEE, I HADN'T PLANNED---I MEAN, I DON'T KNOW. DO YOU WANT ME TO, LIKE, SPELL IT ALL OUT FOR YOU? I MEAN.

BONNIE: WELL, I DON'T KNOW. WE COULD PLAY IT BY EAR, I GUESS...SURE, WE'LL PLAY IT BY EAR, THAT'S WHAT WE'LL DO. I'LL JUST SIT DOWN HERE ON THE BED, AND YOU CAN STAY THERE, AND WE CAN TALK FOR A WHILE, OK?

IS ANYBODY THERE? AND COULD YOU POSSIBLY BE STILL READING. DO YOU GET ANY . . . SENSE OUT OF IT ALL .... IS ANYBODY STILL READING? I LOST THE LORD AT MY OTHER PRAYER OK.

MARTIN: OK, OK. SEE, YOU'RE A VERY ATTRACTIVE WOMAN, YOU KNOW? AND I'D JUST LIKE TO GET REAL NEAR YOU.

BONNIE: WELL, THAT'S EASILY ARRANGED. I'LL JUST PULL YOU OVER HERE NEXT TO ME. THERE, IS THAT NICE?

MARTIN: THAT'S VERY NICE. THAT'S SO NICE, I CAN'T TELL YOU HOW NICE IT IS. THAT IS NICE.

BONNIE: AND WHAT DID YOU SAY ABOUT GETTIN--REAL--CLOSE. ... OH OH, WHAT WHAT'S WRONG? YOU'RE SHAKING AGAIN. WHY ARE YOU SHAKING AGAIN? WHAT'S WRONG??

MARTIN: PLEASE, PLEASE, DON'T MIND IT. I'M GONNA STOP IN A MINUTE. I'M JUST VERY EXCITED, YOU KNOW, AND WHEN I'M EXCITED, I SHAKE AND I HAVE SPAS---

BONNIE: HEY LISTEN, I DON'T HAVE TO HEAR ALL THIS. UH, WOULD YOU LIKE ME TO GET YOUR FRIEND? MAYBE HE CAN HELP YOU.

MARTIN: WELL NO, I DON'T REALLY HAVE ANY REASON TO SEE HIM. I'M ALRIGHT. SEE? I'M NOT MOVING ANYMORE. I'M FINE NOW.

BONNIE: YEAH, OK. I CAN SEE YOU'RE FINE. HEY, TELL ME WHAT YOU THINK OF MY OUTFIT, EH?

MARTIN: I REALLY REALLY REALLY LIKE THE ROBE. IT'S REALLY SEXY. OH GOD. I CAN'T STAND IT. BUT YOU KNOW, I'D THINK I'D LIKE IT BETTER IF IT WAS OFF OF YOU. YOU KNOW?

BONNIE: OH YOU DEVIL, YOU BASTARD. WELL, I THINK WE CAN TAKE CARE OF THAT EASILY ENOUGH. THIS CAN SLIP OFF MY SHOULDERS JUST LIKE THAT. AND I CAN COME OVER TO YOU AND LEAN OVER TO YOUR FACE AND GET EVERYTHING OFF MY CHEST. NOW, HOW DO YOU LIKE THAT? HUH??

MARTIN: OOOOOHHH, OOOOHH!! AAH SHIT! OOH GOD!!

BONNIE: OOH GOD! WHAT'S THE MATTER?? I DON'T LIKE IT WHEN YOU DO THAT! WILL YOU PLEASE STOP SHAKING LIKE THAT?

MARTIN: I TOLD YOU, I CAN'T HELP. WHEN I'M EXCITED, I CAN'T CONTROL MY MUSCLES. CHRIST, WILL YOU TRY TO REMEMBER THAT? YOU KNEW THE JOB WAS TOUGH WHEN YOU TOOK IT. ... OH. I'M SORRY. I'M REALLY SO SORRY. I SHOULD HAVE SAID THAT TO YOU. PLEASE, PLEASE FORGIVE ME.

BONNIE: NO. NO. YOU'RE THE ONE WHO HAS TO FORGIVE ME. PLEASE. I'M NOT A VERY STRONG PERSON. I MEAN, I'M NOT VERY SMART. I MEAN, I--I--PLEASE, I JUST NEED SOME TIME. PLEASE. ARE YOU ALRIGHT FOR A MINUTE? I'M JUST GOING TO GRAB MY ROBE, AND GO OUT TO THE BAR FOR A MINUTE. I'LL--I'LL BE RIGHT BACK..PLEASE..I JUST HAVE TO--I JUST HAVE TO...

MARTIN: OH--GOD, WHAT HAVE I DONE? I'VE SCARED HER TO DEATH. BEFORE THIS NIGHT BEGAN, I KNEW THAT EITHER THE BEST OR THE WORST THING WAS GOING TO HAPPEN TO ME TONIGHT. THIS IS THE BEGINNING OR THE END FOR ME. I PUT THIS KNIFE IN MY POCKET. I MAY USE IT SOON.

I WAS JUST PAYING MY TAB AND LEAVING A TIP WHEN SHE CAME RUNNING. I SAID A QUICK, "OH SHIT" TO MYSELF, WHEN I NOTICED UNFORTUNATELY THAT THERE WAS A TEAR IN HER EYE. SHE WAS RUNNING STRAIGHT TOWARDS ME APPEARING TO BE IN A STATE OF PANIC.

LES: HEY BONNIE, IS SOMETHING WRONG? CAN I HELP YOU?
BONNIE: UH, LES? IS IT?
LES: YEAH. WHAT'S WRONG?
BONNIE: OH, I THINK I BLEW IT. I THINK I REALLY HURT HIM. I MEAN, I THINK I OFFENDED HIM, I HURT HIS FEELINGS. AND I REALLY DON'T KNOW WHAT TO DO. I- -I... YOU SEE, I'M NOT THAT STRONG. I'M NOT THAT STRONG A PERSON, AND I- -I DON'T KNOW. I DON'T KNOW WHAT WOULD HURT HIM, OR WHAT WOULD MAKE HIM HAPPY. I DON'T KNOW WHAT HE WANTS ME TO DO. I--I...
LES: NOW TAKE IT EASY, TAKE IT EASY. I REALLY DON'T KNOW WHAT YOU MEAN, BUT I'LL TRY TO HELP YOU. NOW, TELL ME WHAT HAPPENED.
BONNIE: WELL, IT WAS GOING ALRIGHT. WE WERE TALKING. AND I COULD HANDLE THAT. THEN HE SAID HE WANTED TO GET CLOSER. SO I WHEELED HIM OVER TO ME, AND I TEASED HIM A LITTLE, AND I THOUGHT HE WAS ENJOYING IT. AND THEN, I DON'T KNOW. HE-- HE STARTED TO SHAKE, LIKE HE WAS DOING OUT HERE. AND IT CONFUSED ME, IT UPSET ME.. I JUST COULDN'T HANDLE IT. WHAT AM I SUPPOSED TO DO? I'VE NEVER BEEN AROUND ANYONE LIKE HIM.
LES: AH GEE. I'M SORRY. UH, PLEASE DON'T CRY. LOOK, LET ME BUY YOU A DRINK. UH, WAITRESS...
BONNIE: YEAH, SALLY. GET ME A MARY. HE DOESN'T HAVE TO PAY FOR IT. I REALLY DON'T KNOW WHY I CAME TO YOU. GOD, I LEFT HIM THERE. HE PROBABLY FEELS TERRIBLE. BUT--BUT, HE'S NOT TO BLAME. I AM.

YOU SEE, I'M JUST NOT THAT STRONG. AND I'M NOT THAT SMART TO KNOW WHAT TO DO, WHAT TO SAY. AND THEN YOU TOLD ME THAT YOU WERE HIS BEST FRIEND, OR THAT YOU ARE ALWAYS AROUND HIM, AND YOU HELP HIM OUT A LOT. I THOUGHT YOU WOULD KNOW WHAT I SHOULD DO. ... I'LL GIVE YOU YOUR MONEY BACK. ... CAN YOU TELL HIM FOR ME?
LES: UH, TELL HIM WHAT?
BONNIE: WELL... EXPLAIN TO HIM... WHY I CAN'T DO IT, WHY I CAN'T BE WITH HIM TONIGHT..
LES: UH, WHY CAN'T YOU BE WITH HIM TONIGHT?
BONNIE: WELL, I JUST EXPLAINED TO YOU. I DON'T KNOW HOW. I MEAN, IT'S JUST TOO HARD FOR ME.
LES: DON'T YOU THINK IT'S HARD FOR MART?
BONNIE: OH YES, I'M SURE IT IS, BUT...
LES: YOU KNOW, IT'S LIKE EVERY MINUTE IS HARD FOR MART. I MEAN THAT SHAKING HE'S DOING, HE CAN'T HELP THAT. THE MORE HE TRIES NOT TO MOVE, THE MORE INVOLUNTARY MOVEMENTS HE'S GONNA HAVE. IT'S ALL GOT TO DO WITH PARTS OF HIS BRAIN AND PARTS OF HIS BODY THAT HE DOESN'T HAVE ANY CONTROL OVER, YOU KNOW? DOCTORS COULD TELL YOU EXACTLY WHAT'S WRONG WITH HIM, BUT REALLY, WHAT YOU SEE IS WHAT IT IS. I MEAN, THAT'S REALLY ALL THAT'S WRONG WITH HIM. HE CAN'T WALK OR USE HIS HANDS, AND HE HAS A LOT OF MUSCLE SPASMS. BUT HE MAKES OUT ALRIGHT. HE KNOWS WHERE HIS HEAD'S AT. SOMETIMES HE TAKES THINGS TOO SERIOUSLY, LIKE TONIGHT. ... OH, MAYBE I SHOULDN'T SAY THAT.
BONNIE: NO. WHAT DO YOU MEAN?
LES: WELL, I MEAN THE WHOLE BIT OF US BEING HERE TONIGHT. TOMORROW IS HIS BIRTHDAY, AND HE'S BEEN SAYING FOR THE LAST THREE MONTHS THAT HE WANTS TO BE CONSUMATED BEFORE HE TURNS 19. IT'S BEEN THE MOST IMPORTANT THING IN THE WORLD AND THE ONLY THING I'VE HEARD ALL THIS TIME.

BONNIE: THIS IS REALLY IMPORTANT TO HIM, EH?
LES: OH GOD YES, YOU SHOULD HAVE HEARD HIM BUGGING ME. WELL, SEE, MART HAS KIND OF AN UNUSUAL SITUATION, YOU KNOW? YOU HAVE TO UNDERSTAND HIM. HE LIVES A PRETTY FULL LIFE, ALL THINGS CONSIDERED. I MEAN, SURE, IT'S LOUSY SITTING IN THAT CHAIR AND NOT BEING ABLE TO DO ANYTHING FOR YOURSELF. BUT I HELP HIM GET AROUND A LOT AND WE HAVE A LOT OF GOOD TIMES. WE CAN DO SOME MEAN PARTYING WHEN WE WANT. AND HE LIKES TO WATCH SPORTS, AND HE LIKES TO GO TO MOVIES. SO, IN A LOT OF RESPECTS HE CAN REALLY DO WHATEVER HE LIKES TO DO. HE CAN PARTICIPATE IN THE KINDS OF THINGS HE ENJOYS DOING, AS LONG AS SOMEONE'S THERE TO HELP HIM OUT. BUT HE'S REALLY NOT HAD TOO MUCH SUCCESS WITH WOMEN. I MEAN, HE HAS HAD SOME GIRLFRIENDS AND I DRIVE THE CAR, AND WE DO OUR BEST TO MAKE IT AS CLOSE TO A DATE AS POSSIBLE. WE TRY. BUT IT'S NOT REALLY REAL. MART CAN'T REALLY HAVE THAT CONTACT, THAT UH, SEXUAL CONTACT THAT, YOU KNOW, OTHER PEOPLE HAVE.
BONNIE: YEAH, I SEE..
LES: AND IT'S HURT HIM. I MEAN, HE'S GOTTEN DEPRESSED ABOUT IT. HE'S UPSET BECAUSE HE CAN'T DO WHAT OTHER PEOPLE DO HIS AGE. THERE ARE SOME GIRLS WHO WON'T EVEN KISS HIM. AND FOR HIM, THIS IS HORRIBLE. MART HAS NEVER LIKED THE FEELING OF BEING LEFT-OUT. HE DOESN'T LIKE TO, YOU KNOW, MISS OUT ON ANYTHING JUST BECAUSE OF HIS HANDICAP.
BONNIE: SO HE WANTED A SEXUAL EXPERIENCE BEFORE HE WAS NINE-TEEN. THAT'S WHAT YOU'RE LEADING UP TO.
LES: YEAH RIGHT. I--I GOT IN TOUCH WITH YOU BECAUSE I HAD SEEN YOUR SHOW A NUMBER OF TIMES, AND UH, IF I MAY SAY SO, I JUST HAD A HUNCH, JUST FROM WATCHING YOU DANCE, THAT YOU WERE A

KIND, CONSIDERATE, UNDERSTANDING, SWEET, PATIENT, ANGELIC, ABSOLUTELY DARLING LADY...JUST A BEAUTIFUL CREATURE. ACTUALLY, ACTUALLY, IT WAS YOUR BREASTS. YES, BONNIE, THE FIRST TIME I SAW THEM, I GODDAMN FELL IN LOVE WITH YOU. YOU DON'T NEED TO HEAR THIS FROM AN ASSHOLE LIKE ME, WHO'S OBVIOUSLY HAD TOO MUCH TO DRINK AND AFTER A LONG NIGHT'S WORK. I KNOW THIS.

BONNIE: UH, NO, ACTUALLY, I REALLY ENJOYED HEARING IT. I THINK YOU'RE KIND OF CUTE YOURSELF.

LES: OH CHRIST. BONNIE, BONNIE...I THINK YOU MADE MY NIGHT. I THINK YOU MADE MY WEEK. I THINK YOU MADE MY LIFE! OH CHRIST, I'M SORRY I'M BABBLING ON LIKE THIS.

BONNIE: NO, YOU ARE. YOU'RE A SWEET GUY. HA HA.

LES: I GOTTA TELL YOU HOW MUCH I LIKE YOUR LAUGH. OH GOD. AND MART LIKES IT TOO. MART...MART, WE WERE TALKING ABOUT MART.

BONNIE: YEAH, RIGHT, MART...

LES: LOOK, I TOLD MART THAT ALL THAT WAS GONNA HAPPEN TONIGHT WAS WHAT COMES NATURALLY. I THINK THAT MARTIN WOULD JUST REALLY ENJOY YOUR COMPANY FOR THE NIGHT. HE JUST NEEDS SOMEONE TO TALK TO, SOMEONE TO TOUCH HIM. MAYBE SOMEONE TO TOUCH. HE'S LIVED WITHOUT IT FOR A LONG TIME. HE'S LIVED WITHOUT A LOT OF THINGS FOR A LONG TIME.

BONNIE: I WASN'T REALIZING HOW HARD ALL THIS WAS FOR HIM. I SHOULD HAVE, BUT I DIDN'T REALIZE. IT MUST BE HARD NOT BEING ABLE TO EXPLAIN THINGS TO DUMMIES LIKE ME...MY GOD, IT MUST BE HARD FOR HIM.

LES: WELL, WHENEVER THINGS GET ROUGH FOR HIM, HE LIKES TO SAY TO HIMSELF, "YOU KNEW THE JOB WAS HARD WHEN YOU TOOK IT."

BONNIE: UH, UH HA, YES. YES.

LES: WHAT?

BONNIE: NOW IT'S TIME FOR ME TO DO MY JOB.
LES: UH, WHAT DO YOU MEAN?
BONNIE: TONIGHT, HE WON'T HAVE TO SAY THAT TO HIMSELF. HE'S SAYING IT TO ME.

SHE STEPPED UP FROM HER STOOL. SHE KISSED ME AND SHE THANKED ME. I DIDN'T SEE HER AFTER THAT.

BONNIE: HEY STRANGER, LIKE SOME COMPANY?
MARTIN: OH. ... OH GOD, I DIDN'T KNOW IF YOU WERE COMING BACK OR NOT. I WAS THINKING I WAS GONNA HAVE TO SPEND ALL NIGHT HERE ALONE. I THOUGHT YOU FORGOT ME.
BONNIE: NOW, HOW COULD I FORGET A SEXY GUY LIKE YOU?
MARTIN: WELL. ... SHIT, I DON'T KNOW. UH...
BONNIE: YOU JUST HAVE TO EXCUSE THAT BRIEF INTERMISSION. YOU ARE SUCH A DEVASTATING BRUTE, A GIRL JUST HAS TO TAKE YOU IN SPURTS. NO WOMAN COULD HANDLE YOU ALL AT ONCE, FOR A LONG PERIOD OF TIME...BUT I'M GONNA DO MY DAMNEST TO TRY.
MARTIN: WHAT???
BONNIE: OH YES. IT MIGHT WEAR ME OUT. IT MIGHT EVEN KILL ME...BUT I MUST HAVE YOU...MARTY.
MARTIN: BUT... I DON'T UNDERSTAND. YOU WANTED TO GET AWAY- --
BONNIE: I MUST HAVE THOSE CLOTHES. I JUST GOTTA RIP OFF THOSE CLOTHES. COME--HERE. I GOTTA SEE THIS BODY OF YOURS.
MARTIN: OH GOD, WHY ARE YOU COMING AT ME LIKE THAT? -- LET'S SEE, IT'S GONNA TO TAKE A WHILE TO GET MY CLOTHES OF. IT ISN'T VERY EASY TO DO, BUT WE'LL MAKE IT. CAN WE START RIGHT NOW?
BONNIE: SURE. WHAT DO WE DO FIRST?
MARTIN: WELL, THE HARDEST THING ABOUT TAKING OFF MY SHIRT IS GETTING IT OFF MY ARMS. DO YOU THINK YOU CAN HELP ME?

BONNIE: WELL, I DON'T SEE WHY NOT. THERE'S NOTHING I'D RATHER DO THAN RIP OFF THE SHIRT THAT'S COVERING THIS GORGEOUS CHEST.

MARTIN: WHAT ARE YOU DOING WITH MY ARM? WHAT?...

BONNIE: COME ON, HOW THE HELL DO I GET THIS SHIRT OFF YOU?

MARTIN: TAKE IT SLOW. YOU'RE NOT GONNA HURT ME, BUT YOU'RE GONNA THINK THAT YOU ARE, SO GO AS SLOW AS YOU WANT. WELL, YOU KINDA HAVE TO BEND MY ARM THIS WAY, THEN BEND IT THAT WAY. WELL, FIRST IT MIGHT BE GOOD TO UNBUTTON MY SHIRT.

BONNIE: OK. I DON'T KNOW WHAT YOU JUST SAID BUT I GUESS YOU DO, SO OK, HERE GOES. ... UGH, UGH. THIS IS TOUGH. AM I HURTING YOU?

MARTIN: SEE WHAT I MEAN? NO, YOU'RE NOT HURTING ME. YOU'RE DOING VERY WELL, YOU   REALLY ARE. WE'LL HAVE THIS SHIRT OFF IN...FIVE MINUTES...NO, I'M KIDDING. WE'LL HAVE IT OFF IN A SECOND.

,SPECT THERE'LL BE FIVE OR SOME PAGES LEFT TO GO. ,SPECT Y'ALL STILL READING. THE GOOD PART'S COMIN' UP, DON'T YOU KNOW. MAYBE SOME PRETZELS OR POTATO CHIPS WOULD BE TASTY TO HELP WRAP UP THIS

BONNIE: OH YEAH. HA HA HA. I THINK THAT WOULD BE A LITTLE EASIER. LET ME JUST KNEEL DOWN HERE AND DO THAT. LET'S SEE HERE. I THINK I CAN UNBUTTON WITH ONE HAND, WHILE I'M GONNA GET STARTED ON YOUR ZIPPER HERE. THERE, THAT'S DOWN, YOUR SHIRT'S OPEN. YOU'RE ALMOST READY FOR BED-EE-POO LITTLE MARTY.

MARTIN: GEE, WHERE DID YOU LEARN TO UNBUTTON AND UNZIP WITH ONE HAND?

BONNIE: HONEY, WHEN YOU'RE A STRIPPER, YOU CAN DO ANYTHING WITH CLOTHES.

MARTIN: YEAH, I GUESS SO. UH, I'M STARTING TO MOVE AGAIN, YOU KNOW I'M SHAKING. I HOPE IT DOESN'T BOTHER YOU.

BONNIE: SHAKING? I DON'T SEE YOU SHAKING. I DON'T KNOW WHAT YOU'RE TALKING ABOUT.

MARTIN: WELL, I THOUGHT I SCARED YOU A LITTLE BIT. I SAW YOU FREAK OUT AND I THOUGHT YOU DIDN'T WANT---

BONNIE: WELL DON'T YOU WORRY ABOUT THAT. YOU'RE STILL SEXY, HA HA.

MARTIN: OH GOD, I LOVE YOUR LAUGH.

BONNIE: SEEMS TO ME I'VE HEARD THAT BEFORE. OH WELL, ANYWAY, WHAT DO WE DO NEXT? THERE! WE GOT THE FIRST ARM OFF. HEY, I'M KINDA PROUD OF MYSELF.

MARTIN: OH, I'M VERY PROUD OF YOU. THE REST IS DOWNHILL FROM HERE.

BONNIE: OH MY GOD. I DID IT. WE GOT IT OFF, MARTY. WE GOT THIS GODDAMN SHIRT OFF.

MARTIN: WELL, THE SHIRT IS OFF. WE'RE HALFWAY THERE.

BONNIE: YOU MEAN WE GOT TO TAKE THE PANTS OFF?

MARTIN: BINGO.

BONNIE: OK, HOW DO I GO ABOUT DOING THAT? SHOULD I STAND YOU UP?

MARTIN: THE BEST THING TO DO IS HELP ME TRANSFER FROM THE CHAIR TO THE BED. YOU'LL HAVE TO STAND ME UP A SECOND BUT IT WON'T BE HARD BECAUSE I CAN SUPPORT MY OWN WEIGHT. OK?

BONNIE: OK. ON THE COUNT OF THREE. READY? ALLIE-OOP! OH SHIT, YOU'RE HEAVY.

MARTIN: YEAH YEAH, I KNOW. I'M SORRY.

BONNIE: DON'T BE SORRY FOR BEING HEAVY, LOVER. IT TURNS ME ON... THERE WE DID IT. YOU'RE ON THE BED.

MARTIN: ALL--RIGHT!! YOU'RE GETTING BETTER AND BETTER AT THIS. EVER THINK ABOUT BECOMING A NURSE?

BONNIE: OH, PLEASE. LET ME WORRY ABOUT ONE THING AT A TIME, WILL YOU?

MARTIN: NO, I BET YOU'D MAKE A GREAT NURSE.

BONNIE: YEAH, RIGHT. OK, PATIENT, NOW I'M GONNA TAKE OFF YOUR PANTS 'CAUSE I GOTTA SEE WHAT YOU GOT UNDER THERE. LAY DOWN, TIGER.

MARTIN: OH GOD, YOU GOT ME GOING AGAIN. I DO HAVE SOMETHING BIG UNDER HERE. AND I BET YOU CAN'T GUESS HOW BIG IT IS.

BONNIE: OOH, I BET I CAN. LET ME SEE. ... OOH, YOU'RE RIGHT. I WOULD HAVE GUESSED HOW BIG IT WAS. OH GOD, THAT'S THE BIGGEST HONEY I'VE EVER SEEN. I CAN'T WAIT TO LOOK AT IT A LITTLE CLOSER.

MARTIN: WELL GET MY SHOES AND SOCKS OFF, AND SLIP OFF MY PANTS AND YOU GOT ALL OF ME TO LOOK OVER CLOSER, SWEETHEART.

BONNIE: RIGHT AWAY, DOCTOR PASSION.

MARTIN: OOH, WHAT A NAME.

BONNIE: MARTY, UH, YOUR FEET ARE SHAKING TOO MUCH FOR ME TO UNTIE YOUR SHOE. COULD YOU TRY TO RELAX FOR A MINUTE? JUST RELAX.

MARTIN: YEAH, OK. SURE. I'M TRYING.

BONNIE: COME ON, DARLING. WITH ME HERE, WHAT HAVE YOU GOT TO BE NERVOUS ABOUT?

MARTIN: OH, WHAT YOU SAID, THAT HELPED ME COOL DOWN. KEEP ON TALKING LIKE THAT, DARLING.

BONNIE: UH HUH, THE SHOES ARE OFF. THE SOCKS JUST SLIP OFF LIKE...THAT. WA-LAH, IT'S TIME FOR THE PANTS. THESE SUCKERS BETTER COME OFF QUICK, BECAUSE I DON'T THINK I CAN WAIT THAT LONG.

MARTIN: YOU CAN'T WAIT THAT LONG? CHRIST, YOU'RE DRIVING ME CRAZY, WOMAN. COME ON! TAKE THEM OFF!!

BONNIE: OK OK, HERE THEY ARE. THEY'RE OFF. ALL YOU GOT LEFT ON IS YOUR UNDERWEAR. BUT YOU'RE POPPING OUT OF THEM. I BETTER GET THEM OFF TOO.

MARTIN: WAIT, WAIT. BEFORE YOU TAKE OFF MY UNDERWEAR, TAKE YOURS OFF.

BONNIE: WHY?

MARTIN: I DON'T KNOW. I HEARD IT IN A PORNO FLICK ONCE.

BONNIE: OH, OK. HERE COMES! THE ROBE...THE G-STRING... LIKE IT?

MARTIN: OH GOD, YOU,..

BONNIE: GOD, YOU KNOW, YOUR FRIEND TOLD ME SOMETHING ABOUT YOU. HE TOLD ME THAT YOU WORRY TOO MUCH ABOUT EVERYTHING. HE TOLD ME TO REMIND YOU TO TAKE IT EASY. NOW I'M TELLING YOU TO TAKE EVERYTHING EASY. I'M GONNA GO INSIDE HERE AND SEE WHAT YOU GOT INSIDE THESE SHORTS. OOH, OOOH, IT FEELS LIKE SOMETHING SLIMY, AND LONG, AND BIG, AND HARD, AND WET. OH GOD, IS IT WET. AND IT'S OH, SO HAIRY. OOH, I JUST GOT TO FEEL IT ALL OVER. AW, OH, AH IT'S THE BEST THING I'VE FELT IN A LONG TIME. I CAN'T WAIT TO SEE THIS THING.

MARTIN: OOH MY GOD, OOH MY GOD, OH SHIT, OH SHIT!! OH, I LOVE THIS BUT I DON'T KNOW HOW MUCH I CAN TAKE..OH, BUT KEEP ON DOING IT. PLEASE, PLEASE, DON'T STOP DOING IT. OH, OOH.

BONNIE: YOU LITTLE WEEZEL. YOU LOVE IT, DON'T YOU?

MARTIN: YEH! YEH! YIPEE!!

BONNIE: WOW! I DID IT. I'M NOT AS DUMB AS I LOOK.

MARTIN: YOU DON'T LOOK DUMB. YOU DON'T LOOK ANYTHING BUT BEAUTIFUL.

BONNIE: GOD, YOU'RE A FLATTERER. DO YOU EVER STOP?

MARTIN: NO NEVER. IT'S THE ONLY WAY I HAVE TO KEEP PEOPLE STICKING AROUND ME.

BONNIE: WHAT DO YOU MEAN?

MARTIN: WELL, I DON'T KNOW. I'VE NEVER HAD THAT MUCH TO RECOMMEND ME. I MEAN, I'VE ALWAYS BEEN AFRAID OF LOSING FRIENDS. SO I FIGURE, IF I KEEP ON SAYING NICE THINGS, PEOPLE WILL KEEP COMING AROUND TO HEAR MORE. THEY WON'T BE RUNNING AWAY. I DON'T KNOW.

BONNIE: MARTY, YOU'RE A VERY NICE PERSON, BUT YOU DON'T HAVE TO KEEP PUTTING ON THE CHARM ALL THE TIME. I REALLY LIKE BEING AROUND YOU. YOU'RE A REALLY INTERESTING PERSON. YOU ARE ALSO PRETTY SEXY.

MARTIN: OH OH. HERE COME THE SPASMS AGAIN. YOU GOT ME WHEN YOU SAID THAT..

MARTIN: OH GOD, YOU'RE BEAUTIFUL. AND I'M NOT JUST FLATTERING YOU AGAIN. YOU'RE GONNA HAVE TO LET ME SCREAM OUT MY HORNINESS. GRRRROWL! GROWL! OH, COME HERE, WOMAN! OH! OH! LAY DOWN BESIDE ME. OH GOD, OH GOD!!

BONNIE: MY GOD, YOU'RE JUMPING ALL OVER THE PLACE, AREN'T YOU. PLEASE, MARTIN, I REALIZE YOU'RE BORED, BUT WOULD YOU MIND GETTING JUST A LITTLE BIT MORE EXCITED? I MEAN, REALLY,....

MARTIN: YOU MUST BE BULLSHITTING ME. YOU'RE MESSING WITH MY MIND, HONEY. I'M SPAZING OUT ALL OVER THE BED. I'M SO EXCITED, I'M GONNA BE ALL TIRED OUT IN A WHILE. I DON'T THINK I'LL MAKE IT THROUGH THIS NIGHT.

BONNIE: WELL, YOU GOT ME ALL NIGHT, MAN, YOU MIGHT AS WELL STICK AROUND, AND SEE HOW IT TURNS OUT. BUT RIGHT NOW, I HAVE TO RIP THESE SHORTS OFF YOU. LET ME SEE THIS GIGANTUOUS COCK OF YOURS. ... OH GOD, IS THAT BIG. GOD, IS THAT THING REALLY GOING IN ME? ALL OF IT? NOW, MARTY, YOU CAN'T HURT ME, YOU HEAR? I'M A NICE GIRL, REMEMBER?

YOU WOULDN'T HURT A NICE GIRL LIKE ME, WOULD YOU?

MARTIN: AH, YOU'RE KIDDING WITH ME. I BET YOU'VE HAD LOTS OF GUYS WHO WERE PACKING A LOT BIGGER RODS THAN THIS ONE, STICK IT TO YOU.

BONNIE: NO, MART, I THINK YOURS IS THE BIGGEST. I SWEAR. I JUST THINK YOU'RE SO SEXY. ALL I WANT TO DO IS HUG YOU AND SQUEEZE YOU TIGHT. OH---AH.

MARTIN: OH GOD, OH SHIT. I'M MOVING AROUND AGAIN. I CAN'T STAY STILL. OH, HOW CAN YOU PUT UP WITH ME??

BONNIE: IT'S EASY. NOW, COME ON, TAKE IT EASY. RELAX. JUST LET ME DO ALL THE WORK. WOULD IT BE NICE IF I WENT DOWN ON YOU?

MARTIN: DOES THAT MEA--UH, UH...

BONNIE: YEAH, DO YOU WANT ME TO?

MARTIN: UH, WELL SURE. WHY NOT? THAT WOULD FEEL GOOD.

BONNIE: OK. HUM, YUM YUM YUM. I'LL TELL YOU THE TRUTH, I HAVEN'T HAD ANYTHING TO EAT ALL DAY. AND THIS IS MIGHTY TASTY. YUMMY YUMMY.

MARTIN: AW, YOU POOR THING. DON'T THEY FEED YOU?

BONNIE: WELL YOU SEE, I HAVE TO WATCH MY FIGURE, HA HA. HEY MARTY, WHY ARE YOUR ARMS MOVING LIKE THAT? THEY'RE FLYING ALL AROUND.

MARTIN: WELL, SEE, YOU'RE DOWN THERE, AND I WANT TO BE STILL FOR YOU. SO I'M TRYING TO MOVE ALL MY INVOLUNTARY MOVEMENTS UP TO THE TOP PART OF MY BODY. IT'S ALL VERY COMPLICATED. IT ALL SUCKS WHEN YOU GET RIGHT DOWN TO IT. BUT, WHAT THE HELL. JUST, WHENEVER YOU SEE ME MAKE ANY OF THESE WEIRD MOVEMENTS, REALIZE THAT I'M TRYING TO CONTROL THEM. I'M TRYING TO CALM DOWN. OK, HONEYBUNCH?

BONNIE: OK, HONEYBUNCH. NOW, WHAT DID YOU SAY ABOUT 'SUCKING'?

MARTIN: WHAT?? OH.. OH, HA HA HA!! OH MY GOD! WHAT ARE YOU DOING?? YOU'RE GONNA BITE IT OFF.. YOU'RE GONNA BITE IT OFF!!

BONNIE: UH NO, IT'S ALL ATTACHED. I'M JUST ENJOYING MYSELF DOWN HERE. THIS IS LIKE LICKING ON AN ALL DAY LOLLI-POP. I'LL NEVER FINISH IT.

MARTIN: YOU COULD SPEND ALL DAY TRYING, BABY, IT'S ALRIGHT WITH ME.

BONNIE: AND THESE LEGS ARE SO NICE TO FEEL, AND TO RUB, AND VERY CONVENIENT TO SIT BETWEEN.

MARTIN: OH. GOD, YOU WOULDN'T BELIEVE WHAT YOU ARE DOING TO ME.

BONNIE: OH, BUT I CAN TRY. I SEE HOW EXCITED YOU ARE. WOULD YOU LIKE ME TO STOP?

MARTIN: SHIT NO. I DON'T CARE IF I SPAZ MYSELF TO DEATH TONIGHT. I KNOW I'D GO SMILING.

BONNIE: WELL, I'M TELLING YOU, DARLING, I NEED YOU WITH ME ALL NIGHT. THERE'S A LOT MORE OF YOU TO NIBBLE ON.

MARTIN: I THINK I'LL MAKE IT TIL AT LEAST 4-30 OR 5. NO PROBLEM.

BONNIE: OH THEN, IF I ONLY HAVE THAT LONG, I BETTER MOVE ON UP YOUR BODY JUST AS FAST AS I CAN.

MARTIN: YOU KNOW, THAT'S NOT A HELL OF A BAD IDEA.

BONNIE: YEAH, I THINK I'LL JUST STRETCH MY WHOLE BODY OUT LIKE THIS SO THAT I'M COMPLETELY ON TOP OF YOU. THERE....AM I SMOTHERING YOU? CAN YOU BREATHE?

MARTIN: OH YEAH. THIS--THIS IS FINE. CHRIST, YOU'RE TRAPPING ME SO TIGHT HERE, I COULDN'T MOVE IF I TRIED.

BONNIE: WELL GOOD, THEN YOU'RE JUST WHERE I WANT YOU. GR- RRR-ROWL-ROWLLL!!! MAKE LOVE TO ME, PASSIONATE MAN, DR. PASSION. WHAT ARE YOU WAITING FOR? HUH? HUH?

MARTIN: OHH! OHH!! GOD HELP ME. I DON'T THINK I CAN MAKE IT!

BONNIE: WHERE'S THAT COCKER OF YOURS? STICK IT IN ME. COME ON, ARE YOU A MAN OR NOT? CAN YOU PLEASE A VALUMPTUOUS WOMAN LIKE ME OR NOT! HUH? HUH?? ARE YOU NINE-TEEN OR WHAT? HUH??

MARTIN: HOW DID YOU KNOW I WAS NINE TEEN?

BONNIE: I KNOW EVERYTHING. NOW, SHUT UP AND DO YOUR THING.. COME ON!

MARTIN: UH, HONEY, UH, WOULD YOU MIND, UH, HELPING THE OLD WEINER TO, UH, I MEAN, WOULD YOU DIRECT IT TO WHERE IT HAS TO GO?

BONNIE: WHAT? DO I HAVE TO DO EVERYTHING AROUND HERE?? GOD--DAMN! CAN'T YOU DO ANYTHING FOR YOURSELF?

MARTIN: UH, YOU'RE ABOUT TO FIND THAT OUT. WOO, WHOOA. I DON'T THINK I CAN WAIT MUCH LONGER. ... NO, NO, I CAN'T. HONEY, YOU'RE ABOUT TO GET IT...A VERY SPECIAL PACKAGE. OH SHIT. OH SHIT!

BONNIE: YOU MEAN, IT'S COMING??

MARTIN: I DO BELIEVE I'M STARTING TO PUMP. YES, YES. HERE WE GO. I DO BELIEVE THIS IS WHAT WE'RE ALL HERE FOR. ... BINGO!!!

BONNIE: OH MART, I LOVE YOU. I LOVE YOU.

MARTIN: UH, WAS---WAS THAT---WHAT IT WAS SUPPOSED TO BE?

BONNIE: OH, OF COURSE. IF YOU ENJOYED IT, IT WAS ALL RIGHT. IT WAS ALL IT WAS SUPPOSED TO BE.

MARTIN: WELL--DID YOU ENJOY IT?

BONNIE: OF COURSE. IT WAS WONDERFUL, ABSOLUTELY PERFECT. YOU'RE A WONDERFUL LOVER. DIDN'T YOU THINK IT WOULD BE ALRIGHT?

MARTIN: WELL, I DON'T KNOW. I KNOW WHAT THIS MOMENT MEANS TO ME. I'LL NEVER FORGET IT FOR THE REST OF MY LIFE. BUT, UH. I'D LIKE TO KNOW---I'D JUST LIKE TO KNOW IF YOU GOT ANYTHING OUT OF IT.

BONNIE: WILL YOU STOP BEING SILLY. THAT'S CRAZY. LISTEN TO ME. COULDN'T YOU TELL? COULDN'T YOU SEE IT IN MY EYES? IT WAS BEAUTIFUL FOR ME. IT WAS PROBABLY THE BEST IT'S EVER BEEN FOR ME. I LOVED IT. LISTEN, YOU REALLY LOOK ALL TIRED OUT. I'VE NEVER SEEN YOU SO STILL. WHY DON'T WE JUST STAY STILL FOR A WHILE? NICE AND QUIET. LET'S JUST LAY STILL. THAT'S IT. GO TO SLEEP.

MARTIN: HI.
BONNIE: HI. WHERE DID YOU COME FROM?
MARTIN: I DON'T KNOW...OUTER SPACE. WHERE DID YOU COME FROM?
BONNIE: HONEY, I'VE BEEN HERE ALL NIGHT, DREAMING 'BOUT YOU.
MARTIN: REALLY?
BONNIE: REALLY, BABY.
MARTIN: I WAS DREAMING ABOUT YOU TOO. HEY, WHAT DID YOU DREAM ABOUT?
BONNIE: I DREAMED THAT I HAD JUST MET...PRINCE CHARMING. AND THAT HE CAME RIDING UP TO ME ON A GREAT WHITE HORSE. AND HE GOT DOWN OFF HIS HORSE, AND HE TOOK ME IN HIS ARMS, AND HE MADE PASSIONATE LOVE TO ME FOREVER. ... AND THEN WE FELL ASLEEP, OR WE DID SOMETHING LIKE THAT. I DUNNO...
MARTIN: AH. AH. HOW LONG DID WE SLEEP?
BONNIE: OH, ABOUT AN HOUR, AN HOUR AND A HALF. HEY, YOU DIDN'T TELL ME WHAT YOU WERE DREAMING ABOUT ME.
MARTIN: OH, I DREAMED THAT I WAS THIS VERY, VERY UGLY FROG, AND SUDDENLY THIS VERY BEAUTIFUL LADY KISSED ME. AND MY WHOLE LIFE WAS CHANGED. I WASN'T UGLY ANY MORE. I WAS THIS GREAT BIG HANDSOME PRINCE, AND I HAD EVERYTHING I HAD EVER WANTED.

BONNIE: AW, YOU'RE FOOLING ME.

MARTIN: NO NO, THAT'S WHAT I DREAMED. ARE--ARE YOU FOOLING ABOUT DREAMING ABOUT ME?

BONNIE: NO. WHY WOULD I DO THAT? SILLY, THAT'S EXACTLY WHAT JUST HAPPENED. I'VE JUST MADE LOVE TO THE MOST BEAUTIFUL MAN IN THE WORLD. AND RIGHT NOW, I'M LYING RIGHT BESIDE HIM. AND I SURE WOULD LIKE IT IF HE WOULD PUT HIS ARM AROUND ME. DO YOU THINK YOU COULD? I'LL HELP YOU.

MARTIN: OK. FIRST I HAVE TO LIFT MY ARM THIS WAY. THEN SWING IT OVER.

BONNIE: OK, YOU'RE DOING FINE. ... OUCH!!

MARTIN: OH GOD, WHAT DID I DO? SHIT, IT HIT YOU IN THE EYE. OH GOD, I DIDN'T MEAN TO. OH GOD. ARE YOU ALRIGHT?

BONNIE: YEAH YEAH. I'M FINE. IT'S FINE. I KNOW YOU DIDN'T MEAN TO. JUST HOLD ME. HOLD ME TIGHT. ...OH, NOT THAT TIGHT.

MARTIN: WHY? AM I HURTING YOU? STRANGLING YOU?

BONNIE: JUST A LITTLE. BUT RIGHT NOW IT'S OK. THAT'S FINE. THAT'S PERFECT. AHH...

MARTIN: YOU REALIZE THAT SOMETIMES MY MUSCLES GET TIGHT, AND I CAN LOSE CONTROL OF MY ARMS.

BONNIE: YEAH, I KNOW, I KNOW. EVERYTHING'S ALRIGHT. I UNDERSTAND. IT MUST BE FRUSTRATING.

MARTIN: YEAH. SOMETIMES, I THINK THAT MY LIFE IS TOTALLY DIFFERENT FROM EVERYBODY ELSE'S. NOBODY COULD POSSIBLY HAVE IT AS BAD AS I DO. NOBODY GOES THROUGH THE SHIT THAT I DO. I MEAN, NOBODY EVEN THINKS THE SAME THOUGHTS THAT I DO. THEY DON'T HAVE TO WORRY ABOUT THEIR BODIES MOVING WHEN THEY DON'T WANT TO. SOMETIMES, I THINK THAT I'M NOT HUMAN. I MIGHT BE MORE THAN HUMAN, OR I MIGHT BE SUB-HUMAN. BUT I JUST CAN'T BE THE SAME. I JUST KNOW I CAN'T BE THE SAME AS ALL THE OTHER PEOPLE IN THE WORLD. I JUST CAN'T BE.

BONNIE: WOW. YOU THINK STRANGE THINGS. YOU REALLY DO. BUT I GUESS YOU'RE RIGHT. IN YOUR OWN LITTLE WAY, YOU'RE RIGHT.

MARTIN: YOU KNOW, IT'S JUST HARD TO EXPLAIN IT ALL TO OTHER PEOPLE. THEY WONDER WHY I'M SO STRANGE. "BUT IF I SEEM TO ACT UNKIND, IT'S ONLY ME, IT'S NOT MY MIND THAT IS CONFUSING THINGS. SOMETIMES I WISH I KNEW YOU WELL. THEN I COULD SPEAK MY MIND AND TELL YOU. MAYBE YOU'D UNDERSTAND."

BONNIE: WOW! THAT IS REAL POETIC...

MARTIN: IT'S ALSO GEORGE HARRISON OFF THE REVOLVER ALBUM, BUT WHAT THE HELL.

BONNIE: WELL, TELL ME MORE.

MARTIN: "I WANT TO TELL YOU, I'M ALL FUCKED UP BUT I DON'T KNOW WHY. I DON'T MIND I COULD WAIT FOREVER. I GOT TIME."

BONNIE: I GOT LOADS OF TIME, HONEY. HEY, WOULD YOU LIKE TO DO IT AGAIN? FROM THE LOOKS OF THINGS, YOU COULD HANDLE ANOTHER GO-AROUND.

MARTIN: YOU MEAN---

BONNIE: YEAH MAN. COME ON, I'M HUNGRY AGAIN. YOU MIGHT AS WELL GET YOUR MONEY'S WORTH...ONLY KIDDING. COME ON, TIGER. I THINK YOU'RE READY FOR AN ENCORE.

MARTIN: WHAT DO YOU THINK I AM, A DYNAMO?

BONNIE: I ONLY KNOW WHAT I SEE, AND I SEE SOMETHING GROWING DOWN THERE SLOWLY BUT SURELY. MAYBE I CAN HELP IT ALONG WITH A LITTLE HAND JIVE...OH, YEAH, OH YEAH...AH, YOU'RE WAKING UP. YOU'RE COMING BACK TO LIFE. WATCH THOSE ARMS FLY. OH GOD, WE GOT A LOT OF ACTION OUT OF HIM NOW! OH YEAH...

MARTIN: HA HA HA!! WHAT THE HELL ARE YOU DOING TO ME? HA HA! YOU KNOW, THESE ARMS CAN DO JUST A FEW MORE THINGS RATHER THAN FLY AROUND AND GO WILD. YOU NEVER KNOW WHAT PART OF THE BODY THIS HAND IS GONNA GO FOR NEXT...

BONNIE: EW EW! OOH OOH!! YOU TRICKER. YOU DEVIL! YOU'RE A WILD MAN, YOU KNOW THAT? I GOTTA WATCH OUT FOR YOU!

MARTIN: HEY, YOU KNOW, YOU HAD A NIBBLE, A BIT TO EAT. BUT I HAVEN'T. WHAT'S DOWN HERE FOR ME TO CHEW ON?? OH WAIT. I THINK I SEE SOMETHING. IT'S REAL BLACK, BUT I THINK IT'S EDIBLE...

BONNIE: YOU DIRTY THING. I CAN'T BELIEVE WHAT YOU'RE SAYING.

MARTIN: YOU KNOW, THEY SAY WHEN I WANT TO, I CAN REALLY STICK THIS TONGUE OUT PRETTY FAR... GEE, DO YOU HAVE ANY MUSTARD FOR THIS?

BONNIE: MARTY! YOU'RE BEING OBSCENE! ... AND I LOVE IT. GO AHEAD, BABY, LICK YOUR HEART OUT. OH!! OOH OOH OOH!!

MARTIN: OH---GOD, THIS IS WEARING ME OUT. I THINK I'LL GO TO SLEEP RIGHT HERE. GOOD NIGHT. ... OH, MAYBE I'LL CRAWL UP HERE A LITTLE FARTHER ON THIS STOMACH HERE, THIS LOVELY LITTLE TUMMY, WITH THE BELLY BUTTON THAT GOES INNIE TO OUTTIE, JUST LIKE THAT. HOW ABOUT THAT? HOT DAMN... WELL, GOODNIGHT. ... OH, MAYBE I'LL JUST MOVE ON UP JUST A LITTLE BIT FARTHER, AND CLIMB THESE TWO MOUNTAINS UP HERE. HUH? HUH? I WONDER IF I CAN CLIMB THAT HIGH, EH? THINK I CAN MAKE IT? EH?

BONNIE: GET THE HELL UP HERE AND STOP SCREWING AROUND. KISS ME, YOU FOOL. KISS ME, YOU ASSHOLE!

MARTIN: OH, BONNIE, HOLD ON TO ME. THIS ONE IS GONNA BE EVEN BETTER THAN BEFORE.

BONNIE: I KNOW. MARTY, I THINK I'M IN LOVE WITH YOU.

MARTIN: YES, TONIGHT, WE'RE IN LOVE.

BONNIE: YES. IT'S ONLY FOR TONIGHT, I KNOW. I LOVE YOU.

MARTIN: I LOVE YOU...

BONNIE: WHAT IS THIS 150 POUND LUG DOING LAYING ON TOP OF ME??

MARTIN: I THINK WE FELL ASLEEP AGAIN.
BONNIE: BUT, BOY, DID WE GO WITH A BANG.
MARTIN: CHRIST, THAT WAS NICE.
BONNIE: IT WAS, IT WAS! ... UH, MARTY, CAN I TELL YOU SOMETHING? ... LAST NIGHT WAS THE FIRST TIME I DID IT, AND I ENJOYED IT. I'VE BEEN WITH MEN, MORE MEN THAN I WANT TO COUNT. IT'S MY JOB, IT'S MY LIFE. BUT I NEVER GOT ANYTHING OUT OF IT. IT WAS ALWAYS PAINFUL, JUST PAINFUL. WHEN I GOT TO KNOW YOU, ALL MY FEARS ABOUT BEING HURT WERE GONE. I KNEW YOU WEREN'T TO USE ME. I THOUGHT THAT FINALLY I WOULD BE ABLE TO ENJOY IT, AND I DID. I DID. IT MUST MEAN I LOVE YOU. YOU DO SOMETHING FOR ME. I'M FALLING IN LOVE, FOR THE FIRST TIME IN MY LIFE, WITH YOU.
MARTIN: CAN I CUT IN HERE FOR A SECOND, AND SAY A COUPLE THINGS?
BONNIE: SURE, HONEY.
MARTIN: FIRST OF ALL, YOU HAVE NO IDEA HOW GREAT IT FEELS FOR ME TO ACTUALLY SAY THAT YOU CAN RETURN MY LOVE. IT'S ALWAYS BEEN A GAME OF ONE SIDED FEELINGS WITH ME AND GIRLS. I'M ALWAYS GLAD THAT THEY ARE WILLING TO BE WITH ME, BUT THEY REALLY CAN'T WAIT TO LEAVE ME WHEN THE NIGHT IS OVER. IT'S NOT A NICE FEELING, BUT UP TO NOW, I'VE BEEN ABLE TO DEAL WITH IT. THIS EXPERIENCE HERE WITH YOU HAS MEANT MORE TO ME THAN ANYTHING ELSE IN THE WORLD. I LOVE YOU, AND I LOVE THIS NIGHT FOR EVERYTHING IT'S DONE FOR ME. I TURNED NINE TEEN.
BONNIE: YOU KNOW WHAT ELSE YOU DID?
MARTIN: WHAT?
BONNIE: YOU TURNED INTO A HUMAN...YOU'RE NO MORE, NO LESS. NOW YOU ARE-
MARTIN: A HUMAN.
BONNIE: A HUMAN. ... MART, I WANT TO SEE YOU AGAIN. I'M NEVER GONNA FORGET YOU.

MARTIN: YES YOU WILL. OF COURSE YOU WILL. YOU DO THIS ALL THE TIME. YOU JUST SAID, THIS IS YOUR JOB.

BONNIE: BUT MART, I TOLD YOU, THIS WAS DIFFERENT. THIS WAS VERY DIFFERENT. I LOVE YOU.

MARTIN: I THINK YOU LOVE THE IDEA OF ME.

BONNIE: WHAT? WHAT DOES THAT MEAN?

MARTIN: WELL, I'M MORE OF AN IDEA THAN ANYTHING ELSE. IF YOU JUST MADE LOVE TO A HANDICAPPED PERSON, YOU WAVE HELLO TO A HANDICAPPED PERSON. THERE'S ONE IN YOUR NEIGHBORHOOD. IT'S ALL THE SAME.

BONNIE: MART, YOU CAN'T FEEL THAT WAY. YOU'RE A VERY REMARKABLE PERSON, AND WE SHARED SOMETHING VERY SPECIAL. YOU HAVE TO KNOW THAT. YOU SAID IT YOURSELF. ... MART, WHAT'S THE REAL REASON YOU DON'T WANT TO SEE ME ANYMORE?

MARTIN: I DIDN'T SAY I DIDN'T WANT TO SEE YOU ANYMORE.

BONNIE: THAT'S WHAT YOU'RE IMPLYING. I'M INTERESTED IN HAVING A RELATIONSHIP WITH YOU, AND YOU'RE BACKING AWAY. WHY?

MARTIN: YOU'RE--YOU KNOW...YOU'RE A--UH...

BONNIE: I'M A PROSTITUTE.

MARTIN: WELL YEAH. I MEAN, I SHOULDN'T BE HERE. NO ONE IS EVER GONNA KNOW I WAS HERE. I COME FROM A NICE FAMILY. I WENT TO A NICE SCHOOL. I'M NOT SUPPOSED TO BE DOING THIS KIND OF THING.

BONNIE: WELL THEN, WHY THE HELL DID YOU EVER COME HERE? AND WHY DID YOUR FRIEND CALL ON ME TO HELP YOU OUT? IF YOU GOT SUCH A NICE LIFE, WHY DIDN'T YOU GET IT FROM ONE OF YOUR NICE GIRLFRIENDS?

MARTIN: BECAUSE I'M A SPASTIC, DAMN IT. NOT MANY PEOPLE WANNA GET TOO NEAR ME, ESPECIALLY YOUNG GIRLS. DO YOU THINK IT'S EASY?

BONNIE: DO YOU THINK IT'S EASY FOR ME? DAMN IT. DO YOU THINK I LIKE IT HERE? DO YOU THINK I WANT TO

BE HERE? I GOT A KID, DAMN IT. I HAD TO QUIT HIGH SCHOOL. GOD, I'M ONLY ABOUT SIX MONTHS OLDER THAN YOU. I WASN'T BULLSHITTING WHEN I SAID I LIKED YOU...I LOVED YOU. YOU ARE THE YOUNGEST GUY EVER TO COME IN HERE. ALL I GET ARE OLDER GUYS WHO ARE LOOKING FOR CHEAP THRILLS. IT STINKS. I LIVE ON TOP OF THIS CLUB IN A SMALL ROOM WITH MY KID. SHE CALLS FOR ME AT NIGHT. BUT I CAN'T GO TO HER. I'M TOO BUSY SCREWING BASTARDS LIKE YOU. GODDAMN, I'M MORE HANDICAPPED THAN YOU ARE. FORGET I SAID THAT. ... IT'S MORNING NOW, IT'S ABOUT SEVEN O'CLOCK. I'M GONNA CALL YOUR FRIEND AND TELL HIM TO GET YOU DRESSED. GOODBY. I DON'T WANT TO BE AROUND YOU ANYMORE.

GOD, I HATE GETTING UP EARLY ON A SATURDAY MORNING. BUT SURE ENOUGH, I WAS THERE BRIGHT AND SHINY AT SEVEN SHARP. NOBODY WAS AT THE BAR WITH ME, NOT EVEN A BARTENDER. BUT I SAT PATIENTLY, WAITING FOR SOME SIGN FROM THE BACK ROOM.

SUDDENLY, BONNIE CAME RUSHING OUT, LOOKING LIKE SHE HAD DRESSED IN AN AWFUL HURRY. AND SHE WAS RUBBING HER EYES LIKE SHE WAS CRYING OR SOMETHING. BUT SHE WAS VERY SHORT WITH ME. SHE HANDED ME SOMETHING AND SAID, „GO PICK UP YOUR FRIEND."

I WENT INTO THE ROOM BACK THERE AND I SAW MART JUST LYING THERE, LOOKING AT NOTHING, DOING NOTHING, JUST LYING THERE.

LES: WHAT HAPPENED, MART?
MARTIN: LET'S GET OUT OF HERE.
LES: BUT WHAT HAPPENED?

MARTIN: LOOK, PUT MY CLOTHES ON, PUT ME IN MY CHAIR, AND LET'S GET OUT OF HERE.

I SAW THAT HE WAS PISSED OFF ABOUT SOMETHING, AND I KNEW HIM WELL ENOUGH NOT TO ASK ANY FURTHER QUESTIONS. SO I DID AS HE ASKED AND I PUSHED HIM OUT OF THE ROOM.

AS WE PASSED THE BAR ON OUR WAY OUTSIDE, HE SAW BONNIE STANDING AT A FAROFF CORNER OFF THE JOINT. THERE WAS NO WAVE OR GOODBY OR ANYTHING FROM EITHER OF THEM, JUST TWO BLANK STARES. SO I PUSHED HIM OUT THE DOOR.

WE WERE IN THE CAR, HALFWAY HOME WHEN I FINALLY REMEMBERED WHAT BONNIE HAD HANDED ME.

LES: UH, SHE GAVE ME THIS ENVELOPE BEFORE WE LEFT. DO YOU WANT ME TO OPEN IT?

NO ANSWER.

LES: OK, I'LL OPEN IT. .... HEY MART, IT'S OUR SEVENTY BUCKS BACK. THERE'S A NOTE. WANT ME TO READ IT?

NO ANSWER. I READ IT TO HIM.

HAPPY BIRTHDAY, MARTY. I'LL NEVER FORGET YOU.

                    I LOVE YOU,
                    BONNIE

The Taking Care Of Dr. Dinn

His family was gathering for dinner. Someone had just returned from Chicken George's with everybody's meal. Tonight was the midpoint of their week long vacation at his sister's condominium in Ocean City. Everybody was in different stages of discomfort and irritability with other members of the family. But things were to be expected, and all things considered, this was the start of a pleasant evening.

His family was seated. He had a brother and a sister. His brother was ten years older than he, a thirty year old attorney. He had a date to go play miniature golf so he ate in a hurry and left in the middle of the meal. His sister was a thirtytwo year old physician. She was beginning to be unhappily married and she had two little girls. His father was at the happy stage of thinking about retirement. He had had angina for approximately eighteen years. His mother always fed him at the dinner table, and she lived for her family. The two little girls had already eaten and were playing in the bedroom hallway. And his brother-in-law had been sulking out on the terrace reading a book by Bob Woodward for most of the week. He had always had psychological problems and everyone was aware of it.

The conversation was nonconsequential, but interesting. It began with discussions about everybody's plans for after dinner. It detoured into some of the high school remembrances of the older children. He got agitated whenever his mother allowed her attention to be strayed from appropriately feeding him and keeping his mouth and chin dry. He was always hungry at dinnertime, and he always held it socially important to eat as neatly as possible. He remotely participated in most lively conversations unless he had something important to contribute or something involved or interested him.

Something interested him as his sister and mother talked about Sue Cannele expecting her third child. Sue had gone to high school with his sister and she had always been a laughing friend around the house. And Sue's wedding was still fresh on his mind. That was about two years ago during the fun days of his senior year of high school. He remembered that as being the last and probably the only time he met an interested woman at a wedding reception. The woman was at least five years older than he and she worked in the office with the guy that Sue married. It was just a nice memory from high school senior days and it put him in a good mood.

And he dove into his mother's space again to get another mouthful, and the subject was still Sue's pregnancy. His sister was saying that Sue had chosen Dr. Dinn for her obstetrician and it was emphasized. More than an eyebrow was raised by his mother and his father cleared his throat and made a smart comment which was understood by no one at the table. His mother had a habit of asking and annoying his father to repeat or expand upon many of his smart and misunderstood comments. But before she could ask her predictable question, something else was asked.

His sister asked his mother when was the last time she had seen Dr. Dinn. His mother said not for many years and she didn't even know that he was still in practice. Then his mother repeated the question to her daughter. And she answered her mother that she hadn't seen Dr. Dinn in at least eight years since she studied under him for a few weeks and worked on his ward. None of those at the table who knew Dr. Dinn had any praising words for him and this was what was so interesting.

"Why doesn't anybody like Dr. Dinn?"

His sister said something out the side of her mouth. It was a joke addressed to no one in particular. She asked how anyone could be fond of anyone with as poor a track record as Dr. Dinn. After what he's done.

"What has he done? What did he do?"

He had to ask this question a couple of different times in a couple of different ways because he had a habit of making his most obvious questions just a slight complicated and hard to understand which always made him seem melodramatic which really wasn't always his fault. After everyone at the table did understand his question they mostly dodged it because they, especially his father, had a habit of teasing him. His father said as if he had taken a consensus of all those present who knew Dr. Dinn that they didn't exactly approve of his method of childbirth or of his record of delivery. Then his mother made an attempt to appease him and she added that Dr. Dinn wasn't one of the family's favorite people and they never cared to talk about him too much.

Now Dr. Dinn was beginning to sound like a familiar name out of the past like some old gent who might have once had a run in with his Grandmother. Maybe he offended her at one of her ladies social meetings. Or maybe Dr. Dinn might have once offended his mother at his office during an appointment with one of her children and he made her cry, and after this long she still can't talk about it. Yes, now something like that was coming back to him. And he figured that stories about people who have offended either his Grandmother or his mother could always be interesting. And he was finished his chicken and he was in a joking talkative mood. So he decided to find out.

"Why don't we like Dr. Dinn? Come now, how bad can it be?"
His sister asked him emphatically if he was sure he didn't know. His mother started to clear the table and had no reason to speak to the matter. And his father didn't care at all about the continuing conversation at the table and got up to take and read his newspaper in the living room.

"Yeah I'm sure. What's wrong with the guy? What did he do?"

His sister answered him directly in his eyes, he delivered you.

This just seemed like a joke. He got the connection that everyone had been teasing him all the time, and the big catastrophe that they were so upset about was only the event of himself being born.

Well he thought it was a rather unusual joke and especially for having gone on for so long. After all everyone at the table had been going along with it including his mother who never took part in jokes about how much she valued one of her children. And they had all kept such straight faces. And they were keeping these straight faces even now when he took it that the joke and laugh had been completed.

But then he noticed that no one had really been laughing. And his sister was actually telling no joke at all. And she hadn't really taken her eyes off of him after she made the comment about Dr. Dinn delivering him because she evidently still had more to say about it.

She continued talking mainly to his mother. She went on to admit her wonder and anger over the fact that Dr. Dinn was still practicing and indeed asking why he shouldn't have been questioned for his competency many years ago. His mother had to be pried into sharing her opinion. She made only a few comments which were very typical of the righteous woman she was. She said quietly that it wasn't her place to criticize the man or question his abilities after this long. Then she said that she wasn't sure in her heart or in her mind whether or not he was actually at blame.

At this he remained completely confused. As usually he showed this facially, but it was better for him to be quiet and listen.

His sister was drinking her third glass of wine. This good woman deserved three glasses of wine whenever she would wisely choose to consume. She was an excellent physician, a dedicated oncologist, she had a rotten husband and she had two demanding small children who seldom let her rest too easy. Yet now still seated at her dining table facing only him and addressing mostly his mother her words were coming out much too freely. Her argument began to show her complete disregard and lack of professional respect for Dr. Dinn. And she hoped to prove to his mother that she had definitely been wronged by Dr. Dinn.

She was very sincere and frank. She said that there should have been an inquiry and investigation after the delivery. She told with absolute certainty of her findings more than eight years ago when she examined the records of Mercy Hospital during the time when she was an intern there. She would make it very clear in any testimony that Dr. Dinn was obviously negligent in the pre-procedure and in the actual delivery. Dr. Dinn had arrived too late having not even been on the way to the hospital when his mother had arrived and was about to be prepped. The man knew that the woman was going to give birth within a matter of days. She had had a perfectly normal pregnancy but still she was approaching forty and should have been watched with the utmost care. He had said a few days after the birth that he had been out of the state for most of that day, and the day before and he had only returned to his home a half hour before he was called by the hospital. And he might have even been unavailable when he was called earlier. His sister's convictions were strong.

And he was devastated.

His mother did more dishes. Occasionally she questioned his sister about her access and the validity of her statements to which his sister verified everything that she had said with the authority she naturally had. Then his mother questioned whether every point his sister was making would say that Dr. Dinn was actually guilty of negligence or malpractice. His sister would not break her position. His sister said to his mother that she should have sued Dr. Dinn just as soon as she found out that there was something wrong with the kid.

And he was devastated. He had just been given something great to think about.

His mother would always have the last word. She'd make sure that she did by prolonging a discussion long enough over some seemingly nonrelevant point until everyone became exhausted with the entire topic and wished she'd shut up and get her voice off their nerves. Her righteousness usually was the cause of the exhaustion. And she explained in more ways than she had to that she and his father would have never have sued a doctor for such a set of circumstances. She called legal and public retribution sometimes unchristian. And certainly his birth and his presence on earth as one of God's children was a miracle and wondrous beyond any thought of question. She said that she and his father would never think of libeling a doctor.

His sister told his mother that she was full of bullshit. So his mother explained her simple position in a few more ways.

And he had something great to think about.

And when he had something that he wanted to say it was hardly heard by his family who talked much more and much louder than he could. But what he had to say was going to make his mind a seesaw for a long time. And his family could not help him then because no one actually understood him. He said, "You mean, I'm not really doing this for God? The doctor was just fucked up?"

He doesn't talk too much because his speech is imperfect. He is a writer. He is a very young and hard working well intentional poet and story teller. He will only write things that are introspective. He'll always take somebody's point of view. And he has been becoming aware and proud of the narrow track of values and standards with which he takes his writing. He is a neurotic person because this philosophy and type of personality can only satisfy a person's appeal to dignity about fortyfive minutes out of every hour.

Almost all of the greatest things that he has ever said he has written. So he has been a better friend to people who have read him than to people who haven't.

In the early days of his career which had officially started three years prior to the time he is being examined, he wrote very much about himself. Everything he wrote was about himself. The first piece in which he took any pride came to him as a mainstreamed student in a biology class. He had written a seven page movie script about the entire meaning of his existence as he was proud to see it.

The play was an explanation of his nervousness and anxiety over his involuntary motions and the irregularity of his breathing whenever he wanted to be quiet such as in a classroom or a theater. The message was very self satisfying and not very important. But it was the greatest thing he had ever done. He had actually created a whole scenario of himself that was all his own and was in nobody else's words. He liked it so much he wrote it again. And this time he began it with his actual birth. God was the narrator of the whole work. And he believed every word of what he was writing.

God was busy at the manicurist and failed to oversee the entire procedure of his birth. God said, oh damn and oh shit a few times, but that was about the extent of his apology. From then on God was his best friend, and his life was just like a very hard exam that nobody crammed for, and everyone sort of had to sweat it out together. This was a well working truth for the man born on March second in nineteen-sixtytwo with Athetoid Cerebral Palsy because oxygen had been trapped from entering his brain. He had written his own Genesis.

The beginning stages for his doctrine must have come on a Sunday when he was no more than seven. His father wished to start taking him to church on a regular basis but he could recognize his smallness among the pews and the people and the priest. So his father started him off with a bird's eye view of it all. They sat in the sacristy looking out at the rear of the mass. This was cool for a kid. The words and songs made even less sense to this simple minded seven year old because all the voices were muffled. But at least he could feel part of the show backstage. And he had his father all to himself for a whole hour every week. And he could talk to him about whatever he wanted. Sometimes they'd talk about God.

"Dad, why do you think I'm handicapped?"

His father told him that there must be a reason. God must have had a reason. He wanted him to be still and sit around all day so he could think better thoughts than anybody else could.

His father asked him if that made any sense to him. His father asked him if he could live with that. And so he sat back, ignored mostly everything for the rest of that day and thought about it.

He never really stopped thinking about it. Athetoid Cerebral Palsy was after all a very large part of who he was. And mostly every day and mostly every hour he needed some sort of answer to it. And so the answer grew everyday that he grew. The question might have become a far distant relative who only wrote now and then whenever things got tough. But the answer became his twin brother. He hardly spoke to it because he knew just what it would reply. And when his imperfect uncontrollable stupid handicapped body grimaced when he spoke or stiffened when he gave a command to relax, the answer took over for him and made it all alright.

And he was so cute. He was so easy to introduce to his brother's folk group and to the priests in the sacristy. He wasn't hard to understand. He hadn't thought of anything important to say yet. He just enjoyed being cute. And he liked school. And he liked music. And he knew about all the TV shows. And when he was mainstreamed to a regular junior high school he got the best marks in the whole school and nobody was really surprised. Then he went to La Salle High School and became the obnoxious stupid punk that he always deserved to be. But his parents and his relatives and all the people in the church congregation just closed their eyes to his behavior and said, oh my, isn't it great that he has come so far; they might even be able to put him in some kind of college and find him a place to live one day.

During all that time he was always able to occupy himself one way or another.

And now thirteen years later at the dining table of his sister's condominium in Ocean City Maryland he was being told things about his birth which the nearest people knew and accepted for a very long time but of which he was completely ignorant. And a moment of stun and probably some silent soliloquy was thrusted upon him with no warning. He was given the dilemma. He had to create the question.

This was his attempt: Well shit, was the entire path he had chosen to try to become a mature rational person with a strong belief about who he was and what he was actually meant to be through all stages in his life, all of the foundational conscious thought that has by now been buried and overtoned by emerging personality traits and personal experiences and insight from all he's seen all these years and all the people he's met and all the things he's thought and all the people he's ever been, all that stuff that kept him going to church with his parents every week, the belief that God was listening to him whenever he talked to himself, all that stuff that he has kept like the first sentence in one of his books, all that was bullshit?

He wanted someone he could turn to and share the question right then and there. Not that he thought that anyone outside of him would be able to give a satisfactory reply to it, or even for that matter to understand what the hell he was talking about, but as he received such a large and meaningful impact on his thought and on his mood, he really wanted to share it immediately.

His mother was still in the kitchen speaking on the phone with his aunt who vacationed all year at the condominium building next to theirs. His sister wasn't going to talk to him anymore because it was time for her to take care of her children and to decide how to handle his brother-in-law who suddenly came in from out on the terrace and was childishly demanding something to eat.

So he had been left alone at the dining table with nothing really to observe except an obscure view of the ocean. He began to conceive of the story that could be written about this new discovery of the conditions surrounding his birth and about his reactions to it. He should have been in front of a typewriter. His best work was created in times of crisis and moments of great introspection. He'd written piece upon piece about how his life had become so hard and depressing ever since he had reached the age where all of his friends and peers were having sexual intercourse and he for some reason wasn't getting any at all. Through his writing he had grown and managed to deal with the things which unfolded before him. And he had written enough to firmly define who he was.

But how could he write about this? This had changed everything. In this story God would have no role. There would be no reason to even write God in, not even for a cameo. This would read like just another procedure which took place on the revolving Earth stage where all of the players were human, very imperfect, and nobody had any clue at all of where the plot was going. And the doctor was just fucked up. What a horrible story. He would never write it.

And even if he did, what could it possibly do to his credibility. It would be something as terrible as changing the copyright laws. It had already been written down for years that the events of his birth have been spelled out and proven as having some solid and valid reason to them. And many events in his life forthwith have been documented and analyzed with much consideration and have been judged as following a logical ordinance to them. None of these findings and doctrines has ever been contested to date. Of course his family very rarely studied the chronicles composed and compiled by him because they detested his use of pornography and vernacular. Still the discrepancy remains as to why they kept buying him typing paper and carbon for every birthday and Christmas, and how could they have allowed him to continue writing plays and scenes involving universal provinces and divine control when they knew all along that the doctor was just fucked up.

He needed someone to talk to. So remembering the sacristy scene as being the moment to which this moment was actually casting battle, he turned to the person amazingly still in his presence with whom he had been, his father, who was now submerged too comfortably on a couch under a newspaper. He said, "Dad ? Dad? Dad? Dad?"

His father was asleep. He woke his father up. It was difficult for him to push his wheelchair from the dining table to the couch on the stubborn shag carpet and it took him seven minutes. In that time his father had fallen asleep again. He woke his father up again.

"Dad. Hey Dad, did you know all this?"

His father said, all what?
"Dad, did you know all this that Kathy is saying?"

His father didn't remember what his sister had been talking about.

"My birth, Dad. Did you know about the doctor at my birth?"

His father was actually coming out of sleep so his thoughts were somewhat disjointed. But the difference was hardly noticeable as he said, oh I don't know, I guess. What was she saying about your birth?

The situation was quickly retold to his father by his sister who had many other things on her mind including beginning a large argument with his brother-in-law and changing the littlest girl's diaper. His sister really couldn't understand why he was making such a big deal of it to his father now that the conversation had been over for a couple of minutes.

Yet his father had sat up straight and opened his eyes and set down his newspaper and was making an attempt to concentrate on what he had to say. And so he proceeded trying to express himself.

"Dad. Like, I never knew all this much. I mean sure, when I was younger and asked questions, when I was a real little kid, the situation was explained to me that there Mom was in this hospital, and she was already in the room and she was all psyched to have me, and there were doctors and nurses around all ready to help her, and it was cool. Then the next minute it was some kind of magic moment or something when like magic some kind of oxygen just disappeared or something like that. And I didn't get any in my head. And like it was a big bad time all over the country or all over the world or something 'cause like, everybody could feel that I was in a lot of trouble and I wasn't gonna make it. And then I started crying because it was just horrible and Mom started crying.

And everybody started crying 'cause I was just like almost not there. And the little meter there said one when it's supposed to say ten. And then everybody was crying over that. And then like all of a sudden God just sort of showed up and put some of that oxygen back in my head and he said I was gonna be alright just as long as they let me stay in an incubator for two weeks and then everybody took care of me for the rest of my life. Isn't that how you always told me it happened?"

At the time when he was finishing his question to his father he started to realize just how utterly improbable all his suggested set of circumstances seemed. And even as he was finished speaking he began to retrace all of the events and construe at every stage it most likely didn't happen exactly as he described.
And also by this time his father had begun to drift back to sleep. His father had become quite confused and he said, what? what? what? Was I supposed to be listening to that? I really don't know what you're trying to get at.

There still was a lot of feeling possessing him. "Dad, what I'm trying to say is that I almost feel betrayed. Yes betrayed by you and Mom. By all of you. I didn't know that anyone knew more about my birth than I did. Not my sister. I didn't know that she worked alongside the doctor who delivered me. I didn't even think she knew his name. I didn't even know his name."

He paused for some time. Someone who was still in the room and just happened to be listening to him asked him simply, so? what's the difference?

He began to get riled and jerked his head back to get more air so that he could speak loudly and emphasize his point and say, "But you don't understand. None of you understand. This is my birth. This is my birth you're talking over. This isn't just one of your childhood memories that you can kid about. And this isn't like one of Kathy's old stories from medical school. This is all me. Don't you understand?"

All of these words were not heard by anybody. Most of them weren't because in the middle of them his aunt and his uncle had come in the door and greeted everyone in their usual manner. His family had planned to all get together that evening to play Jeopardy. A family gathering and a game of Jeopardy was enough to knock out of any one person the energy to conduct an intelligent conversation or maintain a coherent thought. His mother and his aunt and anyone else they might invite into a conversation were just no competition for anyone to try to conquer. And he already noticed that the argument he had been trying to present held no popularity or interest whatsoever. He decided that any further dwelling on his dilemma would only hold significance inside his mind. So he asked to be helped to sit on the sofa where he could relax his back.

He thought about his back. It was getting worse. His worry about his curved back actually began in the summer following his junior year of high school. He was asked to stay in a state rehabilitation center for three weeks to be evaluated for possible future employment and also a study of his all around physical condition and an inquiry into what self help aids he might need. He basically agreed to go there so that the state might flip the bill for an electric wheelchair and four years college tuition. He never got the electric wheelchair because the old ugly chain smoking occupational therapist diagnosed him as having too poor curvature of the spine. All of a sudden he decided to look in a full length mirror beside him and say to himself, "You know, she's right. I really do sit like shit. Maybe that's why my esophagus kills me everynight when I go to bed."

He had recently written a poem about the pain he endured everynight in his esophagus but it was very vulgar and hurt the eyes as much as the esophagus hurt the man. His esophagus hurt him mostly after he'd take a tall drink and then lie down. It hurt him after he'd eat something and then tried to type or do something with concentration. He was a good eleven years before he was told and convinced that everybody didn't have pains in their esophagi all the time.

He was older than that, possibly a good thirteen or fourteen before he could accept the fact that everyone was not personally attached to somebody as severely handicapped as he was. He started thinking about this in detail. He was six years old when he started going to the Greenmont School. He was always in a class with about seven other kids. They all had different handicaps but all the children were sort of in the same boat. No kid knew alienation or even rejection. Everyone got picked to play baseball and just about everyone could be anybody's girlfriend. Up to a certain age even the retarded kids from the other wing were their equal. And every kid grew and accepted three times as much as a normal kid would.

Yes it took him at least thirteen years to even receive a glimpse of an idea that the sheltered idealistic world wasn't what everybody knew. When he was mainstreamed into a regular high school everyone immediately showed him that his perceptions and expectations were the ones that were limited. If he thought that walking people were just people who thought like he did only they could walk around, if he thought that every kid his age had an easy and nonresponsible life just like he did with time left over to at great length ponder the great contributions to society made by Cole Porter and Dick Cavett, he was rudely awakened to the fact that he would never again be the only one around with a most unique point of view tangled up in blue. And even if he was, nobody could take the time to understand him. He began to see that the real people were the ones with the real problems. And real life consisted of marijuana smoking and drug busting and violent tempers and broken homes and anxiety and communication gaps and unfortunate stupidity. He began to see that just about everyone he met could have been classified as handicapped in one way or another.

Sometime around here he decided that his only hope of salvation in this brave new world was employing and becoming dedicated to clear sensible thought. He cried all that night worrying about this great new task laying before him. But in the morning he got up again, went back to the regular junior high school and started his thinking on that day.

In school he had no problem because his old teacher came along with him to every class and took notes for him. And on whatever answer he didn't know on a test she didn't mind nudging him. His teacher had been with him for nearly all his life. And she wanted him to succeed as much as he might have. Actually her remaining presence did reduce his need for independent thinking a great deal. She would help him with his homework and assist him with all of his moral and literary and financial decisions. She must have realized long ago the fact that he had just so much potential for near greatest on some day to come, that he really should be monitored and it should be made sure that he never thinks for himself too much. She saw that there were just too many tests he would fail if he were ever left absolutely to his own devices. But he was attractive and intelligent.

He shared his teacher with two others. He shared her guidance with John and with Jackie. John was more attractive and less intelligent than he. John had been his best friend since he could remember having a best friend. John and he were the only people whom the other one could beat up. John had better hand dexterity than he and could easily bang his head against the desk and then flop his body back against his chair vigorously hard rather repeatedly. He would be weak and defenseless during the whole ordeal. But then John would always reduce his force and finally stop torturing him. John would beg him to forgive him and say that he would never do it again. John would then receive a beautiful black eye which would last a good two weeks.

He began to laugh on the couch thinking of his great right backhand. There was nothing funny about the Jeopardy game which his family was playing. He wasn't answering any questions so his family knew that he was imagining he was somewhere else. They ignored him.

He would have liked to talk to John then about his dilemma. John would understand what he had to say. John might have said some of the same things as he wanted to say if John was accustomed to coming up with as many original ideas as he. John really rarely had to think; he could talk, and he always knew what to say. John was always closer to Miss Irene, their busdriver because he was on her bus for her entire route, a total of four and a half hours a day. John sat up front and he spoke her language. Miss Irene was the warmest and most understanding woman who could ever drive a lift bus for a bunch of smart alec dirty minded handicapped young guys.

He knew he was special to her. The private joke which he was able to have with her, not needing to pronounce any hard words for the fun, was that he enjoyed making childish lewd passes at her, offering "a nickel for a nipple."

She would always pretend that his behavior was acceptable and funny. But Miss Irene has gone now. So he really couldn't imagine asking her to talk to him about his dilemma.

But he could share with John how much they both miss her. They'd have a good time talking about how fun it was to ride on old 4968. Miss Irene and Miss Bertle the matron would make sure they had lots of coke and cookies and lollipops and candies for everybody. It was different from any other schoolbus that anybody else ever rode on. Miss Irene would stop at McDonalds if everybody would pitch in and buy milkshakes. And there was a special time when she stopped to buy milkshakes. The last time.

Kevin thought that a milkshake would taste good riding home on the last day before Christmas vacation. So the bus turned into the nearest McDonalds, Miss Irene's treat was very nice, and that ride was very fun. Kevin had Muscular Dystrophy; he was seventeen and he died over the holidays.

John and he shared many friends who had Muscular Dystrophy. They lost many friends. That's something they could have talked about if they happened to be together then. Greg used to sit between them on the bus. Whenever John and he thought about laughing together it never seemed like Greg wasn't there somewhere.

And so John was telling him while he was sitting on that couch in his sister's condominium in Ocean City, Maryland that it was really all relative anyway. John asked him if he would rather be alive or dead. John asked him whether he thought he was handed the most burned pig hind or Greg was. John said that Greg lived everyday knowing that he might have to be dying next week. But John and himself were always allowed to make many long range plans. Their parents knew they could keep them. John asked him if he really had a problem worth worrying about.

John answered his own question. John said, of course you do. You're you. You're the most sensitive and serious bastard I've ever talked to. You've always been ten times smarter than me. I've never liked you for that. You've never liked me because I can talk to everybody and you can't. Hell, I can't tell you what to think. If you think you were screwed over because your family never told you how you were born, then for god sake give everybody shit. But don't tell me your problems.

He recognized the couch and his family again. He knew an answer in Jeopardy so he answered it. Then he turned to his brother-in-law to say something quietly. He could always ask or say anything to his brother-in-law. They were compatible enough and once upon a time they used to be friends.
"Hey man, can I ask you something? Did you hear this story they were telling about the doctor that delivered me?"

Who? Dr. Dinn? Oh sure. I've known about it for a long long time. Ever since Kathy told me when she found out. Boy, you were really screwed over, weren't you?

That was the last time that he ever spoke to his brother-in-law.

The game went on. His brother-in-law and his father knew every answer and so he wasn't too interested. He started thinking of Jackie. Jackie always spent all summer at Ocean City. So it wouldn't have been very far fetched at all if she just appeared in front of him in this living room which must have been every bit as nice as the very one which her father the building contractor owned. And he could see her sitting in front of him somewhat annoyed that she had been requested to his presence. But she was willing to listen to him as long as he had anything constructive to say.

Actually he hadn't seen Jackie for a number of years. But he had always been reminded of her. Whenever he saw Jackie he was really seeing every girl who had ever come very close to knowing and understanding him, but never took the trouble to go all the way. His attitude about such women was not healthy. It was not healthy for him to dwell on such women and such opinions about them he had formed over the past years. Much of his frustration involving his handicap actually stemmed from his unfortunate experiences with women. And whenever he thought of Jackie, he became instantly intimidated by the sex.

"Jackie, do you suppose it's wrong for me to feel hurt and betrayed over the information that was kept from me?"

Well I guess anything is ok just as long as you don't belabor it too much and make me think that you're a drag.

"Well what would you do if you were in my situation? I mean has anybody not told you anything?"

Oh my no, I've been told everything and a long time ago. I don't imagine what I'd do. Oh I suppose I'd have Daddy sue. But I suppose he would have done so long before my sayso.

"You mean? You could sue a doctor? After this long?"

Oh you silly. You can always sue. Isn't your brother a lawyer? Doesn't he tell you these things?

"Well no. I haven't talked to him yet. He's been out."
Why did you have to bother me now with your problems if you don't have all your facts in front of you? Why do you want to come out looking like a moaning asshole? If you got a problem do something about it. But don't sit there all night thinking about it. Nothing good ever gets accomplished when you think too much. You only take the teacher's time and attention away from me.

Then he stopped talking to Jackie out of guilt. Moaning in front of Jackie was absolutely the worst thing he could do.

Now it was getting late and the games and visit from his aunt and his uncle ended. His aunt blew him a kiss on her way out the door. He wasn't in the mood to accept a blown kiss from his aunt.

He didn't mind at all that everyone left in the condominium, getting things ready to go to bed. His father cleared away all the knick knack food and the Jeopardy game. His sister took him to the bathroom and then rolled his bed from the couch he had been sitting on. Then she rolled out her own bed from a couch across the room. His mother had a habit of retiring to bed as soon as his aunt and his uncle left to go home and it looked as if his father and his sister had things under control as far as cleaning up and getting things ready to go to bed.

His brother-in-law went back on the terrace with his book by Bob Woodward and stayed out there all night.

Then he was lying in his bed in the living room comfortably beneath the sheets in the dark. He wasn't going to sleep. By regular living hours practiced by those who aren't vacationing for a week with their family it was quite early. So he stayed still and felt very alone. He was thinking of the millions of things which he knew very well were part of his make-up and his responsibility but he surmised that he would never receive credit or recognition for.

He had undergone some heavy duty thought and reflection tonight. And he had to do it all by himself. The entire process of call and response concerning this meaningful subject had to be transacted within his stereophonic brain. The transmission utilized all of the brain's capacity leaving no power left to operate any music functions. Tunes were now beginning to play in his head because the conversational overload had begun to lighten. Blonde on Blonde had just been flipped to side two when the door opened and his brother had arrived home.

"Michael. Michael. How are you?"

I'm fine. Why don't you go to sleep?

"Because I been waiting to talk to you. Can I talk to you?"

His brother walked over and flopped down on his bed and said, yeah what do you want?

"Well. What did you do tonight?"

I played miniature golf with Diane. I think I'm gonna marry her. What else do you want?

"Well. They were talking here after you left. Kathy and Mom were talking. About my birth. They were talking awhile about it. Do you know they were saying stuff that I... Not only did I not know this stuff. But I was very surprised and shocked about it. And I didn't know just how to take all this. And I been thinking about it all night. Why, do you know what they told me?"

What? That the doctor was fucked up and wasn't at the hospital on time?

"AW SHIT!"

What? Because I knew all that? Well I think it's been known for a long time that there could have been extensive negligence suits brought against him and we could have been awarded substantial damage.

"Aw shit, man. You mean I could have been rich right now instead of here talking to you?"

Well. Yeah. Basically. If you want to put it like that. Why? Are you just finding this out?

"Yes I am. Listen. You can understand this. I've been living this thing, this life, like with Cerebral Palsy for all this time, right? I mean you haven't. And Kathy hasn't. And nobody else has. For me, this is just like a normal life, you know. Like all these extra things that I have to do and I have to put up with? They're just like part of the plan. And I always thought like they were given to me because I was the only one that... That God saw around who was strong enough to take it. To put up with all this shit, you know? Like all my life nobody ever bothered to tell me that. Like, not only could I be great. But I could get a whole lot of money, just for being great. You know? Like, why didn't anybody clue me in on this a hell of a long time ago?"

Well you know why. Your parents would never take any doctor to court and ruin his reputation and his career and then take him for a whole lot of money. You know they just didn't do that in nineteen sixtytwo the way they do today. It just didn't happen. And besides, your mother probably thought it was God's will that you were born this way. And she probably prayed about it all night and said rosaries. And your father probably went along with that because he doesn't have much of an imagination either. If they could tie God's will into the explanation, you know they were going to.

"Yeah. Well I was always taught to believe that."

But listen. I tell you what. You're a man now. You can decide anything for yourself now. If you would like to look into legal action, I mean serious legal action, I would be happy to go with you on this and back you up and help you take this guy to court. It could be done. It's not too late. Hell, this would be the perfectly logical time for you to pursue action and to go after what might be coming to you. You're a young man now. Almost out of college. You've got a very analytical and fertile mind. You should be looking forward to the beginning of a great career. But you've been paralyzed by a very serious handicap all these years as you say. A court of law might very well see it in your favor and take the motherfucker for all he's got. Who knows?

"You really think so, Michael?"

I don't know. Who the hell knows? That sounded good. I tell you. Why don't you let me get some sleep? I'm tired of talking to you. We'll go over this in the morning. Shut up and goodnight.

Then he was left alone for the rest of the night. It was a short pleasant time he laid there warm and contented playing a few more of his favorite albums. And eventually he fell asleep.

Steve Sireci came in to talk to him. Steve Sireci had been partying in the next room. It was late and Steve was by now nice and wasted. But the American Beauty album was just coming on so Steve decided to move the party and join him in bed.

He was very glad to see his best friend from college. He knew that Steve was staying at Ocean City for the summer but he'd been trying and trying to reach him all week with no luck. Steve was always working or partying whenever he'd call. Steve was making a lot of noise talking and drinking to him. His sister remained sound asleep on the other sofa bed and his brother never woke up off the floor. But he and Steve Sireci laughed and cursed for a fun long time.

He could talk to Steve about anything at all because he was his closest friend now. "Hey Steve, can I tell you something that's really bothering me? You know I get around pretty well these days. I really like school. Hell, we're already one half the way through college. Isn't that great? Why, in just two more years we'll actually be real people. We've got so much to look forward to. And you know that'll be the time when we'll all have to define ourselves. I mean we'll be working at jobs and planning out the rest of our lives. Deciding if what we're doing now's what we want to be doing five or ten years down the road. Deciding who we want to marry and how many kids we want to have and how many years we really want to do bonghits. You know. And for me that's all just a little bit unique because in some instances it won't be a matter of deciding how to do these things but deciding if indeed many of these opportunities will be opened to me. And in considering all this I have to realize that my attitude towards these coming challenges must be a continuation of my feelings and convictions that I've developed all through my life about what obstacles and what differences I'll just have to overcome both physically as well as in my head. I have to face everything that's to come with just as much strength and determination as I have always had. But what worries me is... I just found out that a very important thing which has held my moral fiber together for all my life, the main core of my faith has just been shattered. And now it just seems like they've taken away every reason I have to be proud of myself as a handicapped person."

Steve Sireci interrupted his beer long enough to say to him, handicapped, shit you're not handicapped.

He asked Steve Sireci to go home. And that dream was over.

He found himself tomorrow sitting on the beach deck with his mother beside him. She was pretending to read a book about a woman surgeon but most of the morning she was sleeping.

It was prime time. And attractive girls were walking back and forth and laying down to sunbathe close enough to excite and arouse him. He enjoyed sexual feelings for a good while. Then he realized how much he had been drooling. He took steps to correct himself but he had a familiar slight cough which caused him to have to swallow many times and made his face grimace and hard to control. He received a few replies to his flirts, but it wasn't particularly a good day. He got no response from many of them.

He never expected too much response from those who were on the other side of sex. In fact whenever he did get something he became deliriously surprised. They had always been put on another range. He thought that pretty people didn't need to make different kinds of friends. For the most part he always stood by his theory.

The attractive girls on the beach deck who didn't respond to him seemed to notice him just the same. Perhaps they were annoyed that he had such a sexually interested mind. They all seemed to have Jackie's voice when they told him not to look at them so much. You are really insulting.

What gives you the right to look at my bikini and have any reaction at all? Leave me alone.

And by the way, about this dilemma you've been having? I've been thinking and what's so wrong with you being handicapped? You've been doing it so long. You're so good at it by now.

He was never able to get too hard when he heard his mother snoring. So he woke her up to have a conversation with her. If he was lucky she wouldn't yell at him for bothering her. "Mom, Mom. Get up. I want to talk to you. Mom. You know what you all made me feel like last night? Mom, I feel like I'm adopted. I feel like I've been living with a family for this long. I'm twentytwo years old. And all of a sudden my family tells me I'm adopted. This is absurd. I'm not adopted. Doesn't every kid have nightmares about this and worry about the day their parents tell them they're adopted? Well I never had those nightmares. I never thought I was adopted. And now the strangest experience that I could ever imagine having to go through I have to go through. What the hell?"

Oh, don't use such language.

"Mom, I want to say stronger things than this. I am really upset about this."

I know you are by the way you've been talking about it. What I don't understand is why does it worry you so much. If you explained it to me maybe I'd understand.

"Ok Mom. I'll try. See, knowing that the doctor might have been negligent, knowing that there was nothing wrong with you before, that you had a normal pregnancy, that it wasn't your age that was a factor in the problem, knowing that some outside person was involved in, in changing not only mine but all our lives so tremendously, all that really changes my ideas about my own identity. And just say, if you have had another doctor. Mom, the whole script would have changed. I wouldn't have been the person I am."

Of course you would have, dear. We are all God's children. We just have to live the way God wants us to live.

"But I wouldn't have been handicapped. I am upset because this is the first time that I've been told that I could have had a choice about being handicapped. It was really the doctor's fault. And we also had a choice about what to do about it. We could have sued the doctor. We could be rich people today. And we could be living out here on the beach deck everyday of our lives. And I would have never had to start thinking."

And do you really think if you would have gotten all that money from that man that things would have been different and you'd be all that happy like you say you would be? And do you really want to go around all your life blaming somebody else for the way you are? That man was only human. He's one of God's children too. He can make a mistake too.

"Yeah Mom. But it was a terrible mistake. Look at me."

Darling, you're not a terrible mistake. You're a marvelous human being. I love you very much. Why would you have accepted it if it was my fault and I gave you a bad birth?

"Because you're my mother. You're a part of me. You come along with the package so to speak. And God gives all great men to the right mothers."

Ok, dear. If you say so. I'm getting tired. Would you mind if we talk about this later and I go upstairs to the room to take a nap?

To tell the truth he was shocked and amazed that his mother had spoken to him for that long without becoming annoyed at listening to him and tired enough to ask him to excuse her. And on her way off of the deck she was stopped by a younger woman wishing to talk to her and tell her that she also had a child who was born handicapped and mentally retarded.

Ocean City Maryland has always been visited by people who don't understand.

LAUGHIC

Have I yet told you about the Friday night? I haven't? I saw Suzy again. I went out with her, yes. Wild to say the least. It started by me wanting to go out with Kathy oh a couple weeks ago to the symphony. I'm figuring I'm going to begin to get that part of my life rolling at this stage. So I rang Suzy; she's gotta have Kathy's number, right? Alright, I was in the mood to renew with her. And much to the coolness, she was still living at home, I was able to get her, and she was very pleased to hear from me. We're talking two and a half years here; you know you're always going to be psyched if they remember from two years and they still got the smile, the laugh, the nice words for you after that long. So the phone conversation was a high; you know, an old friend gotten back can make you feel awfully good if your mood is right for it. And the deal was to keep in touch and to go out sometime before Christmas. So a week went by before it was December first. And don't you remember what an oh god busy day that was. Everyone in the world was gonna make deals with me that day. So when I woke up in the morning and thinking how significant it was gonna be, I referred to the birthday calendar. (There is no birthday calendar; I just remember all these things well, which is just another reason why it's nice to be me.) I saw there, uh, John Densmore, uh, Suzy... Hey, holy sheep --, I just spoke to her last week; I'm back on the planet with her now, and it's cool. Hey, I could really shine if some flowers showed up from nowhere at her door signed: love, Paul. This is something my brother Lief would do and get loved for. A good project for the morning; I put Lief right on it.

Now I'll tell you about the night we went out because you want to hear about that. I had it scheduled for Friday of that week when everything happened in the world. It worked out to be a good time when she was free, and I just figured that I could dig the significance of it all. So we made the date the week before. I feel good about my life nowadays when I need to give no second thoughts to dates until the time that they will occur. That's a large sign of utilized personhood, it's always seemed to me, and I always wanted to get here. Why not appreciate everything? So I was sitting at my computer, printing out a copy of the poem 'The Life' to give to Suzy as a Christmas gift for when she would arrive, later, much later. I had plans to get dressed in an hour or two. In a minute or two I had turned my head to the door of the Blue Room. And there was someone who it took about three seconds to really be Suzy. There is nothing compared to the speed of hysterical thoughts at moments of embarrassment. People change their looks so much when you're not watching them. God, especially old lovers. Did you ever make plans to do something big, then the moment you get on the scene you realize how stupid it was to think that a mere mortal human would be able to pull it off alone? Especially you? I believe that feeling comes over this man right at the start of absolutely every single dinner date. And it might be before every single interaction I have with another human being. But I digress. (I always wanted to write that.) Suzy sat down and waited for me to relearn to speak. As I remember she had always been patient in times such as this. Happily I had the distraction of the line printer which was still spurting out that monstrously long poem, so she could listen and watched those regurgitated reams as they cluttered up the floor of the old Blue Room. I don't doubt that feelings of overwhelming displacency weren't crossing paths in her mind as well. She looked as if she suddenly recalled how copious my thoughts could grow once I was seated at a keyboard, and she had never laid eyes on a word processor. The time had come for verbal intervention. For rescue.

"Suzy, I can't tell you how shocked you got me. Uhhh-- HERE!! This is for you."

"I don't need a computer at the moment, Paul. What are you talking about?"

"NO NO NO... I mean this poem right here. I just put it out two days ago, and everyone seemed to like it, so I'd like you to have it, uh for Christmas."

"Ah Paul, how sweet,"

(can you believe this already?)

"What a sweet gift for you to think of me like that. Gee, I'm sorry I'm so early. I always did make the mistake of showing up on time for you. It is so very nice to see you. How have you been?"

"I've been great. I'm beautiful. I couldn't be happier at school, and I'm moving out on my own pretty soon, and it's Christmas. I'm beautiful."

Boy, I'd love to know me. If I were to talk to me, I'd think of myself as such a great inspiration. How could anybody want a brighter greeting than what I just gave her? Inspirations only last so long. I asked her how she was doing, and she actually proceeded to tell me. This, as you might guess, took some of the superhuman expectations off of my behavior, and calmed me down to a dull and short acid trip with that call girl in Lake Tahoe. From what I heard that Suzy was saying, it was mostly about the Eskimo who was supposed to marry her two years ago. He just never got around to it and she's been perturbed ever since. I came back after a while to hear the tail end of it. I don't think she was telling me all about him to be offensive; she wasn't, Suzy's not like that. It seemed like she was just enjoying being open with someone who didn't give a shit. Cool.

"What do you want to do tonight?"

"That is totally up to you, sir."

"Well, I tell you what; the first place I'm taking you is the hospital, young lady."

She kept her query puzzled look all the way, as she wheeled me out my back door having been thoroughly pinched, cuted, reminisced about, and sent by my parents--who never have, by the way, forgiven me for breaking up with her. Still queerly puzzled she was for the whole three miles and until she stopped the van in the parking lot.

"Alright, where in hell are you taking me?"

"I told you. You'll find out when we get there. We're going up to the second floor. Come on.."

I was taking her to the main children's ward. I had scheduled a beautiful moment to happen there; and everything would go down perfectly if we could walk to the nursery playroom and find a little small book set on a table right where I had left it about a week and a half earlier, and if we could get there and be alone in that dark room just for a little while without any nurse asking us what the hell we were doing there about two hours after visiting hours were over. Well, all of this came true; could you believe it? Life can be so greatly cool at particular times. And when it happens to me that life is in a good mood, I often see it appropriate to return the favor by sinking my eyelids, letting the palsied body go mellow for a while, and basically drift by in a Morrison haze. People seem to appreciate it; and that's what I did while Suzy read this little small book that I had planted there that week earlier. (Actually, it wasn't really on the same table where I had left it, but it was behind the nurses' counter, so Suzy had to go ask for it, but things were still cool.) So I stayed mellow and lax while Suzy sat down in the dark playroom with me, and read it. It was 'Me Little Trouper'. I had written the rough draft of it the last Christmas that we were going together in hopes of giving it to her then. But I just never finished it. I asked her there if she remembered this story. And she hesitated and then said 'Oh--uh, yeah,' as if to say 'of course not.' And she read the book anyway. I had it written in a little 'nothing book'; you know the 'nothing books' that you can buy at the store? One of them. That Christmas was the one when Lennon died, and 'Me Little Trouper' was supposed to be this little children's story for her (Suzy, it's what I always called her.) And it was phrased and written with all funny words like 'Spaniard in the Works' or something like that. And it had all kinds of stick pictures in it just drawn by my parents. And you could tell which was whose because my mother was in one of her bitchy testy moods, and she had no interest in the project from the get-go and only drew these little stick characters with nothing on them, the least she could do, you know? My father went gungho on the thing and went all out with the drawings on his pages. I think it was the first time he's read anything of mine in fifteen years, and he was so impressed there wasn't a fuck in it or anything, he was grooving on the prospect of having something to be proud of me for. (Gee, I'm sorry that sentence wound up with that word in it and ended up with a preposition. But what can be done? There's a story to be told. And we gotta get back to Suzy; she's almost finished reading.) And then Suzy was finished reading the little small book.

"Paul, why did you leave this book here at the hospital?"

"Well, that's what I meant to tell you. This is what I do. I mean every week. I give something, or I write something for the benefit of others. There is a full sentence that I use and it has twenty words in it and here it is: I release pieces of production for the entertainment and benefit of people whose situations are as unique as my own.."

"Paul, what the hell are you trying to say?"

"Every week I try to do something different to help people. Don't you think it's groovy?"

"Paul, in one way or another, for as long as I've known you, you have always been groovy."

"Well, how do you like the little book?"

"Paul, in one way or another, for as long as I've known you, you are always surprising me; shocking me. I don't know what to say to you. You're always spinning me for a loop. What can I say to you? You say so much, and you don't leave the words for anyone else to use. Why did you bring me here?"

I had brought her there for a minor mindflip between old friends, nothing more. This was getting to be a moment--I mean a moment--that was getting to be about five times as serious as it had to be. 'Me Little Trouper' was a three year old fantasy I had created, with a minimal amount of sincerity at the time, at most. Suzy thought she was reading a deep true confession of my undying love for her. Come on now. I could see it in her eyes; if I had any hope of rescue from this scaring moment at all, I had better break this totally confused silence right then with an encompassing answer to her question.

"It's only a book. It's only a book for some kids at a hospital. What do you think it is? It's only a book."

"Yeah--yeah...Ok, it's only a book. And I like it very much. Thank you very much for letting me read it. Thank you for bringing me here. It's nice to be in the dark again with you. How have you been?"

"Very up, and very down. And I write volumes about in between. None of it is very interesting."

"Well, how about the Bustop?"

"None of it is very interesting. Why didn't the Eskimo marry you?"

"Oh, that's very interesting. I don't think he ever will. He's a very conservative guy. You would like him. No, you'd hate him. You ought to meet him anyway. He wouldn't understand you, that's for sure. He doesn't understand many people. But he understands me, I've always thought. He tries to. He's in himself a lot. He doesn't see too many things that are around him. This is why he likes snow covered cabins in Skaskatuan where nobody else can find. And we are only in love when I'm close enough in his radius for him."

Those of you who have heard of my rugby house know exactly where we were going. If you haven't, it wasn't far, we'll be there soon, so you'll find out. I just showed her where to go once we got back in the van; I just pointed down York Road until we got to the Mickey D's. And I just said 'make your turn here honey, we're home.' Are you enjoying this date so far? Does it occur to you that maybe-just maybe I might just have my foot in the door? Oh, not that I would want it there, mind you; Oh no. I mean it has been three years. And anyone who knows about the people with whom I have associated myself knows that I definitely need not get involved with another artist. Oh no, it's just much too safe to inhabit with the regular people to even consider taking one of those kind for any meaningful relationship of any kind. Life is just so great to people who don't call themselves artists. And anyway, I have the feeling: it's never again gonna matter what Suzy and I feel about each other. Like, I guess she's so far back in my consciousness, it's like the place where you put your brothers or sisters, or your trusty drinking mate, or your barber. They're people who you never think of changing your relationship with. I could never say 'I love you' to Suzy. I'd laugh right in her face. Still, she did think of that little small book as a beautiful kind gesture.. Ah, gimme a break! It was time to go into the party.

'Twas the week before Christmas, and the ruggers had the house all decorated. Actually I knew that the girls had done all the work that afternoon. And I saw how each girl had contributed each their own bit, after each of them told me of the major part they played in the preparation of the entire decor, that is. I love these people I go to school with: the smucks and the clucks. I really am happy calling everyone of them my friend. And I was more than psyched for a swinging holiday bash. And yes, I was a little concerned how Suzy would take it as I afflicted massive quantities of screwdrivers and wallbangers with Joey Morel, and kissed and goosed and proposed to all my best girls, all 30 of them; but I had promised Suzy that we wouldn't stay too long at all, just long enough for me to say 'hello, merry Christmas, goodnight' to a couple of close friends, that we'd split real soon, that being alone with her after this long meant more to me than any party. We stayed eight and a half hours, I was a lying son of a bitch, and plastered on my ear. Then Suzy told me we were going home, and she said it smiling. Then was when I did remember. I loved her.

We got back in the van but I didn't see it. The Friday night was almost over, we were alone in the cold dark; wouldn't this be the part of the story for the sincere last discussion of our great relationship throughout the years? What a shame we'd been parted for this long? How much we'd might like getting back together? 'Come on.. it's the mind after all; we were meant for each other.. what d'you say?'

"No, Paul, he really means a lot to me."

"Ah--ah--yeah--uh, uh, who uh, who does, man??"

"Chris, Paul. Chris."

"SCHAUB!! WHERE IS HEEEE??"

"No, Paul. My Chris. I love him."

"Oh WOWWWWWWWWWWW, man, Heavy duty! You mean this was all just a good time? Just a couple laughs?"   "That's all that you wanted, Paul. It's what you started this story about. That's even your title. Paul, you're very drunk, you always are, eventually. And you don't mean to get this dramatic here at the end. It's only a story, and you're very grateful for the plot being so leveled, so transient, in which you get most the attention. You've done good, again. And I'd be happy to keep on hearing from my Peacefrog. I'm taking you home now. He's almost out of film."

"But Chevy always gets Golde at the end."

"I know. And he still does."

And I think that I had a wonderful date on the Friday night. But I have no remembrance of it. It must have been a movie.

ECCLESIASTICMAN

This is a term paper and nothing but a term paper. It is for Fr. Lowell Glendon to consider as my final assignment in his course on Christian Spiritual Direction. Its title suggests to the reader a creative, poetic, or frivolous text; to a familiar reader of mine, the fact immediately comes that it is certainly written in springtime, and very probably I'm writing it in Easter season.

I need to explain exactly this paper's circumstance; I speak directly to Fr. Glendon now, informing him that this piece will be published in several media once this semester has ended. For the next six pages, I will be playing the part of a spiritual director. You will see immediately that the following dramatics are contrived. Therefore, resign to the fact that the context of my theses is literally a poem. I mean all but to offend you by submitting a less than adequate representation of my comprehension of your course. My sole goal is to introduce, reference, and put to practice many, if not most of the techniques and topics of Christian Spiritual Direction, according to your own definition and those of some authors we have discussed in class, and to show you my regard, aspiration to, and attempt, if hypothetical, at the practice.

Hello; the last time I checked, my name was Paul Peroutka. I'm very pleased to meet you.

This is going to be a very funny term paper you're writing. My name is Paul Peroutka too.

I know that; that's the reason I'm here. Let me explain. I'm 25, and I'm a graduate student at St. Mary's Seminary Ecumenical Institute. I also work five hours a day, but I had the afternoon off, as well as Good Friday tomorrow. And I wanted to come back here to Ridge School to wheel around and see and say hi to a few people. But also, I wanted to see if I could find you.

Me. You wanted to see if you could find me? I got it. Ok, very well; you found me. What can I do for you, man? I'm only 15. I'm really not sure what you want.

Ok, ok, let me explain. By the way, you gotta endure my slow mode of speech. And I'm gladly enduring yours. Let me give you a fact: I am indeed able to speak and pronounce words much considerably better than you.

You say you talk a lot better than I do now, but you're not doing very well at all. Every word and every syllable becomes strained as you're trying too hard. I know that I can speak deeper and easier than you have. Have you really gotten better speech? It sounds to me like you've let it gone to hell.

You are a critical son of a gun, aren't you? Yeah yeah yeah. I think I'm gonna dig this. See: I have to do this paper on Spiritual Direction. Ah damn. See: instead of me going into exactly what Spiritual Direction is, and taking all of that time with my really terrible crappy speech that you say I have, it's gonna be better for me to just use you, just ask you to share with me some things. And then maybe you'll get the idea of what it is we're actually doing.

Yeah yeah, well suppose I already have a pretty good idea what you want to do in your Spiritual Direction? You forget, we're on a same name basis. My first question to you is: I thought the directee was supposed to come to the director, and ask him or her if it'd be alright to begin a relationship.

Ah yeah. Well, that be the only exception I'd like to make. Besides you forget, we're on a same name basis.

And listen: aren't we supposed to be compatible? What the hell are you doing going to Theology school anyway?

This is the great start. I have got to find out why you're so opinionated, why you're critical, and demanding. I know I'm supposed to sit here and let you talk for the first fortyfive minutes. But I've only got six and a half pages. Why is it so important to you what I'm doing? Where I'm going to school? Whether I do the right thing? I've already been through all of this with your parents.

Mom and Dad are still alive. Oh thank you God. I am so happy, blessed. I am now filled with great joy.

You still dig the parents? Oh. Oh. Oh yeah, well I guess you do. I'm sorry; I'm very sorry. I didn't mean to put it like that. Please, I want to shut up. I'm glad I made you happy. Please, would you like to talk about Mom and Dad?

I'd like to talk about Dad. Dad's God, you know that? Well, you still believe that, don't you? I'm the one who said it and wrote it, and made up all the dogma around it. It's so hard to get other people, the others to go along with, with the whole concept. But I'll say it to anyone: my father is God. Well, he's a piece of God, of course. What I believe is that my father is blessed, and I'll say it: above all, well, most men alive. He's blessed with an intelligence and a conscience that have the capacity to withstand anything. He's blessed with a sixth sense of perception. It becomes so, so hard for me to put him into words. I just love my father with all my heart. Sometimes I imagine myself, myself in his body, in his brain. I'm looking at him, right? I'm across him at a table in a restaurant. It's where I'm so happy to be with him, so happy that he is treating me to something, and it is a very nice and hot day, and we are on a two week vacation with all the family, up to Boston. And in this ice cream parlor, I'm looking at him, so carefully. And I'm wondering what the hell he could be thinking about today. He's looking off in space. He always looks off in space, when you think you're talking to him at a restaurant. He's so great. He has to think about all kinds of things. You understand. When he's ignoring you, it really, really is because he has to think about something much much more important. In any kind of room, he really, somehow, I don't know how, he can know absolutely everything important about every single person in the room. It is overwhelming. It's not a mistake, and it isn't by accident. I can't be the only one who sees it, who knows that it is true. But I am the only person who says this, who puts it into words. I tell you, on more than one occasion, that day in the Boston ice cream parlor, I have been inside my father's body. I felt my head shake and lose its balance. It could only last about two seconds. It must have been God who put me there, to experience my father, the man and the figure that I must be completely in love with, to experience my father totally and fully, if only for two seconds.

Good god. Man. You, still. I mean you actually.

What the hell you saying? You're mumbling. Don't mumble.

That's Dad.

Where's Dad?

No. What you said. You really love him. Paul, I can feel how much you love him.

He's the greatest and smartest man who ever lived. And you're the last person in the world I ought to have to convince of that, aren't you?

Holy ... Well, ok. You can say that. Jesus, I'm having a little problem here. ... Oh, it's a problem with myself. And, I'm sorry, I know it's wrong for me to talk, to myself, in front of you. You'll have to forgive me. Please, go on. As a 15 year old guy, yourself, who's been this seriously handicapped for all your life, and who's been going to this sheltered school, where you don't really know too many people outside of here, can you tell me, possibly tell me where else you've been looking for God. Or can you tell me how you relate to God?

Well, I don't believe that I don't know all that's going on outside. I am very smart. I'm very smart about a lot of things. You have to be very smart when you live with cerebral palsy. You have to believe in, first of all, your own code and rules of behavior. Because as I believe, and as every other intelligent handicapped person should believe, it becomes imperative that I imitate the normal people, or the real people, as much as I can. Well really, I should do this all of the time that I am in public. There is no excuse for anybody who is as handicapped as I am not to look his or her best and not to look almost normal everytime that they're in public.

You believe this?

Yes. With all my heart. Ain't I smart, and impressive?

Why do you believe all that, Paul? You say it all in words, but why do you believe it? Why did you call them, the real people? The normal people?

Oh. Oh my god, I will never think of myself as real, as a real human being. I mean, do you? If you're really supposed to be me, at an older age, well are you real? Are you normal? Do you think of yourself as a real human being, after all those years, however old you are?

If I don't, tell me why I don't. Tell me why you don't.

Well, how do I explain? Where should I start? Why do I even have to explain it to you? You're the big me. I want to count on you to fill in the holes in my thoughts. I've come to rely on you.

Well Paul, I need to know everything that you're thinking. My objective is to find out where God has you right now, in your life. I wouldn't mind at all finding out how you got there. But I can't do it for you. You gotta do it for me. And do it for you. Now where did you ever hear that you weren't a real human being? Paul. Who said it to you?

Ah, nobody ever said it to me. I came up with it myself. And hell, people have been trying to deny it for years. Nobody wants to understand.

Yes. What would you have them understand?

That I'll never be real. I don't even want to be real. Nobody can take me seriously. How can they? When I'm out in public, I'm more like a machine that someone has to tug along: push, take care of, feed, give a drink to, translate for. Those things aren't a part of the real society.

Paul. Of course they are.

No no no, you're not listening. I can come to resent this claiming to everyone that doesn't know me, or that's meeting me for the first time, that I'm a real human being. 'Cause I'm not. I mean, I'm not real. I can't be. I'm there. But I'm not a human being.

Ok. You're here, or there. Which is it?

I could be anywhere.

Ok, you're anywhere. You're there being. You're not just in somebody's imagination.

Oh no. I'm here.

You're here. But, you're not real. You're not a human being. Talk to me. I'm very lost.

I am handicapped, for god's sake. How do you expect me to be real? I only function when somebody takes care of me, when somebody helps me. And even that is a weird thing. Even that is para-real. That's more like a show than anything else.

You're saying, that when somebody helps you, like when somebody dresses you, or feeds you, then that becomes more like a show? A show, right? A show that they put on, about you, around you, that is you. Right?

Yes. You've got it.

Sweet Jesus. I'm beginning to understand what you're saying. Needless to say that scares the hell out of me. Now. Listen Paul, now is the time that this is really getting hard for me. I mean, Fr. Glendon: I can hear him right now. He's saying 'look, you're the director. No, that doesn't mean that you should direct the conversation. It doesn't mean that you should direct the directee's thoughts and feelings.' It means that I am here to help you hear and understand and respond to the voices of God within you. And for the life of me, I'll be honest with you, I don't see how I'm going to help somebody hear and respond to the voices of God who doesn't believe he's a human being.

I never said that I don't believe that God isn't with me. I believe that God is with me.

Ok. Ok. Sorry. So sorry for giving up too soon. Paul, where's God?

Oh he's all around. I've thought a lot about God, and I know where he is. I have to think a lot anyway; so I've taken care of thinking about God a long time ago.

Great. Can you tell me where you think he is? I must have forgotten your whole answer.

He isn't a he. Don't you remember? God has absolutely, positively no characteristics of a human being.

God's not a human being either.

No. Well, of course I'm not saying that God is like me. I will say that God is like nothing. GOD IS NOTHING. God is nothing we can understand. God is SPIRIT, the spirit, inherent, and shared, equally domained in the spirit of every human being. And then, in turn every handicapped creature, person.

Ok. STOP. HALT, Paul. You've got to tell me one, only one thing at a time. You are fifty miles ahead of me, and I get the feeling I could come up and join you if you'd only explain one thing at a time to me. Now, I don't know if I want to hear about who God is...Pardon me; what God is, or what you are. But I'll toss a coin, and say that---give me God first. I think I like what you said an awfully lot. I think I still agree with you. Let me say, repeat what I think you said, in my words, and see if you can nod your head. God: very separate from human; no human characteristics at all. We could discuss who in the world Jesus Christ was, but we won't, right now, to simplify things. God: not human, yet, in humans. In every human?

Yes.

Every human being that ever lived?

That's right.

Alright. We're doing perfectly so far. Now, do you mean, that every human being that ever lived, is a part of God?

Um. I think I'd rather say, that a piece of God, is in every human being that ever lived.

Ok. Ok. Might that be the good, and the loving, and the selfless consciousness that we are all capable of? The combined spirit of all of mankind, THAT'S GOD, to you.

Yes.

Beautiful. I mean, beautiful we're getting somewhere. I feel good about where this is going. Whatever we're saying right now, it may have theological implications and problems coming out of its ear. Or it might not; I'm really not sure. But that matters nothing right now, 'cause we're rolling. We know what God is, and where he is for you. He'd be everywhere then, wouldn't he?

Yeah. In any person you'd meet. And in the handicapped, like me.

Why in the hell are you not a regular human being? Everybody who ever reads this is going to give me hell unless you answer that.

Oh. I can be human, if you want to close your eyes, to just about everything. And if you want me to, too. If you want to forget the fact that never in my lifetime will I be able to go get a glass of water by myself, without anybody else knowing it. Never can I even think about going upstairs to my room just to be alone without talking to someone first. I'll never feed myself a meal, be alone in the bathroom. Someone will always know how much beer I've drunk. Can you imagine how many people have taken me to the bathroom? Do you ever recall anybody, man or woman, brother or sister, ever inviting me in there, just to return the favor? Do you think I'm a man? Is any guy a man until he gets his first car? Do you think any girl my age is going to take the crash course to learn my spoken language, witness the necessary drools in order to get the th's, and the d's, and the p's out, and then get the idea that she'd like to kiss me? Do you think I like coming straight home from school every Friday, and not leaving my house again until Monday morning? Do you see a hell of a lot of people worrying about this? Do you think that I could explain this to them, until it becomes their problem too? Do you think I'll ever come near, near living the life that my father has? Or my brothers? Or anybody in my whole family? Do you think that my cousins will ever come to know the person I am? Or care? Do you realize I have cerebral palsy 24 hours a day?

Paul. Paul. You just laid a hell of a lot on me. I tell you. I'll tell you flat out. Don't expect me to understand all of what you said. I can say that I appreciate it; and I feel for you, as much as I'm capable, because I think I see a tear in your eye. Aside from being a very intelligent son of a bitch, you're also highly emotional. I don't have to tell you. Nevertheless and all this aside, once again you're going to have to go slow with me. Fr. Glendon would suggest that I stop asking so many questions, and start affirming, and facilitating images that you give me. So Paul, I've accepted the fact that you're not really a human being. Or how do you want me to say that? You're not a real human being?

I don't know. I don't know; for some reason it sounds strange, or funny when you say it.

Ok, why's that?

Well. Whenever I try it out on other people, somebody else like my mother, I get a wrath of shit for it because they can't conceive that anybody would bother to say all of that about themselves. And they would never have the patience to get through the third sentence of it.

Ok. Paul, Paul. Let me ask you this: does God understand it when you say it to him?

Oh yeah. Yes. Yeah; God understands everything I say.

Everything you say. God understands everything you say. How infinitely greater he is than I. Excuse me, please. Paul, when God agrees with you that you're not, that you're something else besides a human being, what do you and God agree that you are? If you agree on anything, that you are? But somehow I think you know. Come on now; what are you?

You're.. You're really stripping me down here. Nobody's ever taken me this far down the road before. What am I? What the hell am I? An obedient dog?

Are you a dog, Paul?

No. I don't think so.

Well then why did you say that? Why did you say dog?

A dog waits.

You wait. You wait for what?

I wait to go to the bathroom. I wait to be comfortable, a lot of the time.

Do you have to go to the bathroom a lot, Paul? Is that a problem for you? Do you get uncomfortable a lot?

Well no, but it's a bitch when you have to go and there's no way for it. You get the runs in school, but there's no teacher you feel like bothering that long to take you. You don't know how long you will be; and you don't know how stanky it will all come out. Or you're lying in bed in the middle of the night, and all of a sudden you wake up with a case of the runs, or thinking to yourself, god how great it would be to urinate right now. But Dad's asleep and won't be up for another six hours, and he already did a lot of good favors for you that day. You don't feel like interrupting his night's sleep.

Paul, you're getting heavy again. You're saying that a lot of your time is spent waiting, waiting for people, waiting for people to have the time to take care of you. I bet you wait for more things than going to the bathroom. I bet you'd just like to grab yourself a beer or a piece of cheesecake whenever you felt like it.

Or a friend.

Why do you suppose to play this role? Does God ever say anything about it? Do you ever ask him?

We've settled that a long time ago.

Oh, well damn. I must have missed something. Then. Why?

I'm something special, too. Haven't you noticed? Being half alive, all of the time, it takes a hell of a lot of talent. Grace.

And patience, my friend. I have to thank you for your great help. And a good memory.

Fr. Glendon, I write asking you to serve as my direction supervisor. I ask you to consider the case and session which I have transcribed, and allow me to conclude and pray with you over my impressions and feelings having completed my first milestone as a spiritual director. I think I ought to begin by commenting on Paul's age. I wondered, going in on this project, if you would need to speculate on serious practice of spiritual direction being done with a mid teenager. It is my knowledge of the intensity and quality of his personality which convinced me to pursue, and now gladdens me that I completed the experimental project needed to fulfill your assignment.

Paul's mobility was always very minimal; I mean not only spatially and in his dexterity, but socially and experientially. Paul really had a small world; but he never knew it, and you could never tell it to him. Paul would be quite content to sit for hours at a time pondering moral and ethical implications of abortion, divorce, embezzlement, or his own drooling. Paul, from what I've been able to observe, was extremely influenced by his father's domineering figure and stance on proper philosophies on behavior. He looked at me squarely in the eye as he made the remarks about his father being 'a piece of God'. I do not believe he was speaking of a private personal image; I think he was claiming a universal. I think that his father was by far the largest, and oldest, and certainly the most opinionated image in his life. Perhaps you noticed my difficulty, almost my inability to keep silent, not to defiantly shatter that image and interpretation, and others like it, which I took as preposterous and nearly offensive. I know Paul's father. He is as bullheaded, self-centered, and judgmental as Paul ever knew him. One of the farthest things from my mind when thinking of that man is 'being a piece of God'. But as Paul of 15 told the story, as he remembered the Boston ice cream parlor, I felt the moment very vividly. By total surprise, through composing this paper, I met a new friend; he was ten years younger than I, he endured the exact same physical and health limitations as I do, but he had completely foreign images of God, himself, people, friends, morality, faith, from my own.

Of course, my situation is impossible. This was a problem play. I thank the reader's tolerance for my distortion of nature. But for me, it was unguided education. I really was talking to my 15 year old self and listening to him, and uniquely sharing with him, and learning from him. He is that separated from the graduate student responsible for this assignment. The reader will have to believe my ignorance, at the beginning, of whom I would find the younger Paul to be, and what were the many voices inside him. Believe also that this was not a selfish practice. I am beginning the thought and prayer of discovering what I can say to the condition of being handicapped, confined to a wheelchair, confined without speech, or hearing, or sight. I say I do not consider my youthful images and experiences, or my growing ones, as possibly unique. This was indeed my first attempt at communication with these, such real phenomena to my mind, to my life, to my circle of friends. If I can come to use my gift of creativity to facilitate finding the Holy Spirit in somebody's handicap, then I'll make no apologies for this paper.

I was not able to do all I wanted to do, to introduce or represent each facet of the confined, and the searching individual which I deemed Paul of 15 to be. And I didn't touch on absolutely every aspect of Spiritual Direction which I thought should be in a merited term paper. I gave this deep concentration and sincere effort. Thank you for witnessing it.

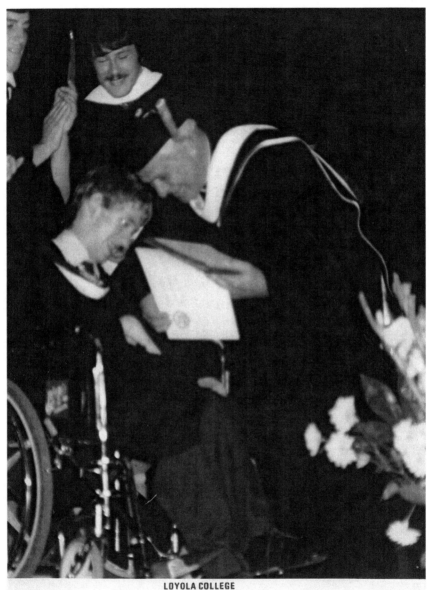

LOYOLA COLLEGE
136th Commencement
May 26, 1985

SCHOLASTICMAN

GREAT DAY!!! I'M OUT OF CLASS NOW. IT IS WONDERFUL TO KNOW THAT I'M THROUGH WITH SITTING STILL. NOW IT DOESN'T MATTER WHERE MY ARMS GO. OR IF I YAWN TOO LOUDLY.

I DON'T MIND DOING THIS TIME IN THE CAFETERIA. IT'S NOT GOING TO BE THAT LONG ANYWAY, RIGHT? JOE IS DUE TO SHOW UP IN A LITTLE OVER AN HOUR AND A HALF TO FEED ME. AND THEN IT WILL BE AFTERNOON ALREADY. AND I'M SURE I CAN GET SOMEBODY TO BRING ME DOWN TO THE RAT SO I CAN FINISH A COUPLE PITCHERS BEFORE THE BUS COMES. DOESN'T IT COME AT FOUR TODAY?

IT'S A LONELY MORNING HERE. DO YOU SEE MORE THAN SIX PEOPLE SITTING DOWN? WHAT A WAY TO LEAVE THIS PLACE. THIS LOUSY PLACE. HOW LONG HAVE I BEEN HERE? HOW MANY OF THESE KIDS HAVE COME AND GONE AND LOOKED AT ME? HOW MANY YEARS, I MEAN REAL YEARS, HAS IT BEEN SINCE I WAS ONE OF THE KIDS? THOSE WERE DAYS OF ANCIENT GREECE. THAT WAS THE AGE OF THE CHARLESTON. THAT WAS FOUR YEARS AGO.

I'M GLAD WE'RE ALONE. THE TUNES AREN'T REALLY THAT BAD THIS MORNING. I'D ALWAYS LIKE THEM TO

BE BETTER. BUT THIS JOCKEY ISN'T OFFENDING ME VERY MUCH. AND DIDN'T HE SAY SOMETHING ABOUT PLAYING THE STONES NEXT?

I CAN'T BELIEVE I'M ACTUALLY THINKING CONSISTENT SENTENCES ABOUT THIS RADIO STATION. I MUST ACCEPT THE FACT THAT IT IS ACTUALLY A PART OF MY DAY WHENEVER I'M SITTING HERE. STILL, IT CONCERNS ME, AND IT SADDENS ME THAT I'VE ADAPTED TO THIS STILL LIFE, AND TO THIS WAY OF LIVING ALONE, SELF-SUFFICIENT, UNTIL SOMEONE I KNOW I CAN COUNT ON IS FREE AND TELLS ME HE CAN SPARE JUST A FEW MINUTES TO HELP ME GET ALL MY BUSINESS IN ORDER. YOU KNOW, I SIT HERE, AND ALL THESE KIDS SEE ME SIT HERE. IT REALLY DOES LOOK LIKE I HAVE NOT A LOT OF THINGS TO DO. IT'S BECOMING A SAYING WITH A FEW OF THE ONES WHO PASS AND SAY HELLO AND SAY A COUPLE OF WORDS AFTER THAT. I'VE HEARD THEM SAY, "HEY, OH, PAUL DOESN'T HAVE ANYTHING TO DO BUT SIT AROUND ALL DAY AND WAIT FOR PEOPLE. WOW, IT MUST BE NICE." WHAT IN THE HELL DO THEY THINK THEY'RE SAYING? DO YOU SUPPOSE THEY TURN THEM OUT DUMBER YEAR AFTER YEAR?

I'M BECOMING HOSTILE NOW. I'M SORRY. NO NEED TO AT ALL. LOOK OUT, WILL YOU? GOD, YOU COULDN'T WANT A NICER DAY. THERE CERTAINLY IS A LOT TO BE SAID FOR SPRING. YOU KNOW, IT'S MORE THAN ONE PERSON CAN THINK OF. DO YOU THINK SPRING IS GOING TO HURT ME THIS YEAR? I TEND TO DOUBT IT. IT COULD HAVE GONE EITHER WAY THIS TIME AROUND, BUT I'M GUESSING THAT THE LOVE THING HAS RUN ITS COURSE. IT'S USELESS GETTING DEPRESSED ABOUT LOVE TODAY WHEN THERE'S SO MUCH TO DO TO GET MYSELF FINALLY THE HELL OUT OF HERE. I MEAN THIS IS THE LAST YEAR THAT IT'S GOING TO MATTER ANYWAY, RIGHT? IF IT HASN'T COME TO ME YET, IT'S NOT GOING

TO COME TO ME HERE AT THIS SCHOOL. AND I'M JUST MEANT TO FIND IT SOMEWHERE ELSE.

AND ALL THE SPRING MEMORIES OF THIS PLACE, ON THE ASTROTURF, BY THE POND NEXT TO THE LIBRARY, ON THE HILL OUTSIDE THE DORMS, HAVING BARBECUES AT MCAULEY, EATING LUNCH WITH THE SUN IN HER EYES, TAKING THAT PICNIC BASKET TO SHERWOOD GARDENS, THEY'LL NEVER BE ABLE TO FIND ME NEXT YEAR. WILL THEY?

I'M LOSING IT. IT MUST BE TIME TO TAKE A NAP. AM I IN A GOOD POSITION? WILL IT HURT MY NECK VERY MUCH LEANING MY HEAD DOWN? I THINK WE'RE COOL. I'LL SEE YOU IN A COUPLE MINUTES. WAKE ME IF ANY GOOD SONGS COME ON. ALRIGHT.

ALRIGHT, JUST THINK ABOUT THE SONGS ON THE RADIO. NOTHING IS HAPPENING EXCEPT THE SONGS ON THE RADIO. THERE'S A BIG GIANT RADIO IN THE MIDDLE OF THIS PLACE, AND IT'S OVER EVERYBODY'S HEAD AND IT'S CRASHING THEM DOWN. AND NOBODY IS AROUND TO SEE YOU OR HEAR YOU. THEY'RE ALL GONE. THEY'RE ALL GONE. T.H.E.Y.A.R.E.A.L.L. G.O.N.E. AND YOU'RE THE ONLY ONE LEFT. AND WE'RE ONLY IN THE CAFETERIA, NOT IN THE CIVIC CENTER. WE'RE NOT AT GRADUATION. THIS DOESN'T HAVE TO BE GOING ON. THIS ISN'T GRADUATION. AND EVEN IF IT IS, IT'S ONLY HIGH SCHOOL. SO IT REALLY DOESN'T MATTER. WE'VE DONE THIS BEFORE. REMEMBER HIGH SCHOOL GRADUATION? REMEMBER HOW WELL WE DID THERE? WE DIDN'T MOVE A MUSCLE. NO MOVEMENTS, NO JERKS, NO GRUNTS, NO ERRORS. EVERYTHING WAS PERFECT. P.E.R.F.E YEAH, I KNOW. WELL, THIS IS EXACTLY THE SAME NOW. EXACTLY THE SAME. AND I BELIEVE YOU'RE DOING FINE NOW. YEAH. YOU'RE DOING FINE. ALRIGHT. YOUR LEGS HAVE STOPPED. NO

MORE TENSION COMING FROM DOWN THERE. AND I'VE GOT YOUR ARMS TRAPPED IN A GOOD POSITION. I'LL KEEP THEM THERE STEADILY. DON'T WORRY ABOUT THEM AND, AND, YOU'RE FINE NOW. BACK TO NORMAL. PICK YOUR HEAD UP AGAIN.

GOD, THIS IS NICE. OH MY GOD, THIS IS NICE. LOOK AT ALL THESE PEOPLE HERE. HOLY SHEEP. ALL HERE TO SEE ME GRADUATE. NO NO, ONLY KIDDING, ONLY KIDDING. SETTLE DOWN. BE COOL. NO, BUT REALLY, THINK HOW MANY PEOPLE MUST BE IN MY CLASS. I MEAN, IF YOU COUNTED UP ALL THE PEOPLE YOU KNOW, I BET YOU'D BE SURPRISED. ARE YOU LISTENING TO THE NAMES? --NO, I WAS TOO BUSY TAKING CARE OF YOU. OH, I'VE CAUGHT A FEW HERE OR THERE. WE'RE ON THE B'S NOW, RIGHT? THAT MEANS THEY'VE CALLED AMY? THAT GUY AMY? IS HE REALLY HERE? DID HE MAKE IT? DO YOU REALLY WANT TO TALK ABOUT THAT? WELL, I WISH HIM WELL. I'M SORRY THAT WE CAN'T TALK TO EACH OTHER ANYMORE. OUR DIVORCE WAS A HARD ONE. IT TOOK ME OVER A YEAR TO GET OVER IT. IT PROBABLY TOOK HIM ALL OF NINETY SECONDS. TRUE, I WOULDN'T CALL HIM A GOOD FRIEND. BUT THAT'S ONLY ME. I'VE SAID THAT ABOUT A LOT OF PEOPLE.

YEH! BARUBE. NOW WE'RE STARTING TO GET THE RUGBY TEAM GOING UP THERE. WOW! THAT'S NICE TO HEAR. HEY, IS EVERYBODY WHO'S SUPPOSED TO BE GRADUATING GRADUATING? I BELIEVE SO. ALL THE GUYS FROM OUR CLASS, PLUS A FEW CHOICE ONES WHO DIDN'T MAKE IT LAST YEAR. HEY, MAN, IT'S ONLY LIFE. WHY DO IN FOUR YEARS WHAT YOU CAN DO IN FIVE? THEY GOT ONE MORE SEASON IN. CAN YOU IMAGINE, MY RUGBY TEAM GRADUATING? DOESN'T IT SEND SOMETHING DOWN YOUR SPINE WHEN YOU REALIZE THAT IN JUST A COUPLE YEARS ALL OF THESE SCRUNGY MUDDERS WILL ACTUALLY BE PROPER RESPECTABLE

SUIT-WEARING BUSINESSMEN EARNING OVER THIRTY THOUSAND A YEAR? HOW DEPRESSING. BY THAT TIME, THEY'LL ALL BE MARRIED, WHIPPED FOR LIFE, HAVE TWO KIDS, TWO DOGS, TWO CARS. AND TROY WILL BE EVERYBODY'S BOSS, ALL OVER AGAIN. JUST YOU SEE. I BET I GOT IT ALL FIGURED OUT.

HEY, ARE ALL THE GIRLS OUT THERE WATCHING US? ALL OUR FRIENDS? CAN YOU SEE THAT FAR INTO THE AUDIENCE? OH, I CAN SEE IT SOME. I CAN SEE THE FIRST COUPLE ROWS. LET'S SEE, I DON'T THINK I CAN RECOGNIZE ANYBODY IN THAT ROW. GOING SLOWLY... BUT NO, I DON'T THINK---OH HEY, WAIT A MINUTE. THAT'S STACEY. HEY, AMAZING. WHO DOES SHE KNOW THAT'S GRADUATING? HEY, ISN'T SHE KIND OF LOOKING OVER HERE? LIKE, AT ME? SHE'S LOOKING IN MY DIRECTION. SHE'S LOOKING AT ME. AND I'M LOOKING AT HER. ALL AT THE SAME TIME. AMAZING. SIMPLY AMAZING. WHO'D A'THOUGHT? SHE'S SMILING AT ME. WHAT A NEAT THING THAT SHE WOULD COME HERE AND SIT THERE AND SMILE AT ME. COOL. OF ALL THE PEOPLE HERE TODAY ALL AROUND ME, I THINK I'M GETTING THE BIGGEST SMILE FROM HER. MY LEGS ARE MOVING A LITTLE BIT. I WISH THEY'D SHUT UP.

YEAH. WHO WAS THAT? OH, STACEY. WOW. YOU KNOW, A FEW YEARS AGO SHE USED TO SIT WAY OVER ON THE OTHER SIDE OF THE CAFETERIA FROM ME. AND DON'T YOU REMEMBER? JOE ALWAYS THOUGHT SHE WAS CUTE, AND HE HAD A CRUSH ON HER. AND THEN I'D SAY, "JOE, IF YOU REALLY LIKE HER, WHY DON'T YOU GO UP AND START TALKING TO HER?" AND THEN HE'D GO INTO HIS ALFALFA IMITATION AND SAY, "AW, WELL, I DON'T KNOW. SHE MIGHT THINK I'M GOOFY." SO THEN I TRIED TO DO MY MARLON BRANDO AND TRY TO GET HER OVER THERE AND START PAYING US SOME ATTENTION. IT'S

AMAZING HOW LITTLE SOPHOMORES AND FRESHMEN UNDERSTAND. SHE LOOKED AT ME AS IF I WAS A BUG.

IT'S A SHAME IT TOOK SO LONG FOR US TO SEE WHAT GOOD FRIENDS WE COULD BE. NOW SHE'S ONE OF THE PEOPLE I KNOW I CAN COUNT ON. SHE'S ALWAYS GOOD FOR A NICE BIG HELLO. SHE'LL PUSH ME WHEREVER I'M GOING. SHE'S A PRETTY PERSON WHO DOESN'T MIND MAKING NEW FRIENDS. I LIKE THAT. I FELL FOR HER, SERIOUS COMMON DECENCY. I MIGHT EVEN GO SO FAR AS TO SAY I AM DEEPLY IN COMMON DECENCY WITH THAT GIRL RIGHT THERE. STACEY.

DAMN, I'M SORRY I'M MAKING YOU LAUGH. I REALLY SHOULD KNOW BETTER. YOU HAVE TO BE AS NULL AS YOU CAN BE TO BE STILL. I JUST THOUGHT YOU'D LIKE TO HEAR WHAT VONNEGUT WOULD SAY IN THIS SITUATION. IF ONLY WE COULD TEACH EVERYBODY IN THIS PLACE RIGHT HERE TO HAVE SOME COMMON DECENCY. I MEAN WHEN I JUST GRUNTED AND BREATHED HEAVILY. I MEAN I'M PRETTY DAMN GOOD AT KEEPING MY BODY STILL AND CONTROLLING MY BREATHING IN TOUGH SITUATIONS LIKE THIS. BUT AFTER ALL, I'M GRADUATING FROM COLLEGE HERE. I MEAN DON'T YOU THINK I HAVE SOME PRIVILEGE TO LET SOME GRUNTS AND SNORTS GO BY? WHENEVER JOHN NOLAN MAKES A NOISE, EVERYBODY IN THE HALL LISTENS. HE'S NO BETTER THAN I. AND EVEN HE DIDN'T BOTHER TO SHOW UP AT COMMENCEMENT EXERCISES. HE SAID IT WAS TOO LONG. AND HE HAD TO CLEAN HIS ROOM. AND EVERYONE NODDED THEIR HEADS AND SMILED.

WELL, WHY AREN'T THEY SMILING AT ME HERE? THIS IS MY SHOW. AND NOBODY'S MAKING IT ANY EASIER FOR ME WHEN THEY LOOK AT ME EVERYTIME I MAKE A SOUND WITH MY CHAIR. STOP LOOKING AT ME,

PEOPLE. NOW I HAVE MY HEAD DOWN AGAIN, AND I'D LIKE TO BRING IT UP AS SOON AS POSSIBLE. THIS IS GETTING OUT OF CONTROL. I KNOW THAT THEY'RE AT THE END OF CALLING THE N'S, AND I'M NOT READY YET FOR THEM TO BEGIN THE P'S. I NEED SOME KIND OF HELP.

HEY, HOW WOULD YOU FEEL IF I CALLED STACEY OVER TO TALK TO ME? MAN, SHE COULD BE RIGHT HERE, RIGHT NOW. ALL YOU'D HAVE TO DO IS BRING UP YOUR HEAD. SEE? THERE SHE IS. YOU KNOW, SHE'S A GOOD FRIEND. SHE WOULDN'T MIND AT ALL HELPING YOU THROUGH THIS.

STACEY, IS IT REALLY HARD FOR PEOPLE TO KNOW HOW TO TREAT ME?

"WELL, NO, PAUL. I DON'T THINK SO. I THINK YOU'RE A VERY CUTE, FRIENDLY, CHARMING GUY."

WELL, I KNOW ALL THAT. BUT WHY DO SOME MISUNDERSTAND? IT SEEMS LIKE IT'S A LOT OF PEOPLE. WHY DO THEY WALK BY AND GIVE ME NOTHING WHEN IT WOULD BE JUST AS EASY FOR THEM TO BE POLITE AND SAY HEY.

"IT'S JUST THAT SOME PEOPLE NEED BIG LIVING PROOF THAT YOU'RE JUST LIKE EVERYBODY ELSE. A LITTLE DIFFERENT, BUT JUST LIKE EVERYBODY ELSE."

WELL, SOMETIMES WHEN THE PEOPLE ARE WALKING PAST ME, I ENVY THEM SO MUCH. I THINK THAT IT MUST BE SUCH A GREAT LIFE FOR THEM IF THEY'D RATHER WALK BY AND NOT BOTHER TO NOTICE SOMETHING AS INTERESTING AS ME.

"NO, PAUL. IT'S THEIR LOSS, AND YOU KNOW IT. SAY, ISN'T THAT YOUR NAME?"

I SUDDENLY SPRANG UP BRIGHT AND BOLD AND EXPECTED TO SEE FATHER SELLINGER COMING TOWARDS ME. I WAS QUAKED WITH THE BIGGEST SHOCK OF MY LIFE. JOE IS TUGGING ON MY SHOULDER NOW AND ASKING ME WHAT I WANT FOR LUNCH. AND BEHOLD IT WAS ALL A DREAM.

They Graduate

Tonight was their prom night. I guess I'm an old one, too old to have been asked. It's funny, but last year I was too. Last year, I remember, at the helicopter party in the courtyard, I went with those three girls all around outside while they hunted and soared for their dates to that prom. I must have missed this year's hunt, because I don't remember it. Maybe it's that I am never there at the right time, or rather I wasn't. Maybe that's why I've only been to my own proms. Maybe that's why I only attend the parties I throw. Do I need to resolve this? Is this really unnecessary? Don't I have to worry about it too much?

Now the readers are the graduates. Two days later, they're listening to the commencement sayings; and I'm laying down tracks they'd never recognize from me. And when they read this, they'll get worried and scared, right about now, because they fear they won't like it when it's over. How very very close we all are. How terribly terribly intimate, that you know exactly how much my written word means, and I know how much you've come to depend on digging my words. My deepest fear has been for years that once I will wake up and suddenly discover that I actually was a narc, I actually was an agent from Moral Majority, or the damned Supreme Court who really does have this thing against marijuana and sodomy. Sometimes I have worried my heart out that my father hangs out in my head while I'm with you guys. Don't you find that you talk to me about the same length of time that you talk to him? Am I your friend or your parent? Why in the hell couldn't I have come to your prom? Either, any one of them?

219

You're getting mad, very disappointed in a letter from me, and wondering seriously whether to continue. Listen, I came here to deliver an address that Sellinger wouldn't dream to ask me for either. Some of you know what I feel about that man and this school. Some of you know what I feel about rejection slips. Some of you know what I think of Oliver North. And I think that you really know some what I feel about you. If you don't, then you don't deserve the credit I've been giving you. For god's sake, you've fed me lunch, and dinner, and then breakfast. You are my hands for pouring beer, therefore you are my inebriation. Therefore you are my youth, and therefore my vitality. You and I are separated by two years, but then so much more. I'm Paul, and therefore I'm sitting, and I'm still, and I roll everywhere to get there, you push me. I'm patient when you can't get what I'm saying, and I'm happy when you do, and we laugh, and I make that sound, and you laugh some more at that. And then I point that I want another beer. I wrote those books that you dug, and you showed your mother, and your friends at home. I write the wild stuff. And I became remarkable when you thought about it a little, and when you talked it out the first couple times. Did you ever, ever, ever realize what you missed? When you dreamed about me, I must have walked. Where did I go? What did you think of me then? Was I ever closer to being a part of your life? Would you have fallen in love with me?

Come on now, for the last time that I'll have you. Think of me. I gave Morel his charm, I gave Farrel his horn, I gave Sireci his good looks. In my pants is a universe, and I'll tell everybody. I mean not to be uncool. I would never leave you with a gross face. This letter will end with the love that you want from me. But I've never bothered to talk to a block of people in this manner before. Understand, you are my class. You are the class who took care of me the most, and you understood me the best. A man could want nothing more. So if I ever really indeed feel like a man, I'll look at you girls, at you guys, and I'll know, as you must know how, everything was alright between us, everything worked, you handled me properly.

But now you're not going to be two years younger than I anymore. You're starting way damned ahead. I'll become that much more sedentary tomorrow. My hands and my feet are moving away from home. And don't think it doesn't affect me. Don't think that I'm not watching you leave regretting horribly that I'll never be a part of your life again, and you will never have a mind to marry me. Don't think this isn't the saddest spring of my life. Don't think that I can take it all the time. Why in the hell do you think I drink?

Some of you know that I wanted to be long far away from here by this time. I would have dug just flying in for the weekend, and kissing you and patting you and saying congratulations like I hardly remember your name. That's not the way it ended up. I've been with you intensely the last four months. You always understand when I need you. I must have a look on me at those times. I have to love you for taking me in, and for knowing when it's right to spend time with me. Everytime you fed me, every drink you poured, everytime you wiped my face or my behind, everyday you lugged me to Beatty to meet my bus, every hill that we took, or we crashed, or you ruined your shoes on, every ride you gave me, every shower you gave me, everytime you took me for one more piss, and everynight you sat me on your sofa and turned out the light, you very excellently held my life in your hands. That's what you did.

Maybe I didn't have to write this letter. Maybe I'm nothing more than a huge crybaby who's embarrassing the hell out of myself. Maybe they've stopped kicking Edgar Allen Poe by now. I cannot say. I think I know how this letter is going to come out. I feel that I am in an uncontrollable situation. And I am a person who must be in control, someway, always. For the most part, I become, I must be the people who happen to be taking care of me at the time. I am the people who are in my immediate circle. I cannot be people who are not. You are all going away from me now. What you can accomplish by ability and space, I must accomplish emotionally. This is my only solution. I love you, and for the most part I'll leave you.

But we will still go see the Dead.   Paul P.

Words to the Graduating Class

Maryland Rehabilitation Center
November 26, 1986.

With these words coming out of this synthesizer many of you have probably not heard before, I will try to convey what I think this day means to all of us. I suppose that will be quite easy to do. A graduation is no less than the completion of a very major job, and that is cause for the utmost in celebration.

I can't help but to get the feeling of humbleness and unity in this room today. We will all celebrate Thanksgiving tomorrow with our families, and the pride and happiness that we are all feeling now is surely going to carry over into tomorrow's party, and long after as well.

I am used to speaking and writing about life with my own cerebral palsy, and my own limitations, and trying to make people see the wonder and intrigue in overcoming such nasty obstacles to lead what I call a very happy and full life. I realize that this morning I must address a much broader topic than just my cerebral palsy. And this ceremony signifies the achievement of each graduate in many areas. But as I said, there is unity in this room. And I think that on this day of graduation from MRC, there are many common denominators that we ought to touch on.

I will take a guess. I bet that no matter how severe or how light your disability is, you have felt very low and sad about it more times than you care to admit. And I would guess that your problem hurt you the deepest, either when it first came to you, or when you first realized that some ability or quality that had been very important to you was taken away. I don't need to take that very far at all. Whatever images or memories this presents to you, I am here to get across to you with my most energy that the spirit is so high and so ripe for you here this morning to treasure in what you have accomplished.

I am a person who looks for answers constantly. I like to find answers for all types of situations, good and bad. In my writings, I deal many times with antitheses. For every mood or kind of traveling I experience, I like to answer it back to the other side of the scale. I really don't like being handicapped. I really don't like being sedentary, and dependent on someone else to go somewhere. I resent these aspects of my life so much that I can curse at it all as easily as I could say good morning to you. Yet there are so many good things that come to me everyday. High on the list is a position in the Health Care Financing Administration, from where a number of my supervisors and colleagues are here today. And for this I thank them very much.

God can be accountable for many reasons why we're happy, and why we're able to accomplish happiness for ourselves. I take a very firm belief in self preservation. There will never be any other person who understands or appreciates how you feel more than you yourself do. And I believe that everyone ought to think long and hard about answering themselves. I believe that today is a perfect time for you to find some very good answers. "Why was I hurt?", or "Why was I born this way?", "Why have I had to take this course in my life that seems so far away from the mainstream, what other people go through and think nothing of it?" And I believe, and I truly want to get through to you, that if you can't find many answers for yourselves today, with your diploma in your hand, and all of the memories of your work and your achievement here at MRC, then you surely don't care about finding answers as much as I do. Perhaps you choose to observe this day in a totally different way than I would. If I was an MRC graduate today, I would be very content and proud of myself.

I would say that it is impossible for me to go into any more depth with you now through this near monotonic voice. I hope I was able to bring some things to light as much as I know I was honored to talk to you. Thank you very much. Remember that, just as it has always been, your future success, your future happiness, everything is up to you.

THE JUST LIFE

This is true prayer. I am going to examine a form and a definition of living prayer of mine, then I want to display and explain a radical change due to a very recent tragedy for me. The tragedy is present and overwhelming. I would rather be writing an analysis of a book by Walter Brueggemann for a course I'm taking this summer. But I've been told to write something else. I was bestowed with a conclusion of my paper before I chose to begin it.

If I had not been born handicapped, likely I would have not devoted my life to writing. If I were not bestowed with curiosity, endurance, and a need for fulfillment, likely I would never want the intensity that I live. If I did not ask the questions that I do, likely my thirst for the answers would have slept long ago. If I could use my voice to speak clearly, I'd have been a rock and roll singer.

I was a senior in college on a night in September, 1984. No less than three weeks earlier, my father, who is about forty years older than I, has undergone a triple bypass heart operation. I lived in my parents' house at that time for a very particular and unfortunate reason. The preceding January I had moved from home to a residence owned and operated by United Cerebral Palsy. By that August, I had lost very much weight, hope and faith due to conditions there. I decided that I could not possibly remain the individual I had been before that January if I continued to live in the residence where I received little and poor care, much depression, where I was unsure about my attendants' drug habits. My tolerance broke completely at the worst of possible times-- days before my father, my arms and legs while I am at home, was due for surgery.

My father benefited very much from his surgery; he has been very healthy and content since. To compensate for the hardship of my presence at home in those weeks and months when care and attention needed to be directed to my father, my mother hired the son of her friend to come to our hose in the evenings to help me in the bathroom and to put me to bed. Now, please have the heart to forgive me for going to all that trouble just to set my scene, but for the first part of this prayer, I want you in that bathroom with me on that night in September, 1984.

It was a time when I would have preferred to have a bowel movement. Though I did have one that morning, it was the way I was feeling that it would be an easier night in bed if I had a bowel movement right then. I would have to go to bed early that night, at 9:30, being exactly in the middle of writing a term paper on the seventeenth century essay, Reglio Medici. My will, my driving aim makes me regret deeply being irregular in the middle of any project, or retiring to bed before I'm finished with it or at a good breaking point. Term papers or bowel movements, they are, like so many other things, much too much effort physically for an athetoid to attempt, having to be cut short or prevented.

I want to introduce you to my mother's friend's son. At the time he was a senior in high school. I think he still might be. Now for this prayer, essentially the first of the three instruments I shall use for this entire paper, is in reaction to this seventeen year old Towson High student, complaining aggrivatively at me from outside the bathroom door, explaining in his teenaged voice that he wishes I'd hurry up and take my dump because he needs to leave my house early tonight; he's got to ask this new chick if she would go out with him.

"If you don't know who I am, let me remind you. Lord, I am Paul. You've let me live to be 23, and I'll admit that sometimes I wonder why you've decided to force many people to endure me for that long. But for all the bitching and manipulating I do, I think that I'm not such a bad specimen. I think I'm a man now. If you had to call me something, you'd likely call me an adult. I am a very respected and admired figure in the community. And it's getting to the point now when you wouldn't have to bend the truth so very far for that acclaim to be justified. God, with your grace, or else without it, I have written and self-published twenty four books. Yes, that is one more the number of years I have lived. I am so 'talented' and energetic. I have so much I want to do and make of my life. Why the hell are you making me listen to this snotnosed, asinine, impatient kid who's really got no problem except that he's a little horny, but that'll be solved in a day or two, won't it? I've had that very problem since I was his age, and you haven't seen to take it away from me since. No no no, I'm not even asking why his sex life is more important than my sex life. I'm asking you why his sex life has to be more important than my bowel movement or my term paper on Reglio Medici?"

The kid continued to bark and complain despite the ugly condescending looks I gave him. So God and I talked more to each other, more about it. And it became one of the best nights of my life.

"Reglio Medici is about justice, isn't it? Yeah it deals a lot about justice. God, you know, I'd like to have some justice here, now. What kind of justice can I find here where I'm sitting. You're not letting my bowels move and get out of me; I'll likely be uncomfortable later in the night. I'm gonna have to go to bed right away at 9:30, while all of my friends at school are having their midweek keg party, all of my teachers are wondering why my term papers aren't done yet, and all of those people in the community who respect and admire me are wondering where I am. How did it get to the point where a seventeen year old kid is actually telling me what to do, when not to take a dump, and when to go to bed. NO no no, I'm not asking you physically how it happened; I was there, I read the script. I mean what do I do with it: How do I answer it to myself, finally tonight when I'm all alone in bed, and nobody will know where I am, and this bozo is gonna be out riding in his car, around my Towson, on my payroll, on my time doing things that I should have done and gotten over with five years ago?"

I really was determined to find justice; some justice; any justice. And what do you know?

"No, wait a minute, let's get some justice out of this. I think I'm ready to do that now. No no no, the kid can wait a second, because I believe I'm on to something. There must be justice, in the eyes of God, in this situation, in any situation. When God puts one in a situation, it's got to be just. I mean think of what a far better person I am; it's got to be just. I won't think too hard about it because I already have a pretty good idea. I was born with a much larger ego than handicap. And that's justice. Thank God for it. Where would I be if this was all I saw, if I really took this kid seriously, if I didn't think I had God to talk to about this? I'm sitting on this toilet now, frustrated as hell, for a reason. I don't know what the reason is right now, but who's to say that I won't find out, or figure it out the very next time that I'm extremely happy? The very next keg party I'm at; when I'm finished this damned term paper on Religio Medici; when I meet one of those people in the community who respects and admires me; or tomorrow morning when I finally have this bowel movement. Bill, I'm ready to get up now. And no, you don't have to wipe me tonight."

In bed, I received the remainder of my theory. It has only taken me two and three quarter years to transcribe it from cerebrum to paper.

"Gee, I'd like to create a body of work, a collection of several books of prose and poetry which would primarily represent the thought and personality of the mature, intelligent, sensitive, imprisoned mind trapped in a severely, or else mildly handicapped body. Well gee, wouldn't I be absolutely the best and most perfect individual to do such a thing? I can give such great sermons on the john. And give me a night in bed, I can make anybody forget what they learned in Sunday school. Maybe I should make it clear that I'm referring to my talent of staying awake until any hour of the night debating and dissecting any subject of personal or social relevance, totally within the confines of my head. Of course, you've heard, I'm always alone in bed.

No no no, you know, maybe this task of writing should be undertaken as a team. And what should be the title of our doctrine? What mind do we start with? Wasn't I just speaking about justice, the justice of it all? Wouldn't such a writing team be doing a great service to a potential audience if it could aggregate and present theories on the justice of each individual, handicapped or not, striving to find peace in his/her life in accepting the forced responsibility and endurance that comes to him/her? Self preservation. This is what Adam Smith started with when he made Capitalism. This is what Martin Luther wanted to get off the wall. God gave, no no no, God gives every single one of us what we see for very specific reasons. The goods are not divided equally. I don't even think that it is humanly possible to interpret any true equilibrium in the distributed goods at all. I guess such an equilibrium exists, but it's buried in the numenon. No human being will ever look at this world, such as it is, and say with a right mind that it is fair.

I never thought that Capitalism was all that fair myself. Yet, almost all of us, in this hemisphere, were raised from Sunday school that Capitalism was blessed by Jesus. He said, 'oh the poor, they'll always be with us. You want to please God, you do the best you can, without appearing too selfish. Now, I shall zap you with parables if your mind gets out of wrack with the ego thing. But God has said that you can keep the land you've gotten for yourself. There's nothing wrong with that. Your selfishness only goes so far as your consciousness. I can't fault you for something going on behind your back while you're looking forward. I told you to look forward. I'd just like you to keep in mind that there are those running absolutely all around you. And once or twice a day you might step on the toes of those behind you, this not being your fault. Every thing of yours has its price; and I know exactly why everybody is in their place in line.'

This is my definition of Capitalism. This is my definition of life in this hemisphere. This is the mind with which I start thinking about possible justice. So I thought on that night in 1984 that I would fancy creating explanations and conclusions on 'the just life'. I still had a lot of seventeenth century literature in my system, and I was looking for a more sophisticated, polished way to say it all. Latin was my only hope. Think; how can you start a church if you don't start with Latin? You might be able to, but I wouldn't want part of it. How could I say 'the just life' in Latin; three words in one? Well, in Latin, there is no 'the', so that took one third of my problem away. Then, usually they had a nice way of chopping off a little piece of their j's to make nice little i's out of them, so 'iust' had to get into my word. 'Life' is vita', but nobody would yell at you if you forgot the 'a' for a minute, or if you had to change it to an 'i' maybe. And I already have an 'i' just waiting for me at the beginning of 'iust'. Now let's see; I have about seven letters so far, that nice little 'i' being the link between the two parts. There would be no harm in adding one more letter to round this off to eight. And look, I got this 'a' at the end that I forgot about for a minute. Sure. This is a first declension feminine noun, what I'm going to call my new church, or 'church'. VITIUSTA. Sure, that's the ticket.

Now you know.

I have just shared with you a prayer from a September evening in 1984. I hope that it becomes clear to you what its content and purpose have stayed prior on my mind and intention. Now in the summer of 1987, my ambition is taking physical shape and direction. But is had been a very very long time since the night I have discussed. This composition, for its purpose and merit, needs to examine two more evening prayers; the next I shall remember as 1985 was ending and so was much of my understanding of myself. And then there is tonight, a time when all of my questions have been answered in a horrible way.

I had been an unemployed college graduate for seven months, or so it seemed to many people. I've always been employed. I feel that more people have been told by my tongue that I am a writer than have laid eyes on anything I've published. And so much gravity of this feeling had become a part of me by the end of 1985. I was shutting down my publishing service because of lack of external support and interest. I was crying to myself everynight, or any time I hung the phone after a friend seemed too busy to talk to me. I really was in the center of several stages and many emotions. And it happened to be December 8, the fifth anniversary of Lennon's death. I considered death, and I considered dying, and how I would eventually go about it. First, yes of course, I felt very sheepish and unoriginal considering something like death or suicide on such a necessarily meaningless day. Then I came to some conclusions in God's presence.

"Listen, death might seem unoriginal, especially on December 8. But where else can you really go beyond that. I mean we all are necessarily human, so this is a necessarily human matter, and being humans, yes we necessarily do have a limit as to what is possible for us to do. A person cannot do much more than die, when he dies. It's not like he really can come back for an encore, or on the next night, to top himself. Though it's been done by our favorite rock stars, desperate lovers, and despondent poets, it isn't like I shall do anything better than simply die when the time presents itself.

"Well alright, is it going to present itself, or are you going to present yourself to it? I mean are you ready to die? Do you want to commit suicide?

"No. Certainly not tonight, no matter how miserable I am now. I know that I have been this miserable on other nights in other years. But I want to say that I don't think that I have too many more years left to be doing this. I mean you can't live, or be alive without growing and advancing. Man, I'd like to grow and advance, but nobody seems psyched to help me. I mean I'd like to be married at this time, or soon. But the girls aren't even returning my calls, much less planning to devote the rest of their lives to me. It's not a good thing to think about. And here I am, already a well seasoned writer, and it barely gets a mention in the family newsletter.

"There's no family newsletter.

"It's a metaphor. If my family did have a newsletter, my writing wouldn't be in there.

"So, you'd like to die now because nobody loves you and nobody reads you.

"No, I didn't say that. I'm not ready to die. There's still VITIUSTA, and there's still '86, when I plan to write fifty books consecutively and pass them out in Greenwich Village every weekend. Then at the end of this decade, I thought it would be nice for me to write some classical poetry and good novels. I have these plans that I want to see through.

"But then?

"But then, I think that it would be nice to stop. Just stop. Do you realize how horribly my back hurts because of my perverted posture? Do you realize my fear and lack of interest in planning to do five consecutive things without knowing when's the next time I can have a bowel movement? Do you know how much it hurts to be forced to live as a celibate without making the choice to do so? I just don't think I want to do this for too many more damn years.

"I thought you wanted to apply to graduate school. I thought that would mean that you had maybe countless more things to add to society.

"I just want to do that for VITIUSTA. Just about everything else I have to offer, I've put down already. Anybody who wants to can find it and recopyright it anytime in the future. I must, I must be one of them who has to die before he lives, in the hearts of old men and young girls.

"Nobody else would ever buy this if you bothered to say it out loud; you realize that. I mean Sylvia Plath would, and Brian Jones would. Even somebody as far out as Theresa of Avila or Denise Hemphill would understand what you're saying. But nobody who would call themselves close to you would understand that you can predict, that you want to manage all of the events in the rest of your life so precisely that you can now say on what day you'll be ready and able to die. No no no, don't get me wrong here; I'm not saying that this all doesn't make enough sense to me. (I'm not sure I want to say that it does either.) I just want to hear you all out. I'd like you to spell it out as much as you can for yourself. I'd like to remind you that certain people, such as yourself, and in particular, artists who think like you think and carry around very deep and final plans concerning their own mortality are more than often deemed by their surrounders as weird, dangerous, and to a large extent undesirable at backyard parties. Tell me, can you deal with that? Until your reservations are confirmed for your next planet, how are you going to explain it to the neighbors?

"Oh, I wouldn't bother the neighbors with this tripe. Would you? These sorts of plans are by their nature subject to change. I've arranged the events and the course in my life so long and successfully by now, that I know never to go to the newspaper with the press release until all of the details are filled in. I won't even let this project be discussed outside the head. Right now, all we do is go to the people with plans for the Greenwich Village writings in '86, and graduate school and VITIUSTA in '87. Okay, babe?

"Ok, Paul. God, it's a good thing this is prayer. Who the hell else would understand this?"

Indeed, perhaps I lost my reader at certain times in 1985. Perhaps you could return and reread those words later, after I have a chance to pray with you tonight. A few hours ago, God bothered to speak to me, and it was a reply to my call of December 8, a year and a half ago.

John Paradiso died on Monday this week. My father stumbled across his obituary about an hour before I came home from work today, and he informed me immediately when I came home. John committed suicide, partially because he had just lost his job. He worked in a booth in a parking lot. And he killed himself, partially because he had just lost his job.

John Paradiso was born on December 15, 1961; he was born with a rare form of arthritis which deformed both his hands, his feet, and paralyzed his legs. John and I went from grade school to half of high school together; it came to be we were best friends and blood brothers for over eleven years. I went on to Calvert Hall and Loyola College. He graduated from Randallstown High, and we drifted apart quickly. The last time I saw him was at a Bruce Springsteen concert in 1984, and we didn't stay to party afterwards in order to have a real conversation. And before that evening, it must have been over a year since he had bothered to telephone me. And I never lost the habit of forgetting to return his calls. And he died last Monday, and I cannot say I have an idea who he has been or what he has been through in these last years.

"Yes you can.

"I can?

"What do you think? It's the same story. John is the same story. He had a different address, a different cast of characters. But you are not ignorant of why he died. You can fill in the blanks, now. Can't you?

"Yes. I know what you are saying. But where do I start? I'm so very hurt.

"Who would you really like to be with right now?

"Mrs Edwards, our teacher. Or Danny, or Joe, or Jackie.

"How about John's mother? Now she is inside a horrible hell, inside a funeral parlor. She doesn't know why John is dead. If you think you do, could you go there and tell her?

"Lord, I can't talk. My body couldn't do a thing right now but spasm in pressure and embarrassment.

"Would you do me a favor and write it down then? Please? With some four part harmony, and feeling?

"I don't want to do this. No no no, I don't want to do this.

"Yes. I am well aware of this.

"I would rather be writing on Brueggemann.

"Oh well, don't worry. I'll square it with your instructor. It will be cool.

"I don't want to be doing this. I don't want to do this. I'd rather not have to do this. I don't want to do this. Can you understand this? I don't want to do this.

"And do you really think that I wanted to listen to you on December 8, 1985? Do you think that was a joy for me? Listen, am I teaching you something here, or not? Am I speaking to you right now, or not? Do you have something to say to John's mother? Or don't you? Aren't you sitting in front of your keyboard right now? Write her your letter tonight; please."

And so I'll write the letter. I have to. I have to accept the conclusion of my prayer. It is very very hard to accept, very very hard to see the hope of any justice.

Dear Miss Darlene,

This afternoon I came home from work at six o'clock, and my father told me that a half hour before, he read John's obituary. He asked me if I wanted him to take me to the funeral parlor. I was speechless, and I ate my dinner thinking only of whom I could call on the telephone to find out what happened. The people whom I called were not home. At seven, my father asked me again, and I foolishly decided not to come. In only the last hour I had experienced great shock and despair, great guilt for my lack of contact with John during the last six years, terrible loss, and some hostility that nobody from school bothered to phone me earlier. Though that hostility quickly turned around in my face, considering my absence from John's life and anybody else's life over these past years. I wasn't ready to see John's body then.

I'm writing you a few hours later, and I am still ignorant of what happened. Perhaps it is best that I can write you my sincere feelings before I find out any circumstances. Perhaps not. Since I found out, I have spoken to a few of John's peripheral friends who are also mine, and they were not aware. I've tried but I can't sleep, and part of the reason is my bad feeling for not attending the funeral home tonight. To tell you the truth, I'd love to be with you, and yet, I'd be afraid I'd get too upset and draw too much attention to myself, or else I'd be inclined to make a social thing out of it, and start talking about nonsense to all other people whom I haven't seen in this long either. I know these are not your problems, and I apologize for burdening you, but if this explains in any way my absence, I'm glad. Glad seems like such a horrible word to use right now.

In danger of over asserting myself, I'd like to add a few more words. John and I haven't been close since the time I started college. A girl who went to high school with John was in my class at Loyola, and while she and I were never that close, I knew that she had remained close to John, and she would always inform me whenever something happened to him. And so I can imagine full well the horrible life that John saw while he was living at the Franklin Center. And I never returned his phonecalls. And I knew well that you went through some domestic problems and changes, and being wrapped up in my own problems, I never made time to call John and offer an ear or anything to help him. This is the point of my letter. I've had some very hard traveling since I've been an adult. And if anybody, anybody knows how bad it feels to be forgotten by your friends, or how good it feels not to have to petition love or care from others that you love and care about, it is I. And now I will never ever have a chance to prove that to John. In heaven he might hear my prayer, from heaven he might see me struggling just as hard as he did. But for the life of me, I'll never rest knowing that I might have very easily saved his life, but very possibly, he saved my life. Looking at a picture of us side by side, in the days when we were best friends, I can't believe I am the one who lived to cry for the other. I would have bargained with whomever I would have had to bargain with, that it be the other way around. I am so sorry that I never had the time to be John's true friend when he needed one. I'll never have a good excuse.

But I pray the hardest I can that Kimberly, Joseph, Mr. Joe, and especially you learn to overcome your grief. I do know a word I can say that I believe can help you. Ignoring physical details, you might as well say that John and I were equal in our confinement. If you can listen to my voice and try to understand why this might have happened, or why there can be any sense in what happened, I'll try to give you a clue. I know that about half of any day in my life, I feel like I'm 80 years old. I have given so much of myself to people whom I loved. Mostly I'm talking about women and romantic relationships, but also I mean friendships with other guys. And I've been hurt, and betrayed, and forgotten. The Paul that gets outside of me and looks at my life from a wall, I mean my analytical mind, tells me that this happens because I am so different and detached from the walking people that I care about, that they cannot see how very important, and self sacrificing, and meaningful the things that I'm able to give them are. And so they always go away to find what they're looking for, what means something to them. And while they stay their own age, I've grown a couple of years. I.e., it's been a long life and I've had many relationships, and I'm sure John did too. And like I say, I feel like 80, and I drink it off, and I fall asleep and start over the next day. Maybe John felt like something close to 80. Maybe now you know what I mean that I might have been able to save his life. I wish I had one more chance. I'm often wrong, but I think I'm right about this.

Please don't take what I assume to be true to be the whole truth. I don't have the right to explain to you why John died. I only know that I'd appreciate if somebody would make an honest attempt to explain it to my mother. I hope I've done more good than harm to you. You mean very much to me because of John. And when you can see the sunshine again, when that day comes, I'd love to hear from you. All of you will be in my prayers.

Truly,
Paul Peroutka

If I didn't thirst for answers from the life that I see, likely I would not be obliged to accept them, even when they are piercing arrows directed exactly towards me. If I didn't love John so intensely, likely I would not have heard God's voice tonight. Maybe I'd have never heard it again. If I did not hunger so much to find the just life, likely I would have written a paper on Brueggemann tonight.

In Memory of Tommy

Dear Editor:

I have recently had a loss. A good friend of mine died just before Christmas.

I have had many losses. I was born with athetoid cerebral palsy, and this has handicapped me from satisfying a soul and a will which have hoped and planned for many things because of a body which can create and perform very little. Yet if you ever meet me you will see a fortunate and happy man. I am now twenty two years old and a senior in college.

I know life with cerebral palsy as being limiting, cumbersome, at times depressing, and at times unbelievably challenging. Consider a life long game of adventure. If you like, consider an intriguing story of an undercover spy who is given a great mission to carry out, and yet can only rely on a few intangible and very shaky reinforcements: minimal ability to communicate with the outside world, and yet no good speech; occasional modes of transportation, yet totally immobile if left all alone; a mind that yearns to be stimulated and enlightened, yet a head that is too shaky to read a book, and speech too slow to hold a conversation at a party or at a meeting.

I have known cerebral palsy to be an inconvenience. My friend Tommy knew it as imprisonment. His story plot would have been just as fascinating. But the limitations which were dealt to him made his chances of satisfying his soul seemingly hopeless. Tommy spent twenty two years completely speechless. The only sound he made came from a congested throat once treated with a tracheotomy. His best means for communication was rolling his eyes upward to indicate the word "yes." His posture in his wheelchair always needed to be restricted and defined in some way. And while a world of kids worried about little league, high school and college plans, curfews and careers, Tommy would have been delighted to devise a way of never having another leg cramp to endure.

Physical barriers made it difficult for Tommy to type his thoughts, to expand on them, to build new ones. The people who loved him knew his devotion to the Baltimore Orioles, his love for his parents and family and his home, his wishes to do well in school. Yet all the words that were ever said were somebody else's, never his own.

Tommy fought a never ending battle with his involuntary movements. He had to struggle to sit still. Any intentional gesture would bring with it, its own wake of extraneous motions, motions which Tommy never really needed.

Tommy would never have died of depression. For he had joy, faith, and wisdom to see true life beyond imprisonment. But he died of cardiac arrest. Now all of his movements and leg cramps have ended. I will always remember my friend as a tremendous sign that the soul is eternally more vital than the body.

From: Cella

Oh father, forgive me for coming home late. Oh heavenly father, please receive me into your house.

I am so weary after my long strange trip. My body has likely never been in so much pain.

I face the prospect of waking up tomorrow morning with the same worries and anxieties and fear and pains that I wanted to escape from today.

I know that it was your decision to assist me in getting back home, safe from all the treacherous things of the terrible road.

I know that you laugh at me, and then you smile on me each time that I cause myself to be trapped in a similar unfortunate uncomfortable situation.

I say that I know you because I see your face, but realize that this is only a metaphor.

I might be a fool in the judging eye of the world. But I am only a child of God. Oh Lord, you have no vengeance, only love.

You are what I speak to. You are what I rely on. You are the light of my life. You are the light in everyone.

You are all good. You are only good. You are every guardian angel. You are in every person's body. Nothing lives without you. Nothing will ever be without you.

I face the world and I am scared, oh Lord.

I am scared by my limitations, and frightened of my illness.

You have showed me so many signs as to why I should live, and why I have a duty and responsibility to live, and to face all the adversity that comes with my name on it.

Yet time after time, I selfishly forget all of the signs that I have known to be true.

I have been made different from everybody in the world. I can get easily blinded by the adversity.

All of my life, you have been nearly invisible to me. I tried to see that it was you in the smiles of inspiring people. I have thought that you breathed in my body whenever I felt well and secure.

But I have never understood your ways, and I thought that I never had the capacity to understand your ways.

Now, tonight Lord, I find that I know of your ways, though I am totally confused of my own.

What makes me doubt the value of my life?

What makes me doubt the value of my intellect?

What makes me doubt the things I know to be true at times when it is so easy for me to fail?

Why am I not as strong as I know I can be, and I should be?

Crazy people acting makes me blind.

Stupid people talking makes me deaf.

Mean old men make me have no feeling.

I want to die when I see how much I've said and how little they've heard.

And those are the times when I realize that all I have is you, Lord.

What am I whenever I don't realize that you are there to listen to me?

Where am I if I'd be all alone, really all alone, truly all alone?

I'd be in agony. I'd be crying. I'd be dead myself.

Oh Lord, you are my savior and you are my only hope. My dreams are moot when I don't share them with you primarily.

Oh Lord, only you are able to understand me fully.

Why do I become less of what I am at times when it becomes imperative that I stay my strongest?

Why do I let other people influence me so?

Will they be with me tomorrow, or the next day, or the next day?

No. Only you will be with me then and all the times between, and all of the times afterward, oh Lord.

You know my truest self. You created the entire me. You have all power over myself and everybody else on Earth.

I think about the world of man, and I cannot comprehend the magnitude of power and knowledge and ability that have evolved from the human mind.

And then I know the truth about the revelation that you sent to me.

And I realize that only creations of God have done such things.

The knowledge and the power of man are finite, and are only within its own bounds of worth.

There isn't life without the Lord. There is no truth outside the Lord.

I love the Lord for being my life.
For the rest of my life I will long to see your reality.
I will love my life because I love the Lord.
I will live my life because I am in love with the Lord.

I will live my life because I love the Lord.
I will live my life because I love the Lord.
I will live my life because I love the Lord.
I will live my life because I love the Lord.
I will live my life because I love the Lord.
I will live my life because I love the Lord.
I will live my life because I love the Lord.
I will live my life because I love the Lord.
I will live my life because I love the Lord.
I will live my life because I love the Lord.
I will live my life because I love the Lord.
I will live my life because I love the Lord.
I will live my life because I love the Lord.
I will live my life because I love the Lord.
I will live my life because I love the Lord.
I will live my life because I love the Lord.

GREAT DAY!!!

THE WORLD IS WAKING UP, I'LL HAVE YOU KNOW. AMERICA AND FINLAND AND ALL THE OTHER COUNTRIES THAT GROW ROSES ARE GETTING OUT OF BED AND PUTTING ON THEIR CLOTHES. THEY'RE GOING DOWNSTAIRS AND PICKING UP THEIR PAPERS AND ALL OF A SUDDEN, THEY KNOW THE CURE WAS FOUND IN THE MIDDLE OF THE NIGHT. YES, IT IS THE CURE. THE CURE FOR LIFE'S PENETRATING AND HAUNTING CRIPPLING KILLER WAS FINALLY ARRIVED AT LAST NIGHT AT EXACTLY 3:27:46 AM BY DOCTORS JOHN KAFFL AND PHILLIP MCCAFEREY AND IT HAS BEEN DECLARED THAT THIS IS A FULL FLEDGED MIRACLE 45 MINUTES LATER BY A TELEGRAM THEY RECEIVED IN THEIR LABORATORY FROM GOD. OH YES, A MIRACLE HAS TOUCHED THE WORLD THIS MORNING, AND, IF YOU CAN BELIEVE IT, EVERY HUMAN SOUL ON EARTH WAS TOUCHED BY IT, FELT IT, AND ARE WELL ON THEIR WAY TO LIFETIME HAPPINESS. LIFETIME HAPPINESS, THAT'S THE TICKET CHARTER TO ETERNAL SALVATION. ETERNAL SALVATION. HOT DAMN, CAN YOU BELIEVE IT?

AND THEN THE WORLD DECIDES INSTANTANEOUSLY TO TURN ON THE TELEVISION SETS. CAN YOU IMAGINE, EVERY TELEVISION SET IN THE WORLD IS TURNED ON? WELL OF COURSE BUT DO YOU BELIEVE THAT THERE IS

ONLY ONE THING BEING BROADCAST AND SATELLITED AROUND THE GLOBE? THE GLOBE, YES! IT'S A STAR FEASTED GALA. A STARFEASTED GALA, YES. AND IT'S NO TELETHON. NOT ONE OF THOSE EGOMANIACS IS ASKING FOR MONEY. THEY'RE NOT EVEN GETTING PAID FOR BEING NOTICED OR PHOTOGRAPHED. THEY ALL, EVERY TV CELEBRITY IN THE BOOK, HAD AN INKLING TO APPEAR AT THE SAME TIME AND THE SAME STUDIO, WHICH JUST MATERIALIZED OUT OF THIN AIR, HUG AND KISS EACH OTHER AND PERFORM IN CELEBRATION OF THE END OF SORROW AND DEATH. THE DISEASE THAT HAS BEEN KILLING THE WORLD WILL KILL NO ONE MORE. AND PARADES ARE REMOTED AND CINEMA GIANTS ARE COMEOED, AND SYMPHONIES ARE ORCHESTRATED, AND PRODUCTION NUMBERS ARE CHOREOGRAPHED. AND JACK KLUGMAN IS HOSTING AND EMBRACES CAMERA 3. AND SHIRLEY JONES IS SINGING LIKE SHE USED TO. AND JOEY HEATHERTON IS SPEAKING COHERENTLY. AND SHECKEY GREENE IS TELLING FUNNY JOKES AGAIN. AND RHODA'S SISTER HAS FOUND THE RIGHT FELLOW. AND EDITH BUNKER CAME BACK FROM THE DEAD. AND JERRY LEWIS CAN AT LONG LONG LAST FINISH 'YOU'LL NEVER WALK ALONE' WITHOUT COLLAPSING, AND HE'LL NEVER HAVE TO DO IT ONE MORE TIME. AND THE STAGE GETS A PHONE-IN CALL FROM BELUSHI. HE'S REACHED THE PLACE. AND HE DIDN'T DO IT TO HIMSELF. NEITHER DID JIMI, JANIS, FREDDIE, OR ERNEST, HE TELLS THE WORLD TO DISMISS THESE MYTHS, AND THE WORLD DOES.

NOW THAT THE WORLD IS CURED OF ITS MOST HORRIBLE KILLER, A CIRCLE MUST BE FORMED. THERE IS NO PLANNING FOR IT. BUT PEOPLE ARE BURSTING OUT OF THEIR HOMES. EVERYBODY'S ARM IS EXTENDED JUST READY TO BE TOUCHED WITH LOVE BY ANOTHER. AND COUNTIES MAKE THEIR CIRCLES EVEN BIGGER BY COMMERSING, AND LOVE TOOK PLACE IN A SQUARE

DANCE, LOVE THAT INVITED MOST OF THE NORTH EASTERN HEMISPHERE. AND SOON WE WILL BE TEACHING THE RUSSIANS TO DO SI DO IF YOU CAN BELIEVE IT. OF COURSE YOU CAN.

SO THERE WILL BE NO MORE DEATH WITHOUT DIGNITY, THE WORLD IS IMPRESSED. THERE WILL LIKELY BE NO MORE DEATH DUE TO HATRED NOW THAT ALL MEN HAVE MET AND EMBRACED AND SWUNG EACH OTHER'S PARTNER. THIS MEANS THERE'S CONCEIVABLY NO MORE NEED FOR LUST. EVERYBODY OWNS EVERYBODY'S LOVE. AND GOD HAS BECOME THE TELLER, JUST THE FOB HE WAS TRAINED FOR. AND YOU KNOW WHAT? MEN HAVE DECIDED NOT TO HURT OR DENY THAT POOR SOUL UP THERE. LORD, HE HAS TAKEN A LOT OF ABUSE EVER SINCE HE STARTED PUTTING THIS WHOLE MAN IDEA INTO EFFECT. THE GUY DESERVES A BREAK AND HIS PEOPLE ARE GONNA GIVE HIM ONE. HALLELUJAH! HALLELUJAH! THE DANCERS SING AS THEY MAKE THE SUN SMILE EVEN BRIGHTER, THE BRIGHTEST. THE WORLD IS MUSIC TODAY.

AND PASSING THE SQUARE DANCERS IN THEIR NEW WAXED AND POLISHED JEEP IS MIKE AND SUE. HAVE YOU EVER SEEN TWO MORE BEAUTIFUL PEOPLE? AND DON'T YOU RECOGNIZE THEM? YOU'VE SEEN THEM RIDING EVERY SUMMER SUNNY SUNDAY MORNING, ALWAYS LOOKING HAPPIER THAN THEY DID LAST WEEK. YOU'VE SEEN HIS ONE HAND COOLLY GLIDING THE WHEEL WHILE HIS OTHER HAND IS PERCHED ON HER LEG. IF YOU'D LIKE TO KNOW WHAT THEY HAVE TO TALK ABOUT TODAY, THEY DON'T MIND; THEY'D LIKE ME TO LET YOU IN ON IT, AND I WILL. THE REASON WHY THEY ARE SMILING MORE THAN THEY EVER HAVE BEFORE IS THAT THEY'VE BEEN CONSIDERING ALL POSSIBILITIES AND LIKELIHOODS, AND IT LOOKS LIKE THEY WON'T HAVE ANY PROBLEMS ANYMORE. YEAH, ALL THEY FEEL

IS LOVE FOR EACH OTHER AND HOPE, ASSURANCE FOR A FUTURE TOGETHER. NEITHER ONE HAS ANYTHING TO BE HOSTILE ABOUT FOR A WHILE. SO BOTH COME TO THE CONCLUSION THAT THEY GOT NOTHING TO WORRY ABOUT. NOTHING. SO WHEN THEY IGNORE THEIR EYES AND THINK OF WHAT THERE IS TO THINK OF, THEY SEE HAPPY DAYS THAT ARE CAUSED AND WILL SUSTAIN BY LOVE. WE GOT A START TO A CELEBRATION RIGHT HERE, DON'T WE?

THEIR NAMES AS I SAID ARE SUE AND MIKE. SO SAY HEY TO THEM AS THEY STOP AND GET OUT OF THEIR CAR FOR A PICNIC AT THE PARK. THERE THEY SIT NEAR SARAH AND DAVEY. THEY'RE REAL OLD; THEY CAN'T EVEN HEAR BUT THEY'VE SHARED A BUCKET OF CHICKEN FROM THE COLONEL AT THIS SAME BENCH AND TABLE FOR EVERY SUMMER SUNDAY FOR THE LAST 37 YEARS. THEY'VE STOPPED TRYING TO TALK TO EACH OTHER, BUT THESE TWO ANGELS STILL HOLD HANDS. AND TODAY THEY CAN HOLD EVEN TIGHTER. OF COURSE TODAY. TODAY IS SO UNIQUE JUST BECAUSE IT'S NOW. AND NOW CAN BRING ANYONE. IT CAN BRING LOVE TO SARAH AND DAVEY LIKE THEY'VE NEVER SEEN IT. AND OUR MIKE AND SUE HAVE CAUGHT A WHIFF OF LAUGHTER AT THE TABLE NEAR, SO THE FOUR BECOME FRIENDS. THE COUPLES SHARE ABSOLUTELY NOTHING AT ALL IN COMMON, BUT EVERYBODY LOVES EVERYBODY ELSE. ALL ARE ENRICHED BY ALL THE JOY THAT THREE OTHER LOVED ONES CAN COMPOUND.

RUNNING BY THE BENCH IS JOHNNY. JOHNNY IS AN ADORABLE DARK HAIRED BLUE EYED BOY WHO ALWAYS WILL BE. YES HE WILL, AND HE HAS TWO SISTERS HE PLAYS WITH AND STABLE, PSYCHOLOGICALLY PERFECTLY ROUNDED PARENTS WHO LOVE NOTHING MORE THAN TO SIT AND WATCH THEIR CHILDREN GROW, AND TO CULTIVATE THEIR LAUGHTER. JOHNNY'S

TWO SISTERS CALL HIM THEIR BOYFRIEND AND TAKE HIM TO THE BEACH EVERY SATURDAY. THIS MAKES HIM THE HAPPIEST BOY YOU WANT TO KNOW. THEY KISS BOTH HIS CHEEKS EVERY TIME HE DOES SOMETHING CUTE.HE'LL ALWAYS BE CUTE.

NEXT TO THE PARK IS A HOSPITAL FOR PEOPLE TO COME WHEN THEY'RE HAVING TROUBLE ADOPTING THE CONVENTIONAL DEFINITION OF NORMALCY, OR WHEN THEY MIGHT JUST NOT FEEL LIKE TALKING TO ANYONE FOR A WHILE. MARGARET HASN'T FELT MUCH LIKE TALKING FOR GOING ON FIVE YEARS NOW. SO SHE'S IN THERE WHERE PEOPLE CAN TAKE CARE OF HER AND CONVINCE HER THAT IT'D BE ALRIGHT TO START TALKING AGAIN UNTIL SHE DOES FEEL LIKE IT. FRED IS HER HUSBAND AND IS GOING IN TO VISIT HER TODAY FOR A WHILE. TRAILING TO HER ROOM HE LUGS A FEW CARDS AND SOME CANDY AND HE CAN'T REALLY SAY EXACTLY HOW THEY GOT IN HIS HANDS. BUT HE SUPPOSES THAT THEY'LL BE FORGOTTEN JUST AS SOON AS HE PUTS THEM DOWN ON HER TABLE. HE DOESN'T HAVE ANYTHING TO SAY, BUT HE KNOWS HE WON'T HAVE TO SAY ANYTHING. HE OPENS HER DOOR WITHOUT LOOKING AT IT. WHAT HE SEES IS HIS WIFE, BEAUTIFUL AGAIN IN A ROBE, STANDING. SHE HASN'T DONE THAT IN YEARS EITHER. SHE IS BY THE WINDOW LOOKING OUT INTO THE SUN AND THE HAPPINESS IT'S CREATING ON GREEN GRASS. THE NEXT MOMENT HER HEAD TURNS, HER HAIR AND FACE GETTING MORE AND MORE BEAUTIFUL. AND THEN A MIRACLE. HER MOUTH TURNS UP AND HER SMILE HAS COME AGAIN. SHE HAS LIFE BACK AGAIN, AND FRED CAN BE HER HUSBAND AGAIN. THERE IS NO TIME BEFORE FRED HAS MARGARET IN HIS ARMS. HE SQUEEZES WITH TENDERNESS THE LIFE OF HIS THAT'S BEEN DEAD ALL THESE YEARS. AND YOU GOT TO KNOW THAT THIS IS THE MOST SPLENDID MOMENT IN THEIR LIVES, IN THE FULL COMPLETED LIFE

THAT CAN BE THEIRS AGAIN FOREVER, PROBABLY IN LIFE ITSELF. I KNOW I COULD NEVER CREATE ANYTHING THAT COULD TOP THIS.

LET'S FLY OUT THE WINDOW TO LEAVE THEM ALONE, AND LET'S SEE THAT ALL THE PEOPLE IN THAT HOSPITAL ARE LOOKING OUT. EVERYBODY'S DAY IS BEING SAVED BY THE SUNSHINE. SMILES RULE ALL, AND NOBODY IS LONELY ANYMORE. ONE CHILD'S LAUGHTER HAS SET THEM FREE.

AND ON THE GROUND IS A NEWSPAPER. THEY HAD OH SUCH A TINY BIT OF SPACE LEFT AT THE BOTTOM TO PRINT ALL THE NONCONSEQUENCIAL STUFF THAT HAPPENED TODAY, AND HERE IT IS. ON THIS SUNDAY IN MID SEPTEMBER, EVERY TEAM IN THE NFL WON. DON'T ASK ME HOW, THEY JUST DID. AND THIS PUT EVERY MONEY STEELING BOOKIE OUT OF BUSINESS, AT LEAST TILL TUESDAY. FINANCIALLY IN THE NEWS, IT HAS BEEN DECREED AND CONGRESSIONALLY APPROVED. PRESIDENT FREEDMAN HAS STOPPED THE DENVER AND SAN FRANCISCO MINTS FROM PRINTING ANOTHER PENNY OF MONEY FOR THE NEXT FOUR YEARS. AND WOULD YOU BELIEVE IT, ABSOLUTELY EVERY CITIZEN, EVEN THE COMMONEST OF MORONS, IS SATISFIED, GRATEFUL, AND UNDERSTANDS EXACTLY HOW THIS IS GONNA WORK... EVENTUALLY. OF COURSE YOU WOULD. IN BASEBALL, THE NATIONAL LEAGUE HAS BECOME A TWO TEAM RACE FOR THE PLAY OFFS. JUST ABOUT EVERY CLUB FELL ON THEIR ASSES THIS SUMMER, REALLY A DEAD SEASON. BUT LEAVE IT TO THE CUBS AND THE METS TO PULL THROUGH AND GIVE US THE LIVELIEST PENNANT RACE EVER. ON THE SHOW BIZ SCENE, LIZ TAYLOR AT LONG LAST FOUND HER SEXUAL PREFERENCE AND MARRIED ZHA ZHA GABOR. AND THE PAPER COULDN'T FIT IN THE BIG STORY ABOUT THE WORLD COMING TO PERMANENT INTERNATIONAL

PEACE. IT FEATURED A CLOSE UP HUMAN INTEREST REPORT ON A LITTLE GIRL, EVELYN, IN HONDURAS WHO ATE TODAY AND WAS PROMISED BY THE CHIEF OF THAT GOVERNMENT THAT SHE AND EVERYBODY SHE LOVES WILL ALWAYS EAT WHENEVER THEY WANT TO. EVERYBODY WAS MORE INTERESTED IN THE LITTLE GIRL STORY ANYWAY. BUT IT WAS PRINTED THAT THERE WILL BE A SPECIAL NEWS BROADCAST TONIGHT ON EVERY TV NETWORK AFTER THAT TELETHON. REMEMBER THAT TELETHON?

WELL I'M READY TO GO HOME, AREN'T YOU? THE SKY IS GETTING DARK. THE STARS ARE REHEARSING FOR TONIGHT'S SCHEDULED ALL NIGHT JUBILEE FESTIVAL JAM. THE BIG MAN IS SUPPOSED TO SHOW UP AROUND 8:30 TO GIVE US SOME LICKS ON HIS SAXOPHONE. SO ALL ARE GETTING READY AND PLAN ON LISTENING IN AND CATCHING THE SHOW. ON THE WAY YOU CAN SEE PEOPLE, FAMILIES, FRIENDS, LOVERS, OUTSIDE ON LAWN CHAIRS. EVERYONE HAS A GRANDMOTHER, AND A BOYFRIEND, AND A BABY, AND A DOG. AND THEY ALL KNOW THE GAS STATION OWNER. AND FATHER BRADLEY STOOPS AND SITS DOWN BESIDE DOROTHY AND HER MOMMY. AND EVERYBODY SMILES AT ME.

I PASS THE HILL ON THE WAY TO MY HOUSE. THERE IS THE MOST BEAUTIFUL PERSON ANYBODY KNOWS. RUTH. SHE HAS TO SAY THE ONLY NEWS LEFT OF WHAT HAPPENED ON THIS GREAT DAY. WELL OF COURSE SHE CAN FINISH THIS STORY FOR US. IT WAS HER IDEA TO BEGIN WITH. AND WHAT ELSE WOULD SHE BE DOING THAN CHANTING BLINDLY AND BLISSFULLY HER GREAT DAY WORDS.

"LENNON IS RISEN, MORRISON IS FOUND, PEROUTKA IS CURED, LENNON IS RISEN, MORRISON IS FOUND, PEROUTKA IS CURED..."

AND I NEED TO HEAR AND SAY NO MORE. I'LL CLOSE MY DOOR BEHIND ME, STAY IN MY HOME, AND CRY TONIGHT FOR THE WORLD'S HAPPINESS. AND I'LL PRAY TO GOD, NOW AND FROM THIS MOMENT ON, USING HIS WORDS, AND PLEASING HIS VOCABULARY. NOW CONVINCED OF HIS INFINITE POWER, HIS IMAGINATION, AND HIS UNDERSTANDING. HE KNEW JUST WHAT TO DO TODAY, JUST WHAT WE NEEDED. AND IT IS CLEAR TO ALL WHO WITNESSED WHAT HE PUT DOWN TODAY, THIS IS NOT AN APOCALYPTIC GUY HERE WE HAVE FOR A SAVIOR. HE ENJOYED THE GREAT DAY JUST AS MUCH AS WE DID. AND WHEN HE SAYS WE MUST DO THIS AGAIN SOMETIME, BEFORE IT'S ALL OVER, I THINK HE MEANS IT.

SO THERE'S NOTHING LEFT TO SAY ABOUT TODAY EXCEPT TO END IT. AND SO I DO, LOVING YOU, DENISE. FROM THE MOMENT I SAW YOU PLAY ACTING WITH A DANDELION, I THOUGHT, THAT COULD ONLY BE A SMILE THAT COULD INSPIRE A GREAT DAY. AND ON IT, I WANT TO HOLD YOU AND CARESS YOU AND KISS YOU. BECAUSE I KNOW ALL MY CONTENTMENT CAN ORIGINATE FROM YOUR FACE. SMILE ON ME, DENISE, AND LET ME KNOW THAT TOMORROW CAN BE PRETTY GOOD TOO.

CHIASTICMAN

WHEN HE WAS SEVEN YEARS OLD, MY BROTHER STEPHEN SAID TO MY MOM, "IF ONE HAD FIFTY DOLLARS, ONE COULD BUY ONE HUNDRED 50 CENT ITEMS." WHEN MY BROTHER MICHAEL WAS TEN YEARS OLD, HE STOOD ON THE FRONT STEP OF MY GRANDMOTHER'S HOUSE ON GLOVER STREET AND HE SHOUTED TO EVERYONE PASSING BY, "LADIES AND GENTLEMEN, LET'S SING A SONG." THAT SAME YEAR I WAS BORN INTO THE ACT. BUT SOON IT WAS APPARENT TO THEM THAT I COULD NEITHER SING NOR DANCE. ABOUT TWELVE YEARS LATER, THEY WENT OFF TO COLLEGE. I WAS LEFT ALONE WITH MY FIRST ELECTRIC TYPEWRITER; WITH IT, I WAS TOLD TO TRY TO DO MY BEST.

MY LAST DAY OF JUNIOR HIGH WAS A GLAD ONE BECAUSE I BROUGHT HOME ANOTHER PERFECT REPORT CARD. I WAS PUSHED UP THE DRIVEWAY TO THE BACK DOOR OF MY HOUSE BY THE SCHOOLBUS MATRON WHO SAID JUST BEFORE SHE DROPPED ME OFF, "GOODBYE PAUL, WE ALL HOPE YOU DO AS WELL IN REAL LIFE AS YOU DID IN SCHOOL." SHE WALKED AWAY BEFORE I COULD TURN AND TELL HER THAT I WOULD TRY MY BEST. STILL THAT WAS A PARTICULAR MOMENT WHEN I FIRST GOT THE FEELING THAT SOMEBODY OUT THERE, BESIDES MYSELF, WAS ENJOYING THE ACT. MY TWO BROTHERS

HAD MOVED FARTHER AWAY SINCE THE LAST TIME I HAD SEEN THEM.

I WROTE A BOOK IN 1982. PEOPLE USED TO REMEMBER IT, BUT NOW THEY DON'T ANYMORE. IT HAD TO DO WITH MY EXPERIENCES LIVING AWAY FROM HOME IN A COLLEGE DORM. THE DAY I HAD FINISHED IT, STEPHEN BECAME MY SECOND BROTHER TO PASS THE BAR EXAM. ALL HIS FRIENDS AND FAMILY GAVE HIM A HUGE PARTY AT A HAWAIIAN RESTAURANT. NOBODY THERE HAD ANY IDEA THAT I WAS WRITING A BOOK, AND NOT A ONE OF THEM SEEMED TO CARE AT ALL WHEN I TOLD THEM ABOUT IT. SO I KEPT MY MOUTH SHUT, AS BEST I COULD, AND WATCHED MY BROTHERS CELEBRATE. EVERYONE HAD SUCH GREAT THINGS TO SAY ABOUT THEM.

IT WAS THEN WHEN I STARTED THINKING IN TERMS OF THE BEATLES AND SATURDAY NIGHT LIVE. NO MATTER WHAT THE NEW ACT IS PLAYING, WHEN THE OLD CAST IS RERUN, THE PAST BECOMES REVERED, THE PRESENT APPEARS PAIL. REBECCA CAN NEVER BE REPLACED. BUT THAT'S ROCK AND ROLL.

A FEW YEARS BACK I WAS SITTING IN THE DULANEY INN ENJOYING A GRATEFUL DEAD NIGHT. RECENTLY I HAD JUST PUBLISHED 'VITIUSTA', A FIVE BOOK COLLECTION WRITTEN BY SOME NEW VOICES SPEAKING TO THE CONDITION OF BEING HANDICAPPED. THE PROJECT BEGAN AS A PARTNERSHIP BETWEEN MYSELF AND ONE OF MY FAVORITE PALSIED FRIENDS NAMED JOHN WHO IS OLDER THAN I AND HAD FOR LONG LED THE PATH FOR MOST OF THE THINGS I HAVE DONE IN MY SUCCESSFUL LIFE. FOR THIS REASON, I HAD GIVEN JOHN TOP BILLING AND MYSELF SECOND. WHEN THE COMPLETE PACKAGE WAS FINISHED, PUBLISHED, AND DISTRIBUTED, I HAD WRITTEN 133 PAGES, AND JOHN,

WHO HAD QUARRELED WITH ME AND BACKED OUT OF THE PROJECT LONG BEFORE ITS COMPLETION, HAD ONLY COMPOSED A TOTAL OF THREE PAGES. THAT EVENING IN THE DULANEY INN, A LOVELY YOUNG DEADHEAD CAME UP TO ASK ME IF I HAD EVER READ JOHN'S BOOK. SHE SAID IT WAS QUITE GOOD AND A DISABLED PERSON IN MY SITUATION WOULD PROBABLY FIND IT VERY ENLIGHTENING. I JUST SMILED, AND I THOUGHT TO MYSELF, "NOT BAD PLAY."

STEVE SIRECI AND JOEY MOREL AND JOE TROY CARRIED ME IN MY WHEELCHAIR ONTO THE STAGE OF THE CIVIC CENTER AFTER DEAN ROSWELL READ MY NAME. FATHER SELLINGER WALKED OVER, HUGGED ME, AND PRESENTED ME WITH MY DIPLOMA AND A PLAQUE INSIGNIA OF THE SCHOLARSHIP BEING FOUNDED IN MY NAME FOR ENTERING HANDICAPPED STUDENTS AT LOYOLA COLLEGE. AND THEN... THIS 'AND THEN' DESERVED THREE DOTS. AND THEN... MY ENTIRE GRADUATING CLASS STOOD RIGHT UP AND OVATED ME. IT WAS THE VERY FIRST TIME IN MY LIFE THAT I HAD EVER BEEN OVATED AND, BELIEVE ME, AN EXPERIENCE NOT TO BE MISSED. MY BROTHERS, MICHAEL AND STEPHEN, WERE OLD MEN BY THIS TIME. THEY BOUGHT THINGS LIKE VIDEO 8 MOVIE CAMERAS; WITH ONE THEY TOOK PICTURES OF THIS CEREMONY. STEPHEN CAN BE HEARD ON THE SOUNDTRACK SAYING,"NOT BAD PLAY, NOT BAD PLAY."

I SIGNED A CONTRACT. MANY MOONS AGO I AGREED TO LIVE THE LIFE AND THINK IN THE HEAD OF A TROUBADOUR POET UNTIL THE CLOCK STRUCK 90. THEN, IT WAS UNDERSTOOD, I SHOULD BEGIN WORKING FOR A BILLING. SO NOW MY BOSS IS 21 YEARS OLD, THE OFFICE MANAGER AT MY BROTHERS' LAW FIRM. LAST WEEK SHE OFFERED TO TAKE ME OUT TO DINNER AND TO MARRY ME. BUT THIS WEEK SOMETHING CAME UP

AND SHE WAS TOO BUSY. SO NOW I JUST DO WHAT I AM TOLD. I WRITE COMPUTER PROGRAMS FOR THE BUSINESS, BUT I DON'T GET TO SEE MY BROTHERS TOO OFTEN. AFTER ALL THESE YEARS OF TRYING, IT MUST BE APPARENT TO THEM AND TO THEIR AUDIENCE THAT I STILL CAN NEITHER SING NOR DANCE. THE ACT IS THEIRS AGAIN. AND IT'S NOT BAD PLAY.

HELL CAN FIND ANSWERS

I'm still Paul Peroutka. And there are still some quite amazing things about my life. You may know me because you've read things I've written about these things. I've taken more than enough folks from my mid high school thoughts straight on through to my reflections upon graduating from Loyola College in Maryland. But this will be the first opportunity I have to share with you my experience as a gainful employee for anyone besides myself. I am set here to relate the story of how I inquired for employment, was hired, and am now enjoying my position as a computer programmer trainee, grade 5, in the Health Care Finance Administration of Health and Human Services of the federal government.

And in the spirit of this lovely Saturday afternoon as I start and must end this explanation of occurrences surrounding this present job of mine, I sincerely hope that we both enjoy it to its potential.

On May 26, 1985, I was given a diploma from Father Sellinger at Loyola's graduation, followed by his announcing that my friends in the rugby club had organized to found a scholarship for the school, bearing my name, which will benefit any entering handicapped student. This was in turn followed by a standing ovation from every one of my classmates, and then by an individual mention of me by Father Sellinger in his closing remarks declaring that I had been myself somewhat of an institution on the campus and all who came in contact with me learned from me.

When an absolutely overwhelming tribute such as the one I have just described is paid to you, several attitudes emerge. The moment seemed so magical that I was compelled to dig as fast as I could to find my truest self and ask him what he really thought of it. My truest self, if you have never met him, is quite largely cynical, questioning, and practical. A large memory I now hold well about the moment I saw my entire class stand up is thinking, as best I could form these coherent thoughts in my brain, that I wish only half of these people had stopped and taken the time to learn from me. I think I would have valued that much more than this unfathomable sudden burst of appreciation. I balanced that thought with another that said, well ok, I do deserve this -- I am the one among them who suffers from athetoid cerebral palsy -- I am the only one who actually has to endure this burden always -- it would be logical to conclude that my forsaking of many pleasures and opportunities I see others enjoy but cannot enjoy myself entitles me the right to bask in blatant glory such as this -- I am indeed the most unique person here, and all the people are really doing is acknowledging it.

That last thought took several lines to write, but as you can imagine, having lived with both CP and this terrible, churning, iconoclastic mind in my head for twentyfour years, that whole stanza gets processed in no more than two seconds.

The night before Live Aid I was throwing a party at my house. A bit disturbed was I when my Uncle Jack and Aunt Joanne had stopped by and said that it was very important that they talk to me for a while, only because I had a million other things on my mind right then. But I knew that Jack was going to ask me something about getting a job for the federal government.

Jack had worked for the government for all his professional career, and in fact so has my brother, Michael. Now I have had a rather long career, six years of writing and forming my style and my stature to emulate that of Ginsburg, Dylan, Lennon, Beatty. I had a hard time seeing myself as a federal government employee. It had, after all, only been a number of months since I had been weaned off the college keg. But all of my surrounders told me in no uncertain terms that this was in 180 degrees of the direction at which I should sneeze. And on that night, Jack gave me a lady's name, a bureau chief, and an address for writing to her. Writing to this lady waited until after Live Aid was over.

On August 28 I met with Mr. Glenn Keidel and Ms. Michael McMullen at the Oak Meadows Building at the Social Security Complex in Woodlawn, Maryland. As many capital letters there are in the last sentence was as major the intensity of my first job interview. Dad accompanied me as he wanted to, and Michael took the time to come over from his building to our meeting. I didn't have to say much, and was told not to, instead constantly to keep my head up and my face in perfect view, to look distinguished, and to seem interested in everything that was said. Dad and Michael had the pictures from graduation, the diploma, the scholarship plaque itself, my old communication board, their favorite articles that I had published in the newspaper, and every other prop they needed to sell me. Dad has been a salesman for over thirty years, and Michael has been charming and endearing for at least that long. Their task must not have been too very difficult. Everyone seemed encouraged by meeting's end.

My works with Peroutka Home Art took me through half of November. I had been told by more than a few folks that waiting for the government to make a decision and then act upon it took a surprising quantity of patience. I did not realize this quantity at first. By mid-October I had given up all but a fraction of hope in being hired by HCFA. Maybe I believed that a position would finally come to me, but I thought it might take many months. And starting one weekend, I disappointedly took to drink after attempting earnestly to avoid both the alcohol and the carefree foolish behavior of college life since I graduated. I think I hung out at one long Halloween party on campus for something like a week.

When I came home again, we still had not gotten any news. So I slept for a while.

The week before Thanksgiving saw the last four releases I was going to make for PHA. On Saturday night after returning from symphony with my family I was telling Michael that I was putting an end to the publishing service. After expressing ignorance at what PHA actually was, he asked me why I was ending it. I replied 'because you didn't know what it was.' That was an exceptionally sad weekend which I definitely did not need. On next Monday afternoon, Michael called the house from work saying that I was hired by HCFA. And the remainder of this is a happy story.

On December 5, late morning my father drove me back to Woodlawn, back to the Oak Meadows Building, and again Michael took the time to come be with us. This time we were meeting Mr. Harry Sanford, the man I was essentially assigned to, Mr. Irv Goldstein, his boss and my supervisor, and Mr. George Towner, an expert of microcomputers and just about anything else anybody could come to ask him. This time we knew that Dad and Michael wouldn't have to sell me. I was only there to meet these new people and get information of what my job would be. But the simplicity and good nature of it all did not alleviate much my stupid nervousness.

I remember now, sitting with Dad in the lobby waiting for the time of our appointment, I saw this black haired lady wearing purple pants and a wild yellow Hawaiian shirt walking from a hall and approaching nearer and nearer to me. I think I had a quite unconscious opinion about her to this effect, 'I don't mind this person walking on the planet like she does, but she certainly wouldn't have any business with me--would she?' As I was thinking my question, I suddenly realized that she was coming, looking straight at me, and there was nothing I could do. She had something to say to me.

"Hi Paul. How are you?"

Now I'm sorry. But you must understand that it was about 10:45. I don't even try to formulate words until about 11:30 each day. Having cerebral palsy, you could rightly think, can be described as one's brain never being fully awake. This is why it often takes away my balance, causes jerks or spasticity or speech aphasia. Sometimes, at least this is my experience, my brain can be more awake or asleep than other times. This can be very sad if I inadvertently give someone too blank a stare or no vocal response, like what happened with that lady with the purple pants and the yellow shirt. My first meeting with the office secretary, Lil Wolff, went like this. But not to worry. I have not begun to say my all about that morning.

Only a few moments past that came George Towner, a kindly looking big fellow, mustache and eastern shore slang and all, and he also recognized who I was without me having the slightest idea who he was. He told my father and I that the men we were there to see were all set to meet us, and to follow him. Unfortunately this confirmation that I was finally going to meet my future bosses at any second brought forth a surge of anxiety which an athetoid hates to experience. I've lived through countless anxious moments and no doubt I'll live through countless more, but at each one I pray and I dig for a train of thought which will help me trivalize the actual moment and somehow relax my involuntary show of nervousness. A pro can pull this off 75% of the time. This just happened to be an off day. And while Harry Sanford was explaining to me what software was going to be on my PC, Lotus, dBase, Multimate, Basic, and what utilities he was purchasing for me, Deskmate and ProKey, I had to interrupt the flow of his words to ask Dad to wipe my chin with a napkin. I kept looking directly in his eyes, and at that moment Harry said nonverbally to me for the first time, 'alright, cut the bull, peroutka.'

On Monday morning, February 3, 1986, I started my first day as a government employee, grade five. I had chosen 1:00 pm to 5:00 pm for my daily work hours as I was originally hired as a part time temporary employee. It was understood that I would eventually be provided with a personal assistant for at least part of my workday, but arrangements for hiring or acquiring that aid was only at the starting gate and it probably wouldn't come about for a number of weeks. Naturally, I accepted this as another example of bureaucratic procrastination, and I resigned myself that I could certainly handle this new job on my own. Hope was for getting an attendant soon though because Michael had been making arrangements with the personnel department suggesting that they quickly hire one Neal Moylan. Michael billed Neal as a recent college graduate, a close friend of mine who has cared for me many times in the past, and all in all is most qualified for the position of my assistant. Neal has been an adopted member of our family whom I have known all my life. Approximately a half hour before I was set to leave my house to ride to work on the MTA Mobility bus, Michael phoned to give the news that Neal had just been hired and would be waiting for me in front of the door of the Oak Meadows building when I arrived. I had to thank God for quietly taking care of that.

Towards the end of that week Neal and I began to appreciate the intensity of our boss Harry's hobbies. He told us that on Friday he was taking off to go to Atlantic City. His game is craps. Neal knows a good deal about that kind of stuff, although his game is roulette. So those two had much fun on Thursday talking over gambling strategy and such while I was deeply in the midst of formulating clues about the hardware and software before me. I decided to tackle one piece at a time. As of then, ProKey had not been fully installed on my system, so I figured that it would be a weekend's homework to read all of its documentation and teach myself how to make directories, copy software from floppy to fixed disk, recognize execution files, write batch files with path instructions, change my autoexec batch file to load all my memory resident software. I might remind you that I was an English major in college. Then again, why would I want to?

Deskmate had already been installed for me, so I was still trudging through all of its possibilities and with the concentration necessary for the most important assignment imaginable. I was up to discovering the calendar organizer on Friday. And I was making a note to myself that it was a federal holiday on February 17 when came the time that Irv decided I ought to meet Regina, the bureau chief, one and the same.

"Regina McPhillips, I'd like you to meet Mr. Paul Peroutka and Mr. Neal Moylan. Paul is our new computer programmer trainee. And although he's only been here four and a half days, we've found his work very satisfactory, and his progress is smooth and steady. He'll be formulating his clues any day now. We're very happy with the decision to hire him. Why, right now he's heavily engaged in the project of lining up his holidays for the rest of the year. Oh no, I'm sure that's not it. I'm sure he's doing something else. Here Paul, why don't you show me how to display what you're really working on? Do I push this button here? No? OOWWW!! IT BIT ME! IT YELLED AT ME! His PC actually yelled at me! How did it know to do that? What did he program in on this thing? BITE THE BOSS'S FINGER OFF. What kind of software package is that?"

I had temporarily activated a command which would make it impossible to exit a window without a password which only I knew. To this day, Irv is convinced that my pc bites the finger of anyone who tries to play with it besides me, and so he won't come near it. Once I made him see me type an entire document while the screen's foreground and background colors were both set to black just to set him off. He wouldn't come near me for a week. I got a lot of work done that way.

By the second week, I had learned to install ProKey by myself and include its proper exec command in my batch. This impressed Harry so much so that unfortunately he then put me to work. He held my hand during my first trips into PCFILE. This was exciting to say the most. My first real assignment had come, to begin managing the database for the in-shop computer training. All permanent, full time office employees are eligible to attend courses on both pc and mainframe programming, and my newly acquired database manages the scheduling and recruiting of all employees taking their courses. At least, it would if I did my job right.

By the third hour of repeating long laborious commands, I suddenly remembered from reading the ProKey documentation what a macro was. So I quickly punched in an Alt-/, and proceeded to type everything that was common about all these commands I was typing. I punched a nice Alt-enter when I was through, and I was so psyched. Little Paul Peroutka from Towson had made his first macro. The rest of this job took no more than fifteen minutes. When Harry saw my work, he was convinced that I had formulated my first clue. I said, no, you must be joshing, man. He said, well, this looks like a clue to me. And then I started to think how silly it would be to argue with my boss, or the first person who said I had a clue for a long time. So I decided against it.

I must interject this story for I'm hoping on it being the hit of the book. Soon after we started working, Neal and I were very kindly visited by two ladies from the personnel department. It was one of their duties to read and go over the rules, regulations, and applications to us as newly appointed government employees. After the necessary papers and forms were explained and then signed, the lady, and it doesn't matter whether or not she forgives me for not remembering her name because I'm sure I'll never see her again, had Neal repeat, and me hum the official oath of office. This is the same oath you last heard Mr. Ronny say way back when, no lie.

And the last order of business in this initiation mode was none other than fingerprinting. If you have never seen me, you have missed a bundle. If you have, you are already laughing heartily at the prospect of anyone trying to fingerprint me. I would not go overboard in a description of the idleness of my hands, but I will explain that they fairly seldom do what I wish them to do. An overall statement of their relation to me would be that they 'always' do just the opposite of what I want them to do. If I want them to open and relax, they will tend to close and clench. If I'm aiming to hold something tight, yes chances are that they will open and refuse to close. And to get them to cooperate with anything as alien as a fingerprint taker, I don't care what the official word for that is, is about as impossible as the proverbial camel through the needle. Nevertheless this dear woman relentlessly tried no less than eight separate methods to organize just one of my thumbs to press down with that gross ink gloss on it. Anyone who knows an athetoid could imagine a more involved scenario than I can relate in words. So I'll leave it up to you to laugh as much as you want. Yes, it was that funny.

Wednesday morning I arrived at work a few minutes before Neal had expected me, so he was not waiting for me on the parking lot. The bus driver kindly pushed me into the building where I could wait for Neal. Lo and behold, only a few seconds later, who walks out of her suite but Regina McPhillips, the bureau chief, one and the same. When our eyes met it seemed as if two good friends had met after a long absence.

'Oh wow,' she said, 'Paul, would you like me to push you in to your station?'

I saw no reason to say no. And so now my boss' boss' boss' boss' boss' boss' boss' boss and I meet this way every so often. It's a kick.

My office neighbor is an example that the spirit of Gracie Allen is not dead. Sheila Frank is a person to whom you must become attached, you have no choice in the matter. Sincerely and truly, I can have nothing but admiration for the gal. From, I don't remember, either the first or the second week, she has come over to our station keeping sure that we did not face the brand new experience without a guiding and friendly hand. I'll remember her willingness to show that support for as long as I come here to work. Sheila has worked for the government for over ten years, and from what I have observed she is a brilliant programmer. From what she has told me, she is also a brilliant mother.

You cannot know Sheila without knowing her immediate family immediately. She is the devoted mother of the genius prodigy seven year old Kevin, and the exquisite model three year old Annie. And if you haven't already heard of one of them, be patient enough to wait for the next people to come out. From what I understand, Kev is substituting on Firing Line for a couple weeks, and Annie has already signed to do three cameos on Dallas next fall.

Sheila worked alongside a nice guy named Charlie for a number of years before she became his wife. I figure if I just stay at my job for a few short years, she might agree to become my mother. I have given it much serious thought, and I definitely believe this would be the right move for both of us. She knows quite well that her two multitalented self sufficient kids will not need her for too much longer. Oh, they might send her royalty checks here and there, but that is nothing to build memories on. I'd be looking for a lasting relationship, something that will grow and nourish if she feeds me right. I'll never leave home. I'd never be blinded by lights. My vision is perfect. I'd never leave home. A couple of people have tried for twentyfour years, and they still cannot make me leave home. I said I was attached to Sheila. I said I had no other choice.

I recall one afternoon coming into work with some very good news to tell her.

'Hey Sheila, did you hear our great news? Congratulate us.'

'On what, Paul? Don't tell me that you and Neal were made permanent.'

'Ok. But we were. It happened yesterday afternoon. I was busy still trying to figure out what I was doing in dBase, and Irv and Harry called Neal into the big room. Well, I was a little curious as to why they would want to talk to Neal alone without me coming with him. I wasn't quite sure what was going down or anything, you know? But then I decided not to sweat it 'cause the program I was writing was so encompassing. But then Lil comes over in a minute or two and she's asking me if I'm alright, if I need anything, because Neal is still in there talking to Irv and Harry, don't you see? So I say no Lil, I'm alright. And then Lil starts pointing with her eyes to the room, to the room, to the room, obviously drawing attention to what I thought I was being cool just ignoring. So I tried to say what Lil, what Lil, what Lil, as to try to say what the hell is going on, Lil, or is there something wrong with your eyes, Lil, or anything more or less to that effect. But you know, after all of that, she still didn't say too much, only that something good was going on in there, and I would be happy when I heard it. Well then I started to figure out that this rules out a lot of things like the possibility that I'm screwing up badly on the job, or that I'm fired, or that they found out about that girl in Ocean City last weekend. I really wasn't suspecting that they'd find out about the girl in Ocean City because I hardly remembered what happened myself. But then, after all of this nonsense had left my head, it wasn't too long before Neal walks up behind me and says 'these men would like to see you now.' Well, at that point I knew not to bother to ask Neal what was going on because he doesn't ever like to talk to me in a rush. He doesn't even talk to me in months with thirty days in them. And he had a good feeling smirk on his face, so I knew I wasn't heading for any trouble. So when I got to the big table in the big room where Irv and Harry were sitting, I really wasn't worried at all. I knew to start looking at Irv only because Harry had already nodded back to sleep. Irv didn't yell at me or anything. He had his newspaper handy, but he only used it to smack Harry whenever he snored too loudly, and I was glad of that. So then

Irv starts telling me the good news, that they're happy with my work, what little I have done. They wouldn't mind seeing my face around for a little while longer, and they were offering me a new permanent position with the agency in which now I would receive full benefits and promotion rights coming to any permanent government employee. I'm in. Now I am really and fully IN. Oh, aren't you so happy for me? Isn't this just absolutely, positively, without a doubt just BEAUTIFUL, Sheila?

'I'm sorry, Paul. But you were talking a bit too fast for me and I didn't catch all that. Would you mind repeating it?'

Sheila has no complaints about listening to my domestic sagas either. I've enjoyed sharing with her my developing relationship with Nicky. I have placed pictures of Maria, Nicky and Lauren all around my desk. I have joined the ranks of being a bragging parent. It is sobering that in these days when I bother and struggle with the one word at a time and the abc method of talking with my new friends and surrounders, most of my conversations are for exchanging parenting advice and anecdotes. I'm mainly digging on how this life thing is evolving.

On the Friday of my second month of working for HCFA, cabinet secretary Dr. Otis Bowen of Health and Human Services came to the Woodlawn complex for an official tour. If you are not sure who I am describing, I am describing a member of the White House cabinet. The day before, his personal assistant came to our buildings to walk through the tour as it would go for the secretary. The actual visit would take place between 11:00 and 12:00. Well alas, I would not be able to meet the secretary on the following day. I work from 1:00 until 5:00 and the Mobility bus could not possibly get me there any earlier. Ah, but no. When I got home on Thursday night, I immediately was told that Michael had just made all the arrangements; there was nothing to worry about. The Mobility bus was canceled for the morning, my home attendant Jim had been asked to come an hour earlier. And Neal was set to drive me in to work early so that I could be there to shake hands with Secretary Bowen. Oh yeah, a first draft of the little note that I should type out on my pc had already been written. It only needed to be edited, and he was putting one of his lids on it right away. I think that Michael always wanted to borrow my cerebral palsy. I think he has kept designs all these years on how to use it a whole lot more advantageously than I have. But at least I had nothing to worry about.

Well, as all mornings before you meet the secretary of HHS will be, that one was hectic, and again nervous. Mom briefed me that Dr. Otis Bowen had been a great physician and at one time he was a governor. I said cool. My father changed my tie three times, and he still didn't get the right one. Finally Neal showed up at the house, and he showed me a few lines he composed in his notebook that might be appropriate to word process for the secretary to see. Neal had done a terrific job on that, and as soon as we arrived at work, I keyed it all in just like he wrote it, only adding a small bit of five part harmony and feeling. And the job looked beautiful.

Secretary Otis Bowen came to tour the Oak Meadows Building about a half hour ahead of schedule, but we were ready. Regina had known that we had prepared this little greeting for him and how much we wanted to be a part of his visit. So she especially steered him towards my station, and the introduction and extension of courtesy were very well received. Neal's note said how very happy and fortunate we were to have obtained our positions, and how cooperative and instrumental so many people were in our success. I wish that I could write so well.

How Do You Like Me So Far, Mom?

All of us knew when we went to bed on Wednesday night that Mom would die sometime in the next 24 hours.

Thursday morning at 6:30 the phone rang in the other room. Dr. Savedel told Dad that the nurse who had just bathed Mom had reported that she thought that Mom would die very soon. Dad called Michael. He picked Dad up and they drove to the hospital.

I thought that it just might happen to me; and yes it did. The moment when my mother left this world, I felt undeniably a powerful surge through my body. The words of the 'Our Father' and then the 'Hail Mary' came to me suddenly without me asking for them. It was nothing but a most perfect moment. Mom had chosen to come to me first. I could not see her face, but I could not have felt a presence more definitely.

Mom and I spent the most miraculous and the longest hour that I've ever lived. We two were alone in our house, in my room. It was the first time I had actually been able to speak to her in over a month.

I can't usually sing when I'm crying. But the first song I sang to Mom was 'When Irish Eyes Are Smiling'. And the second song I sang was 'Danny Boy'.

Mom and I were telling each other that we would be alright. We were embracing each other in unifying celebration of our new and everlasting relationship. She said that now she can be with me all the time. And I realized that from then on, I would be so much closer to my mother than I ever had been. After the hour, everyone was in our house. But ever since then, I've never parted company from my mother.

Praying To Mom

This can be my contribution to this summer's block of warming ghost stories. Once about every three weeks I am blessed with a dream featuring my mother's face, voice, and bright red jogging suit.

Don't get the idea that my mother ever had the propensity to jog during the last thirty years of her life. No, the suit was given to her for Christmas, I guess by one of my sisters, as we all knew her habits of wearing large and loose clothing around the house. When she wasn't wearing that bright red jogging suit, she had on one of her many nightgowns and a bathrobe. She would be sitting comfortably in her Lazy-Boy doing one of several things: reading her newspaper or Reader's Digest, looking up recipes in the church cookbook, doing a crossword puzzle, or crocheting. I mean to say that she might be doing any of these leisure activities if I wasn't asking her to 'be my hands' in one of my many projects.

Well, last night, in my dream she was helping me with a literary project. It had something to do with the design of a page that I had made on my pc. I don't remember, but I think I was actually doing all the work myself. She was just watching and encouraging me on. She had at last been given the opportunity of seeing me capable of creating the thing which I had conceived in my mind through my acquired computer technology. It was fascinating to her.

Seeing Mom's face and hearing her voice is the kind of blessing that I know not to bother to ask for. I know that I will get dreams with her periodically, and they are such wonderful gifts that I have learned to let them come in their own course. Last night's was especially good because she was in a whimsical, creative mood, and so was I. In real life together, our dispositions didn't exactly jell that smoothly always.

That is not to say that we never had great moments when our energies were at the same level while we were busy designing my pages or collating compilations of my writings. We did. And last night's dream enabled me to share with Mom my new Harvard Graphics program. I remember so vividly how exuberant her face was at the different stages when we were cracking the intricacies of the software and getting the exact results we were after.

Mom would have never grasped too much about writing computer programs. But she probably would have made a great software user. If her software was to organize and retrieve cooking recipes, or to calculate how much yarn to use in an afghan. Or if it was a well designed interactive bridge game, I think she would have picked it up and ran with it. In fact, now I remember that she did take an introduction to DOS class about two years ago. I was never quite sure why she did that. But I do remember now that she loved to impress me by reading me her notes and showing me how many terms she picked up at every class.

My mother's world and mine did not intersect as much as we probably would have liked them to do. I guess that's why her classnotes meant so much to her. And maybe that's why I had her there last night helping me design the page with Harvard Graphics. Maybe that's why she helps me in periodic dreams accomplish things like rearranging the schedules for my stage productions, wheeling my chair up to the mall for a sixpack, shaving and blowdrying my hair in the morning, sorting out my hostilities against those enemies that aggravated me that day.

Mom's face immediately became about forty years younger for me after she died, I think. Because during the month and more of her hospital stay, I had looked at her wedding photo in our living room probably quite a bit more than I had visited her drained, shriveled dying body in intensive care. The sight of the twenty year young bright Betty is certainly the one I envisioned entering Heaven and meeting God on the day she died.

In my gift dreams though, I tend to see Mom as the composite of how I saw my mother during my young adulthood, when I was interrupting her doing her dishes and saying her rosary, long enough to help me design all those pages and collate all of my writings, all by hand. And I do recall the very same voice which used to complain so often about me wasting her precious time dilly-dallying and taking her away from her housework. But now, when I hear her, she tells me that she can stay with me and help me all I need. She has all the time in the world.

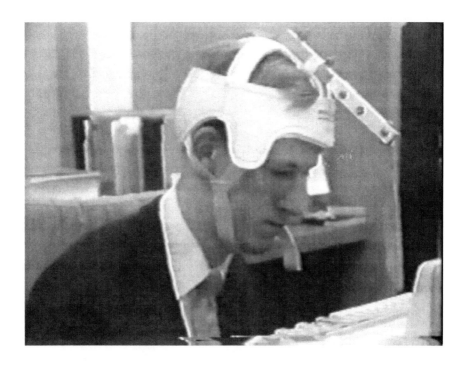

WHY WE WRITE

WE WRITE TO CHANGE THE WORLD. Learning is a change in behavior. By writing, we can take a single aspect of a single thought about one specific phenomenon; we can spotlight it and analyze it, and if we do correctly, we explain that object well enough so that when it is placed back in the whole, it makes the whole justly that much more understandable. If viable information is indeed provided to the reader by the writer, a change in the world can be made.

I URGE YOU TO READ THIS. I AM PAUL PEROUTKA. I AM MOSTLY SEEN IN A WHEELCHAIR; I HAVE HAD CEREBRAL PALSY SINCE I WAS BORN. I HAVE A VERY SUCCESSFUL LIFE. HAVING ALWAYS DONE WELL IN SCHOOL AND EMPLOYMENT, I NOW LOOK STRAIGHT FORWARD AT LUCRATIVE MIDDLE AGE. MY LARGEST DISABILITY COMES FROM THE COMPLETELY BLIND PREJUDICE OF SOME UNFORTUNATE, IGNORANT PEOPLE IN THIS SOCIETY WHICH CAUSES THEM TO LABEL STUPIDLY SOME OF ITS MEMBERS, WHOSE SITUATIONS RESEMBLE MY OWN, WITH THE HORRIBLE WORD, YUPPIE.

I BECOME SO INCENSED AT SUCH BLATANT BIGOTRY THAT IT CAUSES ME TO SUFFER HYPERTENSION AND PAINFUL GASTRIC ANXIETY. THIS IS THE REASON WHY I TAKE TUMS, OR IN SOME COMPANY, RIOPAN. HOWEVER, I DO RECEIVE COUNSELING, UNDERGO THERAPY, AND

TAKE OTHER CORRECTIVE MEASURES TO ALLEVIATE
MY PROBLEM. THIS IS WHY I WRITE.

I WRITE TO THIS FINE NEWSPAPER IN HOPES OF
THANKING AND EXTENDING MY FRIENDSHIP TO
MANY OF MY FELLOW CITIZENS AND COMPATRIOTS.
YOU HAVE PROBABLY OFTEN SEEN EITHER ME OR
OTHER HANDICAPPED PERSONS WHEN YOU ATTEND
YOUR FAVORITE NIGHTCLUB, BAR OR RESTAURANT IN
OUR VERY FRIENDLY NEIGHBORHOOD. I WOULD LIKE
TO TAKE THIS OPPORTUNITY TO EXPRESS SINCERE
GRATITUDE TO NOT ONLY THE ENTREPRENEURS AND
STAFF OF OUR POPULAR ESTABLISHMENTS, BUT ALSO
THEIR CONGENIAL CUSTOMERS, THE YOUNG CROWD,
FOR THEIR HOSPITALITY AND ACCEPTANCE TOWARD
THEIR DISABLED FELLOW PARTIERS.

INDEED, THIS SOCIETY HAS TAKEN GREAT LEAPS IN
GIVING THE DISABLED EVERY RIGHT AND BENEFIT
WHICH WE DESERVE. I COULDN'T BE MORE PROUD TO
SAY THAT I AM FROM THIS AREA, WHERE EVERYONE
BEHAVES SPLENDIDLY, ALLOWING ME AND MANY OF MY
HANDICAPPED FRIENDS TO FEEL MORE THAN WELCOME
IN THE FINE PRACTICE OF GETTING BLITZED.

We write to clarify our opinions, our positions, both collectively and
personally. Some will write until it all makes sense. Me, I'll only keep
typing until my text suits today's requirements of lines and columns. But
you should not emulate my whole personality. You're you. You should
write how and what you want. Composition workshops are absolutely
useless. I call them inherently unAmerican. We live in a country where
no one can tell you what to say, where to worship. No one should assume
the right to edit your voice. You know what you have to say, and how
you want to put it down. You are the writer. It is your choice to make.
And if they try to tell you how you should express yourself through your
writing, then you should pick another major.

We will probably not go to war with Saddam Hussein. A war over oil is inconceivable. War is only a continuum of bad ideas based on protocols of pride which camouflage those ideas as being sensible and just in the bleak light of paranoia. I've written this all before, and take it from me. There'll be no war.

I must explain very much my true self now, so please bear with me. This book is meant to present the rock and roll that I am able to produce. What you need to understand about my work is that it's not typing; it's singing. The concept of me actually singing this material is that it is basically a showcase of the energy in my body. I do not pretend at all that almost anybody wouldn't consider the exploitation of my spasms and strained utterances sheerly preposterous.

I am, yes indeed, asking you all, and I do realize the gravity of this request, to forsake some of your own identity as readers in order to help me put this 'experiment' on. And I have to think that we shall all be able to accept and to understand the whole grand thing much better if we all think of it, my life my life my life my life, as an 'experiment'. I am not a singer with a normal voice. I am an energetic charismatic personality who is going to perform this music in the unique way that I can...

You will want to familiarize yourself with my inflections, my patterns, my abilities, my disabilities, how I sing, what to listen for. Please realize the high respect that I have for you as an audience of mine. As always I say, thank you very much for all your time and attention. Please accept my request as a compliment that I believe you to be able to understand and accept what I'm trying to achieve, and that you'd be willing to do it with me. What I need is a back-up band, and fast.

We write to develop the species, to improve life itself. We comment on those aspects which need change. I write today because I cannot condone abortion. I want us to open our eyes a lot wider than either one of us are seeing now. We are ruled by hormonal media. We have been fornicating far more than freely for the last thirtyfive years. I say that Hollywood now produces life and death, off the screen, and this is wrong. Famous actresses with more luxuries than morals have no right to promote via their media acceptance of uncareful sex and unconditional abortion. Neither do electable Democrats or successful businesswomen on either side of forty.

When I discuss abortion, I'll discuss it with the desperate and poor teenaged girl who hasn't learned her own choices. I'll ask her what happened. I'll look at her home and surroundings. I'll ask her if she realizes the mindset of the moment. The law of the land says that you can stop your pregnancy at anytime. The law also gives a three month old fetus battery protection and inheritance rights. So we leave it up to you. Inside you now is a form of growing human life. But through legislature, we have justified reasons for killing it for just about any reason. You are given the choice. No person has ever lived in a more wonderful land on Earth. America. Where no one can tell you what to say, where to worship, or how to write. You are truly the writer of your life, and truly only you have the choice. This is also written. It is the law of the land.

I write because I want Hollywood, Wall Street, and Capitol Hill to start behaving themselves. This free society reads all the time. No one tells us what to say, where to worship, or how to write. Today we are all writing about finding a political answer to make a biological decision. When should we begin respecting life? If we writers would better show that we respect our own lives as much as we do, maybe the people who are reading will come to cherish their own. It's now 1990. Where are we in the development of the species? Wouldn't it be wonderful if this society could make room for all our children to grow?

I Cannot Condone Abortion

This time of year I travel to many concert arenas where the Grateful Dead are performing. I travel very much, though I live in a wheelchair because of cerebral palsy. Also I can't pronounce too many words, so I do a lot of listening.

I'd like to go back to an arena in Philadelphia where I was last summer. It was there in one moment of a long day that one typical Deadhead was walking around with one typical petition on her clipboard. I decided that I had time to listen to her story.

I started to smile because it makes me glad to help out a determined Deadhead by adding my name to a cause that is worthy of so much time and travel. So as she approached, she asked if I would like to add my name to the thousands who would march on Washington's mall in promotion of choice for abortion.

I'd like to go back to that moment because it was so much of an astounding shock to me to be turning down a fellow Deadhead, an attractive, lovely young girl. That is very foreign to my nature, many who know me would attest. I am sure that it shocked her as much as it did me. She turned and walked immediately away as soon as she saw my silent head shaking no.

I'd like to go back to that moment because I think I have now decided what I would have said to the woman if I could have communicated to her with more than just my silent head shaking no.

Look at me all over. Don't expect me to be on the side of abortion. Consider that I could make a deciding case that my cerebral palsied life might have been prevented due to the mindset of justifiable abortion.

The question becomes: Is it satisfactory that I was born with such a defect? I'll answer this question. Yes, I think so. I'm an acclaimed poet. I contribute to my brothers' law practice. I try to follow the ways of Jesus, and here I am talking to you outside this Grateful Dead concert.

The question broadens: Should the mindset of a right society be to make an attempt to eliminate the handicaps and defects of its offspring? Is selective regeneration truly akin to the responsibilities and scientific privileges which are indeed felt by today's society? I cannot possibly answer this question, for my name is not "today's society". Great, ingenious and powerful men have justified holocausts a million times in history. City-states, empires, and nations have accepted, condoned, fought and died in the names of such men and their holocausts. That was their choice.

The questions thicken: Why use the word, if not the metaphor, "holocaust" when describing the mindset of justifying abortion of the imperfect, the deformed? Decisions and actions of a society inherently must be made by that society. When should human life be protected by civil law? Can the judgment of that arbitrary circumstance and time be anything at all, in fact, but arbitrary in itself?

The question of abortion rests immobly on the perception of the human condition. Were you to meet me and try to persuade me to condone abortion for the betterment of our world and the enhancement of our freedom, I would ask you, very personally into your eyes, for whom are you preserving a world? To whom would you entitle freedom?

I would then suggest that you consider conversing with a birth defected citizen. You might be more enlightened for your own perspective.

As a severely disabled individual, I can logistically answer only one question about abortion. I cannot condone it. I might have been nothing at all if my parents had. I am glad if I speak satisfactorily for anyone in a similar situation who shares my outlook.

Traveling With The Death Bucket

TRAVELING WITH ME IN MY VAN IS TAKING ALONG "THE DEATH BUCKET". THAT IS THE SPADE SHAPED CAN THAT ALL MY MATES USE TO CATCH THE EXCESS SPILLAGE CAUSED WHEN THEY ARE POURING ME ALCOHOL ON ROAD TRIPS. IF YOU DON'T ENJOY THE ODOR, AS NO ONE DOES, PLEASE JUST FORGET IT IS EVEN THERE.

TRAVELING WITH ME IS BECOMING AT ONE WITH MY AGENDA. IN THE SPRING OF 1987 I WAS VERY BUSY AT WORK. I WAS STILL TOURING WEEKLY WITH MY "PAUL '86" MATERIAL, AND I WAS BEGINNING GRADUATE SCHOOL. BUT BY FAR THE MOST IMPORTANT EVENT ON MY MIND WAS THE DATE OF JUNE 1. OBVIOUSLY, THE FIRST OF JUNE OF 1987 WAS TO BE THE TWENTIETH ANNIVERSARY OF THE RELEASE OF THE SGT. PEPPER'S ALBUM...AND ALSO THE ACTUAL DATE OF THE RELEASE OF THAT GREAT CD. OBVIOUSLY; YOU KNEW THIS, DIDN'T YOU?

TRAVELING WITH ME IS GOING ALONG WITH THE WAY I INSIST THAT THE WORLD MUST BE; IT IS SUSPENDING ALL COMMON SENSE, PACKING THE COOLER, TURNING THE KEY, AND DRIVING ANYWHERE THAT I POINT. I RANG UP TOMMY CHESNAVAGE, THE MAN WHO HAS SPOKEN FOR ME AND TO ME FOR LONGER THAN MOST, AND I TOLD HIM ABOUT THIS IDEA FOR AN ALL

OUT BANG-UP CELEBRATION OF THIS MONUMENTAL, HISTORIC DAY YET TO COME.

TRAVELING WITH ME IS ALWAYS KNOWING THE FACT THAT WE SHALL ENDURE, YET OVERCOME QUITE AN ASSORTMENT OF VEHICULAR AND PERSONAL HAZARDS WHICH WOULD SHAKE THE SHOOTIES OFF OF ANYONE WHO NEVER EVER HAD THE PLEASURE TO MEET ME. THIS WAS THE CAR RIDE WHICH INDELIBLY MARKED THAT FACT INTO TOMMY'S HEAD. WE HIT I-95. WE WERE SINGING ALONG. WE WERE CRUISING VERY WELL, HEADING NORTH. ABOUT 20 MINUTES INTO THE RIDE, THERE WAS ONE TREMENDOUS EXPLOSION, AND ALL THIS WATER SHOT UP ON THE WINDSHIELD OF THE VAN. TOM NATURALLY ASKED ME, AS IF I KNEW, "WHAT THE HELL WAS THAT?" WE PULLED OVER, AND HE NOTICED THE TEMPERATURE GAUGE ON THE VAN, NEEDLESS TO SAY, WAS RUNNING VERY HIGH. THE NEEDLE WAS STUCK UP IN THE HOT SECTION.

TRAVELING WITH ME IS HAVING LIVED THROUGH THE FIERY BLAZES OF HELL FOR SEVERAL YEARS OF YOUR LIFE AND DECIDING THAT IT JUST WASN'T CHALLENGING ENOUGH FOR YOU. TOM SAT WITH ME, WAITING BY THE SIDE OF THE ROAD, WAITING BY THE SIDE OF THE ROAD ON 95 NORTH. HE FINALLY LOOKS TO SAY, "PAUL, THE RADIATOR CAP BURST OFF. WE JUST HAVE TO GET A NEW RADIATOR CAP AND GET SOME WATER IN THERE, AND I'LL JUST HAVE TO WATCH THE TEMPERATURE GAUGE AND KEEP MY SPEED DOWN." BUT ON CLOSER EXAMINATION, WE SAW THAT THE LID HADN'T BLOWN OFF, THE WHOLE BLOODY TOP OF THE RADIATOR BLEW OFF! IT BURST RIGHT OFF! SO WE WERE IN DEEP TROUBLE. WE CAN'T GO BACK, AND WE CAN'T STAND STILL. DOES THAT RING A BELL?

TRAVELING WITH ME IS NOT ALWAYS FUN, BUT IT USUALLY IS LIFE THREATENING. WE GOT OFF THAT EXIT BY JUST DRIFTING AS BEST WE COULD...THERE WAS A HILL. SO WE DRIFT DOWN THIS BIG HILL; THE VAN HAD ABSOLUTELY NO POWER, WE WERE JUST GOING ON GRAVITY. AND DOWN AT THE BOTTOM OF THIS HILL, AS LUCK WOULD HAVE IT, WAS A SERVICE STATION. TOM EXITED THE VAN TO MEET TWO BIG MUSCULAR LONG HAIRED GUYS. ONE OF THEM HAD MORE HAIR ON HIS CHEST THAN CRYSTAL GAYLE HAS DOWN HER BACK. THEY TOLD US THAT THEY COULDN'T REPAIR THE VAN THAT NIGHT, THAT IT WOULD BE READY IN THE MORNING. AS YOU CAN SEE, ALREADY OUR PLANS WERE GETTING A LITTLE DISCABOBBULATED.

THE NEXT MORNING, THESE HAIRY, HICKY GUYS FROM THE GAS STATION PICKED US UP FROM THE SHONEY'S HOTEL WHERE WE HAD TO STAY. THEY SAID, "OK, WE FIXED YOUR VAN, AND IT'S GOING TO COST A PHENOMENAL AMOUNT OF MONEY." AND WE REPLY, "OK, WELL, WE'VE GOT MASTERCARD AND VISA." AND THEY SAY, "NO, IT'S NOT WORTH IT TO US TO DO THIS FOR CREDIT. WE'RE GOING TO A WEDDING TODAY, AND WE NEED ALL YOUR PETTY CASH." WE DIDN'T QUITE UNDERSTAND THIS. TRAVELING WITH ME IS NEVER QUITE UNDERSTANDING ANYTHING THAT'S GOING ON.

WE HIT NEW YORK CITY RIGHT ABOUT RUSH HOUR. YOU HAVE TO REMEMBER THAT WE ARE DRIVING THIS HUMONGOUS GIANT JUMBO SIZED VAN. IT IS JUST ABOUT AS BIG AS A CITY BUS. WE ARE DRIVING IT IN RUSH HOUR NEW YORK TRAFFIC. I WANT TO PARK IN TIMES SQUARE, BECAUSE IT'S THE 20TH ANNIVERSARY OF SGT. PEPPER, AND THERE'S SOMETHING GOING ON DOWN THERE. DRIVING IN NEW YORK IN A JUMBO SIZED 747 BOEING VAN IS JUST ABOUT IMPOSSIBLE, AS

WE FOUND OUT. WE HAD ALL THESE WONDERFUL ADVENTURES WHERE PEOPLE ARE CURSING AT US. WE PULLED INTO PAY PARKING SPACES, BUT WHEN WE GET HALFWAY IN, PEOPLE STARTED CHASING US YELLING, "NO, NO, YOU CAN'T PARK THAT THING IN HERE!" SO WE HAD TO BACK OUT IN RUSH HOUR NEW YORK TRAFFIC IN THIS VAN. WE WENT DOWN ONE SIDE STREET AND ONE OF THE MIRRORS ON THE SIDE OF THE VAN SMASHED INTO SOMEBODY ELSE'S MIRROR. WE JUST KEPT GOING. WE DIDN'T WANT TO STOP. WE DIDN'T CARE. WE JUST KEPT GOING.

WE WERE RIDING FOR ABOUT TWO HOURS... TOM'S EYE STAYED CAUTIOUSLY ON THE TEMPERATURE GAUGE AT ALL TIMES, IMAGINING THE RADIATOR EXPLODING IN NEW YORK RUSH HOUR TRAFFIC. THEN WE GAVE UP. WE SAID, "HEY, THIS IS IMPOSSIBLE. WE CAN'T PARK THE JUMBO VAN ANYWHERE." SO WE GOT BACK ON THE HOLLAND TUNNEL, OR WHATEVER IT IS AT THIS POINT, AND WE HEADED BACK OUT TO NEW JERSEY. WE STOPPED AT A ROY ROGERS OVERLOOKING THE CITY OF NEW YORK. AND WE JUST SAT THERE, AND WE LOOK AT EACH OTHER. AND WE'RE JUST LOOKING AT EACH OTHER. AND WE LOOKED AT EACH OTHER. AND WE SAT THERE. AND WE SAT THERE SOME MORE. AND WE LOOKED AT EACH OTHER. WHILE FEEDING ME A ROAST BEEF SANDWICH, TOM WAS SITTING THERE; HE LOOKED AT ME SAYING, "PAUL TRAVELING WITH YOU IS ALWAYS HAVING TO SAY YOU'RE SORRY."

"OK, WE'RE GOING TO CANCEL THIS SEGMENT OF OUR TRIP, AND WE'LL JUST GO INTO NEW YORK CITY TONIGHT..." WE WERE GOING TO STAY WITH ADRIENNE WHO WAS THEN MY ATTORNEY. WE FINALLY GOT IN TOUCH WITH HER OVER THE PHONE. WE WENT BACK TO HER APARTMENT IN MANHATTAN, AND IT WAS WONDERFUL. WE ACTUALLY GOT TO SIT DOWN WITH

A ROOF OVER OUR HEADS, AND WE GOT SOMETHING TO EAT, AND IT WAS NICE ENOUGH FOR ROCK AND ROLL. TOM LOOKED AS IF HE WAS ALMOST READY TO SPEAK TO ME AGAIN. WHEN YOU'RE TRAVELING WITH ME, YOU ALWAYS HAVE TO COME AROUND TO SPEAKING TO ME AGAIN, AT SOME POINT.

THAT EVENING, WE ARE SCHEDULED TO GIVE OUT COPIES OF MY NEW VIDEO AT THE HARD ROCK CAFE. BY NOW, NO ONE FEELS LIKE GOING TO THE HARD ROCK CAFE... BUT IT WAS ON MY SCHEDULE, SO DARN IT, WE HAD TO GO. ADRIENNE DROVE THE VAN, AND SHE STOPPED ON THE STREET TO LET US OUT. SHE NEVER FOUND A PARKING SPACE SO SHE RODE AROUND THE BLOCKS FOR THREE HOURS. I WAS SORRY ABOUT THAT, BUT TOM AND I HAD A SMASH--OF A NEW AND BETTER KIND. HE KNOWS BY NOW: WHEN TRAVELING WITH ME, WE ALWAYS END UP SMASHING.

TOM OPENED THE DOOR OF THE HARD ROCK CAFE ON THAT JUNE 1 EVENING OF 1987. HE PUSHED ME IN. THE WHOLE BOTTOM FLOOR LOOKED UP AND SAID "HI, PAUL." THE DJ CUED UP "PEACEFROG". THE WHOLE TOP FLOOR BEGAN TO BOOGIE. DARLING PAMELA GAVE ME A BIG WET KISS, AND ISAAC LED US TO THE BEST TABLE IN THE HOUSE. WE DRANK FOR FREE. IT WAS AT THAT POINT THAT TOM PROBABLY REMEMBERED WHAT IT'S LIKE TO TRAVEL WITH ME.

FANTASTICMAN

Wait for this one. This was no dream; or if it was, then I haven't yet woken. It's true. It's true.

On a Monday morning in this year's springtime, I was returning home with Dad from my appointment at the dermatologist. This was a new doctor I had gone to see, and he had just committed a pack of cardinal sins for which I was finding it very hard to forgive him.

During my visit, the doctor repeatedly and without exception addressed my father solely, asking my own medical history, symptoms and ailments to my father without even so much as a glance to me for acknowledgment or recognition.

And if that wasn't enough, the bad doctor then had the audacity to say to my father, Sir, have you taken him to see "My Left Foot" yet?

I felt like giving him my left foot in a place he would definitely not appreciate. But I decided against it. When we left his office, the doctor was unharmed. And by the time I had forgotten all about it, Dad and I arrived home where the Mobility bus was already waiting in front of our driveway for to transport me to work.

Understand, because I had had the appointment with that goofy, half-literate dermatologist that morning, I hadn't had time to take my morning nap. And as usual after any weekend, I had a healthy hangover which needed more sleeping off. But this was no problem. I always rode on the bus alone, with no one to disturb me. And while I didn't even feel like going into work that day and having to listen to Neal Moylan, my fat douchebag cousin and co-worker bitch, all day about how raggy I looked, I knew I would catch a few winks on the bus and I would feel somewhat better by the time I got to the office.

Maybe the bus will crash while I'm in it;
or I could swim Loch Raven, then I'd save an extra minute.
Maybe my legs will quiver and quake,
For I'm all shot up, half awake.
What a day this'll be; how I wish I wasn't me.
Why, it's almost like being alive.
There's this jock itch I have; I could sure use some salve.
Why, it's almost like being a- live.
All the ground's gravity seems to keep down my eye lids to put me to sleep.
And from the way I feel like hell when Neal Moylan starts to yell and this headache he's giving.
I could swear this must be living.
It's almost like being a---live.

I was shouting to Dad instructions on what to do at Kinko's copiers that day as I was ascending the hydraulic lift on the bus. When I backed into my seat, I immediately saw I had big problems. There were two women on the bus already, so there went my chance for privacy to snooze. The one on my left was an older woman in a wheelchair who smiled at me and said hello to me whenever I looked at her. She on my right was young, my age, and healthy, quite healthy. She said, hello, this is Peggy and I'm Jenny. You don't look like you're going swimming (I always wear a tie to work). That's where I'm taking Mom now, to go swimming at the hospital. You're going to work, right? The bus driver says you're a computer wiz.

Yes I am.

That was about the only quick and clever response I could come up with. This girl seemed very nice and friendly. Her mother was less talkative, and when she did speak, she mostly complained about her shoulder hurting her. Jenny explained to me that her Mom had a stroke about two years ago. Jenny lived in Colorado, but she was visiting home for that week to take care of her mother while the housekeeper was on vacation. As she continued talking, I was enjoying listening to her more and more. It turned out she grew up just five minutes away from my house, in Riderwood. Her mother was able to say that their house was right next to the school. I kept that in mind for future reference. The ride lasted for about twenty minutes until we got to the hospital pool. I knew I liked Jenny and she had enjoyed the time too. It was a time when I could have kicked myself because I didn't have a copy of one of my books with me to give her. But as she was pushing her Mom in her wheelchair away from the bus, and waving goodby to me, I had a very good strong feeling that I would be seeing her again, with a little bit of luck.

I thought about her all day. I had seen her breasts because she had leaned down in her bathing suit and blouse to adjust my seat belt. At my request, of course. Of course. So when Joe Morel came over to see me that night, I had had the phone book open for quite a while. And I said, Joe, hey Joe, guess what; I met the girl of my dreams today and you and I, we have to drive over to a house next to Riderwood School so we can leave a copy of "Heaven's To Betsy" in some mailbox and hope that it's hers.

So that's what we did. Morel and I rode off into the sunset looking for the street where ... (Well, you get the idea by now.)

Peggy and Jenny were on my bus again on Wednesday, (YES), and there was good news and bad news. First off, Morel and I had left the book in completely the wrong mailbox, but you would have guessed that. Ah, but today I was so well prepared with a book right on my lap ready to give her. She leaned down again, (YES). She started reading Chip's introduction, and then "Why We Write". She flipped out on the Yuppie line. She laughed hard and she said, oh you're such a great writer, and I used to teach writing, (YES). But now I live in Colorado where I'm a travel agent. Paul, do you mind if I ask something personal about you? You have cerebral palsy, don't you? I knew that because I have this thing about Daniel Day Lewis, and my boyfriend Kevin took me to see "My Left Foot". Did anyone ever take you to see that movie?

I forgave the girl for all of the cardinal sins which she committed in that last question. It was clear then that we both liked and were quite taken with each other. We exchanged numbers and addresses, (OH YES).

On Thursday, I flipped a coin to decide whether to take off the next day and maybe we could get together. On Friday morning while I was still in the john, she called me and asked what's going on. I never shit that day, but I got my way. Jenny came over and, you know. We spent a great day talking in my studio. With every sentence said, we became closer as she sat on my bed. We were lost in the time, in my room. It all ended too soon. When she left, we were both very happy all day. We kissed. Tra la, it's May!

It was ten o'clock Saturday morning, the time that Sireci said he would come from Jersey to pick me up to go to the Preakness, so naturally I knew I had about two hours to wait for him. Dad had gone to the store.

I knew I could have a long, leisurely morning phone conversation with Jenny.

And I did.

During the course of our first telephone interlude, I spelled out the name K E V I N ? And she said that she didn't mind telling me about him at all. They have been together for about three years. They do not live together because their relationship works out better that way. And she told me that he is her everything and her soul mate. Fair enough.

I asked her if she wanted to come along to the Preakness. But she said, no, I have to take care of Mom all day, but I really would like seeing you sometime before I go home.

I said, yeah, hey great. Why don't I give you a call after the race, and maybe we can hook up tonight. I have to warn you though; whenever I get drunk, I have the habit of calling people up and telling them I love them.

"Oh my, I can't imagine you doing that, Paul."

Believe me, it wouldn't take many beers at all for me to tell you that.

"Oh really?"

We hung up knowing very definitely that we'd see each other very soon.

I do believe I'd cracked it, I'd cracked it. I'd cracked it. It looked as if I'd cracked it, and indeed I had.

Sireci was only ninety minutes late so he was early. He brought with him his graduate school friend Thaddeus down to Baltimore for this great day full of sun and fun. Right away I started to tell Sireci of the incredible week I was having. I said, Steve, this kind of shit only happens to Steve

Sireci. Oh my god, I can't believe it. You have to meet this chick, man. She's the best thing I've ever found.

"Paul, you say that in every story you write."

I know, but this time it's true, it's true. Now let's go to the Preakness. You know I really don't like talking to you.

Upon arriving at Pimlico race track, Sireci spent the usual first half hour trying to talk each and every cop and security guard into letting us park for free because I'm handicapped. This is most definitely one of his favorite things to do and one of the major reasons why he stays friends with me. Once we got out of the van, the ultimate manifestation of our relationship was fully realized. We'd have a mile to walk from where we finally did park to the infield and the party. So my best friend thought nothing of setting the twentyfive pound ice-cooler, filled with beer and my alcohol, on my lap for the entire length of the trip, leaving me no room to turn my head forward. Each breath became precious, every movement miraculously relieving, and we won't even talk about my cock and balls. I began to regret the night they invented Jim Beam.

Needless to say, every resident of the Pimlico neighborhood commented to Sireci boisterously on his horrible cruel treatment of me. Only about eight little black children offered to carry the ice-cooler on their bikes, for free. But Sireci would hear no part of it. He exclaimed, "Look, he's an author and a shopping cart." Thaddeus thought the whole affair was quite funny as he carried his mini-playmate. But finally, finally, we did make it to the races. And we all had a glorious time.

That we did.

Everyone who should be here is here.
Everyone is feeding Paul some beer.
It's a solar rocker and a roller party at the Preakness Stakes today.
At our annual big holiday there is not a lot Paul has to say while he's luring people to be pouring drinks to him.
The Preakness stakes today.

All the faces today here at this joint will be shitfaced when they get back to Fell's Point. Every Loyola grad is feeling far too glad & our hero Paul will outdrink them all.

> Steve Combs. Marcus. Beaver's carcass,
> Matt Quin's, Kevin's, over there they're
> playing sevens.
> Any second now we might see a fluke;
> The race might not have started yet,
> but Paul is sure to puke............
> And here it comes !!!!!!

BLAAAAAAAAAAAAAAAAAAAAAAAAAAAAAAAAAAAAA
AAAAAAAAAAAAAAAAAAAH.

What a brilliant show of precision, Paul has thrown up dinner from yesterday. And after it left his mouth, he was soon going south. Drank another down all the way. Just our normal Paul. He's true to form all tanked up at the Preakness Stakes today.

At the end of the day, right before it was time to leave Pimlico, I met someone named Kathleen whom I really shouldn't talk about in this story. I'm sorry.

Suzie Gottlieb (remember Suzie Gottlieb from the early days of Queen York Underground?), Suzie walked with Sireci, Thaddeus and me back to the van so to catch a ride back to Fields (remember Fields, our old college rugby bar?), back to Fields with us. On this walk, I found it extremely curious how Thaddeus didn't mind in the least carrying the ice-cooler back to the van. He was able to carry it in one hand and his mini-playmate in the other. And yes, all the way back, all the Pimlico residents were still giving Sireci shit for torturing me before. And I joined along with them. I let them all know just who he was.

His brain is messed, his mind is slow, and they call my friend Pariah.

When we got back to the van I told all three, hey, we gotta call Jenny.

They all said, who?

I said, Jenny, the girl who's at home taking care of her mother waiting for me to call her and tell her I love her because I'm drunk.

Nobody really understood all that, but Sireci picked up my car phone, (it is paid for by the Peroutka & Peroutka Law Offices), and asked me what Jenny's number was. Sireci really is my best friend.

Then I told Suzie exactly what to say to her. "Hello Jenny? This is Suzie. I'm a friend of Paul's. Yeah, we just got out of the Preakness, and right away he said we had to call you to tell you that he has been talking about you all day, and that he loves you a lot, and that he hopes he sees you tonight. ... Alright? Alright Jenny, I'll tell him. ...

"Paul, she says you will."

And I did.

The four of us in the van drove to Fields which is where all of us alumni stop every year after the Preakness on the way home to Fells Point. Suzie and I held each other and she blew in my ear now again, but that had to be because she was missing her boyfriend Ty who was working at home, and I was busy missing you know who.

Hours went by at the bar where everybody got geometrically drunker than the plane they had started out on. Soon there was literally no room to move or to feel comfortable at all because it was getting as sloppy as it ever was when we were all back in school. I had no other decision to make than that this was not the scene I wanted Jenny to see. The time was drawing near to when I would ask Sireci to call her to tell her where to meet us. I grabbed him, decided to ask him to feed me two more beers, which turned into seven, and to take me for one last piss, which turned into three or four. I can't remember. Then I remembered to ask Sireci to call Jenny to tell her to meet me outside Fields in about twenty minutes.

Ty had come into the bar by then, and he was the one I asked to help me trample and stample all the way through all of the crumbly dead drunk bodies and out the door. When we got outside, I explained to him whom I was waiting for and that I'd be alright waiting alone. He said cool; but he was nice enough to fetch me a few Wild Turkeys for the meantime.

I almost wished she wouldn't come; I wasn't as together as I would have liked to be. Alumni came and went in front of the door. I waved and said hello, but I didn't recognize too many. You know how I get when I have only one thing on my mind. And then. There she was. In a red top and sexy shorts. And carrying a box of chocolate strawberries which I never did understand.

We two talked for a while outside. And that was nice.

Then Sireci and Thaddeus came out, and we all drove to catch last call some place in Towson. Then at two we went back and all sat in the van till three. Sireci, Thaddeus and Jenny held conversations about reggae music and graduate school. And our hands slipped into each other's. And we mostly looked at each other. She fell in love with me. For the first time in any story, anywhere, I am telling the truth. A woman fell in love with me. We could have tranced all night.

I imagined lying with her in bed that night. Actually, it was early Sunday morning after a few hours' sleep. I sat up in bed and smiled at her as though she was there. I looked down at it and told her that we were looking at one happy camper. I got Dad up to give me a shower and get me ready for one of the most meaningful days ever in my life. She was coming over this morning, and we would pick up exactly where we left off.

It had been exactly one week since Mother's Day when I sat at my mother's grave and asked her to send me something to keep me going. Elizabeth, you're magnificent.

I was waiting on our patio when she walked up the driveway. Dad had gone to church and Sireci and Thaddeus went back to Jersey. We were alone. I said that we had to talk. She asked me about what? But she knew. I said that I had to know more about her relationship with Kevin.

She said that she would be as honest as she could be. She loves Kevin. And she loves me too. I said there were questions I needed to ask her.

So I did.

How does the normal man kiss since his head isn't shaking like this?
Does he put his nose on this side or leave it up to you?
Are his eyes left wide open as I see your two?
Do you decide, or does he, how intense the whole pretense will be?
When mine are touching your lips, how do you get a feel of what is there in my kiss? Do reveal.
"When you kissed me last night, I felt my heart skip. It really did something to me. I didn't know if you should. But then I was glad when you did. Do you remember, when you first started to, I whispered to your mouth, why aren't you moving your lips all around? And then you knew, and I knew. And then you did, and I did. You said, we'll pick up on this tomorrow. And I said ok. But I still couldn't talk very loudly. I stood up in the van, and I said in front of your friends, Paul, you got drool in my hair. Then Steve said, yeah, but it was worth it, wasn't it? And I said, yeah, and I'll see you guys tomorrow. I thought of you all night."

How does the normal man kiss since he always knows he won't miss?
You understand his whispers and never need to spell.
His hands caress you gently, he holds you so well.
He makes no discordant moves in the way he draws near you and woos.
And now we're getting closer so what do you receive of what is there in my kiss? Make me believe.
"In young relationships, I yearned for what would satisfy my heart, and I neglected the development of closer relationships. I learned that this was a selfish part of me. When I grew up and got to know me, I met Kevin.
"And then there was Paul.
"This is how hard it is when you meet someone after you're already in love with someone else. I wish I'd met you first."

How does the normal man kiss, since he is number one on your list?

He knows that no saliva will flow into excess.
And he is able bodied to bathe, feed and dress.
When you're not one you are two; that's not what I can promise to you.
So before we grow together, do we belong apart?
Oh what is there in my kiss for your heart?
"I love you because you are warm, and you're funny, and you're a poet.
And you're my inspiration, my man."

What is there in my kiss for you, Jenny?
"I love you, Paul."

I got no sleep at all that night. I had said goodbye to her. She was flying out at two thirty Monday afternoon. It hit me all night that I might never see her again. I looked down and cried. I had no one to share my pain with. I talk to my knees, but they don't listen to me.

If I could choose from every woman who breathes on this earth, the face I would most love, the smile, the touch, the laugh, the very soul itself, every detail down to the smallest strand of hair, they would all be Jenny.

I didn't call her that morning. I let her get her Mom off to swimming, and I let her pack, and I let her Dad drive her to the airport. I wanted to let the week begin by letting her go. But then, as I sat on my john right before the bus came...I thought...Wouldn't the perfect happy end to this Asticman be if I were to get up and go right out there to my bus and find Peggy and Jenny waiting for me? Why, of course. She might be sitting on my bus, in front of my house right now. I'll go and find her. She'll be sitting right by my seat, waiting for her dearie.

No, she wasn't.

Dear Mr. and Mrs. Bacon,

I feel compelled to tell you in this way how very much meeting and spending time with Jenny has meant to me. It now seems uncanny that it was actually just a calendar week that marked the time we had with each other. Because of the wonderful experience, I say that I'll never be quite the same.

I want to tell you that I think of Jenny as a very exceptional person and as an abundantly loving woman. And I certainly feel like thanking you sincerely, not only for sparing her company while she visited me, but for raising such a jewel.

Many things occur unexpectedly which can turn one's life around and force one to look at everything differently. While most of these things can be inconveniences or tragedies, one must feel blessed when such an occurrence is nothing but a pure delight. Jenny and I had a wonderful week together, and while she has commitments back in Fort Collins, we do plan on continuing our friendship by telephone. So I should hope that we all stay in touch, and I shall keep you in my thoughts.

I thank you for everything, and everything is Jenny. I guess she'd rather be in Colorado.

> Every apology to Alan J. Lerner.
> and one to Merle Haggard.

GAMBLER

I have a brother who is a thirtyfive year old overweight attorney. He makes a little over a hundred grand a year. On every weekend during football season he spends between five hundred and a thousand dollars in gambling pools on both college and professional teams. He has a twentyfive year old office manager to whom he pays thirtytwo thousand yearly. The boy has caught the gambling bug as well; he invests a sizable portion of his own paycheck in the vice. The two of them like to discuss their wins and losses at their favorite restaurant when all their scores are in.

I like to eat out too, now and again. I know nothing of football. My overweight brother does not give me any of his money. Yet while I am sitting in a restaurant today my thoughts are as well focused on the fine art of gambling.

My first wager with fate is whether or not my athetoid body is sitting still and relaxed enough when initially being pushed up and seated at the table due to the fact that immediately my business partner has to leave me to use the restroom and I may have to deal alone with the preliminary water boy or cocktail waitress. And you know what I need to say to the cocktail waitress.

'Um and oke.'

But did I say that clearly enough so that the consonants can be extrapolated? Have I happened to get a cocktail waitress today who is smart enough to extrapolate some of my consonants? Did she actually understand what I said the first time I said it? And is she only making me repeat myself so many times only to mess with my mind? Could this chick be one of those bitches who doesn't believe that I am over twentyone? Or is she one of those who has a particularly hard time serving alcohol to a handicapped person? What's it gonna be, girl?

My second bout with chance while my business partner is still away from the table is whether or not I am quite sure how to handle the situation with the little middle aged woman who is seated over in the far corner but who is directly in my forward view. I do know her type exactly. She is making maternal gugu eyes at my debonair-like smile at her. She turns her gaze to me from her seemingly flabby husband sitting with his back to the world. The woman's gazes come to me once every fortyfive seconds now, and I know exactly what she wants to come over and talk to me about.

She does rise to approach me. And I am right on the money. She has a job working in a day care center where she feeds retarded folks... like me. ... "What's my name? Do I go to school? Do I hear and understand her alright?" ... You must guess the rest of the scam. So I need to make a decision as to whether to attempt to give this woman a more suitable idea of the person to whom she is asking these limiting and nonapplicable questions, or to play mostly mute, simply to respond with shakes and nods and hope to limit this conversation more to the point of nonexistence. And I need to decide quickly because my business partner will surely return soon from the john, and I know that he isn't smart enough to stay out of this conversation. If I play dumb to the lady now, I know that he will blow my cover immediately when he comes back.

He's back already, so my decision is made for me. It is a time like now when I can deeply regret all the major triumphs and accomplishments which I have made in my short adult life. Because they all have to be explained and documented fully by my business partner whenever he and I have the audience of some poor little middle aged woman who has only thought that she was doing something nice and decent by coming up to a cute child whom she thinks is retarded and engaging in a small harmless conversation about my school and my ability to hear and understand what she is saying.

I keep reminding my proud associate whenever these conversations do arise with such middle aged nice ladies, that we need not include every one of my life's accomplishments. Not even half. Not even one. Sometimes... Most of the time, just a debonair smile from a seemingly underprivileged man in a wheelchair is enough to impress, and to brighten a day. He should count this as being one of my great accomplishments.

From the moment when the food is served to an invalid athetoid in a restaurant until the time when he has finished eating just enough of it so as not to feel embarrassed about giving it back to the waitress, the eater and feeder are in constant labor. If the food is tasty, then they do not mind the work so much. Still it is that: work.

An athetoid's tongue experiences various stages of hyperactivity during the course of a meal, mostly due to sweet and salty foods. I often am not able to swallow all the particles of some bites of food all at once, and therefore am liable to need to clear my throat or cough more often than the average person. It is important for me to feel that I am free to do this occasional coughing, as well as some belching and excess salivating in a clear range where no one is particularly noticing me. If I am hindered in this freedom to cough, as I am now by this little middle aged woman who makes her living every day feeding handicapped retarded children like me, it only makes the whole long meal that much harder to swallow. For these and many more reasons, I consider public mastication to be no easy bet.

And then there is that all important matter of making sure that my feeder keeps my chin dry constantly. I have for my entire life held it imperative to be as neat as possible while dining in a restaurant. And it is here when I risk becoming too imposing on my feeder by constantly putting my dirty face into his clean face. I know very well by now to time my gestures, my mouthfuls, and my napkin requests so to make myself as least imposing to my dining partner as I can possibly be.

I am on my third "um and oke", and the woman is still making gugu eyes at me. You would think that by now my drinking would have become so sloppy that it would encourage the kind soul to turn her stupid face around and stop looking at me. But she is persistent. So I have to bet that my fourth "um and oke" will do the trick.

And the ultimate thing that I gamble on is whether or not I have made a lasting impression on my waitress enough to leave her with these few realities about me: I think she is somewhat cute. And throughout most of the meal I have been lusting and fantasizing about having her. I would like her number.

Yet, even though I tend to entertain such vulgar and chauvinistic thoughts, I am after all quite a charming guy. And, despite the occasional facial grimace, I am perfectly able to give her the whimsical, innocent wink and smile goodbye. And lastly I hope that she realizes that it was my credit card used to pay for the meal and for the twenty percent tip. My payoff comes whenever I am recognized for who I am.

ADAPT

My heart was broken on a Monday morning last winter. I arrived for work at the Social Security complex in Woodlawn, and as I descended the hydraulic lift of the MTA Mobility bus, there they were directly between me and the entrance door to my building.

They were the disabled people's militant activist group, ADAPT, about whose coming all employees at the complex had been warned several weeks back since they had been given a three-day permit to protest at this site. We were told that they were coming to demonstrate against a senate bill dealing with reallocating funds to go to nursing home care instead of home health care. The bill dealt with some policies of the Health Care Financing Administration which is a sister agency of SSA, and is located within the same Woodlawn complex, but is not located anywhere near my building.

Even though I had known that they were coming for a few weeks, I had not given the matter much thought lately. And so I had to think very quickly, while my bus driver rolled me up the building's ramp, about what to do, how to behave, what to say around these people who were obviously going to prohibit me from entering. I had never imagined that their presence would involve or affect me very much. But these were at least twenty loud and boisterous people in wheelchairs, plus about forty walking men and women, and those who were not marching back and forth in front of the doors of the building had chained themselves to them. There was just no way I was going to get in to go to work.

To add to the weight of my decision of how I had better behaved at that moment was the fact that my first, second, and even third level bosses were standing right inside the window before me, and so were many members of our office. And they were all watching my every move. I knew that I was expected to act as if I definitely wanted to get into the building to start my duty, and I was expected to treat all of these intruding handicapped and handicap supporting people with disdain for blocking my passage.

So that was the attitude that I decided to take. I put myself in a stage of playacting. I raised my voice and frowned and yelled out to the best of my utterance that I was very mad at this demonstration and I demanded to be let in the building. But in actuality, I was glad to be put in such a poignant situation. I was being photographed and reported about by a reporter from WGN in Chicago who moderated the altercation between me and the biggest, meanest wheelchair-bound men who were chained right in front of the door. It was getting to be quite a show, and I was doing all I could to uphold the drama of it.

After the camera and lights had gone off and away, I was also glad to put down my offence and try to be friendly with some of these people who were by this time all around me. They were all giving their point of view, both directly to me and to the passing crowd in front of the ramp. They were there protesting a new decision to spend more Medicare money for housing invalids and handicapped shut-ins in nursing homes rather than allocating the money to pay attendants to care for patients in their own homes. There was a total disregard for the facts that this was a decision completely made by Congress, and, the last time I had been told, Congress was still working on Capitol Hill in Washington D.C., and that although the national headquarters which deal with Medicare is located at our Woodlawn complex, the Administrator also works in Washington.

But my complex was the only site at which they were permitted to picket this issue, and like it or not, I was bound to sit there, in the cold afternoon and without any jacket, and listen to their side of the story. I grew more and more sympathetic.

Every person who talked to me was kind and articulate. They asked me to consider the problems and plights of my brothers and sisters, trapped inside nursing homes, who will never experience all of the splendid opportunities which I have had in my life. All they were seeking was attention to the injustice of a system which would spend more money suppressing the potentials and promises of over two million of its handicapped population than in seeing to it that these men and women are afforded life, liberty and pursuits of happiness.

And my heart was truly broken that because of my own attained status in life, I had dared to playact against such worthy and humane ideals. I have been writing for a very long time about things so parallel to ADAPT's causes. What could have ever brought me to this position where I would ever strike against folk who might have been singing my very own songs?

Neal, my co-worker, was able to sneak out a back door of the building and to come around the side, and he rescued me by rolling me around and back in the building. I had already caught a cold, but I was regretting my broken heart so much more. I turned to a lovely young girl, an ADAPT supporter, and I said to her, "I wish I could help you." I knew what they were doing outside, but I didn't know what I was doing letting Neal push me inside.

Soul In The Helpless

Where is the soul in somebody who is totally immobile? If a handicapped person is completely dependent on someone else to eat, to walk, or to live, or even to think and make decisions, does that mean that that person has to share a soul with the helper? Is a soul personalized or universal? And if everybody is supposed to get their own soul, what happens to those who are too poor or too weak to buy one?

Are there different souls, group souls for different classes, in different countries, in different costumes? Can movie stars buy their own souls from a designer and market and publicize them for the most profits? Let me see Madonna's soul, and then let me see the Pope's, the Queen's, and then one from an eighty year old invalid and a four year old with Down's syndrome and cerebral palsy. Can we not explore by dissecting them all one day and seeing the difference in what they look like?

Religion has an answer. Every human being who has ever lived has had a soul which was seen and known only by God. Well, that is ideal if you are God. But man cannot always conduct business with supernatural concepts. True; everywhere on earth we have bureaus and divisions of religion, theology, education, evangelism and nature worship. But have too many people given great, serious thought to seeking, or finding, or accepting the value of a soul in a body who is unable in any way of expressing his or her own true feelings? Is an invalid entitled to its very own soul if no one is able to find it?

How many souls live in nursing homes? How much life is slowed down or deadened by old age, debilitation, or profound mental retardation? How many identical faces will be sleeping on the streets tonight? How many Kurds have been killed, not in the last few years, but in the history of mankind? How many souls have lost in the Darwin game? In the Hitler game? In the Reagan game? Would the combined souls of all the lost bodies in the world today ever come close to matching up with even one of Donald Trump's collection of souls? Would he ever find it in his gigantic heart to donate just a handful of his souls to make sure that all the invalids from his home town got a chance to go to Heaven? Well, maybe he might.

How do you think it feels to be taken away from the rec room TV everyday and never being told where they are taking you? How do you think it feels to be seeing life go on all around you and never being able to communicate with it, or to understand it, or to grasp it in any way? How would you like to live life as an ant? Your only question would be whether or not you would live for the next twentyfour hours. But you would not be all that concerned about it. You would have no concern; remember? You are an ant. And if you do have a soul, no one is aware of it. Probably, no one has ever bothered to tell you what a soul is so that you could decide for yourself if you had one.

So can spiritual direction ever be done or attempted on the under-privileged or the profoundly retarded? The spiritual director might have to charge five dollars an hour, but that's not what I mean. I mean is a soul always as under-developed as its body and mind are? Don't you think we should determine that before we go much further with some spiritual direction? God is not about to make the decisions for us. He knows a soul when he sees one. I ask if man can. I am asking how far we really can take religion, and equality. Whose souls do you recognize?

I am asking some ridiculous questions for some good reasons. I want the world to abhor euthanasia, to admonish warfare, to avoid selfishness. Many of the civilizations which live today do so much to enhance and to progress the human condition, while the same societies, along with plenty of others, do very much damage to the core of the species. Throughout a million races all over the globe, there seems to be a surviving thread of thought that no matter how identical faces might be, souls are unique. We seem to hold onto the concept of unique souls so as to hold onto society itself.

I do fear that every year the soul gets more and more invisible. But as soon as it is forgotten, then we all shall be.

RECOMMENDATIONS FROM THE BOARD

The Heavenly Board for the Handicapped wishes to present the following 3 recommendations on how earthly existence would better bless and keep our living brothers and sisters as they prepare their souls to come into the Kingdom:

1. Parents and every family member should be exposed to in-depth love and sensitivity training in order to inform them that the handicapped one is actually a gold mine for the whole family to experience tremendous, miraculous spiritual interaction. All adult family members need to be trained not only how to teach the children how they can exchange wondrous love with the one who is handicapped, but also how they themselves can witness this love and fully learn from it.

2. Love angels from every arch should expose family and friends of their handicapped ones to sensitivity love training in order to inform them that, although they may know of the glowing spirituality illuminating from their interaction, they might not be able to see and realize the clear pathways down which it can lead them making their own decisions in life.

3. Love and affection training should be fully accessible to all living bodies.

Just Give Him A Cookie

I had finished writing "Icon" the month before. By now the book had been in the hands of a prospective literary agent in New York for a few weeks, and a load of copies of my printing had been delivered all around my territories. It was Christmas Eve, and my father and I were perpetuating our most beneficial yuletide tradition; he stood me up from my wheelchair and was walking me down the aisle to my airplane seat so I could depart for nine days to the other side of the country.

Cerebral palsy still does have its ups and downs. Before I could ascend to the friendly skies, Dad and I needed to meet and manage one last drag familiar to both of us. My two airline attendants for this trip, Jeff and Crystal, would not let Dad deplane, and start spending Christmas with one of my siblings of whom he is more fond, until they could ask and re-ask him some rudimentary interrogations: "What special instructions do you have for us, Sir, about the way we should care for your handicapped boy? How is it that we should feed him? How many times do we need to take him to the bathroom? Will he be amused enough with the music from the headset? Will he prefer the Hillbilly or the Disney channel? Will he like some milk or a pillow?"

Before we had left our house to come to the airport, my father had seen me sneak three or four shots of Wild Turkey. Since my mother has been gone for over three years, Dad has taken over the parental responsibility of seeing that my buzzes never actually come to full fruition while he is in my presence. This is why I spend the holidays away from him each year. Thus, I knew that as my last Christmas bonus, he would deliberately see that I would most definitely have a dry flight west. He read in "Icon" about my last trip to LA.

This is what Dad said to Jeff and Crystal, by this point all ears: "Well no, I wouldn't worry about feeding him dinner or taking him to the bathroom. He doesn't need a pillow. He is a college graduate and he has a great bladder. You can't give him anything to drink. But if you're walking past him, and you feel like doing something for him, you could always stick a cookie in his mouth. You'll do fine."

Last month while I finished my fourteenth book and was trying diligently to get it to a publisher, my dear Dad saw to it to have yet another birthday, his seventy first. He's a hard man to keep down and at times a harder one to put up with. But they are certainly two of my major lots in life. And I love him. And I must remember that I love him very deeply as I begin long and dry airplane flights such as this one. I can go five hours without a drink. I won't like it, but after all, the man did give me life. Oh, what a life.

So the tradition continued. My friend and soul-brother, Clay Goldstein, met my brave face as Jeff and Crystal clumsily pushed me in my chair out from the hanger. I was in L A X again, bound for Hollywood, and a drink and a leak. But not yet. I made a motion and said a syllable, and Clay knew what I wanted.

"Hey wait, you guys," Clay said to Jeff and Crystal who after five and a half hours and three thousand miles still had no clue what to make of me. "Paul wants to give you both something."

Clay reached in my flight bag and pulled out two new chap books. I saw to it that Jeff got "Orgiasticman" and Crystal got "Morassticman". I figured that just because I had a dry day, they didn't need to.

I am never really in Hollywood until Clay drives me up to LaCienega Boulevard. And I am not really comfortable until the time that we check into my suite at the Park Sunset Hotel and Clay gets me out of the chair and sits me on my couch. Then, we start talking.

"Well Paul, how was your flight?" Clay asked me politely.

He would soon regret having asked me such a thing. "Clay, my flight to LA was not at all as pleasant as it was last year. I happened to be placed between two very fat people. One was a twentytwo year old girl with a walkman and a load of Salt and Pepa tapes. Even if I would've wanted to, I could not've because the other person was her father. And they were both big and fat and left me no room at all to have cerebral palsy. And it was agonizingly uncomfortable and horrible, but that wasn't the worst part. The worst part came about two hours later when I was in the middle of a nap with my head hanging down and cerebral palsy was finally giving me a break. And then all of a sudden, that guy Jeff came up to me, tapped me on my shoulder, woke me up out of a cool still, caused me to jerk my arms slightly out of their set positions, looked at me and said, 'Paul, are you ready for a cookie?' And I thought, o my god, this guy's gonna try to give me a cookie in the middle of the airplane in the middle of these fat people in the middle of all these other people and they're all watching the movie and I'm right in front of the screen and everybody's watching this guy trying to give me a cookie. And he's got this pack of four little white dry cookies. And the last thing I want is one of these cookies in my mouth, because my mouth isn't ready and I got no reason of getting it ready, because I don't want a cookie in the first place because it will be too much work to try to get it down, and I'll have to move my head and turn it around a lot, and there is no place to turn it. But I don't want to be rude to the guy, because he's only trying to be nice. So I'm able to shake my head no for the cookie, and I think I get a thank you out, and Jeff starts to turn to walk away with the cookie. And I'm psyched. And then all of a sudden, the guy next to me, the fat guy who's the father of the fat girl, he says to Jeff, 'No wait, he's trying to tell you that he does want the cookie.' And Jeff comes back. And this thing has already gone back and forth too many times, and we already got the whole class of the plane distracted from the movie just to see if I want this cookie. And now there's like nothing for me to do. I can't contradict the fat guy, and I can't try for another thank you. I'm gonna have to let this steward put this dry ass cookie in my mouth. And anybody with athetoid cerebral palsy and a college education knows that you just don't do this. But I did it. So now here comes the saliva, and the vanilla, and then all the jerks I gotta make to even begin to try to get this gd cookie to go southward. But of course, it isn't going anywhere, 'cause I'm panicked, and nothing is gonna happen except frustration and salivation. And it's just a bummer. So, what does Jeff say? 'Oh Paul, let me get you a drink of water.' So there I am. The steward leaves me in the middle of the airplane in the middle of the country. Nobody's back to concentrating on the movie; everybody's still looking at me, except the fat people next to me. They're engulfed in the flick. And I got a face full of vanilla. I got no towel, no sleeve, no knee to wipe anything on. The steward is gone for over two minutes. I could look down, but that doesn't really help because when I look up, it's a lot worse. All I was doing was taking a nap, and then came the cookie from hell. Oh well."

Clay then said, "Paul, I'm sorry but I must have lost you along the way. Would you mind repeating that? No no, Paul. Only kidding, only kidding. Listen, you've been through a lot and you certainly deserve a great vacation in LA. And that's just what we're gonna give you. I told so many people you were coming. Everyone who didn't want to see you has already left town. So now all that's here are people who are set to party with you. You're going to meet a new woman everynight."

What Clay didn't say then was that we were going to meet every one of his women everynight. But I soon got wise. Women were the focus of many of our conversations during the week.

"Paul, I'm gonna be introducing you to a lot of girls this week. I love them all, but tell me what you think. If there are any whom you want to go after, you are home free. Remember, you're in California."

Tuesday night we went to dinner at a seafood restaurant, and it was there I met Karin. She spent that night with Clay in his part of the suite. The next day she and I discovered we had a thing for each other.
By my last full day in LA, we had become a happy threesome. We were joined that evening by a stunning twenty year old singer named Tamara and Clay's friend Kevin. We stayed up all night because my plane was leaving early the next morning.

During my last hours in LA, Karin and I became romantic. Clay stayed in the other room watching hockey with Kevin. He let it happen for Karin and me. Tamara came in and slept like an angel on the floor next to our bed.

The five of us got in the car. We dropped Kev and Tamara off at her place. She was still very sleepy. She kissed me very sweetly. I regretted that I wouldn't be seeing her, Tamara. Then we drove to L A X.

Clay and I were back at our same old hanger. It was time for me to say goodby to him, and to her. I found myself on the Bogie side of the end of Casablanca. Only I was the one who was getting on the plane. I was certainly too wired to figure that one out.

When Clay had settled me in my airplane seat, he kissed me on the cheek saying "I love you Paul." The pretty stewardess asked him if there was anything special she could do for me. Clay turned from me and walked out of the plane saying, "No, just give him a cookie."

Printed in the United States
222238BV00001B/32/P